TURTLE REEF

THE WILD AUSTRALIA STORIES 4

JENNIFER SCOULLAR

PILYARA PRESS

Pilyara Press
Melbourne

To the Australian Marine Conservation Society, providing a vital voice for Australia's ocean wildlife

CHAPTER 1

Zoe sat up in bed and groaned. Just how much had she drunk last night? Still, it had been worth it. Without a large dose of Dutch courage, she would never have found the fortitude to give her loser boyfriend his marching orders. A wave of relief helped wash away her hangover. Had she been cruel? No, not cruel, more like direct. But what choice did she have? After all, last night was the third time she'd tried to tell that man they were through. He was just so darn persistent, like a human limpet.

Zoe contemplated going back to sleep, but her mind was too busy. Why did she always have such bad luck with men? *You wear your heart on your sleeve, my girl,* her mother would say. *There's your problem.* Zoe pulled the pillow over her head. What could she do? That's just the way she was made. But Zoe had to admit that her system wasn't working out. Not at all.

People had warned her about Hugo, but she hadn't listened. It wasn't in her nature to be cynical or suspicious, and she liked that about herself. Her friends saw it differently. They said she was trusting to a fault, gullible even. They said she was naïve and no judge of character. Her friends had been right - again.

The last six weeks with Hugo, for all its dysfunction, was the closest thing to a relationship that she'd had for a long time. Before him there'd been a string of the most appalling, dead-end dates imaginable. She wasn't blameless of course. She could be recklessly honest, speak her mind without thinking, screw things up, but still ... What about the guy who talked about himself non-stop for so long that she set the stopwatch on her phone, just out of curiosity? Thirty-three minutes straight. She didn't even have the opportunity to say something tactless with that one. Then there was the guy whose interests were lifted word for word from her Facebook profile. He liked the exact same movies, same books, same bands. It had given her the creeps. There was the cheap date who proudly admitted he'd complained about the food to get their meals for free. Weirdest of all was the one where the man's wife had joined them half-way through dinner to explain she was dying of cancer and wanted to set her husband up with a nice girl before she gave up the ghost.

Zoe hauled herself from bed and looked out the window. Down on the street people hurried like ants, an anonymous throng that she was too often a part of. She felt empty, hollow. This wasn't how she imagined her life would be.

Zoe glanced at the time. Almost nine o'clock. A sudden sick feeling hit her, until she remembered Monday was her day off. How she hated working at that library. When she finished a degree in zoology at Sydney University last year, she'd hoped to work for Parks and Wildlife, or maybe as a research assistant with the CSIRO. She'd even applied to the Australian Antarctic Division. With a major in marine mammals, she might have scored a job on the Weddell Seal Project, or researching the Southern Ocean Whale Sanctuary. But here it was, end of August, and she hadn't even made a second round interview. So Zoe was stuck working at the university library. Not even in the zoology department. She would have loved being surrounded by biology books all day. But no, she'd been assigned to the deadly-dull engineering faculty. Technical journals and pimply first years hitting on her. Yuck.

Zoe wandered from the window towards the kitchen. She craved a greasy hangover-cure breakfast, but the contents of her fridge was disappointing. The Macdonald's down the road seemed like the best option. Zoe caught sight of herself in the mirror as she pulled on jeans. Her tangled, brown hair already looked greasy, although she'd just washed it yesterday. For years she'd wondered how it would look short, really short. Perhaps today was the day to find out? She paused, frowning at the spare tyre around her tummy and the generous curve of her hips. Her tall frame could usually carry a little extra weight, but six weeks with foody Hugo had tipped the balance. Her stomach rumbled. She could really go a bacon and egg muffin right now. The diet could wait.

Zoe brushed her teeth and dragged a comb through her hair. What she really wanted was to get away. From her dingy flat, where she wasn't even allowed to have a cat for company. From the library, and her dreadful dates, and the Macca's round the corner.

The phone rang from somewhere in the bed clothes. She fumbled for it, in two minds whether to answer or not. What if it was Hugo, or the library asking her to work today? She didn't recognise the number. 'Hello?'

'This is Bridget Macalister, director of the Reef Centre at Kiawa.' Zoe had applied for a position at the Queensland marine park months ago. The pay on offer had been modest, little more than a keeper's salary, but she was more than willing to start at the bottom. Hearing nothing, she assumed she'd struck out.

'Congratulations,' said Bridget. 'You have the job.'

CHAPTER 2

The train's rhythmic clickety-clack was soothing as a lullaby. Zoe propped in the corner, half-awake and half-asleep, until a change in tempo roused her. She blinked out the window, then checked her watch. Why was it so dark? She checked her watch again. Five-thirty on a September afternoon in Queensland. It should still be broad daylight. Nose pressed against the pane, she stared at the pall lying over the landscape.

The middle-aged man sitting opposite leaned forward, a helpful expression on his ruddy face. 'Black snow, luv.'

'Excuse me?' said Zoe.

'Bundy's black snow.' He gestured out the window to the strange grey world. 'They're burning the cane.'

Zoe stood on the platform as the other passengers hurried away, fingers curled tight about the handle of her suitcase. First time in Bundaberg. First time anywhere in regional Australia for any length of time. There'd been a few family trips up the coast as a child - magical beach holidays that had inspired her love of the ocean. But apart from that, Zoe was a Sydney girl through and through, born and bred in Bankstown. A city girl who was determined to embrace this new lifestyle, this new opportunity, this new job.

Her stomach churned with excitement. She glanced around the old station building with its cream weatherboards and bullnose verandahs. Full of old world charm, but she was too wound up to appreciate it. Zoe wandered towards the exit, momentarily confused as she caught sight of her altered reflection in a window. What had she been thinking, getting her hair cut so short? It had seemed such a good idea at the time. A bold new look, practical too, because her new job would entail much swimming and diving. But instead of sassy and stylish, it made her look like a boy with too small a head. A head that looked odd on her generously-proportioned body. She'd have done anything to have her old hair back. Zoe frowned at her reflection, then moved further down the platform to avoid seeing herself. A pinhead, that's what she was now.

She could smell fire. Cinders got up her nose, burned her throat, stung her eyes. So much for fresh country air. A handsome man wearing a bush hat was watching her. Was that him? Was that the man Bridget had sent to collect her? She smiled and smoothed her close-cropped hair. He separated himself from the fence and strolled over. 'Quinn Cooper. I'm your lift.' He extended his hand and swept off his hat in an old-fashioned gesture. 'Welcome to our little slice of paradise.' Something deep in her stomach flipped over in an all too familiar way.

'Zoe,' she said. 'Zoe King.' His hand-shake was firm, just the way she liked. In fact, on first impressions, there was a lot to like about this man. Attractive in a laconic, sunburnt sort of way. Older than her, about thirty. Lanky and tall, with a dark, close-cut beard, and that hat made him look like an actor from a pioneer movie. Honest grey eyes and a slow Queensland drawl in his voice. She started to thank him, but an embarrassing coughing fit choked away her words.

Quinn looked concerned. 'Apologies for the smoke,' he said, like somehow he was responsible. 'The wind changed unexpectedly and brought it into town. Best get you a drink.' His hand brushed hers as he took charge of the suitcase. They set off towards the platform gate, and Zoe swallowed hard, trying to quell the tickle in her throat.

An elderly station attendant stepped forward. 'Afternoon Quinn.' He tipped his hat. Zoe searched in her bag. Where was that ticket? But the man waved them through to the car park regardless. The train blew its whistle and pulled away from the platform, to continue its seventeen-hundred-kilometre journey north to Cairns.

'In you get.' Quinn put her bags in the back of the red Jeep Wrangler.

Zoe reached for the handle but he beat her to it. She was a little taken aback. Nobody ever opened car doors for her back in Sydney. She settled into the passenger seat, eyes drawn to the faded glory of an old hotel opposite. They swung right into a broad thoroughfare, past buildings flanked by coconut and date palms. Past the unexpected grandeur of Bundaberg's historic Post Office, with its Italianate Victorian design and imposing clock tower. Quinn pulled over in the main street.

'I'll buy something to wet your whistle. What'll it be?'

'Diet Coke thanks.'

Quinn returned with two bottles of ice tea. 'Coke's no good for you.' Zoe didn't like tea, ice or otherwise. She took a sip and screwed up her nose. Yet despite the taste, it was oddly refreshing, and did a good job of soothing her irritated throat. Quinn glanced across and nodded approvingly as she took a bigger gulp. 'I'll head down Quay Street, give you a look at the river.'

Bundaberg's Burnett River was home to one of the world's rarest living fossils – the lungfish. She'd written a university paper about it. Zoe sat forward, eager to see the waterway for herself. But she caught barely a glimpse across the parkland before they turned and headed out of town.

Zoe finished her drink and looked for a place to put the empty bottle. She settled for holding it between her bare knees.

'So,' said Quinn. 'You're the new dolphin trainer.'

'Trainer? No, I'm a zoologist. Majored in marine mammals: seals, whales, dugongs ... that sort of thing. Although I do have a special interest in cephalopods.' She wet her lips with her tongue. 'Are you on staff at the Reef Centre?'

'Not me. I grow cane out at Kiawa. But I do know your boss, Bridget Macalister. We're getting married next year.'

Oops! Just as well she'd sworn off men. Her boss's boyfriend was about as far out of bounds as you could get. 'Congratulations,' said Zoe. 'I'm really looking forward to working with Bridget. Such impressive research credentials.'

'Bridget's great, the absolute best.' Quinn's eyes shone with pride. How sweet. 'You'll love her. Everyone does.'

'Will she be at the centre when we get there?'

'Bridget said to bring you back to the farm. She's arranged a welcome dinner.'

Zoe stared out the window to hide her disappointment. She wanted to see the Reef Centre tonight. How could she wait until morning?

A stiff wind change had cleared the smoke haze. At first, paddocks and orchards flanked the narrow road, giving way to emerald fields of cane as they drove farther from town. She felt out of place in her black skirt and neat grey shirt. The vivid beauty of this Queensland spring cried out for colour.

Quinn didn't offer any further conversation. Half an hour later the car turned into a pair of tall gates hung between bluestone pillars. They passed beneath a gracious arch with the word Swallow-dale emblazoned across it. A few minutes later a white house came into view on a rise. More of a mansion really. Sweeping lawns and sub-tropical gardens framed the imposing two-storey homestead. Wrap-around balconies featured wrought-iron lacework, and numerous arched floor-length windows gleamed like diamonds in the late-afternoon sun. Tennis courts stretched beside a river on the left, with what looked like stables beyond them. A pretty cottage nestled beside a broad ornamental lake, fringed by trees. Some sort of lookout tower stood near the water. Further afield, a sea of sugar cane stretched to the horizon, topped with feathery seed heads that wafted in the wind like waves. The only blight on the magnificent view was a dark plume of smoke. Zoe was stunned. People paid to have wedding receptions at places like this. Everything screamed of old money.

'What a lovely home.' An understatement, but it was all she could come up with. The only time she'd seen anything quite so grand was in a glossy magazine.

'Built by my great-great-grandfather,' said Quinn. 'Jack Cooper was a pioneer of Bundaberg's sugar industry. Since then, the eldest son of each generation has taken over the plantation.' He heaved a sigh, as if the worries of the world lay on his shoulders. 'My father passed away last year, so the job's mine now.'

'I'm sorry to hear that,' said Zoe. 'I mean I'm sorry to hear that you lost your father. I imagine you love running Swallowdale.'

'Of course.' Quinn swung onto the circular drive and pulled up by the homestead's rose-covered entrance. 'It's an honour for any man to follow in his father's footsteps.'

'Well, I suppose that depends on the father, doesn't it?' said Zoe. Quinn shot her an odd sideways glance before climbing out. He walked around to her side of the car, but by the time he got there, Zoe had opened the door for herself, and was standing triumphantly on the groomed, gravel driveway. 'Take my dad for instance,' she said. 'He drives a school bus. I wouldn't want to do that.'

Quinn gave a tight smile and hauled her suitcase from the back. A black-and-white border collie with a magnificent coat came bounding up to them. 'Meet Captain.'

The dog propped on Zoe's feet and trained his beautiful, brown gaze on her. She knelt down to hug his neck. Captain offered a paw.

'You're honoured. He doesn't often take to people like that.'

Out of the corner of her eye Zoe noticed movement on the balcony. Someone was watching them - a teenage boy with dark wavy hair. Quinn followed her gaze. Zoe waved to the boy but he ducked from sight.

'That's Josh, my kid brother.' Quinn laid an unexpected hand on her arm, and glanced around as if someone might hear. 'Josh is well …

different. Not quite right. ' Quinn glanced up at the empty balcony. 'Cut him some slack, okay?"

'Of course,' said Zoe, wondering exactly how Josh was not-quite-right. 'Thanks for telling me. I'd hate to put my foot in it. I do that a lot I'm afraid.'

Quinn smiled. 'Well, so does Josh, so you'll fit right in.' He gestured towards the house. 'After you.' All this chivalry was going to take some getting used to.

'Zoe tells me she's a scientist.' Quinn took a bite of fluffy mashed potato.

'That's right.' Bridget's voice was low and musical. 'Zoe's our new research officer, funded by a grant from the Environment Department.'

'So the government pays her salary, eh? That's a good lurk,' said Quinn. 'But doesn't the centre really need a dolphin trainer, not a researcher?' A note of concern crept into his voice. 'Don't get me wrong, you're doing a great job with those animals. You have a gift, no doubt about it, but you're not super-human, Bridge. I worry about you, trying to do everything yourself.'

'Zoe majored in marine mammals,' said Bridget. 'She knows plenty about training dolphins, don't you Zoe?'

Zoe almost choked on a piece of broccoli. Her knowledge of marine mammals was entirely theoretical, and it most definitely did not extend to training dolphins. She'd read a lot, and watched plenty of Flipper reruns on television — but that was it. Zoe shifted nervously in her seat. What to say? Both Quinn and Bridget had their gaze trained on her face, awaiting her response. 'I did receive a high distinction for my work on operant conditioning training at the Sydney Aquarium,' she said at last.

'There.' Bridget shot Quinn a triumphant glance. 'I told you so.'

Zoe concentrated on her plate, hoping nobody would notice the blush of embarrassment creeping up her cheeks. It wasn't a lie exactly. She had carried out a research project at the Sydney Aquarium in her second year, and it had involved training animals using operant conditioning – only they weren't dolphins. She could see the title on the paper she'd so proudly submitted at the end of the semester. *Associative Learning And Memory In The Common Sydney Octopus*. The octopuses had constantly surprised her with their intelligence and problem-solving skills. She'd grown very fond of Gloomy, her main test subject. So fond in fact, that at the end of the project she'd stolen him from his tank and surreptitiously released him under a boardwalk into Darling Harbour.

An awkward silence had fallen on the room. Zoe gazed out the window to where a rosy sunset flared on the horizon, looking like a picture postcard. Maybe if she changed the subject. 'Isn't Josh joining us?' Main course was almost over, and there was still no sign of the boy. For some reason she hadn't been able to get him off her mind.'

'My brother is as unreliable with meal times as he is with everything else,' said Quinn, though his tone was good-humoured. 'But he usually turns up for dessert.'

Zoe picked up her dainty crystal wine glass and turned it gently between thumb and forefinger, admiring the fine gold etching.

'An antique,' said Quinn. 'The set belonged to my grandmother.' He topped the glass up with shiraz. Zoe didn't usually drink red wine, but it was all that was on offer, and it would be rude to refuse. Anyway, the more she drank the better it was tasting. To her delight, Bridget had stopped asking questions and started talking about her work.

' ... then Koko got the same idea,' said Bridget, 'and soon we had five dolphins doing backflips all at once. The crowd loved it.'

'How many dolphins do you have?' asked Zoe.

'Six in all,' said Bridget. 'Three bottle-noses and three spinners.'

'I can't wait to meet them. How far along are they in their rehabilitation?'

'I'm afraid none of our current dolphins are candidates for release,' said Bridget. 'Five have permanent injuries and our youngest spinner, Baby, was born right here at the centre. He'll never be able to fend for himself.'

'What a shame,' said Zoe. 'That must be hard to come terms with.'

'It's heartbreaking,' agreed Bridget. 'I've dedicated my career to rehabilitating these animals. But it's not all bad news. We've done lots of successful turtle and seabird rescues this year. You'll meet all our patients tomorrow.'

Zoe put down her knife and fork. 'Imagine, living and working at the Reef Centre. It's a dream come true.'

'Not living there,' said Bridget. 'There's been a change of plans.'

'I thought accommodation came with the job?' said Zoe

Quinn drained his wine glass. 'You'll be staying here at Swallowdale, in the cottage. Fully self-contained and a cleaner once a week, who'll also stock your fridge.'

'But why?' asked Zoe. 'I mean, that's very generous of you, but I was looking forward to staying at the centre. You said there was a bungalow right next door. It sounds perfect.'

'Oh, we couldn't do that to you,' said Bridget. 'I had a good look round that old shack last week. It's more rundown than I realised, so Quinn offered the cottage instead. It's quite lovely, with a view of the lake.' She raised the silver serving spoon and turned to her fiancée. 'More potato?"

'No thanks, hon. Couldn't fit in another thing.' Quinn wiped his mouth with the crisp linen napkin and pushed back his chair with a satisfied sigh. 'Never tasted beef so tender or spuds so fluffy. You're a miracle Bridge, you know that? Working all day and then racing over here to organise a slap-up meal? Don't know how you do it.'

Zoe's hand strayed out of habit to push her non-existent hair back behind her ear. 'Yes, it was delicious.'

Bridget bowed her head a fraction in acknowledgement. 'Hope you all left room for dessert.'

Zoe's eyes followed her new boss as she slipped from the splendid dining room into the kitchen: tall, tanned, enviably slim, and with the sort of luminous beauty you might expect of an actress or super model. She wore her sleeveless cream blouse, skinny jeans and embossed boots with such flair, Zoe half-expected a camera crew to pop out from behind the curtains. Bridget's mane of golden hair bounced a little as she walked, as did her shapely bosom. It was apparent that she wore no bra, but her gravity-defying breasts remained horizontal. What a knockout. No wonder Quinn was besotted. Zoe was a bit besotted herself.

Picking up her empty plate and wine glass, she hurried after Bridget into the kitchen. 'You've gone to so much trouble.'

'No trouble.' Bridget gave Zoe a warm smile. 'I love to cook, don't you?"

'Not exactly.' Zoe copied Bridget and scraped off her plate into the in-sink garbage disposal. She'd never seen one before. It set up a low whirring sound. 'Back home I used to eat a lot of Macca's.'

Bridget's mouth pursed with concern. 'We don't have a McDonald's in Kiawa.' She wiped her manicured hands on a tea towel. An enormous diamond on her ring finger caught the light, blazing silver and gold. Everything about Bridget was larger than life. 'There's a good fish and chip shop, but it's not healthy to live on that stuff.'

'No, I suppose not.' Zoe pushed a piece of carrot down the sink, curious to see what would happen. The Insinkerator gobbled it up. Then a stalk of broccoli met the same fate. She looked around for something else. A fork on Quinn's plate still held a piece of gristle. Zoe reached for it.

'I could show you some recipes,' said Bridget as she pulled a multi-peaked lemon meringue pie from the fridge.

Zoe started to thank her, then stopped. Oh dear. Her arm had knocked the little wine glass into the Insinkerator's jaws. The whirring sound grew louder as savage, steel teeth crushed the antique crystal, grinding it to pieces. Bridget glanced across, but the shredding sound suddenly stopped. The beautiful wine glass was no more. Zoe stared in horror at the sink. What should she do? Should she say something? It would be too humiliating.

When she turned around, someone was watching her - the boy from the balcony. A good-looking kid with tousled chestnut hair and clever grey eyes; a younger version of Quinn. Where had he sprung from? Bridget glanced up from arranging the magnificent pie on a china cake stand, and visibly started. 'Josh, I wish you wouldn't sneak up like that. You gave me a fright.'

The boy's face fell, clearly unhappy to have displeased her. 'Sorry Bridget.' The words were uttered in a kind of slow motion, like he had to concentrate to get them out. He wasn't slow on the uptake though. He knew exactly what had happened to the wine glass.

Should she pre-empt him, confess her crime? No, a little too much time had passed. It would seem odd that she hadn't mentioned it earlier. Zoe didn't breathe. Would he tell? Josh wore a thoughtful expression, as if he was trying to make up his mind. Then he grinned and something passed between them. She heaved a relieved sigh and shot him a grateful look. For some strange reason she knew her secret was safe.

Bridget favoured Josh with a dazzling smile. His face lit up with pleasure, like a puppy who'd been patted. She handed Josh the cake stand bearing the magnificent pie and carefully lowered the bevelled glass lid on top, trying not to squash the mountain of meringue. 'There. Do the honours please, Josh, and I'll get the cream.'

The boy carried the dessert into the dining room with exaggerated care. Quinn applauded when he saw it. 'Bravo. A masterpiece. I'm a lucky man alright.'

The room fell silent as they feasted on the lightest, tangiest lemon meringue pie Zoe had ever tasted, complete with dollops of fresh, clotted cream. All except Bridget, that was. She announced that she was already full.

Quinn removed the lid again, and picked up the silver cake server. He raised his brows and looked at Zoe. She was about to say *yes please* and dig in for a second helping, but the sight of Bridget serenely sipping her sparkling water made her pause. Reluctantly she shook her head. 'You girls eat like birds,' said Quinn, heaping up his dish. 'Just as well, eh Josh? All the more for us.' Zoe was rather flattered by the description. Nobody had ever said that she ate like a bird before. Far from it. She pushed away the memory of last week's two-for-one Big Mac deal that she had taken such enthusiastic advantage of.

There was something very strange in the way Josh shovelled the food in; grunting and chewing with his mouth open, unconcerned as cream dripped down his chin. Wild and uncivilised, like an animal feeding. Zoe poured herself a glass of water from the bottle on the table and tried not to stare. When Josh finished he started to hum loudly, tunelessly. Thank goodness Quinn had warned her. Josh was indeed a strange one.

When they'd all finished, Zoe stood and picked up her dish. 'Leave it,' said Quinn. 'It's dark enough. I'll show you how we burn a cane field. Quite a show.' He looked about. 'Anybody else coming?'

Bridget shook her head. 'I'll stay and clean up.'

'Me too,' said Josh. The laboured affect in his speech could not disguise his eagerness to help, as he set about clearing the table. He was clearly as big a fan of Bridget as his brother was.

Quinn rose to his feet. 'Well Zoe, looks like it's just you and me.

Zoe grabbed the guard rail and hauled herself onto the platform at the top of the floodlit tower. Climbing the lookout's vertical timber ladder left her dizzy and breathless, but she'd done it - challenged her fear of heights. A flush of pride passed through her. What an inspiring start to her new life.

Quinn leaped nimbly up behind her, his shadow merging with hers. There wasn't much room at the top. 'I'm turning off the lights,' he said. Zoe blinked a few times and inadvertently moved against him as the world went dim. She shivered slightly in spite of the warm evening.

'There.' Quinn pointed to the west. Three white jeeps moved in convoy along the edge of a field. Roof mounted spotlights cast bright moving circles on the standing cane. When the vehicles were evenly spaced along the length of the track they stopped. Zoe watched the nearest jeep. Men in orange visi-overalls emerged, carrying containers like giant oil cans with long spouts. Zoe gasped as sudden columns of flame flew from the cans, engulfing the wall of cane before them.

'Drip torches,' said Quinn. 'They shoot a mixture of petrol and diesel.' In a synchronised assault the men ignited the crop. Soon it blazed all the way along the track. Fire climbed into the dark sky, higher and higher, towering over the men. A dramatic sight, orange flames dancing against the black curtain of night.

'Why wait until now?' asked Zoe. 'Why not in the daytime? Or is it just because it looks more awesome in the dark?'

Amusement showed on Quinn's face in the reflected glow of the flames. 'Cane fires get pretty fierce,' he said. 'We wait until dusk for the temperatures and winds to drop. It's safer.' The fire increased in fury, roaring like an angry beast. It took off in a spectacular way across the paddock, leaping four, five, six meters high into the inky blackness. A sight equally frightening and thrilling. Zoe closed her eyes and imagined what she might be doing if she was back in Sydney. Eating takeaway in front of the television perhaps, or updating her Facebook profile. Quinn took hold of the railing with both hands and leaned towards the inferno. 'Beautiful, isn't it?'

Heat flushed Zoe's face and an acrid smell assailed her nostrils. She pictured the scorched earth, the billowing smoke, invisible in the darkness, choking everything in its path. She pictured animals and birds and insects, fleeing for their lives. 'I read somewhere that they don't burn cane any more,' she said. 'That the modern way is to cut it green, and leave the cane tops on the ground, like a kind of mulch.'

'Trash-blanketing?' said Quinn. 'Yeah, some blokes do that, but not round here. We're an old-fashioned bunch in Kiawa.'

'Why?' she asked. 'Wouldn't mulching keep down the weeds? I mean, if it was better to cut cane green, why wouldn't you do it? '

'You want to know why?' An edge had crept into his voice. 'My father burned cane, and his father before him, and his father before him. And that's reason enough for me.'

CHAPTER 3

'Well?' said Bridget. 'What do you think of our star attractions?' Six dolphins cruised around the natural salt-water lagoon of the Kiawa Reef Centre. The three smallest ones were particularly energetic, leaping from the turquoise pool in graceful arcs. Those must be the spinners, *Stenella longirostris*, literally meaning longbeaks. One of them shot forward and approached Zoe. They lacked the fixed smile of their bottlenose cousins, and were around half their size. More dainty, with slender beaks or rostrums, and soft brown eyes. Almost human eyes.

'This is Baby.' Bridget sat down at the edge of the water. The sleek little dolphin rolled upside down and presented his pale pink tummy to be scratched. Bridget obliged, then nodded to Zoe. 'Come and say hello.'

Zoe knelt down and tentatively stretched out her hand, enchanted by this strange and exotic creature inviting her to play. But she was also a little scared. Truth was, Zoe had never had much to do with real live animals. She'd grown up in a two bedroom flat in Bankstown, sharing a bedroom with her older sister Stacey. Mum worked as a cleaner and Dad drove Greyhound coaches between capital cities. The family seldom had enough room, time or disposable income for pets.

When Zoe was little it had been fun sharing with Stacey. She'd adored her big sister, who told her stories about princesses being rescued by white knights, and always let Zoe crawl into bed with her when bad dreams came knocking.

Everything changed though, when Stacey hit her teenage years. She no longer had time for her kid sister. With Mum working nights and Dad away so much, they weren't allowed to have friends around very often. Zoe abided by the rules, even though it put her on the outer at school. But it wasn't long before Stacey was bringing boys home behind their parents' back. She'd bribe Zoe with lollies or money to get lost. If that didn't work, she'd threaten harm to Zoe's most precious possessions. 'If you don't give me and Jayden some privacy, I'll dump those stupid fish books of yours in the toilet. And don't you dare tell Mum either.' How Zoe had hated it. Banished from her own room, trapped in the cramped flat, unable to block out the mysterious giggles and thumps coming through the thin walls, no matter how loud she turned up the television.

When Stacey turned seventeen she moved out and Zoe suddenly had some space to herself. What a luxury. She landed an after-school job at Bankstown public library and soon had enough money saved to set up a small aquarium in her room. She loved her fish, but it wasn't quite the same as having a dog or a cat. You couldn't form a relationship with a guppy. Lack of experience had left her timid about connecting with more challenging animals. And yet here was Baby, staring at her with those curious, intelligent eyes, demanding just such a connection.

'Don't worry,' said Bridget. 'You won't frighten him.' She didn't realise Zoe was the frightened one. Why would she? Dolphins were so universally loved. Like so many little girls, Zoe's side of the bedroom had overflowed with dolphin stickers and posters, closely followed by those of horses and unicorns. Dolphins, horses and unicorns - symbols of magic, power and fantasy in the life of a lonely child. She drew their pictures all over her school books and wrote sentimental stories and poems about them.

But she'd since discovered that horses could be scary close up, having fallen off the only time she'd ever ridden one and broken her collarbone. Likewise she'd discovered that dolphins weren't always the amiable characters of fairy-tale fame, spending their days frolicking happily in the waves and saving people from drowning. They were effective and cunning predators, capable of real aggression, and had been known to bite swimmers when provoked or frightened. 'Do not be taken in by dolphins and their winning smiles,' her first marine mammals lecturer had warned her. Then he told the story of the Brazilian dolphin Tião, who sent twenty-eight people to hospital before eventually killing a swimmer.

Bridget slipped out of her jeans to reveal bathers beneath. Zoe looked enviously at her boss's toned, tanned thighs, and then to her own plump white legs emerging from khaki King Gee shorts. Baby uttered a series of swift clicks and whistles. 'He wants us to join him,' said Bridget. 'Come on, you'll dry off soon enough.'

Zoe hesitated for a moment then sat down on the concrete edge, trailing her legs in the lagoon. Baby immediately approached, rubbing up and down against her like a smoochy cat. Zoe eased herself into the water. She stretched out her hand to feel skin as slippery and firm as wet rubber. Baby was surprisingly warm, like a living, breathing beach toy. He sidled close and on impulse she wrapped her arms around his sleek, streamlined body. It throbbed with a strong, steady heartbeat. The dolphin's physical presence delighted and overwhelmed her, chasing away her doubts.

Now two more dolphins approached, playfully slapping their tails. One held a rubber dumbbell in its mouth by a little handle, and appeared to be playing keepings off. It hid the toy under its belly and between its fins when the others tried to snatch it.

As Zoe relaxed, she began to appraise them with the eye of a scientist. Baby was a healthy young male, born at the centre, but according to Bridget the rest all bore injuries serious enough to prevent their return to the wild. The problem was obvious with the smallest bottlenose, whose tail bent permanently to the right, making it a clumsy swimmer. A second spinner nosed its way into her arms. Zoe winced to see a massive shark bite scar on its left side and a bullet hole through its dorsal fin. 'That's Baby's mother,' said Bridget. 'Koko.'

'Why hello, Koko,' said Zoe as the dolphin offered her flipper for a shake. 'I'm very pleased to meet you.'

Now the biggest dolphin approached and Zoe drew in a quick, admiring breath. Indo Pacific bottlenoses were large dolphins, she knew that. But such theoretical knowledge hadn't prepared her for real thing. The animal swimming straight for her was two-and-half metres long and must have weighed well over two hundred kilos. Bridget jumped up onto the paved pond edge. 'Get out,' she said. 'Kane can get grumpy if you don't have any fish for him.'

Zoe hurried from the water. The big dolphin cruised by, casting a baleful glance her way as he passed, rolling slightly to reveal an attractive pattern of spots along his sleek, muscled side. The animal looked in good physical shape, apart from a drooping dorsal fin and a bloody laceration on his rostrum.

'What happened there?' asked Zoe. Several of the dolphins had cuts and scrapes on their skin, but Kane's nose was by far the worst.

'Kane fights the gates,' said Bridget. 'It's a game he plays.'

'What's his story?'

'A fisherman found him in trapped in a net, suffering from shark bites and a stingray barb to the jaw. He recovered here at the Centre and we released him into the bay. Kane was a bit of a lone wolf, raiding nets and intimidating swimmers. We took him seventy kilometres out to sea, but he returned within days, cadging fish and biting people. We don't know why. Our vet, George Fairthorn, thinks the stingray barb may have permanently damaged his jaw so he can't catch his own fish. Fisheries and Wildlife declared him a public nuisance. So for Kane it's either the Centre or a bullet.'

Kane lazily turned and swam past them again. His perpetually-smiling mouth gaped wide. There didn't look to be much wrong with his jaw, or his gleaming rows of sharp white teeth.

Further out in the lagoon, keeping its distance, swam another bottlenose, smaller than Kane. A dazzling, graceful animal, coloured in delicate shades of blue-grey with a pale blaze extending from head to dorsal fin. 'What about that one?'

'Mirrhi is from the off-shore Bora Reef pod. Fisheries and wildlife identified her by scars on her dorsal fin. She was washed up two years ago on a sand bar in mangroves, half-dead and tangled in plastic. It's been a long road to recovery, and sometimes she still has seizures.'

Zoe jumped as she became aware of somebody standing close behind her. Josh, wearing bathers and swim goggles and holding a towel. 'Where did you spring from?' she asked.

Bridget laughed. 'He's always doing that.' She waved him over, took the boy's hands in hers and gave him a warm smile. 'Aren't you Josh? Always sneaking up on people?' Josh's face flushed a little. Zoe didn't miss how his gaze slipped momentarily to linger on Bridget's bare, brown legs. It looked like young Josh had a crush on someone.

There was a flurry of movement in the pool. The dolphins were all crowding around Bridget now, leaping and slapping tails. Even shy Mirrhi seemed excited. 'It's getting near time for their training session,' said Bridget. 'They love learning new things. It's all part of the environmental enrichment program we offer here at the centre, to encourage natural behaviour. We use a combination of sight, smell, taste, touch, and physical interaction. It's as important to provide mental stimulation for the dolphins as it is to provide nutritious, well-balanced diets. Bored dolphins can develop some very negative habits. That will be one of your duties actually Zoe – to dream up some new fun stuff for these guys.'

'I'll get right onto it tonight.' Enthusiasm for the task made her heart beat fast. Researching the latest developments in captive dolphin enrichment was a far cry from cataloguing engineering journals. She couldn't wait to get started, couldn't wait to prove herself to her new boss. Zoe stared about the sparkling cove and at the brilliant, blue curve of the bay beyond. She closed her eyes and breathed in the salty breeze blowing straight off the wild ocean. Sydney and its crowds and concrete seemed a very long way away.

Bridget checked her watch. 'Josh, go ask Karen for a bucket of fish and some of the dolphins' toys?' Josh dropped his towel and sprang to his appointed task. Zoe noticed that he wore a whistle on a cord around his neck, identical to one that Bridget was wearing. 'Such a sweetheart,' said Bridget. 'He loves spending time with the animals here at the Centre. It's a bit of a nuisance of course, but I just can't seem to say no to him.'

Zoe compared Bridget's sunny personality with that of her former boss, old Miss Addis, head librarian at the engineering faculty. She was just plain mean. Petty, narrow-minded, always finding fault. Miss Addis regarded library users as the enemy, and loathed them with a vengeance. In her mind, students existed only to muddle up her nice neat shelves, and disrupt the rigidly organised cataloguing system.

By contrast, Bridget was friendly and generous. Willing to put herself out, to interrupt her day in order to please an intellectually disabled boy. Did Bridget realise that she might be as much of an attraction for Josh as the animals were? Probably not. She seemed almost unaware of how charismatic she really was. 'Can I stay and watch?' Zoe was determined to make a good fist of this job, and if that meant learning how to train dolphins then she'd learn, and quickly. How hard could it be?

Bridget gave her an apologetic smile, sunlight glinting off perfect white teeth. 'Not today I'm afraid. The plan is to hand you over to our head keeper, Karen. She'll show you around the seaquarium and the rescue centre. Currently we have two pelicans, two turtles and several rays as inpatients. Karen will outline their rehabilitation plans, and also bring you up to speed on our new research project — mapping sea grass meadows and monitoring dugong populations.'

The tantalising prospect of getting close to some real-life research pushed all other thoughts from Zoe's mind. Dugongs worldwide were in trouble. Elusive and mysterious, they still held an almost mythical significance in many cultures. But they also faced butchery based on people's ignorance, much like elephants and rhinos. Myths abounded. That dugong tusks were aphrodisiacs. That their hair and oil had miraculous medicinal value. Even their tears were believed to have magical qualities. To top it off, their meat was a delicacy in many countries. Australia remained the dugongs' last stronghold, but so little was known about their lives. What an honour, to be involved in research that would help protect them.

Josh returned with a bucket of fish, followed by a stout middle-aged woman with steel-grey hair and bright, blue eyes. 'I'm Karen.' She shook Zoe's hand. 'Been looking forward to getting some help around here. If there's time later we'll take a trip out to Turtle Reef. How does that sound?'

Zoe followed the keeper towards a low, rundown building on their left, an ugly brick and concrete structure of seventies vintage. 'Might not be too pretty to look at,' said Karen. 'But you'll appreciate it in a cyclone. This place is built to withstand a category four.' Cyclone? She hadn't banked on any cyclones. 'Don't worry,' said Karen cheerfully. 'They don't happen very often.'

'I'm pleased to hear it.' A swift look back revealed Bridget, stripped down to a bikini, standing on the edge of the lagoon. Josh stood beside her.

'We use only sand-filtered sea water and natural sunlight in our aquarium,' said Karen proudly. 'There aren't many built that way any more.' They pushed through the doors, and were immediately bathed in soft aqua light. Fish of various shapes and sizes sailed around, all in the same direction, behind panes of floor length glass. Snapper, cod, coral trout. A pair of graceful sting rays. A splendid lionfish, bristling with colourful spines. Zoe moved closer until her nose was almost pressed against the window. She gasped with delight as a green sea turtle swam past, mere inches from her nose.

'Wait a moment,' said Karen. 'Our new guest should be by any minute ... there. Meet Chopper.'

A three metre shark cruised by. Pointed snout, stout body and underhung jaw, laden with rows of ragged teeth - a grey nurse. The white-tipped claspers on its belly told Zoe it was male. She frowned at the deep scar encircling the animal's neck, maiming its first two gills. 'What happened to him?'

'Tangled in a shark net off Kiawa beach,' said Karen. 'The

contractor responsible for checking the nets knew these guys are endangered and bought him here. Not before two smaller ones drowned though. On a brighter note, we hope he'll mate up with our female. There might be the splish-splash of little fins before too long.'

Grey nurse sharks were known as the labradors of the sea – friendly and harmless. Zoe felt an angry catch in her throat at the sight of the mutilated fish. 'Shark nets don't work,' she said. 'They actually have the opposite effect, attracting sharks to feed on the by-catch. My professor wrote a peer reviewed paper on the topic, backed up by some very solid research.'

Karen shrugged. 'Try telling that to the Mayor, Leo Macalister. He says nets are needed to convince tourists that the beaches are safe. If you ask me, it's all a big publicity stunt.' She led Zoe out the back of the building and up a flight of stone steps.

'Macalister …' Zoe turned the familiar surname over in her mind. 'Any relation to Bridget?'

'The Mayor is Bridget's father. And what's more, he owns this whole place, including the cafe over the road and the beach shack next door.'

'I don't quite understand,' said Zoe, 'You mean Bridget's father owns the Reef Centre?'

'Lock, stock and barrel,' said Karen.

Zoe wasn't sure why she was so taken aback. What was wrong with that? Somebody had to own the place. Maybe, with Bridget's help, she'd convince the Mayor to look at that research paper on shark nets.

They emerged onto the roof, offering stunning views across Turtle Reef National Park. Concrete pathways bordered an assortment of large, open air tanks. 'We're at the top of the seaquarium.' Karen pointed to a rusty ladder leading down into the water. 'That's the access to the main display tank. It's how you'll get in for the shark feedings.'

Zoe's jaw fell open. 'Shark feedings?'

Karen nodded. 'Our last girl quit on Friday. There've been quite a few disappointed visitors this week, I can tell you. I'd do it myself of course, but my back's not so good these days.' Her hands found the small of her spine for emphasis. 'Gives me grief.'

'I'm a researcher,' said Zoe. 'I'm here to, well … research. Not swim with sharks.'

Broad amusement showed on Karen's ruddy face, but she stopped short of laughing. 'Your dive qualifications are up to date, right?'

'Well yes, but …'

'No buts,' said Karen. 'We all pitch in here where we can.' Zoe opened and closed her mouth like a fish, but no words came out. 'You're not scared are you?' asked Karen. 'You said yourself that grey nurse sharks are harmless.'

'Wasn't there another shark up the back?' said Zoe. 'It didn't look like a grey nurse to me.'

'Oh, you mean Rosie? She's our bull shark. Been here for years. Wouldn't hurt a fly.'

Zoe did not want an argument on her first day, but bull whalers, along with tigers and great whites, were one of the few sharks dangerous to people. They were responsible for most of the shark attacks in Sydney Harbour, and she had no reason to believe that their Queensland cousins were any more friendly. Still, if Rosie was tame and well-fed …

There was another, more compelling reason why Zoe didn't want to become the daily shark feeder. Wet-suits weren't flattering garments for someone carrying extra weight, and being the centre of public attention wearing only skin-tight rubber would be an exquisite torture. Those things exaggerated a person's natural physique. Bridget, for example, would look even leaner and more amazing. Of course she would. Zoe, on the other hand, would appear considerably fatter than she really was. She could cope with that on a research dive with a handful of colleagues all focused on their work. But to be gawked at by crowds of strangers? Kids making jokes? Skinny women smugly noting how heavy she was compared to them? Zoe sucked in her stomach. It was straining against the top button of her shorts. She imagined herself swimming clumsily around the tank, resembling a plump dugong, tempting the good-tempered Rosie to make a meal of her.

'Well?' asked Karen. 'I'd hate to tell Bridget that you won't do it. Might even be enough to make her look for somebody else.'

'No problem.' Zoe blurted the words out so swiftly that she surprised herself.

'Excellent.' Karen gave her a broad grin. 'I knew we could count on you.'

CHAPTER 4

The cane-train's haunting whistle filtered through the fog of
sleep. Zoe opened her eyes as a knocking sounded at the door.
She opened her eyes, checked the clock and groaned. Seven o'clock.
This was her day off. She was supposed to have Mondays and Tuesdays free in return for working weekends. 'Move over Captain, you
big lug.' The border collie was taking up half the bed. He thumped his
tail, but didn't move.

Zoe gave up and stroked his handsome head. She'd always wanted
a dog, and had invited him to stay last night when he came to visit.
His warm, solid presence was very reassuring. 'Who needs a man
when you have a dog, eh?' Captain smiled and snuggled further down
into the doona. His weight on her left leg had made it go to sleep and
when she dragged herself to her feet, she almost fell over. Should she
get dressed? The knock came again, more urgent this time. 'I'm
coming.' Zoe stumbled to the front door.

Bridget stood in the doorway wearing snow-white breeches,
gleaming black boots and carrying a leather crop. She looked like a
model from *Country Life* magazine. Zoe stood agape in her pilled,
pink nylon nightie. 'We're riding to the Hump,' said Bridget brightly.
'Quinn and me. You're invited.'

'Riding?' said Zoe. 'I'm afraid I can't ride.'

'Oh, come on. There's nothing to it.' Bridget fastened a stray strand of shining hair into the knot at the nape of her long neck. 'It's too beautiful a morning to waste. I'll meet you down at the stables in ten.' And with that she was gone. Zoe stood for a moment, decided there wasn't any getting round it and hurried off to boil the kettle. She couldn't face the coming humiliation without a strong brew.

This dream job was proving more of a challenge than she'd expected. So many things conspiring to wrest her from her comfort zone. For one thing, her day started at seven and she was not a morning person. For another, the work was physically hard, much harder than she was used to. There'd been some disappointments. Still no car, and the promised research trips to the reef hadn't materialised yet, but she didn't mind. It was early days, and Zoe loved being surrounded by so much natural beauty. The stunning view of cane fields and rainforests sweeping down to meet the rocky coral coast. Working with the animals. It filled a hole in her heart. .She'd been missing such a connection to nature, without even realising.

It was hard yakka though. First thing in the mornings she sorted, rinsed and weighed out fish that had been thawing overnight. She added vitamins to the portions and helped Karen clean the equipment and preparation areas. Afterwards she assisted with the morning feeds and filled out food and behaviour records for the dolphins and each patient in the recovery unit.

At twelve noon came the big event for the day, the *Dancing Dolphins* show. There was always a good crowd seated along the small portable grandstand set up above the sandy cove. Bridget would emerge from the seaquarium with a bucket of fish, and saunter - there was no other word for it - towards the little lagoon. She wore short shorts and a gold bikini top that showed off her bronzed body in a spectacular fashion, like some sort of surfer version of Queen Cleopatra. For many male members of the audience, this was show enough. Bridget remained composed and ignored the odd wolf-whistle and catcall. She turned to wave at people when she reached the water, and was met with a flurry of applause before a single dolphin had even slapped its tail.

And, amazingly, Josh was there with her for the show, right in the thick of it, every single time. He didn't do much - fed out fish on cue, blew his whistle and clicked his clicker, motioned occasionally to the dolphins. Half the time he seemed to be in the way, but Bridget treated him with unfailing sweetness. Her patience and kindness impressed Zoe deeply. How lovely of Bridget to indulge Quinn's kid brother like that. Although Josh was a genuine help where Mirrhi was concerned. The young bottlenose was skittish and shy, unsure of her tricks and reluctant to perform them. She kept a close eye on Josh, whose presence for some reason calmed her down and gave her confidence.

Each show began with the theme from *Swan Lake* echoing through the tinny public address system. Two pelicans resident in the lagoon always seemed to puff out their chests at this point, as if in in clumsy imitation of swans. The three little spinner dolphins would start things off by launching into the sort of behaviour for which they were renowned and named — leaping into the air and spinning like tops before losing momentum and crashing back with a splash. Meanwhile Kane and Mirrhi, the much larger bottlenoses, balanced on their tails halfway out of the water and scooted backwards. When the animals performed these actions in rough unison, it resembled a dolphin ballet.

Karen narrated the performance, providing an informative spiel. 'In the two-hundred-thousand years that humans have been on this planet, we've caused a lot of damage. By contrast, dolphins have lived for twenty-five-million years in total harmony with nature. Did you know their brains are forty percent larger than ours?' The audience listened politely. Some people were surprised to discover that dolphins were mammals, not fish.

Kane was the star of the act. For a reward of sardines, he balanced on the edge of the pool so the visitors could get a good look. He opened his mouth to show his teeth. He slapped his powerful tail, a tail that had once propelled him at high speeds through the open ocean. Bridget pointed out his blowhole, and Karen's booming voice-over explained that during millions of years of evolution, dolphin nostrils had migrated to the tops of their head. Kane did a few leaps through a hoop, a few backflips. He played a half-hearted game of pool soccer with Mirrhi and the show was over.

After lunch Zoe squeezed into a wet suit and did her own show, diving into the seaquarium. At least she didn't have to wear a bikini. It wasn't as bad as she'd thought it would be. Quite fun really, once she'd gritted her teeth and forced herself to get over her self-consciousness. Inhibitions came rushing back however, when she looked out one day to see Quinn standing in the audience. He wore a broad smile, and gave a wave while she tried to hide behind Chopper. Since then Zoe had kept an eye out, but he hadn't returned. When she was invited to the main homestead for dinner, neither of them mentioned his visit to the shark show.

Zoe was beginning to learn the names and personalities of the aquarium residents: Shrek, the massive but gentle Maori wrasse, dazzling in electric blue scales, who liked for some reason to kiss the back of Zoe's neck when she wasn't looking; Snap, the shy moray eel with his oddly human face and bright sapphire eyes; Sarli, the graceful green sea turtle who took leaves of lettuce and spinach from between Zoe's teeth to the delight of the crowd. Then there were the sharks, all of them as friendly and well-behaved as Karen had promised. Zoe liked trying to read the lips of her audience, imagining their oohs and aahs of alarm as Chopper and his wicked looking teeth nudged at her hand.

Zoe spent the rest of the day helping out with demonstrations, like the turtle and ray feedings in the shallow touch pools, and watching dolphin training sessions. She wrote more reports. She helped unload fresh fish delivered by Archie, a local fisherman. One afternoon she made a start on washing the vast aquarium windows. They were grimy from fingerprints, and streaked with green mould in the corners. Zoe was surprised to find the place was quite rundown. The water in some tanks was cloudy, and they could use a good clean out. And the artificial underwater habitats looked sad and tired. Rocks slimy with algae. Sickly aquatic plants. Zoe had resolved to tackle Bridget about it in the coming weeks, perhaps help her plan a tank renovation program.

By the end of each work day she was physically exhausted. Back in Sydney, if Zoe was tired after work, she'd spend her evenings vegged out on the couch watching TV. Here in Kiawa she read books instead, or took Captain for long walks in the fragrant, twilight garden. Sometimes she headed out again after dark to volunteer for Turtle Watch, patrolling local beaches to protect nests and hatchlings. Back in Sydney, McDonald's, or something like it, was usually on the menu. That was impossible here — Kiawa wasn't exactly the fast-food capital of the world — so Zoe was forced to cook. Simple cooking, but it was more than she was used to. Last night she'd grilled a chicken breast and made salad from ingredients in the well-stocked fridge. She'd picked at the bowl of tropical fruit that was miraculously refreshed each day, and had been asleep by nine-thirty.

Zoe yawned, and poured more milk in her coffee so she could gulp it down fast. Looking forward to a sleep-in, and now this. There was a time, when she was in her teens, that an early call to go riding would have been a dream come true. That was before she lost her nerve. Her cousin owned a skinny thoroughbred, an anxious ex-race horse with terrible stomach ulcers and a ruined mouth. He'd bolted with her on their first ride. She still had nightmares about that day. The terror of racing out of control, the seemingly slow-motion fall onto the post and rail fence, the weeks of pain as her collarbone mended. Zoe had never ridden again. Well, time to face her fears. Zoe thought back to when she'd climbed the lookout tower. To the first time she'd lowered herself self-consciously into the shark tank. There seemed to be a lot of facing-her-fears going on here in Kiawa.

She finished her coffee, and pulled on jeans, a T-shirt and runners. Then she remembered Captain. It took all her strength to drag him off her bed and out the door. He scratched hopefully at it a few times, then gave up and led Zoe through the bright morning down to the stables.

. . .

The building was draped in flowering jasmine and bush honeysuckle. It must have been the sweetest-smelling stable in the world. Bridget was already mounted on an elegant, dapple-grey mare. Quinn stood by the gate, between a tall chestnut and a stout bay. In his Akubra and moleskins, framed by the two horses, he made a handsome picture - the epitome of old-fashioned, Aussie bush charm. Zoe couldn't help herself. Her imagination took flight. Quinn was her bushranger lover, come to whisk her away to his remote hideout. And she would go with him, though it meant forever living the life of a fugitive. Captain barked, chasing off her daydream.

'Hey boy,' said Quinn when he saw Captain. 'I was looking for you last night.' He knelt down to give the collie a pat. 'You weren't shacked up with that bitch next door, were you?'

Zoe stopped dead in her tracks. Surely he couldn't mean her?

Bridget was regarding her with an open amusement that seemed at odds with her usual kindness. 'He's talking about the neighbour's dog,' she whispered as Quinn turned to open the gate.

Zoe burned with embarrassment, and looked around hopefully for Josh. She could use his friendly face right now. At the Reef Centre, wherever Bridget was, the boy wasn't far away. Today, however, he was nowhere to be seen. 'What beautiful horses,' said Zoe.

Quinn slapped his chestnut on the neck and it tossed its proud head. 'This is Yarraman, and Bridget's on Duchess. Have you done much riding? No? Well, Cobber here will look after you.' He rubbed the bay gelding's face with a work-roughened hand.

A crashing sound came from behind the stables. Cobber shied and Zoe's heart beat faster. 'What was that?' More crashing, followed by a series of piercing neighs.

'Nothing to concern you,' said Bridget. 'Come on, up you get.'

Quinn indicated where Zoe should stand. 'Bend your knee ... no your left one.'

His strong hand grasped her leg, sending a little shock through her. 'What are you doing?'

'Giving you a bunk up.' Before she knew it, he'd rocketed her into the saddle. He handed her a helmet. She fiddled with its strap. Now his hand pressed against her thigh and she almost dropped the hat. 'Move your leg back.' He adjusted her stirrups and showed her how to hold the reins, while Bridget looked on patiently. Then he mounted Yarraman and they were off.

Nervous as Zoe was, it didn't spoil the thrill of being on a horse again after all these years. Cobber was a placid and steady mount, just as Quinn had promised. Zoe stroked his shining black mane, then leaned forwards in the saddle to catch a whiff of his warm, horsey smell. It was one of those perfect spring mornings, and she was suddenly delighted to be out so early in the day. It would have been a crime to have missed this. 'Where did you say we're going?'

'Up the Hump.' Bridget pointed to the dome-shaped hill dominating the skyline. 'An extinct volcano. Matthew Flinders named it when he sailed past in the Norfolk way back in 1799. The Taribelang Bunda people had a name for it long before that of course. — Gilibulga, the sleeping giant. It last erupted a million years ago, and must have been a doozy. They've found lava rock five kilometres out to sea.'

'The Hump is why Kiawa's fields are so fertile,' said Quinn. 'All that rich, red volcanic soil.' He pointed to the peak. 'There's a great view from the top.'

They rode in single file through green cane under a bright blue sky, until they reached the river. A path beside the water meandered through remnant pockets of rainforest, where towering, twisted figs and glossy-leaved ironbarks provided welcome shade. The sun was already starting to bite.

The track opened up until it was broad enough to ride two abreast. On their left, a tumbledown stone wall built by long-ago hands stretched into the distance. It added a powerful sense of history to the place. Captain dashed on ahead. Bridget's mare moved up beside Cobber. She arched her neck and jig-jogged sideways, causing Bridget to rein her in tight. 'How are you liking the job so far?'

'It's wonderful,' said Zoe. 'But I'm dying to go out on the reef and get stuck into some proper research.'

'Karen hasn't taken you yet?' asked Bridget. 'That's a shame. How about we head out after lunch today?'

Zoe beamed and stroked her horse's neck. At last her real work would begin.

The path narrowed once more and veered south through a gate and away from the river. They were moving steadily uphill now. Bridget dropped back and they rode again in single file. Native frangipanis crowded close on either side of the track. The horses brushed against their lower branches, releasing fragrance into the air from perfumed clusters of yellow flowers. Tiny, twittering birds flitted through the blossoming wonga-wonga vines, and crowds of colourful butterflies swirled down from the canopy, vanishing as quickly as they came.

Cobber's nose touched the copper-coloured tail of the chestnut horse in front, and Quinn's broad back blocked Zoe's view of the path ahead. He looked around. 'How are you going back there? The tone of his voice was warm and encouraging.

'Fine,' she said, grateful he didn't know where her fantasies had taken her. 'I'm doing just fine.' Sunshine combined with the clip-clop of hooves to lull Zoe into another day dream ... she was a tough, uncompromising pioneer woman, newly-wed, heading out with her man into the unchartered wilderness to claim a selection. Up ahead rode the square-shouldered figure of her husband, hips swinging in rhythm with his horse, noble dog trotting at his heels. The love of her life, strong and silent, devoted to his new bride — determined to forge a future for them both in the unforgiving heat and isolation of the Queensland bush.

An enchanting pretence. Quinn was completely different from anybody she'd ever dated back in Sydney. Better built and better-looking for a start. Down-to-earth, serious, and utterly unaware of his own charm. In other circumstances Zoe could have easily have fallen for him. If she hadn't sworn off men. If he didn't already belong to Bridget.

Quinn glanced back again. Zoe sighed and gave him the thumbs up. Time to stop these silly daydreams. She didn't really know him.

Quinn might be nothing like she imagined. What about that charged moment of anger at the top of the lookout tower? A man with a temper perhaps.

The trail grew rocky and winding. A cooling breeze hit them as they emerged from the forest onto an open grassy slope. Quinn turned in his saddle. 'Are you up for a canter?'

A canter? Zoe didn't even know how to trot, but she was keen to impress, so pride trumped caution. 'Sounds good.' Quinn's rangy chestnut swished his tail and took off at a cracking pace up the hill. Placid Cobber suddenly sprung to life and followed suit. Zoe fell forward and grabbed his mane in fright. She was just getting used to the rhythm, when a flurry of windblown leaves spooked him. Cobber leaped sideways and a flashback to her last, disastrous ride made Zoe freeze. She lost her balance as well as her stirrups, and could feel herself slipping sideways. Clutching at the reins only served to make Cobber poke his nose and gallop faster. She screamed, but Quinn was too far ahead. The wind and drumming hoofbeats drowned out her cries. She tried one final yank on the leather reins. Cobber ducked his head and snatched them from her hands. The reins slid down his neck out of reach. Now she had no control at all. Blood throbbed in her ears. She couldn't breathe, and her chest grew tighter still in anticipation of the coming fall.

A voice sounded through the fog of her fear. 'Hang onto the neck strap.' It was Bridget, steering her mare alongside Cobber, grabbing hold of his dangling reins. Zoe hadn't noticed the narrow leather belt at her horse's wither. She grabbed it and managed to haul herself upright. By the time the horses had come to a snorting halt, she'd found her stirrups and despite the humiliating rescue, was feeling pretty proud of herself for staying on.

Quinn had reached the top of the rise. He'd missed the whole thing. 'I'll go have a word to him,' said Bridget. 'He shouldn't have taken off like that.'

'No, no.' It mattered what Quinn thought. Zoe wiped the beads of sweat from her brow. 'Don't tell him. He might feel bad, and anyway, I'm getting the hang of this.'

'Okay,' said Bridget. 'Stick with me, and remember, next time, grab hold of that neck strap if you lose your balance, not the reins.' Zoe stroked Cobber's sleek bay neck. 'Push your heels down, and sit back, deeper into the saddle. That's the way. Ready?'

Zoe nodded, grateful for Bridget's rescue and feeling guilty for her silly fantasy about Quinn. As she glanced up at him, he wheeled Yarraman around in a half rear. A dramatic sight, man and horse on the hilltop outlined against the vibrant blue sky. Her heart beat faster. The shock of Cobber bolting ... or something more? Zoe shook her head to clear it, and followed Bridget up the hill at a sedate jog, trying to recall what she'd read all those years ago about rising to the trot.

At the top of the hill Zoe pushed her heels down, sat deep in the saddle and asked Cobber to stop with a gentle feel of his mouth. This time he was happy to oblige. He lazed on a loose rein, resting a back foot, while Zoe stood in her stirrups for a better look. The summit of the Hump offered a breathtaking three-hundred-and-sixty-degree panorama, extending to the Pacific Ocean and coral coast on one side, and the Great Dividing Range on the other. All around lay a brown and green patchwork of cane fields. The Kiawa River curled around the Hump's lower slopes. It had carved out a valley along the edge of the ancient lava flow, a place too steep and narrow for settlers to clear for cane. Remnant stands of rainforest followed its shining course, until the river widened into a broad wetland delta and joined the ocean.

'Turtle Reef National Park is a collection of three main reefs and lots of smaller ones.' Bridget pointed out to sea. 'See that semicircle of dark blue past the white yacht? That's Macalister Bar. An artificial reef, brainchild of my grandfather. He was a mad-keen diver, and fifty years ago he decided it would be fun to sink stuff off shore to make for more interesting local dive sites. You wouldn't believe some of the things he dumped. Boats. A three-hundred-tonne gravel dredge. A couple of old seaplanes. There's even an entire cane train, carriages and all, towed out on barges and tipped overboard.'

Quinn rode up to them. 'You wouldn't get away with it now,' he said. 'Too much red tape, but divers and fishermen love it. Should see the barracuda out on the bar.' He whistled long and low through remarkably even teeth. 'My father caught one two metres long there once.'

'I can't wait to see it all,' said Zoe. 'Do you think we'll find some dugongs today?'

'Oh yes, and dolphins and turtles as well,' said Bridget. 'We'll go for a dive, and later I'll take you through the terms of reference for our new research project. How does that sound?'

Zoe beamed her pleasure. She took another look around at the million dollar view and breathed a deep sigh of satisfaction. And to think she'd wanted to stay in bed this morning. What a fool!

CHAPTER 5

The ride home was a great success. Zoe even managed a short canter without losing her balance. By the time they reached the stables, her renewed enthusiasm for horse-riding knew no bounds. Quinn swung lazily from his horse and came over to take charge of Cobber.

'No.' Zoe slid awkwardly to the ground. 'I want to put him away myself. I need to learn.'

'Come up to the house when you're ready,' said Bridget. 'We'll have lunch and head off to the centre together afterwards.'

Bridget gracefully dismounted and swept off her helmet. How did she do it? Over two hours riding in the wind and sun, and barely a hair out of place. Zoe ran a hand over her own cropped head. Quinn, attentive as always, was at Bridget's side in a flash. 'I'll take Duchess for you sweetheart.' She threw him the reins. They certainly made a handsome couple. It must be nice for them to not have Josh hanging around for once. As fond as they were of him, he did monopolise a lot of Bridget's time.

'What do you want me to do with Cobber?' she asked Quinn after Bridget had headed for the house.

'First, tie him up and take off his saddle and bridle. They go in the tack room over there. Then hose him down.'

Zoe watched carefully as Quinn took off Yarraman's bridle and slipped a rope halter over the horse's head. He clipped on a leading rein and tied it to a piece of baling twine looped along the hitching rail that ran the length of the stable verandah.

'Why tie it to string?'

'If they panic and pull back, the twine breaks before their halters do.' Zoe copied him. When she looked up, he was watching her. 'You'll want to use a quick-release knot.' He showed her how. 'Now you try.' She tied the knot right first try, and he nodded approval. 'You did well today. Feel free to ride Cobber whenever you want. He's as good as yours.'

Zoe stoked his soft brown nose. 'Thank you. That's brilliant.'

With Yarraman and Duchess, Quinn showed her how to remove the saddle and bridle, how to hose the horses down, starting at the legs, and how to dry them with a sweat scraper. Lastly, he brushed out their manes until they lay against the animals' necks like curtains of heavy silk. 'Bridget likes me do this.' He looked a little embarrassed. 'You don't really need to.'

'They're such beautiful animals,' said Zoe. 'I can understand why she wants them to look their best.'

'If Bridget wants it done, that's good enough for me.'

Zoe wondered how it would feel to have a man adore her, the way Quinn adored Bridget. She'd never had that. She'd never had anything approaching that. A sudden sadness came over her. She turned so that Quinn couldn't see her face.

'Will you be okay putting Cobber away? He can't be turned out with the others. He's already too fat and might founder on the lush spring grass.'

She swallowed hard and tried to push the sadness away. 'Founder?'

'A hoof inflammation from too much rich feed. It can cripple them. Put him in that last loose box and throw him some hay. I have to put these horses in their paddocks.'

'Go ahead. I'll manage,' she said, though she wished he'd stay.

Quinn headed off with the two horses in tow, while Zoe hosed Cobber down. No point feeling sorry for herself. The day was far too beautiful, the sun far too bright, the air too fragrant with the scent of flowers. The plump little bay enjoyed his soaking, leaning into the stream of water and making her laugh by drinking from the end of the hose. By the end of it she was almost as wet as her horse.

Zoe scraped the excess water from his coat and brushed out his mane the way Quinn had shown her. 'Got to keep you beautiful for Miss Bridget.' When she'd finished, Cobber's black mane lay neat and shining along his glossy bay neck. Zoe had a silly, childish urge to tie ribbons in it. 'You have better hair than I do,' she said. Her new minimalist hairstyle was practical though. Cool and no fuss. Quick to dry after a dive. Who cared if she looked like a sexless boy? There was nobody in Kiawa she was trying to impress in that way.

'We're done. You can snooze away what's left of the morning in your stall.' The loud crashing sound came from behind the stable again. What was it? Cobber whinnied and danced about on the end of his rope. Zoe led him around the back for a look.

In a yard behind the building stood a beautiful black mare. Taller than Cobber, but far more dainty in build. Her heart-shaped white star was perfectly formed, as if an artist had painted it on her forehead. She was bashing the galvanised iron side of the stable with an angry forefoot. The mare stopped when she saw Zoe, her big brown eyes fringed with dark lashes, staring out from under a flowing forelock. Her coat was sleek with sweat, though towering Moreton Bay figs shaded the yard. The mare let out a series of frantic neighs and paced the fence, her flared nostrils showing crimson.

Cobber whinnied in answer and dragged Zoe closer. He pranced like a two year old, rubbed his nose against the mare's neck and made deep romantic noises in the back of his throat. Zoe was intrigued. 'Are you flirting Cobber?' The pretty mare was clearly thankful for the company, although she gave him a couple of warning nips when he got too fresh.

'Hello there, black beauty,' said Zoe. 'What are you doing back here all by yourself?'

She pulled Cobber away and put him in the loose box with some hay. Then she went back to the yard and approached the mare with an outstretched hand. Zoe was rewarded with a bowed head and a soft snuffling nose on her fingers. She slipped through the rails and ran a hand down the mare's shoulder, marvelling at her silken skin, laced with a fine network of veins, the noble arch of her neck and the extravagant, high carriage of her tail when she moved. Zoe couldn't stop staring. She'd never seen anything so lovely in her life.

'Would you like some hay too?'

The mare snorted and tossed her finely chiselled head, as if to say *yes please*. Soon she was timidly accepting offerings from Zoe's hand, and enjoying scratches behind her neat, black ears. Zoe slipped from the yard and gathered up some fresh grass. The mare nickered and followed her along the rails. Zoe fed her a few handfuls, then patiently stroked her until she could run a hand over her rump and down her legs. She found a soft brush in the stable and groomed her dusty coat. She picked burs from her tangled mane.

Time slipped by. When Zoe looked at her watch, it was past twelve o'clock. 'Oh no. I've got to go.' Impulsively she kissed the horse on her black velvet muzzle, before ducking from the yard and running to her little cottage. Lonely neighs followed her up the hill.

Zoe arrived at the main house as the others were sitting down for lunch, Josh included. As usual Bridget had put on a spread, Chinese food this time. Zoe helped herself to some fried rice. Delicious. At this rate, she just might marry Bridget herself.

'You've been a while,' said Quinn. 'Did you have any problems with Cobber? I was about to come looking.'

'No problems,' said Zoe. 'He was good as gold. What's the name of that black mare behind the stables?'

'Aisha,' said Josh as he helped himself to a prawn dumpling. 'I love Aisha.'

'I can understand why. She's absolutely beautiful. Aisha's an Arabic word right? Why is she kept by herself?'

'Quinn doesn't like her stirring up the other horses,' said Bridget. 'And yes, Aisha is Arabic for life.'

'She's Arabian then? I thought black Arabian horses were very rare?'

'They are,' said Josh. 'She's special, like me, isn't she Quinn?'

A shadow fell across Quinn's face. 'Don't anybody go messing with that horse,' he said. 'She's not right in the head.'

'Well of course she's not,' said Zoe. 'She's lonely. Anyone would go a bit mad being locked up on their own like that.' Quinn shoved his chair back and abruptly left the table.

An awful silence fell across the room. Zoe felt her face burning. 'I'm sorry,' said Zoe. 'I didn't mean ...'

Bridget frowned. 'Will you help me in the kitchen for a minute?' Josh stood up, but she waved him back down. 'I want to talk to Zoe.' Bridget closed the door behind them, leaned against one of the benches and tapped her long fingernails against the granite surface. 'You couldn't have known, but talking about that horse hits a raw nerve with Quinn.'

'Why?'

'Quinn's father bought Aisha's mother, a mare named Kariman, for Josh's twelfth birthday. That was three years ago. Aisha was a champion endurance horse, and Josh was the junior Queensland title-holder, riding against much older kids up. Aisha was just a foal at foot back then.'

'Endurance riding? Sounds tough.' A sense of where this conversation was going dawned on Zoe. She wasn't going to like this story.

'Long distance riding against the clock.' Bridget glanced around and lowered her voice. 'Josh and Kariman were leading the field in the Warabong Challenge when a kangaroo jumped out in front of them. Kariman reared and Josh went into a tree.'

'So that's why ...?'

Bridget nodded. 'Fractured skull and a massive bleed in the brain. Josh was in an induced coma for weeks.' She glanced at the door and lowered her voice. 'His father shot Kariman. He wanted to shoot Aisha too, but Quinn wouldn't let him. She was just a baby after all, and he knew how devastated Josh would be to lose both of his horses.'

Zoe spotted Quinn through the window, striding away from the house with Captain trotting after.

'Last year Quinn leased Aisha out to someone who wanted to break her in as a dressage horse,' said Bridget. 'The woman did all the wrong things. Tied Aisha's head down to force a correct carriage. Left her for days in tight side-reins and called it mouthing. Hobbled her when she resisted. Quinn found out what was happening and took the mare back, but by then she'd been branded as uncontrollable and was bucking people off. Little wonder, considering what she'd been through. Josh was thrilled to get Aisha back, but Quinn's got it in his head that she's dangerous — that she's got bad blood. He's terrified Josh will get hurt again and won't let him anywhere near her. '

'That's ridiculous,' said Zoe. 'You can't blame the horse for any of this.'

'No,' said Bridget. 'But he has a point about Aisha being dangerous. I had a go at retraining her myself and got nowhere. She's terrified of the bit, she bucks and has no brakes.'

The kitchen door opened and Josh came in, his face troubled.

'Ah,' said Bridget. 'Let's set the dining room up. Quinn has a special meeting of the Canegrowers' Association. Josh, we'll need more chairs. And then' - she turned to Zoe - 'We'll get out to that reef.'

CHAPTER 6

As Quinn headed down towards the lake with Captain at his heels, Aisha's unwelcome neighs rang out from the stable yard. Today was the first time anybody had spoken that horse's name for a very long time. Well, it wouldn't do any good for Zoe to plead her case. His mind had been made up long ago. The mare was dangerous, a threat to everybody's safety. There was plenty of truth in that, enough to justify him placing her out of bounds. But it wasn't the full story, not by a long shot.

Aisha neighed again, a haunting, lonely cry. Quinn put his hands over his ears, unwilling to hear, trying to block out the wave of unwanted sympathy he still felt for the mare. He wasn't a cruel man. He knew she was neglected and starved for attention. The problem was that in his mind she was inextricably linked to Josh's accident. He couldn't help it. The mere thought of Aisha transported him back to the time when his brother's life had changed forever. To the time when a terrible argument between Quinn and his father had forever ruined their relationship.

He and Dad at the hospital, hollow with worry and grief. Barely eating or sleeping, never leaving Josh's side. Except when he went into surgery to have a hole drilled in his skull. Quinn could picture it like it was yesterday: his little brother lying in ICU, covered in wires and tubes, looking so pale, so frail. A ventilator making his chest rise and fall in an eerily natural way. But there was nothing natural about it. Switch off that monstrous machine and Josh would die.

Quinn stopped, crouched down, and pressed the heels of his hands against his eyelids, hoping the swarms of dots might obliterate the dreadful images. It didn't work. It never worked, and the memories came swirling back.

After hovering for days they'd finally been chased off by an ICU nurse. She took his father aside. 'Go home, Mr Cooper, have some sleep. Let the doctors get on with their job.' They drove back to Swallowdale in silence – exhausted and powerless to comfort each other, separated by a gulf of sorrow.

When they arrived home Dad went inside and came out with the rifle. 'I'm shooting Kariman's filly as well.'

Quinn's reaction was instant and unequivocal. He placed himself squarely on the path in front of his father. 'No, you're not.' Dad's face turned redder and redder, and a throbbing vein in his neck looked like it might burst. 'You shot her mother,' said Quinn. 'That's revenge enough. Stacking tragedy on top of tragedy won't help Josh.'

'It'll help me,' said Dad. 'Now get out of my way!' He waved the rifle around wildly, and tried to push past.

Quinn didn't think it through; there wasn't time. All he knew was that he had to stop his father. He had to protect that foal. For the sake of Josh and for the sake of fairness and compassion, he would not allow another heartbreak into their lives.

Quinn threw his weight onto his right foot. Grabbing the stock of the rifle with his left hand, he shoved it aside. A gathering force moved from his swivelling hips to his powerful right arm as he cocked it back, squared his fist and took aim at Dad's jaw. The unexpected blow sent him crashing to the ground. Quinn stood for a few moments, rifle in hand, gazing down at the unconscious figure of his father. He stooped to check that his pulse was steady and strong. He pulled off his own shirt, folded it and placed it tenderly beneath his father's head. Then he ran down to the yards, loaded the frightened weanling into a float, and drove Aisha north for two hours to an agistment farm outside of Gladstone.

Quinn had returned to find his father drinking whisky out on the verandah. The two of them never spoke about what happened that night, but their father-son bond was broken. The intimacy had gone out of it: the affection, the playful banter, the careless companionship. Henceforth Marshall Cooper remained guarded and aggrieved, despite Quinn's constant efforts to fix things, to win him over. Then he died, and it was all too late. And Aisha? Free-spirited young Aisha? Through no fault of her own, the beautiful mare epitomised his ruined relationship with his father.

He couldn't explain the feelings Aisha triggered in him to anybody. Not even to Bridget, although he suspected that she guessed. It would involve opening himself up in a way unheard of in the Cooper clan. Even before his mother died, they weren't a family of sharers. And after her death, what little emotional communication they did have vanished altogether. *Man up and tough it out* had always been his father's advice until Josh's accident. Afterwards, Quinn would have welcomed even this harsh counsel, because they barely spoke at all. And when they did, his father confined his comments as far as humanly possible to practical matters.

Get a grip. No point trawling through ancient history, worrying about things he couldn't change. Quinn checked his watch. He'd walked further than he meant to, halfway round the lake, and people would be arriving at the house soon. He shook his head to clear it, and headed back. Bridget would tell him to focus on the positive, and it was sound advice. Like today's meeting of the Kiawa Canegrowers' Association. He *was* looking forward to the gathering, for it concerned PWSY, the one positive thing to come out of Josh's accident.

Project We'll Show You, or PWSY as it was commonly called, had kicked off nine months ago. It was Quinn's baby. Through traipsing around after Josh to various rehabilitation programs, he'd come across other young people with disabilities. Some of them lived in Kiawa and its hinterland region. Many couldn't, or wouldn't, attend mainstream schools, and the nearest special training college was a two-hour drive away. Thanks to their various sets of mental and physical challenges, these kids struggled to find jobs as they grew older. Parents faced a daunting choice. Should they uproot the entire family and head for the city to seek out opportunities for their child? Or should they stay in their community, close to social and family supports, but leave their child's future in limbo? Individual stories touched him. The mute teenage girl who'd spent an unsuccessful year looking for work, and now refused to leave her house. The poverty-stricken single mother trying to raise four kids and wrestling with her eldest son's autism at the same time. There but for the grace of God . . . not everybody had the Cooper's deep pockets.

Quinn came up with an idea. As president of the Kiawa Cane-growers' Association, he had some local clout. Why not ask members to take on one or more of these kids, provide them with a job, and train them for a career in agriculture? It was a big ask. Sugar prices had hit an all-time low, and the region was still recovering from last year's devastating floods. But, despite all this, the scheme had taken off. He'd spent a lot of time talking to families, trying to match each kid's abilities with the work on offer. A start-up government wage subsidy helped convince members, but so far most farmers had kept their PWSY employee on after the initial funding cut out. Some had even taken on another, and more growers were coming on board as word got out. Kiawa was rallying to help its own, and now over twenty local cane farms were part of the project. So many young people gaining confidence and independence, realising their potential, forging a future. Pity Josh wasn't one of them. Maybe he wasn't ready for more responsibility. Maybe he'd never be ready.

Quinn reached the house as Mal Owen and his son Shane pulled up. The teenager grinned and nodded a greeting. Not much older than Josh and already his father's right-hand man. A worm of envy squirmed in Quinn's stomach. 'Good turnout,' said Mal. He was right. The drive was crowded with vehicles. 'And no wonder. That young feller you sent me? Dylan? He's keen as mustard, sharp as a tack and a whizz with machinery to boot. Worked at the family truck repair shop, apparently, just for the fun of it, until his grandad retired. Then he couldn't get a job because he's deaf. Well, some other feller's missed out badly, because Dylan's the best new worker I've had in donkey's years. Never takes a sickie, never late . . .' Mal dug his son in the ribs. 'He could teach this shirker a thing or two, I can tell you.'

Shane grinned again. 'He already has. He's teaching me Auslan. I can swear at you, and you don't even know.'

Mal tousled his son's hair good-naturedly. 'Watch out, mate. I'm picking up that signing stuff too.'

Dylan's was a common success story. Young PWSY workers were earning themselves a fine reputation. Quinn employed two autistic kids himself to help with the harvest, both of them reliable and enthusiastic. Not like Josh. Josh, who mooched round the house all day playing online computer games, or spent his time fooling about with the dolphins. Half the time he even slept at Leo's shack next to the Reef Centre, so he could be there early the next morning. The kid was utterly unmotivated to do anything useful.

The raucous bass-and-drum sound of Metallica boomed down from the balcony, startling them all. They looked up to see Josh playing air guitar, lost in a loud, distorted riff. Quinn shook his head and smiled. Josh might not be responsible like Shane. He might not be keen-as-mustard like Dylan. He might never be either of those things. But for all his brother's faults, Quinn wouldn't have swapped him for the world.

CHAPTER 7

Zoe stood on the deck of *Seafarer*, the Reef Centre's nifty little runabout. Bridget was lowering what looked like a four-pronged grappling hook into the ocean. 'Won't that damage the coral?' asked Zoe.

Bridget pointed to the red buoy bobbing beside the boat. An improbable thing to see in this vast expanse of ocean. 'That buoy marks this as a designated anchor point, a bare rocky spot. We dive here all the time. And anyway, I'm using a specially designed reef pick that won't do much harm.'

'Confession time,' said Zoe. 'This is my first time on the Barrier Reef.'

Bridget looked up with a disbelieving expression. 'Where did you learn to dive?'

'In Sydney Harbour, just last year.' It was the only place Zoe had ever dived. Her theory classes were held in an historic sandstone building not far from the CBD. Practical lessons took place at a nearby wharf, among floating litter and stormwater pollution, and with the roar of city traffic in her ears. A far cry from this pristine place.

'Muck diving?' Bridget threw her an amused look. 'Well, you're in

48

for a treat today. This reef is in a Green Zone – no fishing allowed. It's teeming with life.'

Should she tell Bridget of the surprising beauty and diversity of Sydney's waters? Of the mysterious kelp forests and gardens of sea tulips. The cleverly camouflaged weedy seadragons? The bizarre and beautiful giant cuttlefish that grew to a metre long and were so friendly and curious that they followed you about. The shy Port Jackson sharks. Instead, she adjusted her mask one last time.

'Ready?' asked Bridget.

'Ready.' The next moment Zoe entered a vivid and unfamiliar underwater world. Several metres down now, and how very different this place was to Sydney. The stunning clarity of the water for one thing, invisible as air and yet so blue she might have been swimming in the sky. And all around, more kinds of fish and coral than she'd ever believed possible. She blinked in wonder at the dazzling array of colours – colours she didn't know could even exist in nature. Crazy neons, electric blues, and yellows so bright you almost needed sunglasses. And to think this was only the southernmost tip of the Great Barrier Reef.

Zoe ventured deeper, past a soft purple sea fan, over a spreading green coral as broad as a billiard table. She glanced up. A massive potato cod hovered above her, silhouetted against the shimmering surface. And look, there went a pale blue unicorn fish, its horn reminiscent of that mythical creature.

Bombarded by so much colour and movement, Zoe forgot the cardinal rule of scuba diving – she forgot to breathe. Hanging onto the lungful of air increased her buoyancy, and she began to rise. A feeling of being starved for breath and a growing pain in her chest alerted her to the danger. The deep draught of compressed air was expanding as she ascended, threatening to rupture her delicate alveoli, threatening to burst her lungs. She exhaled in a panic, resisting the instinct urging her to rush upwards. That was the worst possible thing to do. Instead she trod water and inhaled - slowly, mindfully. Next she exhaled with the same degree of conscious control. Only when she'd recovered the rhythm of her breath did she rise to the surface in slow motion, tossing aside her regulator and mask, gulping down the sweet air.

Bridget popped up beside her. 'Are you okay?'

'Sure.' Zoe hoped the word didn't sound too much like a gasp for breath. 'I just got a bit dizzy.' Something bumped her thigh and she looked down. Unbelievable — a hawksbill turtle. A critically endangered hawksbill turtle, the size of a car tyre, was munching on a sea sponge right beside her. Zoe laughed in delight, her fright forgotten. There was the hooked, raptor-like beak, the beautifully patterned serrated shell and the pair of claws adorning each flipper, just like in the photographs she'd seen.

Bridget tapped her on the shoulder and pointed to their left. Black fins cut the surface of the water, and a vast shadow passed beneath them. 'Back down, quickly.' Bridget vanished from sight.

Zoe followed her lead and was rewarded with a remarkable sight. Manta rays, five in all, caught up in a courtship train of magnificent grace. Nothing she'd read had prepared her for the sheer size of these animals. They dwarfed the divers. The larger female leading the dance was five metres across, wingtip to wingtip, and must have weighed a tonne.

This time Zoe's breathing remained regular and calm. There was something immensely peaceful about being in the presence of the great rays. Like a meditation. The eager suitors mirrored the female's every move, performing a series of backward rolls, looking for all the world like they had been choreographed. Now she sped to the surface and seemed to vanish. Her admirers performed the same trick. Where were they? Had they breached? Seconds later they reappeared like magic, slicing back into the water many metres from where they'd left it, flapping wings like giant birds as they flew away. If only she'd seen it from up top, seen the rays leap from the blue of the ocean into the blue of the sky. But then she wouldn't have witnessed their underwater ballet. The reef was filled with so many marvels that she needed two of her, at least, just so she didn't miss anything.

Zoe spent a marvellous half-hour exploring, trying not to hold her breath, observing the nonstop drama that was life on the reef. A purple scorpion fish launched itself from a rocky ledge, aiming for a striped angelfish, which escaped into swaying strands of soft coral just in time. Orange clownfish, like Nemo of Disney movie fame, nestled among the protective jade-green tentacles of bubble-tip anemones. Schools of shining silver barracuda and trevally sailed past. A giant Queensland grouper lived up to its reputation as bold and curious by investigating the stream of bubbles from Zoe's regulator. Then it settled on a prominent coral outcrop where little blue cleaner wrasse plied their trade, relieving the big fish of parasites, even venturing between its gaping jaws in perfect safety.

By the time she and Bridget went topside, the spell cast by Turtle Reef was complete. Zoe was in love. Not the kind of fickle, romantic love that had so often let her down. But a kind of joyful and profound passion, which moved her like the finest music, poetry or art.

'How does this compare to Sydney Harbour?' asked Bridget as she took off her gear. Her eyes held a smug certainty about the answer she would receive.

'Okay, you win,' said Zoe. 'There's no comparison.' She gulped from her water bottle, then flung herself onto a seat and hung over the side, unwilling to take her gaze away from the water.

Bridget shook out her long blonde hair, towel-drying it briefly before starting the motor and heading towards the shore. 'Next stop, the seagrass meadows fringing the mangroves. You'll see dugongs.'

'Stop it.' Zoe shielded her eyes from the sun. 'I don't think I can stand any more excitement.'

Sure enough, half an hour later Bridget killed the motor and Zoe spotted dark shapes beneath the surface – her first sight of a wild dugong and calf, grazing on the waving underwater fields of flowering seagrass. The pair used their front flippers to paddle to the surface every four or five minutes, breathing through nostrils on their vacuum snouts. Snouts that looked more like strange stunted trunks than noses. She could see firsthand how they were more closely related to elephants than to whales or other marine mammals. The boat drifted closer. So close, she could have reached out to touch the scars on the mother's back as it swam in a slow circle, keeping its body between the boat and its baby. It rolled to regard her with a wise, brown eye, then flicked its fluked tail and swam away.

Zoe collapsed on a seat. Overwhelmed. Stiff and sore from the unfamiliar physical activities, but more alive than she'd ever been. Her mind ranged through the events of the day. The horse ride to the Hump and her near fall. The sad story of Aisha the Arabian mare. The beauty of the reef dive and her sudden, breathless panic. So very different to a Monday in the engineering library back in Sydney. The contrast made her laugh aloud.

Bridget glanced across from where she sat at the helm. 'Something funny?'

'I'm just happy,' said Zoe. 'Utterly, deliriously happy.'

'Strap in.' Bridget flashed Zoe a Hollywood smile. 'This is just the beginning.'

'When do I get hands-on with the dugong research project?' she asked. 'I can't wait to get started.'

'That's the kind of enthusiasm I like to see.' Bridget checked her watch. 'I'll drop you off at the centre now.'

'I thought you were going to give me a research briefing?'

'We've run out of time. I'll radio ahead and ask Karen to brief you instead. Can't take you back to Swallowdale afterwards though. Dad's mayoral campaign launch is tonight and I promised to be there.'

'Not a problem,' said Zoe. 'I'll get home somehow.'

'Sorry. I haven't organised your car yet, have I?' The radio crackled and Bridget reached for it. 'Next week, I promise.'

'No worries,' said Zoe. Except it was a worry. She hated being shunted to and from work each day, like a child going to and from school. She wanted to explore Kiawa by herself, have some independence.

Bridget was talking to Karen on the radio, while Zoe settled in for the trip home. Tired now, content to stare at the late-afternoon horizon, where turquoise ocean met the impossible blue of the sky. They skirted close to shore. How many people, for how many centuries, had admired the same stunning view? In Sydney the pace of change made you dizzy. Here in Kiawa, nothing seemed to change. Time had forgotten this peaceful place.

Take Bridget and Quinn. Even romance was done differently here. They weren't going to live together until after the wedding. It was the sort of quaint, old-fashioned decision that didn't seem out of place in Kiawa. Bridget stayed the odd night at Swallowdale, but she lived with her father at Cliffhaven, the two-storey ocean-front home that lay only a few hundred metres from the Reef Centre. Zoe had tried a few times to peek in, but rocky sea cliffs either side of the property and a high front fence guaranteed mayoral privacy. According to Karen, the architect-designed house was the height of luxury, boasting its own private beach and mooring.

Zoe pictured the evening that lay ahead for her. Cooking for one. Washing up and a bit of laundry. Watching television alone or reading a book until bedtime. She half-hoped that Bridget might ask her to the launch party. No way to get home and change first, of course. She imagined Bridget saying, *Come to the party tonight. Nothing to wear? No problem. Borrow something of mine.* Then the embarrassment of trying to squeeze into size ten clothes. Still, it would be worth it for a night out, and to have a look around next door.

Zoe was an inquisitive person, more curious than most. She'd always been interested in what was on the other side of locked doors, and to discover how things worked. Her sister had another term for it - being a snoop. *'Why do you always have to go poking your nose where it doesn't belong, Zoe?'* Sometimes it got her into trouble. She was twelve when Dad proudly brought home a new computer. *'Don't mess with it,'* he said, but curiosity got the better of her. What if she clicked that icon? What did this file do? What would happen if she edited this or moved that? After accidentally deleting the operating system and disabling the security program, a virus led to a fatal error and the dreaded *blue screen of death.* Dad had lost all his files, including family photos, and had never quite forgiven her.

Then there was the time he set up a home marine aquarium for her birthday. Soon afterwards, she found a pretty octopus during a family day at the beach. So inquisitive was she about the little creature that she smuggled it home in her swimming bag and put it in the tank. It ate all the damselfish before her father spotted it and identified it as a deadly blue-ringed octopus. Despite her tears, he took the octopus back to the ocean, and the fancy aquarium back to the shop.

Zoe's curiosity didn't abate as she grew older. She lost her first job by asking too many questions about the high staff turnover at the local café where she worked. It turned out the new owner was hiring girls on trial shifts and then not paying them. The owner was fined and the café closed down. One time she'd snooped around in a boyfriend's bedroom, not realising he shared it with a two-metre-long pet python. The snake had given her a nasty bite. But it seemed she hadn't learned her lesson, because she was bursting to get a peek at Cliffhaven.

When they pulled up at the jetty, Zoe took ages gathering her gear, still hoping for an invitation, but it wasn't forthcoming. She chewed her lip in frustration. 'Have fun tonight.'

Bridget nodded absently, waited for her to disembark, then steered her boat towards the rocks that shielded Cliffhaven's private mooring from public view. Zoe let out a long, disappointed sigh. Maybe next time.

CHAPTER 8

Karen was waiting on the jetty, standing by the golf cart used to ferry elderly visitors to and from the main gate, and towing a trailer full of eskies. Archie must be on the way with a fish delivery.

'You're keen,' called Karen. 'Isn't this supposed to be your day off?'

'Bridget took me out to Turtle Reef,' said Zoe. 'I was blown away.'

'It has that effect alright.' Karen began unloading the eskies and lining them up along the wharf.

Zoe pitched in to help. 'I'm really looking forward to your briefing on the dugong research project.'

Karen straightened up. 'Sorry, not today. No time.'

'Didn't Bridget just talk to you?'

'No.'

'That doesn't make sense,' said Zoe. 'I heard her discuss it on the radio not ten minutes ago.'

'Well, it wasn't with me.' Karen pressed her lips together in a thin smile. 'I've only been here a few months myself, but there's one thing I've learned about our Miss Bridget. Sometimes she takes on too much, and things, well . . . things fall through the cracks.'

'I'm not sure what you mean.'

'Bridget's a people pleaser. She makes promises in the moment, because she wants people to like her. No matter how unrealistic that promise is. She's not always so great at following through.'

'Wants people to like her?' asked Zoe. 'Bridget doesn't have a problem with people liking her. Far from it.'

'You're right, she's charismatic. We're all half-under her spell, but don't put Bridget on a pedestal.' Karen put a kind hand on Zoe's shoulder. 'Golden Girl is as flawed as the rest of us. Now I must get out of this sun.' She went off to wait in the shade of the golf cart.

Zoe trailed her hand along the rough jetty rail, mulling over Karen's words. Bridget hadn't organised her research briefing after all. So what? She was a busy person. Had Zoe put her on a pedestal? She did admire Bridget enormously - even envied her a little. Maybe more than a little. Bridget had it all. Drop-dead gorgeous and director of her own research centre. A doctoral thesis from the prestigious Marine Mammal Institute of California. And, to top it all off, she was engaged to Quinn. Zoe kicked idly at a steel bollard and stole a glance at Karen, who was fanning herself with a notebook and looking at her phone. Was that why Karen said the things she did? Was she jealous of Bridget?

A dot in the distance grew larger and turned into a boat. Archie's old timber-framed fishing vessel *Rambler* on its way in with a delivery. Karen was already on her feet, opening the esky lids. Zoe groaned. She should have nicked off while she could. Now it would be rude if she didn't help.

'Ahoy there.' Archie threw Karen a line, and the stink of dead fish wafted over the wharf. He was a beefy man in his fifties, with squinty eyes sunk deep in the sunburnt skin of his face. A faded Coca Cola cap shielded his bald head from the Queensland sun. His short beard was salted with grey, and always looked like it could use a wash. 'Got a beaut load for you today.' Archie lowered the gangplank and carted a large crate down to the pier. It was full of plastic bags containing fish on ice: herring and whiting, squid and shrimp. Karen checked it over, nodded approval and started transferring bags from the crate into the eskies.

Archie turned to Zoe. 'Any chance of giving old Archie a hand?'

She followed him up the gangway onto the flat, square stern. On one side a hold contained more crates of fish – and something else. Two live tanks, one with crabs and crays, and another holding a large octopus. The creature explored its stainless steel prison with questing arms, desperately seeking an escape route.

Zoe had a soft spot for octopuses, ever since her adventure with the blue-ringed variety as a child. She'd also been fond of Gloomy, her test subject back at Sydney Aquarium, and the sight of his doomed cousin filled her with pity. 'How much for the octopus?'

Archie put down the crate of squid he was carrying and chuckled. 'That bugger? Found him and a bunch of his mates in my pots stealing crabs. The rest were too quick for me. Got out before I had the pots up.' Archie scratched his beard and coughed. 'That feller was meant for bait.' Better not tell him that fresh octopus went for thirty dollars a kilo at the Sydney fish market. 'What do you want an octopus for?' he said. 'I can't hardly give 'em away.'

'For the aquarium,' said Zoe. 'I want to display it in our aquarium.'

'Take him then.' Archie lifted up the crate again. 'He's on the house.' When they finished unloading the fish, he put the octopus into a green garbage bag and handed it to Zoe. 'With old Archie's compliments.' He doffed his hat and headed back to the boat.

'What have you got there?' asked Karen.

Zoe opened the neck of the bag and an olive-coloured arm snaked out. She pushed it back down. 'Can I have a tank for him? There's the one the baby seahorses were in.'

'I suppose,' said Karen. 'People might be quite interested in an octopus.'

'Of course they will be,' said Zoe. 'Einstein here will be a star attraction.'

Karen laughed. 'I know those things are meant to be smart, but Einstein?'

'Their brains are fascinating,' said Zoe. 'They run on a decentralized nervous system that evolved in a completely different way from vertebrate brains. Some scientists think they're as intelligent as dogs.'

Karen flinched as an arm escaped from the bag again. 'That slimy thing might be brainy, but I'd rather cuddle up with my cocker spaniel any day. Come on, let's get this fish packed away. Then you can set up a tank for him. I have to go soon, so you'll need to lock up by yourself.'

'That's fine.' Zoe thought about the campaign party going on next door, the party to which she hadn't been invited, and shrugged. 'I've got nothing better to do.'

The octopus flowed from the garbage bag into the tank, and half-buried itself in the sandy bottom beside a rock. It turned from green to creamy-brown, blending in perfectly with the new background. It was of medium size, with a muscular body. Little raised horns above its eyes gave it a devilish expression. Long arms with two rows of suckers crept towards the corner of the aquarium and explored the glass. Zoe had forgotten what an alarmingly alien animal an octopus really was. Jet-powered, master of camouflage, a shape-shifter. Three hearts pumping blue, copper-based blood around his boneless body. Zoe examined it more closely. A representative of *Octopus australis*, commonly known as the hammer octopus, named for the club-like, tentacle tip found in mature males. This specimen possessed no such modification. So Einstein was a girl. Zoe gazed into her strange, horizontal pupils. Hypnotised. Convinced a consciousness gazed back.

'It's beautiful.' The sudden sound of a voice in the quiet made Zoe spin around in fright. Josh stood right behind her, staring into the tank. Einstein buried herself deeper in the sand.

A slow flush of embarrassment crept up the boy's face. 'Sorry.'

'No, no, it's fine. You startled me, that's all.' Zoe looked around, but there was nobody else in the seaquarium. 'Where's Bridget? Did she come back for something?'

'No.'

'What are you doing here by yourself? Does Bridget know?'

He shifted uneasily. 'I'm allowed.'

'Of course you are,' said Zoe. 'I just mean . . .' What did she mean? She had no idea what Josh was or wasn't allowed to do.

He pointed to the octopus. 'What's his name? Can I feed him?'

'*Her* name is Einstein and, yes, you can feed her. I was just going to see if she'll eat.' Zoe fetched some live shrimp from the storeroom breeding tanks. She let Josh drop a few in and they stood back to watch. A large shrimp trundled along the sand towards the rock. To Zoe's delight, Einstein billowed from her hiding place, glowing pink with excitement, and enveloped the unfortunate crustacean beneath her mantle.

'How does she eat?' asked Josh.

'She has a sharp beak, like a parrot,' said Zoe. 'She also has poison, like a snake, to paralyse her prey. An enzyme in her saliva breaks down protein. Turns the inside of the shrimp into liquid, and she sucks it up like you'd suck up a milkshake through a straw. Look, she's going for another one.'

Josh was captivated by the scene being played out before him, they both were. When Zoe finally checked her watch, it was after seven o'clock. 'How are you getting home, Josh? Is Quinn picking you up? I might need a lift.' She rather fancied a lift from Quinn.

'He's at the party,' said Josh. 'I didn't want to go. He said I could stay at the shack tonight.'

'The shack?'

'You know, that little house up on the cliff above the beach.'

'I thought it wasn't fit to stay in?' said Zoe.

'There's nothing wrong with it,' said Josh. 'I like staying there. I get to spend time with the dolphins when nobody's around.'

'That must be fun.'

Josh nodded and grinned. Such a good-looking kid, with no outward sign of his disability. Except, perhaps, for a certain naivety in his expression, a naivety more commonly found in children. 'We could go there if you like?'

'Okay.' She was curious about the place where she'd been meant to stay before Bridget changed her mind. During the past week she'd often gazed up at the little bungalow, balanced halfway up the rocks between the Reef Centre and Cliffhaven. How had it ever won planning approval? Its windows overlooked both the ocean and Dolphin Harbour. A steep drive cut into the cliff provided car access from a private road at the back, and a series of steep stone steps led up directly from a gate set in the side fence of the centre. They'd be a challenge for somebody afraid of heights, but nothing could be as tough as that first day, climbing the lookout tower. And there'd be a spectacular view out to sea as a reward. Zoe put the last few shrimps into the tank, and checked the filter was working properly.

'Right Josh, lead the way.'

'This is gorgeous.' Zoe wandered from room to room. The charming retro decor gave it a fifties surf shack feel, but it also had all the mod cons. Newly renovated by the looks of it, yet the classic laminex kitchen table was the same as her grandmother's. Woven cane hoop chairs, red gloss kitchen cupboards and colourful wall prints. Wide windows offered a stunning, one-hundred-and-eighty-degree view of the foreshore and rocky, coral coast. The place oozed warmth and character

Zoe ventured, white-knuckled, onto the little balcony with its quaint wrought-iron patio setting for two. The structure seemed to be perched precariously in mid-air. She took some deep breaths to steady her racing heart and held tight to the railing. A timber stairway, painted to match the shack's white weatherboard exterior, led down from the covered deck to a sheltered beach below. She ducked back inside to safety. How wonderful it would be to live here. How perfect. Zoe tried idly to twirl a finger in her too-short hair. Why had Bridget said this place was rundown?

The north-facing windows overlooked what must be the rear of Cliffhaven, giving her a bird's-eye view of the party. There was one of those infinity pools where the edge seemed to join the sea. Beyond it lay an ocean swimming hole, bounded by a natural rocky ledge. A crowd was gathered around a large white marquee set up on a lawn area above the beach. Two people were setting up tiki torches, and a man in a chef's hat was tending a pig on a spit. Zoe looked longingly at a girl filling glasses with bubbling champagne.

Josh touched her arm and pointed out to sea. 'Dolphins.' Sure enough, a pod of dolphins were surfing just offshore. He disappeared inside briefly and returned with two pairs of binoculars. 'Here.' Zoe reluctantly let go of the railing and adjusted the lenses. The dolphins were circling now, backs gleaming in the late sunshine as they arched through the water 'I think they're rounding up a school of pilchards or whiting,' she said. 'Yes, yes. Look at those gulls and terns, swooping on a ball of baitfish. You can see its shadow, moving beneath the surface. Now gannets are joining in. Look at the size of them, just like mini dive-bombers.' It felt like she could almost reach out and touch them.

'Sharks,' said Josh.

Zoe raised her binoculars a little. Half a dozen dark forms were moving in fast from the reef. Larger than the dolphins, and deeper swimmers, they ripped into the bait ball, splitting it in two. 'Hammerheads.' From the deck they had a front-row seat for the unfolding drama. The large, oddly-shaped sharks bore eyes at each end of their elongated heads, giving them a three-hundred-and-sixty-degree view of their underwater world. Smaller reef sharks were joining in. Predators from above and below, working together, putting aside their differences to divide and conquer. After ten minutes, all that remained of the huge shoal were a few scattered schools of fish, powerless to avoid the sheer numbers of their pursuers.

Zoe put down her binoculars, breathless with excitement. 'Thank you so much for bringing me here, Josh.' The boy grinned at her. 'Have you had any dinner?'

'No.'

'Fancy a walk into town? We could get fish and chips?' she said. 'My shout.'

Zoe put the parcel down on the table between them and opened the butcher's paper. Steam rose into the twilight. They sat out on the deck to watch the sunset, drinking lemonade and sharing their chips. Josh started on a piece of crisp battered snapper while Zoe unwrapped her hamburger. Since starting work at the Reef Centre, she couldn't bring herself to eat fish any more. Josh shovelled food in at a great rate, chewed with his mouth open, slurped his drink and burped unashamedly, but in this informal setting it seemed quite natural. She was no expert on teenage boys. Perhaps they all ate like that.

'So you were a champion endurance rider,' said Zoe. 'I'm impressed.' The words had already slipped out before she realised how tactless her remark was. What if he'd rather forget all that? What if it dredged up terrible memories about the accident? But one look at Josh's face dispelled her fears. His eyes shone with pleasure and pride.

'I won six trophies,' he said. 'I could win more too, if I could ride again.'

'You don't ride any more?'

'Nope.'

'Did the doctor say you can't?'

Josh hung his head. 'Quinn.'

'I suppose he's just trying to look after you. Keep you safe.'

'I don't want to be safe.' Josh threw a chip to a waiting gull. 'I want to be happy. I want to live.'

The misery in his voice caused a cloud of sadness to settle on her. 'Can't you talk to your brother? Make him understand how important this is to you?'

'We used to talk.' Josh swallowed hard. 'We used to talk a lot. Not anymore. Not since Dad died.'

'What about Bridget?' asked Zoe. 'Perhaps she could get through to him?'

'She won't go against him.'

Zoe flared with indignation on Josh's behalf. If he was physically fit and capable, and he certainly seemed to be, why shouldn't he ride again? This was the first time she'd spent an extended period of time with Josh. Once you got used to his halting speech, poor table manners, and lack of respect for personal space, there wasn't much wrong with the kid.

'Would you like me to try?' she asked. 'See if I can make Quinn understand?'

'Maybe.' He gave her a shy smile. 'Maybe, yes?'

'I'll corner him when I can,' said Zoe. 'In return, could you help me with Cobber? I'm a beginner at this horse-riding caper, and Quinn couldn't possibly object to you giving me some tips from the ground.'

Josh extended his arm. 'Deal.'

They laughed and shook hands. Live jazz music drifted up from below, along with the soft background murmur of party conversation. It merged with the song of the sea into a kind of lullaby. Zoe yawned. She'd had a big day. Life in Kiawa was so in your face. She rarely ever felt physically tired back in Sydney. 'How will I get home?'

'Stay here,' said Josh. He grabbed her hand, pulled her inside and led her to a charming little room with a single bed. Zoe peered through the bamboo blind. The window overlooked the centre. She could see the rising moon reflected in the waters of Dolphin Harbour. 'Where do you sleep, Josh?'

'On the other side.'

'Show me.' She followed him back into the lounge and down the short hall to what was clearly the master bedroom. Built-in robes, en suite and an ocean view to die for. The mess, unmade bed and clothes-strewn floor indicated that Josh often slept here. 'Do you think Bridget or Quinn would mind if I stayed?' Josh shook his head. Zoe yawned again. She *was* tired, very tired. Too tired to walk the ten kilometres back to Swallowdale. What else was she supposed to do? There were no taxi ranks in Kiawa.

CHAPTER 9

The old-fashioned, wind-up alarm clock woke Zoe more effectively than her phone ever had. Great idea — no snooze button. Although why she'd set an alarm she didn't know. Tuesday was her day off. She sat up, worked out how to turn off the twin jangling bells and checked the time. Six o'clock. A warm breeze lifted the blind at the open window. She could taste the sea and feel the tide going out by the slapping rhythm of waves on the beach. Heaven. Just as well she hadn't been invited to last night's party, with all that champagne on offer. Since coming to Kiawa she'd woken up every single morning with a clear head.

A soft knocking came at the door. Josh opened it a crack. 'I've made toast.'

She rubbed sleep from her eyes. 'Be there in a minute.' The door closed. Zoe dragged herself out of bed and grabbed her clothes from where they lay higgledy-piggledy on the rattan chair.

She dressed quickly and went to the bathroom to brush her teeth. Hmm . . . her shorts seemed looser than usual. She hiked them up a few times without success. Was she losing weight? Habit told her to jump on the scales. It had been a depressing part of her daily routine in Sydney. But there weren't any scales. There weren't even any full-length mirrors – not here in the shack, back in her little cottage, or even in the guest bathroom of the main house at Swallowdale. Apparently people in Kiawa didn't worry too much about how much they weighed or what they looked like. The irony was that most of them looked fantastic, with the kind of fit, natural grace that went hand in hand with sunny weather and an outdoor life.

Zoe headed to the kitchen, drawn by the cheerful sound of a whistling kettle, chuffed by the idea that soon she might actually have to buy a belt for her shorts. Rounding the corner she stopped dead in the doorway. Josh was nowhere to be seen. Instead, a tall man she didn't know was lifting the red kettle from the stove. He was older, close to fifty, wearing sharply creased trousers and a white business shirt with rolled-up sleeves. Not conventionally handsome, perhaps; mouth too wide and nose too thin. Still, with his penetrating blue eyes, thick dark hair and erect bearing, he was most certainly a man of presence. And there was something oddly familiar about him. He smiled, his teeth perfect and blinding white beneath a clipped brown moustache. 'Coffee?'

'And you are . . . ?'

'My apologies.' He put down the kettle, strode towards her and extended an arm. 'Mayor Leo Macalister, messenger boy, at your service. Welcome to Kiawa.'

Zoe's intake of breath was audible as she shook his hand. Of course, he had Bridget's eyes. 'I'm Zoe King from the Reef Centre. I hope you don't mind . . .'

'I know who you are.' His grasp was firm and friendly, his gaze disturbingly direct, with a hint of the cynic about him. 'Josh told me on his way out. He wanted me to give you this.' Leo handed her a plate of burned vegemite toast.

'Josh has gone?' asked Zoe. 'That was sudden.'

'Archie's bringing in a new dolphin, and Bridget asked me to give Josh the message. She knows how devoted he is to those animals. And Quinn asked me to remind him about a doctor's appointment in Bundaberg today.' Leo pulled a face. 'Josh didn't seem too happy about it.'

'Your daughter's very good with Josh,' said Zoe.

'My daughter's very good with everybody.'

Zoe forced a smile. For some reason his words rankled. Was she getting fed up with the Bridget Macalister cheer squad? She tried to push the thought away, but yesterday's conversation with Karen crept back. *Golden Girl is as flawed as the rest of us.* Zoe derived a degree of *schadenfreude* from the thought.

'From what I hear you're a very talented researcher.' Leo placed a friendly hand on her shoulder before turning back to the kettle. Did his hand linger a fraction too long? Would she mind if it did? He was older, but still an attractive man. Giving up on men didn't preclude a little harmless flirting, surely? He poured two strong black coffees and sat down at the table. 'Bridget's been singing your praises. Says we're lucky to have you.'

Zoe plonked herself down on a chair and wrapped her fingers around the mug in front of her. Gratitude and guilt tied her tongue in knots. She owed everything to Bridget.

'Here's an idea,' said Leo. 'A few of us are heading out today for some fishing. Why not join us?'

'Thank you, but no.'

A spark of challenge flared in Leo's eyes. 'Bridget tells me you don't work Tuesdays'

Zoe squirmed a little as she tried to explain. 'The truth is, I see fish more as friends than anything else. I don't want to hurt them. And, in any case, I want to drop into work and check on that new dolphin myself.'

Leo sipped the black brew, his brow creased in thought. 'So you're a sentimental girl, like my Bridget.' Zoe couldn't tell whether he meant it as a criticism or compliment. 'How about a sightseeing trip to the outer reef instead?' he said. 'Next Monday. I'll square it with your boss and swing by here at nine o'clock; let you have a bit of a sleep-in.'

Typical of a Kiawan, thinking nine o'clock was a late start.

'But I live at Swallowdale. I only stayed here last night because I couldn't get a lift back.'

'You mean nobody's organised you a car? No? I'll have one delivered out to Quinn's today. But for the life of me, I don't know why you don't just stay here.'

Zoe didn't know either, and wanted to jump at the invitation. Living at the shack would be utterly perfect, but instead she bit her lip. 'Thank you, but I'm perfectly happy out at Swallowdale.' It was obvious that Josh saw this place as his turf, and it might put his nose out of joint if she moved in. And then there was Bridget, who'd been dishonest about the condition of the shack. For some reason Bridget didn't want her here and it wouldn't do to provoke her boss. Still, Zoe couldn't help being curious about Bridget's motives.

'Suit yourself.' Leo pushed his chair back and stood up. 'Well, I'm off.' He fixed her with persuasive blue eyes. 'Looking forward to that trip to the reef. Nothing I enjoy more than showing off Kiawa's natural attractions to visitors, especially ones as beautiful as you.'

A slight flush of heat rose from her neck to her face and threatened to erupt in an embarrassing blush. It was a relief when Leo shut the door behind him. Zoe couldn't deny there was a degree of mutual attraction, despite the age difference, despite her decision to swear off men – despite the fact that Leo was Bridget's father. What would she think if Zoe hooked up with dear old dad? No, it was impossible. Better steer clear of the men in Bridget's life, although an innocent trip out to the reef couldn't hurt. Zoe waited until she was sure Leo had gone, then hurried out into the bright morning and down the steep stone steps to the centre below.

Josh and Archie carried the canvas hammock from the boat to where Karen waited on the pier. The new dolphin lay motionless in its stretcher, eyes shut like it was dead. They gently loaded it onto the golf cart, and Bridget and Josh jumped in beside it. Zoe hung onto the back and willed the cart to hurry as it trundled towards the hospital compound. Just a few days ago, this animal, a juvenile bottlenose by the look of it, had been roaming the wide blue ocean with others of its kind. Now it lay deathly still and terrified in an alien world, literally out of its element. 'What happened?'

'Found beached,' said Bridget.

'It's so quiet.'

'They're nearly all like that when they first come in,' said Bridget. 'For one thing, they're sick and exhausted. And for another, they're helpless out of water. Dolphins' main defences against attack are escape or ramming, and they can't do either. No wonder shock sets in so easily.' Karen took the corner at what was top speed for the golf buggy. 'Don't worry,' said Bridget with a reassuring smile. 'George is ready and waiting.'

'What have we here?' asked the vet. With Josh's help he weighed the dolphin and got it safely onto the examination bench in the clinic. 'A young adult male, severely underweight. No obvious external injuries.' He peered at its red, angry-looking back and the bleeding cuts from where it had scraped against the tailgate of the cart. Zoe winced to see them. She'd discovered to her shame how delicate dolphin skin was when she accidentally drew blood from Baby with a sharp fingernail.

'Sunburn.' The vet lifted one eyelid with his finger, and then the other. 'They're clear.' He treated the wounds on the skin topically, then prised open the dolphin's mouth. The animal opened his eyes wide, but allowed the examination. 'Ah, see this? A fish hook lodged in his jaw. Looks like he tried to steal an easy meal.' George worked the vicious barb free. 'It's time the fishing industry used hooks that corrode away. It would save a lot of lives.' The vet pulled out a stethoscope and began a full medical exam.

Josh brought over a pen, a notebook and a bucket of water. Bridget poured some over the dolphin's back and produced a tape measure. 'Hold the end of this please, Zoe, and record the numbers.' Zoe dutifully did as she was asked: distance from tip to tail, eye to blowhole, circumference of waist and rostrum.

The vet drew blood from a vein in the animal's tail fluke. 'I'll test for morbillivirus. There've been a few outbreaks this year.' He administered a hefty injection.

'What's that?' asked Zoe.

'A giant dose of vitamins and long-lasting antibiotics,' he said. 'Even healthy dolphins sicken easily in captivity. They arrive with no immunity to human pathogens. Simple pneumonia, for instance, can kill them in no time.'

Once the newcomer was treated and measured they lowered him into the quarantine pool. Josh and Bridget hopped in too, supporting the dolphin for a few minutes until, to everyone's relief, he began to swim by himself. He blundered around the small tank, confused and disoriented, scraping his sides and banging his rostrum until it bled. George jumped in and administered a second injection. 'A mild sedative.'

The young animal's obvious distress was very confronting. For the first time Zoe considered what captivity really meant for a wild dolphin, one that had known only the boundless freedom of the open ocean. Hemmed in on all sides, sonar signals ricocheting off the walls in what must be an assault on its senses, a cacophony of sound or something like it. Add in exhaustion, prolonged time out of the water and loss of its family – no wonder so many rescued dolphins subsequently died.

The sedative was doing its work and the dolphin grew calm. It floated at the surface, blowhole rhythmically opening and closing in a way that was almost hypnotic. 'He'll be fine now,' said George.

'Thank goodness for that,' said Karen. She knelt down and stroked the animal's back. 'I'm always worried you'll overdo the dose, George.'

'So am I,' he said. 'It's a bit of a gamble. Sedatives and dolphins are a dangerous mix.'

'Why?' asked Josh.

'Dolphins aren't like us,' said George. 'They must remember to take each breath.'

'It's bizarre but true,' said Zoe. 'Dolphins are conscious breathers. Scientists discovered it when they anaesthetised some dolphins to attach electrodes to their brains. Some sort of neuroanatomy trial. As soon as the dolphins fell unconscious they stopped breathing and died.'

'What a cruel experiment,' said Bridget. 'How could they do that?'

Zoe shot her a sharp look. It almost sounded like Bridget hadn't heard the story before. But that was impossible. Any undergraduate student of zoology would know of the infamous experiments conducted by neuroscientist Dr John Lilly in the sixties. It was basic *Marine Mammals 101* stuff.

George packed up his bag. 'Call me if you need me.'

Bridget got out of the water. 'Come on, Josh, he needs to rest.' The boy didn't move. Her tone turned low and coaxing. 'If you get out now, I'll let you name him.'

Josh climbed reluctantly from the tank. 'I don't know what to call him yet,' he said. 'I have to get to know him first.'

'Of course you do,' said Bridget. 'We'll give him a number until you decide — twenty-two.'

'Will he be alright?' asked Josh.

'We'll know more when the blood results come back,' said Bridget. 'He's very thin, though. I don't think he'll be going back in the bay any time soon.'

'That's a shame,' said Zoe.

'Think of it this way – if we weren't here he'd have no hope at all. He's really a very lucky dolphin.'

Karen cleaned the equipment while Bridget collected her notes and favoured Zoe with her most dazzling smile. 'Did you get home alright yesterday?' Fortunately she didn't wait for an answer. 'The party at Dad's was wonderful. Quinn and I danced the night away.' Zoe glanced across at Josh. Would he tell? She didn't want her boss to know that she'd stayed at the shack overnight, but wasn't exactly sure why.

Bridget put a hand on Josh's shoulder. 'I'll have someone run you back to Swallowdale. Quinn says you have a doctor's appointment this afternoon.' The boy groaned. 'Would you like a lift back too, Zoe? I'm sure you don't want to hang around the centre on your day off. I don't know why you came down here in the first place.'

Zoe was tempted to stay and monitor the new arrival, but she also wanted to go home and have a shower. Her clothes felt unpleasant, sticky with perspiration. Then there was Leo's promise of a car. Maybe it was already waiting for her back at Swallowdale? What a joy to be able to come and go as she pleased. Explore the coast and hinterland, stay back late at work whenever she wanted, duck into town for Kiawa's limited takeaway options instead of cooking. Marvellous.

Zoe stood up from where she'd been squatting by the tank. 'I'll just check on my octopus before we go.' She hurried to the seaquarium where Einstein was so perfectly camouflaged beside a rock, that it took a while to spot her. 'See you tomorrow,' she said. 'We have a training date.'

CHAPTER 10

It was unseasonable weather for late September: hot and humid, with a strengthening west wind. Quinn stood on the verandah as the jeep made its way up the sweeping drive towards the house. Good, Josh was in the back seat. That would have been Bridget's doing – she had a way with him. Quinn had half-expected Josh not to come home at all. The kid hated his outpatient appointments at the Bundaberg hospital, especially the longer sessions that involved rehabilitation therapy. He thought them a waste of time.

Privately Quinn was inclined to agree. From what he could tell, they seemed to accomplish little more than to remind Josh of his limitations. But they were part of the expert care plan, a plan that Quinn intended to follow to the letter. Since their father's death, responsibility for Josh's recovery hung heavily on him. He was determined to maximise his brother's progress in every way he could.

Zoe followed Josh from the car. She looked like she'd slept in her clothes and her strange, spiky hair stood out on end in all directions. Funny that before her arrival he'd been expecting a sophisticated city girl.

Quinn liked Zoe. She had an indefinable, quirky appeal and a keen intelligence. A forthright tongue that both irritated and intrigued him.

A soft, womanly shape that made him catch his breath more than once. He cleared the unwelcome thought from his mind. Someone like him, someone engaged to the sweetest, most beautiful woman in the world, had no right to be thinking of anybody else in that way.

He'd always known he would marry Bridget. The two of them were thrust together from the beginning. Kiawa was a small town. The Coopers and Macalisters mixed in the same circles. He and Bridget went to the same school, although she was two year levels below him. As children they shared not only social events, but also the difficulties of dealing with powerful, domineering fathers. As the pair reached their teens, their friendship evolved into romantic attraction. The match was heartily endorsed by both families. The daughter of Leo Macalister, a man who owned half the town, teamed with the son of cane king Marshall Cooper — it seemed like the perfect fit.

After school Bridget left Kiawa to go to university. She travelled the world to pursue postgrad work while Quinn stayed home on the farm, dealing with a succession of personal blows: Josh's accident and long rehabilitation; his father's death; a fall in sugar prices that forced him to dismiss some of Dad's oldest and most trusted employees. It was like betraying members of his family. It had been a lonely, difficult time and, through no fault of her own, Bridget was gone when he needed her most. Maintaining a long-distance romance wasn't easy, and when Bridget finally returned eight months ago, she'd altered in some subtle way that Quinn couldn't put his finger on. Or maybe it was him. Dealing with so much grief by himself was bound to change a man.

Bridget was as keen as ever to get married and, if anything, she'd grown even more beautiful. Her extraordinary devotion to Josh surprised and moved him, but although she still played the part of the perfect partner, something indefinable was missing. Her focus had subtly shifted away from him. She was so bloody busy with her job, that was the problem. They never had time to talk any more, not to really talk. Quinn could have strangled Leo when he gave Bridget the position of director at that rundown marine park. Talk about a hospital pass. But she was determined to show her father that she could make a success of the Reef Centre.

'That place hasn't turned a profit for years,' Quinn said when she first took over. 'Why don't you ask Leo to sink some more money into it? He should have done it a long time ago.'

The suggestion horrified her. She was determined to show her father that she could make a success of the Reef Centre. Quinn understood her motivation all too well. Like his own father, Leo was a hard taskmaster – demanding and larger than life. Bridget had spent her entire childhood seeking, but not finding, his favour. As an adult, that hunger for approval hadn't changed. Quinn knew it to be folly. It was easier for him. He'd emerged from his father's shadow.

To her credit, Bridget seemed to be succeeding with the Reef Centre. Since starting the dolphin shows, crowd numbers were up, and with Zoe there to take some of the load off? Well, it might just give him and Bridget the chance they needed to become close again. By the time of their marriage next autumn, Quinn hoped things between them would be back on track. It was a long time to wait, but he was a patient man. Nothing ever happened in a hurry in Kiawa.

Quinn stepped down from the verandah. 'Hello, Zoe.' He tipped his hat. 'Ten minutes till we leave, Josh. Go get cleaned up.' Two cars turned into the driveway. One of them was Leo's red Lexus. What was he doing here?

But instead of Leo, a well-groomed young woman emerged from behind the wheel. 'I'm looking for Zoe King.'

'That's me.' The woman looked Zoe up and down for a moment. 'Compliments of the mayor.' She tossed the car keys to Zoe, who fumbled the catch. Josh retrieved them for her as the woman got into the second vehicle and was driven away.

Zoe walked around the car, trailing her fingers along the shiny red paintwork in a way that gave Quinn an unexpected shiver inside. 'That's Leo's Lexus,' he said.

She hesitated for a moment, as if thinking her answer through. 'I met Mr Macalister this morning and told him I didn't have a car yet.

He said he'd organise it. I'm supposed to have one, you know. It's in my contract.'

Quinn shifted his feet. Seems like he wasn't the only one who'd noticed Zoe King. Leo always did have an eye for a pretty girl - the old scoundrel. Zoe slipped into the driver's seat, showing off a pale, shapely leg in the process. Josh hopped in beside her. 'Want a ride?' she asked. 'I could drive you to Bundaberg for your appointment.'

'Yes,' said Josh with a grin. He looked happier than Quinn had seen him for a long time.

'I can't ask you to do that,' said Quinn. 'We'll be hours.'

'You didn't ask,' she said. 'I offered, and it's not like I've got anything else to do. It's my day off.'

'I want Zoe to drive me,' Josh's face set into an expression of stubborn defiance that Quinn knew all too well. 'Or I won't go.'

Quinn scratched his beard. 'Okay, Zoe. We'll take your new toy for a spin.'

'Great. I'm dying to try this thing out. It seems very flash for a council car.'

Quinn snorted. How naive was she? 'When I said that's Leo's Lexus, I meant it's his own, personal car. And Leo doesn't lend his vehicles lightly.'

'Oh.' Zoe looked bewildered. 'It's probably just temporary, until he can organise something more suitable.'

'Probably.' He hadn't meant to sound sarcastic, but Zoe gave him an unhappy look. 'Josh, go tidy yourself up,' he said. 'And hurry, or we'll be late.'

Zoe looked down at her crumpled clothes and ran a hand through her hair. 'I'd better change too.' Quinn sighed. It was going to be a long afternoon.

'You two go in while I park the car,' said Zoe.

Quinn shepherded Josh to the enquiries desk at the outpatients department of Bundaberg hospital. 'Josh Cooper,' he said. 'Here for his three-thirty with Ann Carter.'

The receptionist checked her computer. 'Down the hall to room nine. Last on the right. I'll let her know you're here.'

Josh's cheerful therapist beamed as they came in. 'Hello Josh.'

He ignored her and started to fiddle with a wooden puzzle box on the table.

She turned her attention to Quinn. 'I hope you'll reconsider my offer of a live-in place for your brother at the Biala Special School It's a fantastic opportunity for him to make friends, and the teachers there are terrific. They really understand kids like Josh. I can't hold it forever.'

A mutinous-looking Josh began to back out of the door. Quinn pushed him forward. 'My brother stays with me. Nobody understands him better than I do.'

The smile on the woman's face slipped a little. 'Very well, if you've made up your mind . . . We'll be at least an hour. Josh missed his last session and there's a lot to catch up on.'

Quinn ducked out of the clinic's double glass doors to where Zoe waited in the shade of a tulipwood tree. She wore a green-striped sleeveless cotton shift that looked a size too big for her and a wide straw hat. The tops of her shoulders showed red, peeling from too much sun, exposing small patches of skin the colour of wheat. The wind blew her dress against her legs, outlining their shape. Today was the first time he'd seen her in a dress. It suited her.

'Have we time to look around Bundaberg?' she asked.

'Not the best day for a walk. It's blowing a gale.'

'I don't mind,' said Zoe. 'I'd pay for a tour of that post office. There are some beautiful old buildings here.'

'Okay. Living somewhere all your life, you don't take much notice.'

'It's the same with me and Sydney,' she said. 'You know, I've never been to Bondi Beach.'

Quinn had a sudden desire to show off the town. 'We could take a look at the churches as well. Very historic. The Catholic church is designed like a Roman temple, and built in the shape of a cross. The

Anglican one is more Gothic, with pointed arches and spires. I think St Andrews is the oldest. It has a massive pipe organ and a carillon in the tower - a set of musical bells. They're quite beautiful to listen to.'

'Yes please,' said Zoe. 'But I'd like to see the river first.' She handed him the keys. 'You know where you're going.'

They stood in Anzac Park and watched the broad Burnett River wend its lazy way to the bay. 'See that bridge?' said Quinn. 'Over a hundred years old. Used to be a tollway. They charged a penny for pedestrians and threepence for carts.'

'Who says the cost of living never goes down.' Zoe laughed and two dimples appeared in the middle of her rosy, wind-whipped cheeks.

A sharp squall stole her hat and carried it down the bank towards the water. They both leaped at once. Quinn reached the river first and snatched it from the air in the nick of time. Zoe couldn't stop and cannoned into him. They both lost their balance and crashed to the ground, their fall cushioned by the lush spring grass. Quinn's own hat fell off and Zoe sprang to retrieve it. Despite the tumble and the wind, her short hair still lay strangely flat, all in one direction, like she'd just surfaced from a dive.

Quinn climbed slowly to his feet. Zoe put his Akubra on her own head, stood on her toes and twirled around. The action seemed so natural, so uninhibited, so unlike anything that Bridget would do, that it caught him by surprise. Her skirt lifted and spun, its shadow dancing over the grass. On an impulse he lunged for his hat, but she lightly sidestepped him and ran for the trees. In a trice he gave chase, cornering her behind a white fig, resisting the urge to take her hand and pull her to him. They laughed, swapped hats and sat side by side on a low wall overlooking the river's wide waters.

There was a lump in his throat. Quinn brimmed with an unfamiliar kind of carefree happiness, like the fall had knocked all the stiffness out of him. He turned to Zoe, felt the drawing power of her eyes. What was it about this odd girl that stirred him so?

'Tell me about your mother,' she said.

It was the last thing he'd expected her to say - and it was none of her business - but for some reason he didn't care. 'Mum died a long time ago, soon after Josh was born.' He kicked his heel against the wall. 'Josh was completely unexpected. Mum didn't think she could have a second baby, not at forty, not with kidney disease. Doctors advised ending the pregnancy but she wouldn't have it.'

'How old were you?'

'When she died? Same age as Josh is now.'

'Did your father ever remarry?'

'No. I don't think Dad ever really stopped grieving for Mum. A lot of the joy went out of him. He raised the baby on his own, with a fair bit of help from nannies, and me, of course. Josh was a real bright spark. Dad absolutely doted on him, and so did I. A little bit of Mum, alive in the world. Raising Josh gave Dad something to live for.'

'He had you to live for too.'

Quinn shifted in his seat and gazed out across the river. 'I was fifteen. Didn't need raising.'

He turned to find her unsettling gaze upon him. 'Bridget told me about Josh's accident.'

This surprised him. It wasn't Bridget's place to tell. 'Josh almost died in that fall. When he was diagnosed with a brain injury, it was like losing Mum all over again for my father. The hopes and dreams he had for Josh? Gone. Dad was never the same.'

'Bridget said that he shot Josh's horse.'

Quinn's light mood was evaporating as the conversation grew more and more personal. 'You weren't there.' He stood and strode towards the river, collecting his thoughts, imagining how his father would feel about him sharing their family history with a stranger. Better steer the conversation back to safer territory, stick to being a tour guide.

Zoe was running to catch up with him. Quinn took a deep breath and, before she had a chance to speak, pointed to the bridge again. 'Can you believe it was underwater during the flood last year?'

'I thought the Paradise Dam upstream was supposed to regulate floods?'

'That bloody dam's never worked properly, but I suppose it's better than nothing.'

'It's not better than nothing,' said Zoe. 'It's much worse than nothing.'

Quinn looked at her sideways. 'What would a girl from Sydney know about our dam?'

'Plenty,' she said. 'I wrote a paper last year on one of your local endangered species – *Neoceratodus forsteri*.'

'Speak English.'

'*Neoceratodus forsteri*,' she repeated. 'The Queensland lungfish.'

'Lungfish?' asked Quinn. 'You mean those big green slimy things? They named a town after them – *Ceratodus*. You can still see the old railway siding on the Burnett Highway west of here.'

'I'd like to go there,' she said. 'Lungfish are amazing. Living fossils with lungs *and* gills – an evolutionary link between fish and amphibians. And the only place they're found in the whole wild world is right here in this river.'

'Is that so?' said Quinn. 'The Burnett and nowhere else?'

'Well, almost nowhere else,' said Zoe. 'They're native to the Mary River too, a bit further south.'

'So lungfish are only found in the Mary and Burnett rivers?'

'Pretty much,' said Zoe. 'Although they have been introduced to some other places.'

'Like where?'

'Brisbane River, and the Albert and Coomera. Oh, and Stanley River. And I think some were introduced to the Enogerra Dam as well.'

He couldn't stifle a grin. 'So these rare fish are found no other place on earth – except for the Mary, the Albert, the Coomera, the Stanley . . .'

'Stop it,' she said. 'The point is they *are* rare. Did you know they can live for a hundred years?' He raised his eyebrows. 'They can, but the ones in this river don't. The Paradise Dam is killing them. Useless fish ladders, completely the wrong design for large-bodied fish. Not one single lungfish has been recorded in the dam's downstream fishway. It's the same for barramundi, mullet, bass – turtles too. Nothing big will use it. Instead they're killed on the staired spillway, which should be smooth, of course. They smash to death on its concrete steps.'

Quinn wanted to argue that people were more important than fish, but the passionate way she'd told the story both surprised and moved him. 'It does seem like a waste, to have them die like that.'

'One study found that more than one-hundred-and-fifty large lungfish were killed in a month, and they don't even start breeding till they're twenty years old. At this rate they could go extinct on our watch, after being around for two-hundred-million years. People don't realise.'

'No, I suppose they don't,' said Quinn. 'I certainly didn't.' She had him at a loss and his discomfort level was rising again. Not one conversation with this young woman ever wound up the way he expected it to. It was impossible to make small talk with her. She cared so darn much about everything. He checked his watch. 'Maybe we'd better head back. Josh will be finished soon.'

'What about showing me those churches? And the post office?'

'I don't think there's time.' This wasn't true, but Quinn had had enough. If he spent much longer alone with Zoe his brain would explode. He strode for the car, wishing he'd never accepted her lift into town.

'Wait,' called Zoe. Quinn came to an abrupt stop. What now? His phone rang, the hospital. Josh wasn't cooperating. The session was progressing slowly and running late. 'Can we at least get a drink somewhere?' She shielded her eyes from the sun. 'I'm so dry.' He took in her flushed face and the sheen of perspiration on her high forehead. She wasn't used to this weather, she wasn't a Queenslander.

'Come on,' he said. 'We'll make a pit stop at the Royal and take a look at that post office on the way.'

. . .

It took a few moments for his eyes to adjust from bright sunshine to the dark interior of the old hotel. Quinn led Zoe through the coolness of the bar into a comfortably furnished room that still had the old *Ladies Lounge* sign above the door. She was about to sit down when Quinn frowned and pulled out her chair. After a moment's hesitation she took the offered seat. He nodded his satisfaction. 'What will you have?'

'Water's fine,' she said.

'I'm having a quick beer.'

'I'm not a big beer drinker.'

'I'll get you a shandy,' he said. 'Beer with a dash of lime. Most girls like it.' She opened her mouth as if to say something, but didn't. He went to get the drinks.

'About Josh . . .' she said when he returned from the bar. 'How does the brain injury affect him?'

'It's hard to explain,' said Quinn. 'You had to know him before the accident. He was such a bright kid.'

'He still seems like a bright kid to me,' said Zoe. 'Maybe it's good I didn't know him before. That way I don't make comparisons.'

'Josh can't always find the word he wants,' said Quinn. 'He gets frustrated. And he has trouble with reading and spelling. He's a very concrete thinker now, takes things literally and blurts things out. It gets him into trouble.'

'Did he always love animals so much?'

'Oh yes,' he said. 'That hasn't changed.'

'Your brother is very fond of Aisha.'

Quinn stiffened. 'You don't need to tell me that.'

'He wants to work with her, ride her. It would mean the world to him.'

Quinn sculled down half his beer in one long gulp. 'I don't think so.'

'Josh is good with horses, isn't he? He must be, to have done so well at endurance riding.'

'That was a long time ago,' he said.

'Two years? Not so long.'

'Three years,' he said. 'It was three years ago. And my father forbade Josh to ride after the accident out of a legitimate concern for his safety. Not just Aisha – any horse. As far as I'm concerned, the subject's closed.'

'I think your father was wrong,' she said. 'You don't understand how important this is to Josh – riding again, working with Aisha. It would do wonders for his self-esteem.' Quinn's knuckles tightened. Why couldn't she leave it alone? She was like a dog with a bone. 'And there's something else,' she said. 'Your brother told me that he has trouble talking to you: that you used to be close before your father died, but not anymore.'

Why hadn't he gone straight back to the hospital? 'Josh told you all this, did he? Obviously he has no trouble talking to you.'

Somehow she failed to appreciate the sarcasm in his voice. 'He misses spending time with you. I could tell it makes him sad.' Zoe sipped her shandy and made a face. 'Imagine how thrilled he'd be to go out riding with you again.'

Quinn felt a vein start to pulse at his temple, throbbing in time with his heart. What did she know about him and his brother? He cleared his throat. 'Are you finished?'

'Will you at least think about it?' Her gaze was hopeful, expectant.

He drained his beer and rose to his feet. 'No, I won't think about it, and I'd thank you to mind your own business.'

'I didn't mean to interfere. I just wanted to —'

'Wanted to what? Poke your nose in? Stir up trouble?' He hadn't meant his words to come out like that, so . . . combative. 'My brother has enough to contend with without you putting ideas in his head.'

She bristled. 'I did no such thing. This is his idea. Josh desperately wants to ride – you must know that.'

The couple at the next table turned to stare.

Quinn was at a loss. This had turned into an argument, something he wasn't used to. The natural hierarchy of life at Swallowdale meant conflict was rare. His father's word had always been law, brooking no disagreement. And since Quinn had taken over, nothing had changed. He received the same unquestioning respect from Brian, the farm manager, and the other workers, as if his father's dead hand still ruled. It made for a peaceful life. He and Bridget rarely quarrelled. So apart from Josh, nobody challenged him. He didn't know how to handle Zoe, hadn't had enough practice with dissent.

Quinn dared to look deep into her eyes. They flashed with determination and resolve. 'This conversation is over.' He headed for the door. The afternoon had been a big mistake, one he wouldn't repeat. He marched to the car, his eyes watering in the bright white sun, his hands lightly trembling. And as he walked, his shadow long and dark before him, he tried to push aside the unsettling thought that Zoe was right.

CHAPTER 11

Zoe peered into the empty tank. It made no sense. Yesterday a colourful pair of clownfish nestled and swam within the protective embrace of a pink bubble-tip anemone growing in that back corner. This morning they were nowhere to be seen. Zoe checked from every angle, then fetched the rickety stepladder, and climbed up to the top of the tank. Maybe they were behind the rock. She reached in to move it. Ow— a burning sensation went through the back of her hand where she'd brushed against the anemone's stinging tentacles.

'You look nice.'

Zoe jumped in pain and surprise. The ladder tipped over, collecting her bucket of chopped squid on the way. She landed right in the middle of the smelly mess.

Karen stifled a laugh as she rushed to help. 'Well, you *did* look nice.'

Zoe hauled herself to her feet. Great. Now she stank of fish.

'You're making quite a habit of coming down here on your days off.' Karen eyed her appraisingly. 'Why are you all dressed up?'

'I'd hardly call denim shorts *all dressed up.*'

'But they're smart ones, aren't they, beaded at the back like that?' said Karen. 'And since when do you wear earrings and lipstick to work? You can't fool me. I haven't seen that red top before.'

'Of course you haven't seen it.' Zoe grabbed a paper towel. 'I never get a chance to wear anything except khaki around here.' She dabbed ineffectually at a damp spot on her top, hand still smarting from the bubble-tips sting. The rock in the tank had toppled from its original position, but there was still no sign of the missing clownfish.

'Tell me who you've got all dolled up for,' Karen said, 'and I'll get that stain out of your shirt while you take a shower.'

Zoe sniffed a few times, screwed up her nose then checked her watch. 'Leo's picking me up at the jetty in ten minutes.'

'Leo Macalister, the mayor?'

'He's taking me on a day trip to Lady Elizabeth Island.'

Karen whistled through her teeth. 'You're a dark horse.'

'Oh, please,' said Zoe. 'He's so old.'

'So's George Clooney,' said Karen. 'What does Bridget think about it?'

'I'm not sure she knows.' Zoe stripped off her top and threw it to Karen. 'Thanks. Better have that shower now or I'll be late.'

'Welcome aboard,' said Leo over the drone of the motor. He took her hand as she jumped from the dock to the rear boarding platform, then nodded to the man at the helm. 'We're ready to cast off, Simon. Hold her firm.' The gleaming black and white cabin cruiser rode high and proud in the water, the name *Flipper* emblazoned across her bow. Leo came aboard, then hauled in the line.

'What a gorgeous boat,' said Zoe.

'Isn't she?' Leo's voice swelled with pride. 'Bridget named her, as if you can't guess.' He secured the rope and heaved a satisfied sigh. 'Let me introduce you to our fellow travellers.'

Zoe followed him through the starboard door to the cockpit area, where a balding middle-aged man sat in the revolving captain's chair. He swung round to greet them, his ruddy face alight with pleasure.

'I'm Simon Bennett,' he said, turning the helm over to Leo. 'And this is my wife, Carla.' A thin blonde woman in her thirties lounged on a rear bench seat. She acknowledged Zoe with a warm smile and adjusted her brightly patterned sarong.

'Make yourselves at home,' called Leo as he revved the engine and took the boat slowly out. 'Drinks and snacks in the icebox under the servery. We're off to the southern-most coral cay of the Great Barrier Reef, one of the seven natural wonders of the world.' Zoe settled herself on a comfortable portside seat at the fore of the boat and prepared to enjoy the ride. Lady Elizabeth was one of the most remote islands in Turtle Reef National Park, further out than she'd been before. She'd heard about the wild dolphins offshore and was hopeful of a sighting.

Flipper travelled northwest at a fair clip, past the Cape Bounty lighthouse, into the bay proper. They were aiming for the Pass, a deep-water channel providing boats with safe passage through the treacherous shallow seas of the inner reef. Zoe was getting to know Kiawa Bay.

'Perfect day for it,' called Leo without turning round. He was right about that - sunny and still, with a few cottonwool clouds overhead.

Zoe crossed over to the captain's chair and stood behind him, staring curiously at the high tech helm, its walnut panelling the only nod to the past. 'That's a fancy dashboard.'

'I should say so,' he said. 'Top-of-the-range compass right here in the centre, state-of-the-art Faria instruments . . . there's even a digital depth sounder in case I misjudge the Pass.' Leo pointed to a separate panel. 'Light switches, anchor winch controls, trim tabs.' He glowed with pleasure, seeming ten years younger out here on the water. 'Wait till you see below – all mod cons, even a climate-controlled wine rack.'

'Um, I suppose there's a toilet?'

Leo stood up. 'Simon! Take over will you?' He slid open a section of moulding and a door magically appeared. Down they went to luxuriously appointed living quarters – bathroom, galley, dinette, queen-size bed.

'You could live on this thing,' said Zoe.

'That's my dream,' said Leo. 'Cruise north, island-hop, take my time – with the right companion, of course.' He winked, but it wasn't sleazy, more light and flirty. 'Want some music?' He tapped a panel – instant jazz. 'Just thought I'd give you the heads-up re: our guests.' He lowered his voice. 'Simon and Carla are potential investors.'

'Investors in what?'

'They're looking to construct a multimillion-dollar resort.' Leo glanced around him as if the cabin walls had ears. 'The original plan was to build a bit further up the coast, or go south to Bargara. I've convinced them to take a gander closer to home.'

'A resort?' Zoe must have sounded doubtful.

'Don't worry, you and Bridget will approve,' he said. 'A fair slice of the the profits will be used to protect wildlife.' He tapped the side of his nose. 'Wildlife means tourists, right? Your dolphins, for instance? They'll be a real hit. Anyway, the Bennett's want to go green – sustainability, recycling, restaurants using all local produce. You know the drill.'

'Like an eco-resort?' said Zoe.

'Exactly. It will be just the boost this town needs. But keep it under your hat, will you? It's all very hush-hush for now.'

'Eco-tourism is a fabulous way to protect habitats and show off Turtle Reef.' Zoe felt herself swept up in Leo's excitement. 'At the moment there's hardly anywhere for visitors to stay around Kiawa, even if they wanted to. Before I realised that board and lodging came with the job, I went looking for accommodation myself. Nobody wanted to know me. Even the estate agent seemed unfriendly. No private rooms to let, no flats or holiday rentals. I couldn't believe it.'

Leo nodded. 'Kiawans are a funny lot. They like things just the way they are. They're not one bit interested in having a lot of strangers come in and change things. I was the same, to tell you the truth, and not so long ago either. In love with tradition. We Macalister's are fifth-generation canegrowers, same as Quinn Cooper's mob. Kiawa royalty, some folks call us. I still lease out quite a few farms, wouldn't be without them. But getting into local politics has been an eye-opener. Problem is, we still see ourselves as a sugar town, which we are, of course. Eighty per cent of agriculture in this region is cane. But it leaves new opportunities going begging. All the young people will end up leaving and Kiawa will become an irrelevant backwater.'

'What are you two doing down there,' bellowed Simon. 'Or shouldn't we ask?'

Leo smiled. 'You'll give me a reputation, young lady.'

Topside again, and Zoe curled up in her seat to watch the ocean. Nothing but the occasional diving tern. Wait, was that something in the distance? Dark dots in the water, coming in at a tangent? Yes, the tell-tale fins of dolphins. And then they were all around the boat, a dozen or more, surfing *Flipper*'s bow waves in an age-old dolphin sport. 'Look,' she shouted, wishing the hull didn't ride so high, wanting to be in the centre's little runabout so she could be closer to the water. This was the first time she'd seen wild dolphins, and these weren't just common bottlenoses. Slender rostrums and bumps in front of their elongated dorsal fins told her they were Indo-Pacific humpbacks, a species she'd never seen before.

Carla hung over the side while Simon rushed for his camera. The animals braced their tails against the thrust of the wave, hurtling forwards with fearless abandon, the epitome of *joie de vivre*. Occasionally one rocketed ahead or took a turn at the stern, but mostly they just enjoyed their free ride at the bow. Zoe thought of a line from *Moby Dick*, a novel she'd loved since studying it at school. How did it go again? *Hailed with delight by mariners, full of fine spirits ... they are the lads that live before the wind.*

Two dolphins arced from the water in unison. They seemed to remain poised in mid-leap, silhouetted against the sky, before knifing underwater without a splash. What would it be like - that brief, blinding silence, then back into the arms of the ocean to travel who knew where? How empty were the lives of captive animals by comparison? Maybe she should talk to Bridget, convince her to re-evaluate her dolphins. Make a new effort to return them to the wild.

'Will we see dugongs?' asked Carla.

'Not way out here,' said Zoe. 'They live close to shore, where they can graze on the seagrass meadows. Kiawa is rather special in that it has a large population of dugongs.'

'I'll make a point of seeking them out,' said Carla. 'Some people say they're ugly, but I think they're adorable.'

'Sex-starved sailors in the olden-days obviously agreed with you,' said Zoe. From above, the dugong's curves resembled women. They mistook them for mermaids.'

Carla clapped her hands in delight. 'That's a marvellous story.'

A shadow appeared on the horizon, looming larger by the minute. 'There she is,' called Leo. 'The Lady herself.'

Half an hour later they dropped anchor just twenty metres offshore from the prettiest little island imaginable. Vast columns of coral, so tall they nudged the surface, encircled a turquoise lagoon. Beyond lay snow-white beaches fringed by she-oaks and pandanus palms. The island itself was clothed in a tropical pisonia forest, looming lush and mysterious.

'It's straight from a movie set,' said Zoe. 'Or a David Attenborough documentary.'

Leo stepped to the stern and took a bucket of bait from a locker. 'Watch this.' They looked over the side as he fed the breathtaking array of fish that had gathered. Sleek reef sharks. Two large speckled groupers. Throngs of coral trout, dazzling in orange and blue – a signature species of a healthy reef. Zoe had never seen so many fish in one place. 'It's a Green Zone out here,' said Leo. 'Hasn't been fished for fifty years.'

Zoe took in the pristine scene with a jolt of joy, aware like never before of the reef as a single, breathing organism. From migrating humpback whales to the humblest coral polyp, everything was vitally connected. She looked towards the island. 'How do we get there?'

'Swim.' Leo lifted the rear bench seat to reveal an assortment of masks, goggles and fins. 'Forget Cairns,' he said. 'Some of the best snorkelling in the world is right here in front of us.'

Carla unwound her sarong to reveal a toned, taut body in a purple bikini. She drew admiring glances from the men and caused Zoe to make some unflattering comparisons with her own figure.

She didn't want to stand on deck in her bathers beside the beautiful Carla.

'Do we need wetsuits?' she asked.

Leo shook his head. 'The water's warm and there are no marine stingers this far south. Quite a selling point, eh, Simon? No need for those ugly stinger suits.'

Zoe gave a small sigh. She could use a top-to-toe outfit right about now, however unflattering.

'Hurry up and change,' said Leo cheerfully. 'We're wasting all this lovely sunshine

Zoe emerged from the cabin, wearing her black one-piece and a towel wrapped around her waist. She stepped onto the deck, burning with self-consciousness, but the others were sorting through the jumble of equipment, and paid her no heed.

Simon looked up and adjusted his goggles. He was a big bear of a man, not quite the right size for the flimsy speedos he was wearing, but he didn't seem to care. 'Know what I love about swimming?' He clasped his generous belly in two large hands and jiggled it. 'This big sucker doesn't weigh me down.' They all smiled. How did men manage it, inhabiting their bodies with such confidence, whatever the shape? Although that wasn't true of all of them. The hordes of self-obsessed gym junkies back in Sydney were as vain as any woman. She inhaled, drawing air deeply into her lungs. That's all it was – vanity. Zoe dropped the towel.

There it was, the dreaded once-over from the others. She braced herself against the embarrassment, wishing she could crawl into a nice safe wetsuit. But to her surprise she received the same subtle nods of approval as the lovely Carla had. In fact, Carla herself wore the most appreciative expression of all. 'That's a lovely swimsuit. I like the style. A well-cut one-piece is so much more flattering than the average bikini. Where did you get it?'

She couldn't very well say Target, could she? 'I don't know, somewhere in Sydney . . .'

Simon came to her rescue. 'Last one in's a rotten egg.' He jumped off the dive platform with an enormous splash. Laughing like a schoolboy, Leo followed his lead, leaving Carla and Zoe to make a more dignified entry into the clear, buoyant water of the sheltered cove.

All around them lay a tapestry even more vivid than Turtle Reef. Brightly coloured parrot fish abounded and were utterly fearless. Zoe could hear the soft chomping of their beaks as they grazed on the branching coral gardens. Blue-spotted lagoon rays scooted past and, look, there went a shovelnose shark, with its strange triangular snout.

So intent was she on her observations that she bumped into Leo. They both got a fright, losing concentration and gasping for air through their snorkels, before breaking the surface and pushing up their masks. 'Let's swim to the island,' he said. They struck out for Lady Elizabeth, Simon and Carla following close behind.

Before long their feet found purchase on the shallow shore. They left their equipment beneath a windswept casuarina tree, safe from the incoming waves, and set off along the beach. But it was like no beach that Zoe had ever known. Instead of sand, millions of stark white coral fragments crunched musically underfoot. Leo indicated the splendour all around with a wide sweep of his arm. 'You could run day trips out here, anchor a pontoon offshore, offer glass-bottom boat rides.'

'Do you get those crown-of-thorns starfish?' asked Simon. 'I hear they can devastate a coral reef in no time.'

'Never seen one south of Mackay,' Leo said.

'What about turtles?' asked Simon. 'You get turtles?'

'Three different kinds,' said Leo triumphantly, as if he'd organised them himself. 'Loggerheads, greens and hawksbills. Lady Elizabeth is a major rookery, and there are plenty more nesting sites along the coast near Kiawa.'

'That's right,' said Zoe. 'I volunteer for the *Turtle Watch* program at Kulibari beach. We do night-time shore patrols to protect laying mothers and escort hatchlings to the water. In some places there are nests every few metres.'

'What did I tell you?' said Leo. 'Nothing draws tourists like baby turtles.'

Simon stared out to sea, then pivoted slowly on one heel, completing a three-hundred-and-sixty-degree sweep of the stunning beauty on display, taking it all in. He glanced at Carla and received an approving nod.

A smile played across Leo's lips, as if he sensed victory. 'So . . . what do you think, you two?'

'What's not to like?' Simon shrugged. 'Coral cays, pristine waters, iconic wildlife.' He gestured towards Zoe. 'Beautiful women with trick dolphins. It's exactly what we've been looking for.'

CHAPTER 12

Josh frowned and hunched his collar against the rain as Zoe bumped around the ménage. 'Not like that.'

'How then?' she asked.

'Just ride *properly.*'

Zoe pulled on the reins. Cobber continued his shambling trot for a while and then came to an abrupt halt. Zoe fell forwards onto his neck. 'Josh, you can't just say *ride properly.* You have to tell me how.'

A cloud of frustration darkened his face. He stared at the ground and kicked the base of a post.

'Let's try again,' said Zoe. 'What will I do?'

'Go round,' he said without looking up. Zoe kicked her horse into a trot again. Cobber angrily swished his tail and kept yawing to the left, aiming for the stable. Zoe struggled to straighten him, pulling on the right rein and trying to remember to rise to the trot.

Riding in the ring was a lot harder than following along behind the other horses. So much to remember. It was like patting your head and rubbing your stomach at the same time. Cobber poked his nose and opened his mouth to avoid the action of the bit. He veered towards the gate, jaw braced, and broke into a canter. Josh rushed to close it, causing Cobber to swerve at speed. Zoe lost her balance and hit the ground before she had time to be scared.

She could taste dirt. Grit found its way into her eyes making everything blurry, but it wasn't like the last time she fell off. No excruciating pain in her shoulder, no gasping for air that would not enter her lungs. The reality was infinitely less frightening than the memory. Josh came over. She climbed unsteadily to her feet, blinking like mad until her vision cleared. 'Don't worry, I'm alright.'

But instead of concern on Josh's face, there was anger. 'You'll ruin everything.'

She eyed him warily while catching her breath. Then she brushed herself off and went to catch Cobber. It's not like she fell off on purpose. 'We can stop if you want.'

This seemed to infuriate him further. 'If you fall off, Quinn will stop you riding like he did with me.'

'No he won't. I'm not hurt.'

'He will so,' said Josh, 'and then I won't be allowed down to the stables anymore.'

'I'll try my hardest not to fall off again,' she said. 'I promise.'

That seemed to mollify him. 'Get on,' he said, 'and trot in a circle.'

Zoe tried a second time. Cobber ignored her steering, carted her to the gate and promptly fell asleep. He stood there, immoveable, swishing his tail and resting a hind leg, dozing in the sunshine.

'No,' called Josh, his voice rising. 'That's wrong. You need to leg yield.'

'What's leg yield?' This was hopeless. Why did she ever think that Josh could teach her anything. 'I give up,' she said, dismounting. 'If you can't tell me what I'm doing wrong, this won't work.'

Josh's face became a mask of misery. He seemed to be struggling with something, searching for words that wouldn't come. This riding business had been a mistake. It was just upsetting him. Zoe reached for the latch on the gate.

'I can't *tell* you,' he said, 'but I can show you.' Like a flash he was in the saddle. The transformation in Cobber was instantaneous. Head raised and alert, one ear flicked back listening to Josh murmur, '*Here we go.'* The boy didn't appear to move a muscle, but suddenly Cobber was cantering a neat circle. With arched neck, collected stride and a lively but controlled energy, he looked nothing like the bored plodder of a few moments ago.

'That's amazing,' called Zoe. 'How did you do that?'

Josh trotted to the gate. 'Watch.' He turned Cobber from the gate and into the middle of the ménage, but she couldn't see what he was doing differently. He looked at her expectantly. 'What am I supposed to be seeing?'

He returned to the gate. 'Don't just watch my hands.'

He was right; that's exactly what she'd been doing. With exaggerated slowness Josh tweaked the right rein. This time she paid attention to the rest of him. He seemed to sit down deeper in the saddle. His left leg moved back a fraction, pressing into Cobber's flank behind the girth, causing him to move away from it and to the right. 'Leg yield.' Josh did it again. Whenever he applied his left leg Cobber moved to the right. Zoe walked around him, watching from a different angle as he switched legs. Now Cobber was moving to the left away from the pressure of Josh's right leg.

'Let me try,' said Zoe, and Josh dismounted. This time when Cobber napped left towards the gate she was ready. She pushed her right leg firmly against his side. At first nothing happened, and Cobber continued moving in the wrong direction. But when she dug her heel in a little more firmly, he straightened up and walked to the middle of the ménage. A shrill whistle pierced the air. What on earth? Josh stood with his dolphin training whistle to his lips, the one he always carried round his neck on a lanyard. He nodded, and she used her inside rein to steer the horse's front half, while her outside leg steered the back half. It worked, prompting another whistle. Cobber stopped poking his nose and trotted a passable circle.

'Again,' yelled Josh. He wasn't scowling any more.

After half an hour of practice, and with the reinforcement of Josh's whistle, she found her rhythm, and could get Cobber to reliably trot around the perimeter of the ménage and stop when asked. 'That's enough for one day,' she said. 'I'm pooped.' Zoe leaned down to pat

Cobber's neck, breathing in the delicious smell of horse, sweat and dust.

Back at the stables, she unsaddled her horse under Josh's watchful eye. Whenever he didn't approve of something she did, like the way she removed Cobber's bridle, he'd tap her on the shoulder and take over. To be honest, it was more of a thump than a tap, but she was prepared to put up with it. Zoe observed him complete the task, then had another go at it herself. When she did something right, like taking off the bridle without knocking Cobber's teeth, for instance, she received an encouraging whistle.

Absurd? Absolutely. But the fact was, it worked. Josh didn't have the words or communication skills to instruct her verbally, but with this system she was improving fast. After all, why shouldn't humans respond to the principles of operant conditioning training as well as any other animal? And Josh was a whiz at it, keenly observant and prompt to reward any correct action she performed. Her thoughts turned to the centre's dolphin shows. Josh was always right beside Bridget, blowing his whistle and kneeling to use that clicker of his underwater where it was harder for the dolphins to hear. At first Zoe had considered his presence there as a mere indulgence, but now she knew better.

Zoe hosed off her horse, and they led him past the tennis courts to the turnout paddocks. Sunshine soaked into her, making her drowsy right down to her bones. Even Cobber seemed daydreamy, hanging his head and dawdling. The call of a plump wonga pigeon was all that broke the afternoon peace.

A trumpeting neigh from the paddock ahead woke Cobber up. With pricked ears and arched neck, he pranced down the track like a young colt. 'Show off,' laughed Zoe. 'Who are you trying to impress?'

There, through the trees, in a little paddock by herself. Aisha, racing along the rails like a mad thing, heading straight for the corner by the gate. Zoe's face turned ashen. The mare would never stop in time, careening towards the fence at an impossible angle. But at the last second she gathered herself and made an impossible leap, clearing the gate and landing sure-footed as a cat.

Zoe remembered to breathe. Aisha shook her head and came to a dancing halt before them. Cobber stretched out his neck to touch the mare's velvet muzzle with his own, atremble with admiration. Josh stroked her shiny damp neck. His face shone with relief and delight. Zoe put Cobber in the paddock and handed Josh the empty halter. 'Here.' Aisha lowered her chiselled head into the noseband as soon as Josh held it out, and let him fasten it around her ears. The gesture was so gracious, her expression so kind, it was impossible to believe she was the rogue Quinn and Bridget made her out to be. 'What a pretty head,' said Zoe.

Josh nodded. 'She's so beautiful, I feel all weird inside just looking at her.'

'What do we do now?' asked Zoe.

'Aisha wants to go for a walk.'

Zoe started to say, *Won't Quinn mind?* but stopped herself. Of course he'd mind. He'd forbidden Josh to go anywhere near Aisha, forbidden him to ride at all. She thought back to the flare of anger between them in the Bundaberg hotel. Even hopping on Cobber briefly, the way Josh had, was against Quinn's rules. He was only looking out for his brother, she knew that, but it still didn't make much sense. If anybody could handle himself around horses, it was Josh.

Zoe studied the boy's eager face. 'Okay,'

They walked up the track on either side of the mare. Aisha was glad to be out, that much was plain. She walked with a springy step, ears pricked and head high, gazing about with wide-eyed enthusiasm. Sometimes she stopped to examine something along the way: a tree stump, an irrigation pipe, an oddly shaped rock. Josh hummed as they went.

When they returned Aisha to her paddock, Josh was loath to leave. He picked handfuls of grass, feeding her over the fence and rubbing her ears till Zoe convinced him it was time to go. Aisha stood at the gate, a forlorn figure, watching until they rounded the corner of the tennis courts and disappeared from sight.

Josh took sudden hold of her arm, so hard that it hurt. 'Don't tell Quinn.'

Zoe gently disengaged herself, and thoughtfully ran her fingers through the flowers of a blueberry ash on the side of the path. How clever Josh had been today, training her with the whistle like that. How happy and engaged with the horses, almost like a normal boy. How could she take that away from him? 'You have my word, Josh,' she said. 'I won't say a thing.'

CHAPTER 13

'Give me a minute,' said Bridget. 'I'm just trying to feed him a few fish first.' Dolphin twenty-two, now named Echo, had spent the last two weeks recovering in the centre's veterinary compound. His quarantine period was over and Zoe was impatient for his release from the hospital tank into the little lagoon next door.

Mirrhi raced up and down the dividing wall, making a series of loud clicking noises, well aware something was up. Zoe checked there were enough fish in her bucket and whistled Mirrhi over. Might as well do her eyedrops while they waited. A little stream ran into the lagoon, and fresh water hurt the dolphins' eyes.

She kneeled down and gave the signal for the Mirrhi to lie on her side. Two soothing saline drops in the right eye, wait a minute, and then give a fish. Zoe repeated the process with the left eye, then asked Mirrhi to roll over and expose her belly, a behaviour useful when vet checks and ultrasounds were needed. Zoe checked her blowhole for mucous or bad breath. Good, salty and slightly fishy, but on the whole sweet and clear.

'Echo won't eat,' called Bridget. 'Not even for Josh. I think we'll simply do a quick health check and let him out. Maybe his appetite will improve when he has company.'

It had been a battle getting Echo to eat dead fish. For the first few days he hadn't recognised them as food at all, and required force-feeding, a distressing task for all concerned – and a dangerous one. Slipping fish safely past razor-sharp teeth wasn't easy.

It was Josh who'd first coaxed him to eat. He staged a vigil beside Echo's tank, showing great patience and spotting subtle indications of feeding behaviour that the others had missed. Whenever Echo swam slightly closer to a fish, turned his head towards it or even relaxed his jaw, Josh was there, wriggling the fish enticingly in front of him.

At first this devotion seemed to irritate Echo, and Zoe worried that Josh might be bitten. She was confident of Mirrhi, Koko and Baby now, but she still couldn't entirely shake off her fear of the other dolphins, especially Kane. As it turned out, it was Echo's very irritation that finally caused him to feed. One day he snapped in annoyance, and Josh boldly thrust a fish between his jaws. From then on it was plain sailing, and a heart-warming friendship developed between the two of them.

The longer Zoe spent in the job, the more she came to understand that Josh was no hanger-on at the Reef Centre. He had a crush on Bridget; that was plain. He loved to be around her, and she had obviously used this closeness to coach him. He'd been a star pupil, because Josh was a capable trainer in his own right.

Zoe had returned to the centre one rainy evening to collect the iPod that she'd left behind. To her surprise, Josh was at the lagoon, working solo with the dolphins in the fading light. The sleek creatures were spinning and leaping in a dazzling display. Nobody else was around.

At first Josh tried to make her leave. 'Don't watch me.'

'I won't bother you, Josh. I'll just sit over here, okay?'

His mouth still scowled, but a smile played around his eyes. He was weakening.

'Please Josh . . . ?'

'You can watch, but don't tell anybody.'

'I won't say a word, promise.'

She took a seat out of the rain in the little covered grandstand, while Josh returned to his task. He was trying to get Kane to ring a bell by pushing a pedal attached to a post at the edge of the water. Bridget had been attempting to teach Kane this same trick for weeks without success. It seemed straightforward enough. When Kane approached the lever, Bridget would reinforce the behaviour with whistles and fish. This worked up to a point. Time and again, the dolphin swam nearer and nearer. His nose hovered tantalisingly close … and then he turned away. Bridget's training for this trick had come to a standstill.

Josh slipped some sardines into his belt and slid quietly into the water. Prickling fear crawled down Zoe's spine as Kane torpedoed towards him. Ramming dolphins could break ribs, collapse lungs or knock a swimmer unconscious. She still couldn't get Tião, the Brazilian bottlenose, out of her mind. Although his victim had been drunk, and reportedly tried to force a cigarette into Tião's blowhole before the attack. More than enough reason to retaliate.

Kane swerved at the final moment, sidling up alongside Josh and allowing himself to be scratched. Zoe moved in for a closer look. Josh was standing in the shallow water with one hand over the lever, so Kane couldn't reach it. Why? Kane nosed his belt, as if to check that he still had sardines, and then began his customary dance of *almost but not quite* around the pedal. Sometimes he hung stationary in the water just a millimetre away, close enough for Bridget to have rewarded him. But Josh kept the sardines in his waist pouch. After a few minutes Kane impatiently nosed the hand Josh held over the lever and was instantly rewarded with a fish. He did it again, knocking Josh's hand harder this time and ringing the bell at the same time. Again he was rewarded. After a few more repetitions, Josh withdrew his hand and put it behind his back. Something must have clicked. Kane pushed the lever anyway and got his sardine. Soon the bell was ringing out each time Josh put his hand behind his back.

Zoe thought it through. By rewarding Kane when he almost touched the lever, Bridget had been teaching him just that – to *almost* touch it. They'd reached a teasing impasse. But Josh had thought of a way to bridge the communication gap between human and dolphin. And it took him just half an hour to do it.

Since then, Zoe had stayed back most nights to watch him. She'd learned more about dolphin training from Josh in the last week than she ever had from Bridget. And Zoe learned something else as well — an extraordinary bond existed between Josh and the young female Mirrhi. It wasn't apparent at first. Shy Mirrhi hung back while Josh worked with the rest of the dolphins. Once he ran out of fish, the others quickly lost interest and wandered away. Josh then donned a mask and snorkel, and dived into the water. This was Mirrhi's cue to play.

At first Josh lay quietly at the surface, face underwater, watching Mirrhi as she scooted about beneath him. Then he began to swim, matching her speed, twisting this way and that to mirror her movements. Or did Mirrhi mirror him? It was impossible to tell, they were so in synch – a graceful, hypnotising dance.

They played with a beach ball, taking turns to sink it with their bellies, then let it rocket to the surface for a game of keepings off. They whistled and blew bubbles. Zoe could have sworn Mirrhi was laughing. They swam in circles, creating whirlpools, pushing toys into the centre to see them spin. This wasn't training or conditioning or enrichment. There were no whistles or fish rewards. This was play, pure and simple: a joyful, authentic connection between kindred spirits of different species, revelling in each other's company.

When Josh and Mirrhi started ringing the bell, Zoe had slipped away. The pair's bond was so close, so intimate, that being there felt like an intrusion. Josh hadn't noticed her leave. And as the bell rang out again and again across the empty park, a great wave of loneliness had swept her up and brought her to tears.

Mirrhi emitted a series of whistles, loud enough to bring Zoe's thoughts back to the present, though a sense of loss still lingered. The young dolphin tilted her head and trained a large, dark eye upon her. 'I have a new friend for you,' said Zoe. 'So play nice.' She pulled the handle, raising a hydraulic gate that separated the hospital tank from the lagoon. Echo emerged slowly from his pool, urged on by Bridget and Josh, suspicion showing in each line of his sleek body.

Mirrhi pounced, scooting round him at great speed, slapping her tail and clicking in wild excitement. Echo cruised the perimeter of the lagoon, cautiously exploring his new surroundings. Josh emerged from the hospital compound and sat down at the water's edge. Mirrhi sped over for a pat and a few fish, then splashed him hard several times, before returning to her new playmate.

'That'll teach you, Josh, for paying so much attention to Echo,' laughed Zoe. 'Mirrhi's jealous.'

They watched the young dolphins for a while, on the lookout for any signs of aggression. Echo seemed intimidated at times by Mirrhi's enthusiastic advances, but otherwise the introduction was a success. Mirrhi was clearly trying to help the newcomer, showing him around the lagoon, bringing him her favourite toys, and even passing him a stray fish that she found in the shallows. Echo snapped it up and Zoe clapped.

'A perfect pair,' said Bridget. 'Perhaps we'll hear the splash of little fins in the future.'

Zoe frowned. 'Surely Echo will be released soon?'

'That's the plan, of course,' said Bridget. 'His red blood count is still down. We'll have to get to the bottom of that first.'

'But —' Zoe stopped herself. No point returning a sick dolphin to Turtle Reef. Disappointing, though. Every day Echo spent in captivity, dependent on them, eating dead fish, would make his return to the wild that much harder.

'I was thinking,' said Zoe, 'about the others.' Her mind's eye could see the dolphins of Lady Elizabeth Island. Leaping for joy, surfing *Flipper*'s bow wave, spiralling into the boundless deep. How badly she wanted that freedom for their dolphins. 'Mirrhi, for instance. Are you certain she can't be released? I'll do some research on similar cases if you like, successful releases after prolonged captivity. Find some precedents.' The words flowed from her. 'You said she still has seizures, but she hasn't had any since I've been here, has she? What does George say? Could we get him to re-evaluate her? And then there are the spinners —'

Bridget interrupted her. 'Heartbreaking, isn't it? We spend so much time and energy rescuing these gorgeous creatures, nursing them back to health — then we fall at the last hurdle.' There was real sadness behind her smile. 'Why don't I take you to lunch, Zoe? We'll talk about it more then.'

Bridget went inside to order, while Zoe sat on the pub verandah, staring out to the bright sky and sea. She couldn't help being flattered by the lunch invitation. Bridget was usually so busy, either with the public or the administrative side of things. Ridiculous, to have a scientist of Bridget's experience and standing wasted in the office, or talking to kids about turtles. She'd studied under the legendary Professor Scott C. Thomas at the Marine Mammal Institute of California. She'd spent two years as a fellow at the Centre for Marine Science at Curtin University, investigating dugong populations in Shark Bay. Zoe had hoped they might work together, even become friends. So far that hadn't happened. Maybe this lunch was the start of a turnaround.

Bridget returned with a mineral water and Zoe's iced tea. 'Let me say how impressed I am by your work here so far.'

A warm flush of pride spread from Zoe's neck to her cheeks, and her enthusiasm was unleashed.'I've finished mapping the seagrass beds in the bay's southern quadrant, based on those aerial photographs you gave me. I'm ready to start spot sampling in the field next week.' Bridget raised her brows in approval. 'But the news isn't good. Compared to that ten-year-old study by Kirkwood, seagrass cover looks like it's down forty per cent.'

Bridget frowned. 'That much? The mapping data you've sent me so far is meticulously done, by the way. Absolutely first class.'

Zoe felt like singing. This was what she'd been waiting for - a one-on-one with Bridget, discussing quadrants and maps and research. 'When do we start the tag-and-release program?' she asked. 'That's when we'll find out how the dugongs are really faring. At the moment we're just guessing.'

'You're keen, Zoe,' said Bridget. 'I love that, I do, but first things first. We need those seagrass maps finished before we move ahead. The field sampling as well. No point tagging animals without solid data about their local environment.'

Zoe shielded her eyes from the glare of the water, fighting to hide her disappointment. 'But at the rate I'm going, the mapping could take two months, or even longer. How about an extra day a week for me to work on it? Or two half-days? I could go out after the shark show.'

'I can't spare you, I'm afraid, especially now we have the six baby pelicans.' Bridget's voice faded to a conspiratorial whisper. 'You're much better with the animals than Karen. She doesn't have your gift.'

Zoe felt the tell-tale flush of pride again.

'The other thing I love about you,' said Bridget, 'is your dedication to returning our rescues to the wild. Look at last month. Three cormorants, five rays and two turtles – nursed back to health with your help, given the all-clear by George and released where they were found. That is what we're here for.'

Zoe could hear the *but* coming, and felt the flush fading.

'But sometimes it's just not possible.' Bridget leaned forwards, her face solemn. 'Let me assure you, no dolphin fit for release spends one more day at the centre than is absolutely necessary.'

'I didn't mean to imply they did,' said Zoe. 'It's just that I saw my first wild dolphins last week and, well . . . they were such free spirits. I'd love our dolphins to experience that again.'

Bridget didn't speak for a while, seemingly lost in thought. 'Let me tell you a story,' she said at last. 'Last year Archie brought me a young dolphin found tangled in a shark net, terribly malnourished. We named her Hope. I nursed her round the clock, hardly leaving her side, neglecting my other duties, even neglecting Quinn.' This was apparently the greatest lapse of all. Bridget's eyes misted over. 'I can't tell you how much I loved that dolphin. Hope was like my child.'

'Did she pull through?'

'She did. I wanted to release her, but George wasn't keen. Hope's red blood cell count was still low.' Bridget drew a deep sigh. 'I insisted, saying it was her birthright to be free. We took her eighty kilometres up the coast to where Archie first found her. She chased the boat when we left.' Bridget's voice had grown husky with emotion. She paused as if it was too painful too continue, sipped her drink, screwed the paper serviette into a ball. 'Last month Hope washed up dead on Kiawa beach, just a few hundred metres from the centre. She'd come home, you see - tried to find me.' Zoe's hand flew to her mouth. 'The autopsy showed that Hope died from a combination of starvation and infected shark bites.'

'I'm so sorry ...'

'You see, she wasn't as strong and capable as I'd thought. From that day on I vowed to never make the same mistake.' Bridget lowered her head and a tear rolled down her cheek. The sight moved Zoe to tears herself. At that moment their connection was tangible. She and Bridget, wildlife-warriors, fighting for the animals of Turtle Reef.

A voice from behind them made Zoe jump. 'Whatever's wrong?' Quinn pulled up a chair, concern written all over his face. 'Are you two crying?'

Zoe wiped her eyes. Zoe had barely seen Quinn since that day in Bundaberg two weeks ago when she'd asked him to let Josh ride. The conversation had left Quinn furious, she knew. Furious and hurting, but Zoe had no regrets. Somebody had to tell him how unfair he was being. Somebody had to be an advocate for Josh.

But her boldness had come at a cost. Quinn no longer dropped by the cottage on her days off with an invitation to go riding. He didn't ask her up to the house for cups of tea, made the old fashioned way in a china pot. When they met by accident in the garden, he didn't point out where the wallaby with twin joeys was hiding, or show off a new flower spike on the purple ground orchids. Zoe missed these simple connections and was lonely without them. Kiawa wasn't a friendly town. If it wasn't for Leo Macalister, she'd have no kind of social life at all.

Quinn rested his gaze on Zoe. There was no longer anger in his eyes, only warmth. She turned away, blinking back tears, pushing away a worm of guilt. He'd be wilder than ever if he knew what she and Josh were doing every morning. She wiped her face. 'Bridget was just telling me about —'

'Shall we change the subject to something more cheerful?' said Bridget.

'One of my jokes should do it,' said Quinn. 'Why did the cane farmer win a Nobel prize?

'I don't know,' said Bridget.

Zoe shrugged. 'Me either.'

'Because he was out standing in his field.' Silence. Bridget looked at Zoe and they both groaned. The sad moment had passed. 'That's what I wanted to see.' Quinn reached for his girlfriend's hand. 'A smile on that beautiful face.'

'Your jokes are so bad they always make me smile.' Bridget touched his face in a tender gesture, and Quinn kissed her softly on the lips. Zoe examined her feelings. Good, no twinge of jealousy. Time to concentrate on the important stuff. Next week she'd start sampling the seagrass beds off Turtle Reef. That was the sort of satisfaction she could rely on.

CHAPTER 14

The hands of Zoe's brand-new wind-up alarm clock showed five o'clock. She lay awake, listening to the dawn chorus of birdsong, waiting for the rap on the door. *Knock, knock.* Captain jumped off the bed and padded out, tail a-wag. Zoe yawned, got up and raised the window blind. First light was peeping around the rose-tinted clouds. One of the best things about this getting-up-at-daybreak business was seeing the sun come up.

A familiar impatience took hold. She couldn't wait to go riding, but her impatience was tempered with worry. For the last two weeks Josh was doing more than giving her early morning lessons on Cobber. He was retraining Aisha.

She'd been against it to start with, but Josh was relentless. Eventually she'd handed him the mare's bridle.

Instead of saying *thank you*, he scowled. 'That's the wrong one.'

'It was on the hook marked *Aisha*,' said Zoe.

Josh ran his finger over the twisted metal mouthpiece. 'Give me Cobber's – the one with the rubber bit.'

At first Josh struggled to bring the bridle anywhere near Aisha — heartbreaking, to see how frightened she was. It took the two of them half-an-hour to fit it on the rearing mare. By the time the bridle was properly adjusted and buckled up they were all out of breath. Aisha stood damp with sweat, forefeet spread wide and sides heaving.

'You're okay,' Josh soothed, rubbing her ears. At first he lunged her in circles using the soft rubber snaffle, roller and loose running reins. After a few days, as she grew less fearful, he attached long ropes to her bridle. Walking a few metres behind, he reinforced the rein signals with voice commands as if she was harnessed to a buggy. *Walk, trot, left, right, whoa.* Aisha was a keen and quick learner. Sometimes he clicker-trained her at liberty, teaching her to bow and come when called, using mints as rewards. The mare was hooked on the sweets, and soon learned to faithfully follow him anywhere without ropes or halters.

When he first mounted her, Zoe paced the rails, heart in mouth. The saddle didn't concern Aisha. She tolerated the tightened girth and flapping stirrups with barely a flick of her ears.

'Sure you want to do this?'

Josh answered by putting a foot in the stirrup and mounting. Aisha plunged across the ménage, nose in the air, ears flat against her head. She rolled her eyes and frothed at the mouth. She constantly fussed, chewed at the bit and flung her head around.

Josh responded by working Aisha on a completely loose rein. It was wonderful to see him control and guide her with only his legs. Aisha seemed confused when first given her head, snatching at the bit, unsure of this newfound freedom. But soon she relaxed. Her ears came forward, her champing lessened and she stretched her neck out, long and low. By the third day the mare seemed to realise nobody was going to hurt her mouth anymore. The pair began to work as a team.

They were in constant danger of being found out, of course, but Zoe minimised the risk as much as possible. The ménage couldn't be seen from the house, not even from the second-storey balcony. Zoe had checked. The stables were screened by a line of trees and, according to Josh, Quinn attended to his daily paperwork straight after breakfast. So although he was an early riser, he was rarely out and about on the farm before seven-thirty.

There'd been some close calls. Brian, the property manager, drove past a few of times on his way down to the river. Josh always ducked from sight at the sound of the approaching jeep. The various workers weren't horsey people and took little notice of Zoe bumping around on Cobber, or of the saddled and bridled black horse tied to a rail.

One time Quinn came looking for her. She heard him calling long before she saw him. 'Quick,' she told Josh. 'Take Aisha out the back, into the cane.' She nudged him. 'Hurry.'

Josh sprang to life, coiling the lunge rein in his right hand and running with the mare into the field. The waving stems closed seamlessly behind them. All that showed above the crop were the tips of Aisha's dark ears.

Quinn came round the corner, Captain trotting at his heels. 'Morning, Zoe,' he said in his easy drawl. 'Didn't think you'd be up yet. How's Cobber going?'

'Good, great . . .' Zoe guiltily smoothed the soft check fabric of the new shirt she'd bought for riding. This was the first time since their afternoon in Bundaberg that Quinn had sought her out. Here he was, extending an olive branch, and she was in no position to accept it. Captain pricked his ears towards the cane. Would he give the game away?

'Glad to hear it.' Quinn looked very handsome in the early morning light, with his smiling grey eyes and hair still wet from the shower. 'Bridget rang to ask if you can work this afternoon. Leo wants a private dolphin show for some bigwigs he's trying to impress. Can you help her out? And can you take Josh with you? Bridget thinks he's better off at the centre than playing on that computer all day. She's an angel, isn't she? Putting up with him the way she does.'

'Sure.' Zoe fiddled with Cobber's girth in an attempt to show that she was busy and the conversation was over. But Quinn suddenly wanted to talk.

'Finally figured it out, have you? That mornings are the best part of the day?' Zoe turned to him, placed a hand on the hitching rail, felt the undeniable current of attraction between them. Quinn mirrored her movement. 'How are the riding lessons with Josh going? Can't imagine he's much of a teacher. It's bloody hard for him to say what he means.'

Zoe bit her lip. There was so much she wanted to tell him. That the lessons had been going swimmingly and that Josh was an excellent, if somewhat unorthodox, teacher. That although he had trouble finding words to express himself, he'd worked out a way to overcome the problem. That he'd been coaching Zoe with whistles and clicks, in the same way that he trained the dolphins . . . in the same way that he trained Aisha.

'Josh has been great,' she said. 'Look, sorry . . . I'm going for a ride.'

Quinn lowered his eyes and made a line in the dirt with his boot. 'I'd keep you company,' he said, 'only there's a meeting at the mill . . .'

'No problems.' She tried to mount, but ended up hopping around awkwardly on her toes.

'Stand still, will you?' He legged her up and tightened the girth. 'Where are you off to, anyway?'

'Aah . . . up the Hump.'

'I guess it's the only ride you know. We'll have to fix that. There are some fantastic beach rides I can show you.'

Zoe was sweating in spite of the cool morning. She could see Captain, nose to ground, scouting closer to Josh's hiding place. 'Look, if I don't get going I won't have time to help Bridget out this arvo, so . . .'

'See you later then. Enjoy your ride.' Did he sound disappointed, or was that her imagination? Quinn slapped Cobber on the rump and whistled to Captain. The dog stood staring at the cane field for a moment, then followed him up to the house.

Zoe had waited until she was sure he'd gone, then slipped off Cobber and went to find Josh.

'Why is Quinn so mean?' Josh had asked, hugging Aisha's satin neck. 'I hate him.'

'You don't,' she'd said sadly. 'You love him, and he loves you. Somehow we'll find a way to make him understand.'

. . .

Zoe shut the bedroom door, lost in thought. She hated going behind Quinn's back, but she hated the idea of disappointing Josh even more. He loved Aisha. He was a different boy around that horse – confident, enthusiastic. *'Riding Aisha makes me feel the way I did before I hurt my head,* he'd said. When the right time came he'd be able tell his brother that. Once Quinn saw how happy the mare made Josh, he'd come around, she was sure of it.

Zoe could hear the sound of clinking cups and the kettle going on the stove. She showered, dressed and grabbed her phone off the charger. More out of habit than anything else. Mobile reception in Kiawa was patchy at best. When she arrived in the kitchen, Josh handed her breakfast. Always the same thing – two slices of vegemite toast and a cup of tea. Fortunately she'd learned to like tea. The beverage was as ubiquitous to Kiawa as coffee was to Sydney.

'I'm taking Aisha out today,' he said. 'She's bored in the ménage.'

Zoe opened her mouth to argue, and shut it again. Why not? The horses were behaving beautifully. Quinn was away in Brisbane until tonight. Brian and the other farm workers wouldn't arrive until eight o'clock. They had the place to themselves.

'Okay,' said Zoe. 'We'll ride down to the river, but no further than that.'

Josh began to hum, and put another round of bread into the toaster. Zoe smiled. Aisha wasn't the only one bored with riding in the ménage.

They walked to the stable through dew-damp grass beneath a pale morning sky. Captain, and his waving plume of a tail, led the way. 'I want to catch Aisha today,' said Zoe.

The black mare was down by the irrigation channel, staring longingly at a herd of horses grazing in a distant paddock. Zoe called her and Aisha pranced over to the gate, tail held high. It streamed out behind her like a banner. She looked very beautiful, like a dream horse. No matter how many times Zoe saw that proud head and floating trot, it always sent a shiver up her spine.

They saddled up and set off for the river. Aisha danced on ahead, shying at Captain and eyeing each puddle and rock with exaggerated interest. 'Not too fast,' called Zoe. 'Just walk.' But it was no use. Aisha kept dancing and Cobber had to trot to catch up.

Josh was grinning from ear to ear. 'She wants to go.'

Even lazy Cobber felt fresh, stepping sideways and chewing at the bit. The broad, grassy track stretched invitingly before them, flanked by swaying forests of sugarcane on one side, and a harvested field on the other. A reckless energy pulsed through Zoe, and she matched the boy's grin with her own. 'Well, if she wants to go, let's go.'

Josh whooped out loud, startling the horses. Cobber shied. Aisha arched her back and gave three high-spirited bucks. Zoe held her breath, but Josh sat them out easily. The horses settled into a steady, pounding canter, side by side, stride for stride. Zoe laughed. It was perfect – the feeling of controlled speed and power beneath her, the shadows striping the path ahead, the sweet, heady fragrance of freshly cut cane.

When they reached the old stone wall by the river, they pulled up their horses and let them graze on a loose rein. She checked her watch. Seven o'clock. 'Time to head back.'

'Not me.' Josh urged Aisha up the rainforest trail running along the river.

'Josh, no!' Zoe followed at a gallop. She had no choice, her horse had the bit between his teeth. A shiver of fear ran through her as Cobber hurtled up the narrow track, striving to catch up with the fleet-footed Arabian mare. His breath was laboured and his neck sleek with sweat before the path widened and Josh drew rein. Zoe almost fell off as Cobber stumbled to an abrupt halt. He took a few faltering steps and stopped again. Something was wrong.

Josh swung from his saddle. 'Get off.'

Zoe dismounted. Josh lifted Cobber's near forefoot, pulled a pocketknife from his belt and dug around in the hoof. 'There.' He held out a large, sharp stone. 'Jammed in his foot.'

'Will he be alright?' asked Zoe.

'Yeah, but you can't ride him.'

'How am I supposed to get back?'

'Walk.' Josh remounted Aisha.

'Well, of all the . . .' Aisha whinnied suddenly and Cobber pricked his ears. Two riders were bearing down on them, a man and a woman, mounted on a pair of chestnut thoroughbreds. What to do? Cobber couldn't outrun them, but Aisha could. 'Go home,' said Zoe. 'Make it fast and take Captain with you.' Locals would be bound to recognise the dog. 'I'll stall them.'

Josh didn't hesitate. He took off at a gallop with Captain at his heels. Zoe waved goodbye and started after him on foot, leading a limping Cobber who was looking very sorry for himself. Soon the riders, a middle-aged couple, were upon her.

'Trouble?' asked the woman.

'Nothing serious,' said Zoe. 'My horse had a stone in his hoof.'

'Bad luck.' The man came alongside and extended his hand. 'Ed Owen, and this is my wife, Nancy. We grow macadamias at Tamborine Creek on the southern slope of the Hump. ' Zoe reached up, shook his hand and introduced herself. 'That's Quinn Cooper's bay you have there, isn't it?'

'Yes,' said Zoe. 'Cobber.'

'So you're the dolphin lady from Sydney?'

'That's right.' The bush telegraph worked efficiently in Kiawa.

'What's up with your friend?' asked Nancy. 'Not very nice to take off and leave you like that.'

'I told him to go,' said Zoe. 'He . . . he had to be somewhere.'

'Looked like a good horse he was riding,' said Ed. 'One of Quinn's, was it?'

Zoe pretended not to hear, and the couple exchanged glances.

'Come on,' said Ed. 'I'll double-bunk you back. Nancy can lead Cobber. You'll get wet otherwise.'

Wet? She glanced skywards, where dark clouds were scudding in from the north. 'Thanks, but no,' said Zoe. 'I feel like walking.'

'Shall we let Quinn know what's happened?' asked Nancy.

'Really, I'll be fine.'

'Suit yourself.' Ed tipped his hat, they said their goodbyes and the riders headed off at a brisk canter. Were they hoping to catch up to Josh? The pair were suspicious, or at the very least curious. Josh better hurry.

Zoe started walking. Amazing, how long it took to go somewhere on foot. That wild ten-minute gallop was translating into a very long trudge home. Cobber didn't help. Every few minutes he stopped, held his leg up pathetically and refused to move. Not knowing how badly injured he was, Zoe was loath to force the issue. He could be in a lot of pain. Not enough to take away his appetite, though. He jerked the reins from her hand and ate furiously whenever they came across a patch of fresh juicy grass.

After half an hour or so, Cobber wasn't the only one limping. Zoe's new riding boots weren't broken in and she could feel the blisters forming. Well, it wasn't like she'd expected to go hiking in the darn things.

The sky darkened and darkened again. Fat plopping raindrops turned into a downpour. Such a miserable trek home. So much for *Queensland – beautiful one day, perfect the next.* Zoe distracted herself by trying to track the other riders. It was well-nigh impossible on rocky ground, but in other places hoof prints lay deep and clear in the damp, red earth. Cobber's tracks were easy to pick. After all, his feet were right there with her for comparison – broad, round and plate-like. Some of the prints showed distinct semicircles that had her tricked for a bit. Of course - horse shoes. The chestnuts were shod. That made it simple.

Zoe hoped the shod hoof-prints would veer off at some point. Plenty of other paths intersected the bush track - but no such luck. An hour later, when she finally reached the river, the hoof-prints turned through the open gate to Swallowdale. She sat on the historic stone wall for a few minutes, resting Cobber and her aching feet. Then she plodded on with a sinking heart.

The couple had followed Josh through the cane fields towards the stables. Cobber stopped again. She tugged at the reins. 'Come on, not long now.' Together they hobbled up the track. It was encouraging that the two sets of shod hoof-prints did lead back down again. It meant, at least, that Ed and Nancy weren't waiting at the stables for a chat.

But somebody was waiting in the stable yard when she arrived — Bridget. 'I've been trying to reach you.'

'Sorry,' said Zoe. 'You know what phone reception is like around here.'

'What's happened to Cobber.'

'He bruised his foot on a stone.'

Bridget stepped forwards and examined him. 'It doesn't look too bad.' She looked around. 'Did you go riding by yourself.'

'Yes —' started Zoe. She followed Bridget's downward gaze. The ground was churned up with multiple sets of hoof prints. 'I met Ed and Nancy Owen on the way home, riding a gorgeous pair of chestnuts.'

Bridget did not look completely convinced. 'Pity I wasn't home. I haven't seen Nancy in ages.' She stroked Cobber's nose. 'Anyway, I'm looking for Josh.' She fixed her direct gaze on Zoe. 'You haven't seen him, have you?'

'I, um . . .' Zoe didn't want to lie to Bridget, but she didn't want to get Josh into trouble either. So she said nothing.

Bridget's expression went from expectant, to puzzled, to worried. 'Are you okay? I asked you a question.'

'I . . . ah . . .' Captain burst from the bushes, followed closely by Josh. The collie bounded joyfully from Zoe to Bridget and back again.

'Josh,' said Bridget. 'Just the man I'm looking for. We need to treat Echo for some cuts and scrapes. Can you come to the centre with me? He's so good for you.'

Josh's face lit up. Bridget waved goodbye and they headed for the house. Captain was clearly torn between staying and going. He came over for a pat, then sat down at her feet, whining and looking long-ingly after the disappearing figures. 'Go on then,' said Zoe. 'Nobody's stopping you.' With a sharp bark Captain shot off after them.

'Well, Cobber,' said Zoe. 'Looks like it's just you and me.' She unsaddled him, hosed him down and put him in the yard with a feed. Despite the fact that her feet were killing her, she went to check on Aisha. The exercise had done the mare good. For once she wasn't restlessly pacing the fence. Instead she dozed contentedly in the shade, resting a back foot and swishing her tail at flies. Zoe smiled. The morning was a bit of a disaster, true, but in the end no real harm had been done. Aisha had enjoyed herself, and so had Josh. If Quinn could have seen them together, galloping through the bush, moving as one, free as the wind . . .

Zoe carted the saddle and bridle to the tack room, eyes taking a moment to adjust to the gloom. What was that? A note lay on the bench, addressed to Quinn.

Hi Quinn, Ed Owen here. I met Zoe King on the river track this AM at ten o'clock. Horse lame and phone out of range. She's fine, on her way home. BTW saw Josh riding black horse like the devil was after him. Couldn't catch him. Can that boy ever ride!

Zoe crumpled the sheet of paper into a ball and shoved it in her pocket. She headed for the cottage, dying to get her boots off, anticipating a long, hot soak in the tub to soothe stiff muscles and aching feet. She was going to be sore, and both heels had blisters.

Back home she stripped off her wet clothes, ran a bath and tried to relax – but her mind was too full. Things couldn't go on like this. She had to find a way to tell Quinn about Josh and Aisha. Until then, there could be no more early morning rides for the pair.

Her thoughts turned to Echo? Cuts and scrapes, Bridget had said. The young dolphin hadn't settled into captive life, even with Mirrhi as a companion. He remained fearful and distrustful. How badly hurt was he? It was no use – curiosity had the better of her. Zoe dressed and headed for the Reef Centre.

Karen and Bridget were so deep in conversation they didn't notice Zoe slip through the gate into Dolphin Harbour. In her hat and dark sunglasses, they probably didn't even recognise her. She took a seat in the front row, alongside a few inquisitive members of the public.

Echo hovered at the far side of the round training pool, snorting occasionally and blowing nervous bubbles. Even from this distance, Zoe could see blood on his nose, and raw welts where he'd bashed his rostrum against the iron gates. Josh was watching him from the side of the pool.

Zoe leaned forward and strained to hear what Karen was saying. 'The stronger he gets, the wilder he gets. I've dropped the water level right down. Not much more than a metre deep, and still can't do a thing with him. He won't take fish. I can't medicate him, train him, draw blood – nothing.'

Josh stripped to his togs and slipped quietly into the water. For some unaccountable reason he held a red signal flag in one hand. The boy moved to the centre of the pool. Echo scooted around the perimeter. Zoe expected Josh to tempt him with fish, though the tactic had not been very successful so far – Echo was too nervous to be motivated by food rewards.

But instead Josh followed the dolphin: calmly, deliberately, always moving towards him with the flag upraised. Echo grew more and more agitated — dashing every which way now, weaving back and forth in an attempt to get away from Josh and his waving flag. All this wild swerving occasionally brought Echo closer to Josh. At that precise moment the boy lowered his flag and retreated a few steps. It was subtle. You had to watch closely to pick the pattern. Once the dolphin had passed him and was heading away again, Josh resumed his quiet pursuit.

What was he playing at? It took Zoe a while to see it. Josh was using the same principles a trainer might use on an unbroken colt. Since starting to ride, Zoe had filled in many long, lonely nights by watching horse training videos on YouTube. One in particular sprang to mind: a man holding a stockwhip, working in a round yard with an unhandled young brumby. The colt was clearly terrified, galloping in circles, seeking an escape route. Eventually it changed direction and, in so doing, turned briefly to face the man. At that exact moment he lowered his whip and retreated. Soon the colt was stopping to face the trainer more and more frequently, even taking a step or two towards him. Within twenty minutes he was relaxed, and trailing after the trainer like a puppy. The colt had learned that the only place where he wouldn't be bothered, the only truly *safe* place, was right beside the man.

It had been a stunning sequence to watch and a highly effective training exercise — but it involved a horse. Would round-yarding work on dolphins too? It was an intriguing possibility. Ten minutes in, and no progress seemed to have been made. Echo continued to dash about wildly, and Josh continued his methodical pursuit, retreating and lowering the flag at the instant that Echo accidentally approached him. Zoe saw no signs of the kind of gradual calming displayed by the colt in the video.

Zoe glanced at Bridget, who was watching Josh. How long would she allow this to continue? The plan wasn't working. All it was doing was stressing the dolphin and putting Josh at risk of being bitten. Then something happened. Echo turned to face Josh, but this time it didn't look like random, fearful avoidance. The dolphin made a hesitant, experimental movement towards Josh. The boy deferred, dropped the flag and moved back. Back, back, back ... with Echo tentatively following as if drawn on a string. Ten minutes later, when Josh stopped with his back against the far side of the pool, Echo swam forwards and nuzzled into his arms.

Karen clapped. 'Bravo.' Zoe expelled a breath she hadn't realised she was holding. It had worked. Of course it had worked. Josh had expertly applied the purest principles of operant conditioning, instantly rewarding Echo whenever he approached. But instead of fish, he'd found a reinforcement more appropriate for this particular dolphin. The reward had simply been to take the pressure off. For Zoe, it was a breakthrough moment. The principles of operant conditioning would work with any animal, as long as you could find the subject's currency.

Josh signalled to Karen, who took him the medical kit. The boy treated the injured dolphin, administering eyedrops and salve, feeding Echo pilchards laced with oral antibiotics. These offerings were eagerly snapped up now the dolphin was calm.

If Zoe had ever doubted Josh's natural talent as a trainer, she didn't anymore. Natural talent … She frowned. Until now she'd always attributed Josh's success to Bridget's excellent coaching. She was the expert. Why, then, had she needed Josh to work with Echo today? He wasn't there just to give the dolphin a bit of confidence. He'd been the brains behind the entire session. Bridget hadn't even gone near the water.

It made no sense. Bridget was one of the most highly-qualified marine mammal trainers in Australia. As a fellow of the Marine Mammal Institute of California, she'd worked with the legendary Scott C. Thomas, a world-renowned expert on cetacean behaviour. Bridget said her doctoral thesis had been on the subject of dolphin intelligence. She shouldn't be leaving things to a teenage boy.

What happened next was even more disturbing. The expression on Bridget's face when she caught sight of Zoe – a fleeting look of alarm. It was replaced immediately with a tight smile, as she hurried over. 'I'm very glad you're here'

Somehow Zoe doubted that. Yet to voice her concerns seemed so . . . so disrespectful to a woman she genuinely admired. Bridget put a hand to her abdomen. 'There's a pain, right here. It's been bothering me all day. Could you take me home?'

Zoe forgot about her doubts.. 'You should see a doctor.'

'No.' Bridget grimaced. 'I'll be fine.' She gave a little cry and doubled over, clutching her side.

'I'm driving you to Bundaberg,' said Zoe. 'No arguments.' She ran to where Karen was squatting by the edge of the pool, repacking the medical kit. 'I'm taking Bridget to hospital.'

Karen stood up, slowly straightening her back. 'What's the matter?'

'Abdominal pains. Did she mention to you that anything was wrong?'

'No,' said Karen. 'She didn't.' Her expression held no trace of sympathy or concern. Zoe knew Karen had some issues with Bridget, but her reaction, or lack of it, seemed particularly hard-hearted.

She ran back to Bridget, took her arm and helped her to the front gate. 'Wait here while I bring the car round.'

. . .

'This is my father's car,' said Bridget as she climbed into the red Lexus. 'Why do you have it?'

'I'm entitled to a car. Remember it's in my contract?' Zoe spun the wheel and sped out onto the street. Oops, the speed bump. Too fast. She winced as they lurched over it, and glanced across at the passenger seat, relieved that Bridget didn't call out in pain.

'When did you meet my father?'

'One day at the centre,' Zoe said vaguely. They drove on for a few minutes in silence. 'How are you feeling?'

'Worse,' said Bridget. 'Much, much worse.'

At the hospital they were shown to a cubicle. Bridget lay down on the hard trolley and turned her face to the wall. A young man, an intern, came in with a clipboard and Zoe excused herself. Ten minutes later he emerged. 'I've given your friend some pain relief. We're going to admit her overnight.'

'What's wrong?'

'I suspect appendicitis.'

An orderly arrived, went into the cubicle and emerged wheeling the trolley. How did she do it? Bridget still managed to look gorgeous in spite of the ordeal she was going through. Zoe could have sworn she'd brushed her hair.

'Ring Quinn for me . . . and Dad,' said Bridget.

'Of course,' said Zoe. 'Do you want me to stay, or maybe bring you something?'

'Go home. I'll be fine.' Bridget managed a smile. 'Thank you.'

'No worries. You just get well.' Zoe reached over and squeezed her boss's hand. It was almost a relief knowing Bridget was ill. It explained why she'd needed Josh to work with Echo today. But a nagging voice reminded her that it didn't explain the look on Bridget's face when she recognised Zoe in the crowd — the look of panic, not of pain.

Zoe left a message on Leo's voicemail, and then rang Quinn. 'I'll be right there,' he said. 'Did they say what was wrong?'

'The doctor said appendicitis.'

'That's impossible,' he said. 'Bridget had her appendix out when she was fifteen.'

CHAPTER 15

Zoe ushered the crowd in and turned on the red light, bathing the previously darkened room in a rosy glow. Zoe hadn't expected quite so many people for her first demonstration. She'd practised plenty of times, but there was truth in the old show business adage, *never work with children or animals*. And it didn't help that Karen was lurking in the background. She'd been sceptical about the idea from the start. 'You'd better perform, Einstein,' whispered Zoe, 'or I'm going to die of embarrassment.' The big hooded eyes of the octopus fixed on her as she turned to face the gathering.

'Welcome everybody to our new Octo Show.'

'Why is the light all red?' asked a skinny boy.

'Most octopuses are nocturnal,' said Zoe. 'Their eyes don't pick up light in the red range very well. It tricks them into thinking it's dark.'

'Tricks me too,' said the boy's father. 'I can't see a darn thing.'

'It might take a few moments for your eyes to adjust,' said Zoe in an encouraging voice. She moved closer to the tank and stepped awkwardly over the makeshift guard rope. 'Meet the star of the show, our hammer octopus . . . Einstein.' A titter went through the crowd at Einstein's name. Zoe stepped aside and gestured towards the aquarium with a flourish. 'Octopus are cephalopods, meaning *head foot*, and are in the same family as squids and cuttlefish.' The audience members shuffled closer and peered into the glass. Zoe looked around. Einstein was gone. No wait, she *was* there, lying flat on the bottom. Her skin had turned to the colour and texture of fine sand. People kept staring, but her flawless camouflage meant they couldn't see what was right in front of them.

'There's nothing in there,' called the skinny boy. In a flash he ducked beneath the rope and rapped on the glass. Einstein instantly showed herself, flashing red with anger to the appreciative gasps of the crowd. Zoe held her breath. It could be fatal if she became upset enough to discharge her ink. The ink itself wasn't toxic, but in a confined space it could clog her gills and choke her. Zoe was ready to rescue Einstein from the tank if needed. But instead the octopus jetted off behind her rock. Zoe groaned. Great. Now what was she supposed to do? She hadn't fed Einstein last night, in the hope she would be hungry enough to perform, but after a fright like that? She might not emerge for hours.

The crowd were looking at Zoe expectantly, so she put on her best smile. 'You've just seen for yourselves why the octopus is called the master of disguise. It can change colour faster than a chameleon. It's also an escape artist *extraordinaire* that can flatten its boneless body to squeeze through the tiniest of cracks, and create its own ink smoke-screen. An octopus is jet-powered. It has eight arms with thousands of suckers that can taste as well as feel. It's a shape-shifter, with a beak like a parrot, venom like a snake and teeth on its tongue. But the most intriguing thing of all is its curiosity and intelligence.' Zoe licked her lips. Einstein was still nowhere to be seen.

'You're telling me that overgrown chunk of calamari has a brain?' said a man wearing an *I ♥ Queensland* T-shirt...

There was a ripple of laughter. She'd been afraid this would happen. How could she convince them that the humble, misunder-stood octopus deserved their respect?

'My dog can do tricks,' a girl said. 'Is that octopus as clever as my dog?'

'It's hard to judge,' said Zoe. 'But some people think so. A common octopus has five-hundred-million neurons in its brain. That's not very different to a dog, which has around six-hundred-million.' There was a murmur of surprise.

'Do octopus have hearts?' asked the girl.

'They sure do,' said Zoe. 'Three of them, pumping blood that's blue instead of red.'

Fascinating as these fun facts might be, they weren't much use without Einstein. The audience wore expectant expressions on their faces. Zoe looked around helplessly.

She did have a second hammer octopus she could show them, a smaller male, compliments again of Archie. He lived in the next tank and had been christened Houdini, due to his skill as an escape artist. But he was much shyer than Einstein and had already eaten a crab that morning. Odds on he'd be hiding too. And, anyway, he wasn't trained.

Zoe thought hard. 'Do you have a cat at home, as well as a dog?' The girl nodded. 'Does it like climbing into boxes?' The girl giggled and nodded again. 'Well, in the same way that cats love boxes, octopuses love small, tight places. Excuse me for a moment.' She left the room, ran to the equipment cupboard and returned with an old-fashioned glass fish bowl – Einstein's favourite toy.

Zoe took the lid off the tank, slipped the bowl inside and waited. This proved too much of a temptation for Einstein. She flowed out from behind the rock and poured herself into the fish bowl, moulding her body to its shape until only her eye horns peeped over the rim, pulsing purple with excitement. She looked very cute, and the laughter that followed was appreciative instead of derisive. So far, so good.

Zoe took a glass jar from her bag, showed it to the crowd, and placed a piece of herring inside. She screwed on the lid and gave it to several members of the audience to check that it was tight. Then she put it into the tank. 'Let's test the problem-solving abilities of an octopus,' said Zoe. Fortunately Einstein had decided to play. She enveloped the jar in her mantle, grasped it with all eight arms and repeatedly twisted her body. A minute later the lid came off and fell to the aquarium floor. Einstein ate the herring. A burst of applause greeted her effort. Even Mr Calamari clapped, and Karen nodded approval.

Zoe brimmed with relief and pride. 'An octopus's sensitive suction cups and prehensile arms can hold and manipulate objects as effectively as any human hand,' she said. 'Let's make the task a little harder.' This time she put a piece of herring inside a child-proof pill bottle. Einstein pressed her mantle down on the cap. Twisting her body at the same time, she removed the lid with ease and ate the fish. Then she blew a jet of water at the little empty jar. It shot into the stream of bubbles from the aerator and was propelled straight back to her. She did it again and again.

'Einstein's playing bouncy ball,' said the skinny boy.

'That's right,' said Zoe. 'Octopuses are very playful. Play is defined as an activity for enjoyment or recreation without any practical purpose. Only intelligent animals play.' Einstein directed a powerful stream of water at the pill bottle, shooting it right out the top of the tank. This last antic won over the crowd. They jostled for the best view as Einstein dismantled a Mr Potato Head stuffed with sardines and then played tug of war with her feeding stick.

Her last and most impressive trick involved an octo-puzzle box. Zoe had kept it as a souvenir from her time as a researcher at Sydney Aquarium. It consisted of a series of three Plexiglas cubes, each with a different latch. The smallest cube had a sliding latch that twisted to lock down, like the bolt on a horse stall. Zoe baited it with crab meat, locked it and placed it inside the second cube. This next box had a latch that slid counter clockwise to catch on a bracket. Zoe placed this cube inside the largest box of all. It had two different locks – a bolt and a lever arm that sealed the lid like the top of a glass canning jar. Zoe set her stopwatch and dropped the puzzle box into the tank.

The octopus surged onto it and a hushed expectancy came over the audience. Time ticked by. Einstein focused on the task with almost human concentration. A minute in, and she'd undone the two latches of the big outer box. Using one arm to pull out the smaller cubes, she began working on the second box. Forty seconds later the inner cube came free. It took just ten seconds for Einstein to slide open the last bolt and receive her reward of crab. 'Under two minutes,' said Zoe. 'Her best time yet.'

People cheered as the octopus flowed to the top of the tank and extended an arm out of the water. Zoe reached over and gently shook it. 'Good job.' She fed Einstein a last piece of crab.

The octopus grabbed her reward and retired to an empty coconut shell on the sandy bottom to eat it. To the delight of the crowd she grabbed a second coconut shell and pulled it down on top of her like a lid, waving her arms before disappearing from view.

The charming move with the coconut shells hadn't been taught. It was just what Einstein did when she'd had enough attention, but it was a terrific finale to the show. Zoe grinned. Maybe she could work out some way to reinforce that behaviour, ensure it became a regular part of the act. She turned to the audience. 'Thank you all for coming, and I hope that meeting Einstein today has given you a new respect for our cephalopod friends in the ocean.'

There were murmurs of assent.

'That's a sweet octopus,' said the girl as they trooped from the room. 'Mum, can we have one as a pet?'

'Our puppy might get jealous,' laughed her mother. 'But you're right about Einstein being sweet - and clever too. I had no idea. We won't be eating squid or octopus again, that's for sure.'

'Your plan to convert the world into octophiles seems to be working,' Karen said, when the last of the crowd had left.

'It does, doesn't it?' said Zoe with a grin. 'Wasn't Einstein wonderful?'

Karen gave a one-shouldered shrug. 'I have to admit, the octopus did okay. If she can consistently repeat that performance, I think you're onto a winner. How'd you teach her the trick with the coconut shells?'

Zoe tapped the side of her nose and put on what she hoped was a mysterious smile. 'A professional secret, Karen. Now, have you seen Josh? I promised he could come with me this afternoon to sample seagrass.'

'Josh? He'll be bored stupid. But at least you won't get lost with him along. That boy knows Turtle Reef like the back of his hand. ' Karen looked up at the gathering clouds. 'If you're going, don't leave it too long. I don't know what's going on with this weather. It shouldn't be this hot and stormy in October.'

A pod of dolphins joined them for the trip out. They kept pace with the little boat as it headed up the coast towards Cape Nelson under a gloomy sky. It was thrilling to see them, but also an unsettling reminder of all that the centre's dolphins were missing out on.

Zoe took off her jacket, despite a few spots of rain. They skirted the mudflats and sub-tidal shallows surrounding the Kiawa river mouth until they reached a likely-looking sampling site. Zoe took an echo-sounding. Not too deep, with fair visibility and what looked like an even coverage of seagrass. She marked their position with a yellow buoy, tagged the coordinates on her GPS and dropped anchor. 'Right, Josh, let's get to it.'

Sitting at opposite ends of the little runabout, they could barely see each other over the mountain of equipment: stakes, snorkels, flippers, quadrats, buoys, binoculars, cable-ties, measuring tapes, plastic bags, clipboards, weighted ropes, maps, seagrass identification sheets – and her scuba gear, which unfortunately seemed to be right at the bottom of the pile. Great. 'Help me move this stuff, Josh.'

Half an hour later she was ready. 'Can you give me that ruler, and a quadrat?' Josh looked blank. 'One of those square things.'

He handed it over. 'What's it for?'

'It's a standard habitat sampling tool.' Zoe carefully labelled it. 'You set it down on the seabed, and take a photograph to record and identify the species inside it. Then' – she picked up a thin PVC pipe from the equipment pile – 'you use this to take a seed core sample, put a few plants into plastic bags for analysis, and do it all over again at the next site.' His eyes had glazed over. Maybe it had been a mistake to let him come.

'Can I help?'

'Sorry, Josh,' she said. 'I need you here on the boat to spot me and, anyway, you don't have any dive gear.'

'How deep is it here?'

'Fifteen metres.'

He snorted. 'Fifteen metres? Who needs dive gear for fifteen metres?'

Zoe tightened her straps. 'I do,' she said firmly. 'Now keep an eye on me, will you? I shouldn't be long.'

Over she went. Visibility wasn't nearly as good here as it was further down the coast. Unseasonable heavy rain in the catchments had caused the Kiawa River to run high, discharging its silt-laden run-off into the estuary and intertidal zone. Clouds of fine particles suspended in the water meant that fish materialised from the gloom without warning. A reef shark loomed nearby, and a fantail ray. A cuttlefish shimmied into view, the rippling fin of its mantle flashing blue and silver. The creature seemed as curious about her as she was about it. 'Shoo gorgeous,' she mouthed softly. 'I have work to do.'

Zoe set down her quadrat on the seabed in an area of ribbon grass and paddleweed. She took out her camera. This was a steep learning curve. It was harder than she thought to avoid shadows, or patches of reflection in the photographs. Zoe measured stem lengths and leaves, and took samples. After examining three quadrats in a five-metre radius, she went topside.

'Can we go now?' Josh looked bored.

'Not yet.' Zoe checked her observations against the identification sheets and standard cover estimates. She stored her samples and transferred the information to a data recorder. 'Okay, now we can go.' They fired up the motor and headed north for a few hundred metres. Then she repeated the whole process.

Josh wasn't much of a dive buddy. As Karen had predicted, he quickly lost interest in the whole seagrass mapping thing. Sometimes when Zoe returned to the boat he was off swimming. Once he startled her by free-diving down and sneaking up behind her. He thought it was hilarious. Another time he was taking a nap. Zoe didn't mind that Josh wasn't taking the job seriously. They were in calm, shallow water and she was getting the hang of things. She'd be happy to head out by herself next time.

As the afternoon wore on Zoe made some disturbing findings. This area was a far cry from the idyllic underwater meadows that Bridget had shown her on that first dive. The aerial pictures had been deceptive. The mix of seagrass here wasn't as lush as it appeared in the photographs, and it contained fewer species than she'd expected. Many places were degraded and suffering from some form of dieback. Dugong grazing trails were few and far between. And the sediment layer was three or four times deeper than it should have been. This wasn't a major problem for vigorous species with long strappy leaves and large rhizomes, like ribbon and eel grass. But shallow-rooted, small-leafed varieties? The ferny *spinulosa* and delicate paddleweeds? They were being choked by silt.

By four o'clock, when Zoe stopped for a drink and afternoon snack, her mood matched the dreary grey skies. 'What's wrong?' asked Josh as he ate the last of their chocolate biscuits.

'The seagrass here isn't as healthy as I'd hoped.'

Josh pulled at her arm and pointed shoreward. 'Look.'

A dark shape lay in the shallow water between their boat and the gnarled tangle of mangrove roots. A living, moving thing. She found it with the binoculars. Hmm, maybe not living after all. That odd rolling motion might be due to the rhythm of the incoming tide. A dugong. She grabbed snorkel and fins. 'Let's go.'

There was no pungent smell of death, just the stink of rotting seaweed and mangrove mud. The animal half-floated and half-lay on her side. A newborn calf rested beside the body, drifting gently back and forth between its mother's flippers as if even in death she was trying to comfort and protect her infant.

Zoe had never seen such a large, dead animal before, not like this. Not in its natural environment, raw and unsanitised. Not away from a dissection table or outside of a butcher shop. She was overwhelmed. The dugong mother showed no signs of obvious injury. Zoe took a closer look. She was pretty sure she knew what had killed her. Starvation. At a rough guess the dugong weighed about half of what she should have. Death must have been recent, for she wasn't yet bloated. On the contrary, she was oddly deflated. Skin that should have been thick and smooth, hung off her skinny frame in great folds. The vital blubber layer, designed to insulate her from hunger during lean times, had collapsed like a flat balloon and her tail was limp. Sightless eyes were sunk deep into the dugong's wizened, wrinkled face. Even her short trunk seemed to have shrivelled and shrunk.

The baby was about a metre long, and heart-tuggingly beautiful. Dead? Zoe couldn't tell. She prayed to see the rise and fall of that perfect pale-cream chest. But then young dugongs were notoriously difficult to raise. They almost never survived – and this one was *so* young. Bile rose in Zoe's throat. What should she hope for? Josh paddled in closer to the animals, reaching out uncertainly to touch the calf. It moved a little under his hand, but not of its own accord. The calf was dead too.

She should put her scientific hat on. She should be dispassionate, take measurements and tissue samples and photographs from every angle. But what she saw in front of her wasn't a research opportunity. It was a real-life tragedy that seemed somehow personal. Dugongs had similar life spans to humans. They reached sexual maturity at a similar age, and their pregnancies lasted more than a year. They were slow breeders, just one calf every five or six years, each live birth representing an enormous investment on behalf of the mother. Heartbreaking, to think this one had successfully delivered her baby, only to die when it needed her most. Had she known? What did dugongs know? They were closely related to elephants, and elephants were highly intelligent and famed for mourning their dead. Did this mother dugong despair as she used the last of her strength to bring her doomed baby into the world?

As Josh stroked the calf's flawless skin, Zoe felt the sting of tears behind her eyes. 'Come away,' she said, turning her head. It seemed disrespectful somehow to be there, voyeuristic.

They swam in silence back to the boat. Zoe made the call to Fisheries and Wildlife, gave the GPS coordinates, went through the motions. Then she drew anchor and headed south. She'd had enough for one day.

'Take over, please, Josh. I feel sick.' Wordlessly they swapped places. Zoe stared over the side, at the choppy grey water reflecting the sky. She closed her eyes, but couldn't erase the sight of the mother and baby from her mind. She couldn't shift the degraded seagrass meadows from her thoughts. The two things were linked; they had to be. What was happening out there in the bay?

CHAPTER 16

Quinn knocked on the cottage door. 'Come in,' sang Zoe. He took off his hat and pushed through the flywire. Captain trotted down the hall to greet him.

Quinn ruffled his handsome white ruff. 'Nice to see you, mate. Whose dog are you again?'

Zoe sat in the sunroom, cross-legged on the couch, pouring over a laptop balanced on her knee. She looked up briefly. 'Just a minute.' Quinn stood by the door, fiddling with his hat, quietly observing Zoe while her fingers flew over the keyboard. Sleeveless check shirt, cut-off blue jeans and bare brown feet. She looked very different from the city girl, dressed in black, that he'd picked up from the station six weeks ago.

A lot skinnier, for one thing. Right from the start he'd admired her curves, but this new athletic look suited her too. Not just skinnier, but healthier and stronger, with definition in her arms, and muscle in her long, brown legs. How she folded them up like that was a mystery. Zoe's once-pale skin was bronzed by the sun. The haircut that he'd found so severe in the beginning was growing out. Soft, copper-coloured curls framed her face.

'What are you doing that's so fascinating?' he asked.

Zoe looked up again, eyes like emeralds. 'Researching our seagrass dieback,' she said with a final tap of the keys. 'And I'm not getting anywhere.' She closed the laptop and smiled up at him. 'What can I do for you?'

'I have a favour to ask.'

'Try me.'

'I'm rostered on for *Turtle Watch*. Bridget put me up to it. We were going together but . . .' He hesitated for a moment. 'You know about *Turtle Watch*, don't you?'

Zoe untangled her legs and stood up. 'A nightly monitoring program designed to record the number of turtles nesting on a particular stretch of beach, mark the nests and keep females and eggs safe during laying.' Zoe pulled a folder from the shelf. 'I'm a volunteer too, see?' She showed him the collection of scrawly, handwritten reports inside, with the Turtle Watch Logo in the top corner.

'Great, well the thing is ...' Her clear green eyes made him momentarily forget what he was saying.' Bridget can't come tonight.'

Bridget was spending the evening with Leo. Though home from hospital and much improved, she still didn't seem herself. Quinn was annoyed with Bridget's doctor, who hadn't taken her episode of abdominal pain seriously. 'Most likely caused by stress,' he'd suggested, after conducting a battery of tests. 'The body translates anxiety into physical symptoms, like the knot in your stomach when you have an exam or important meeting.'

'My fiancée has no reason to be stressed,' Quinn had said. 'Do your job and find out what's wrong with her.' In the end, the cause of Bridget's pain remained undiagnosed.

'Shall I come with you tonight then?' said Zoe. 'Watching sea turtles is one of my favourite things to do.'

'Thanks.' Quinn felt a prickle of pleasure. 'It's my first time, and I'm not sure what to do or what to look for. If I missed something important, Bridget would never forgive me.'

Zoe laughed. 'A hundred-kilogram sea turtle dragging herself up the beach is hard to miss.'

'Fair dinkum, they get that heavy?'

'Some get even heavier.' Zoe reached down to stroke Captain. 'When do you want me?'

'Tonight.' Suddenly he was looking forward to the evening that had seemed like such a chore. 'I want you tonight.'

The first turtle turned up soon after they arrived at moonlit Kulibari Beach, a remote inlet north of town. Quinn saw it first, a movement in the shallows - the bobbing, beaked head of a turtle. He directed the torch to a point along the beach where high tide met silver sand.

'I see it.' Zoe's voice was an excited whisper. 'Well spotted.'

The turtle made several false starts before settling on a course and dragging her bulk from the water. Quinn moved in closer, careful not to shine the amber torchlight in the animal's eyes. 'She's a whopper.' Her curved, heart-shaped carapace alone measured more than a metre in length. All up, the sea turtle must have weighed as much as he did.

'A loggerhead,' said Zoe. 'But you've seen them before, right? Living right on the coast like you do?'

'I saw turtles back when I was a kid.' Her bright eyes pierced the gloom like searchlights. 'But now I steer clear of the ocean.' Quinn's breath caught in his throat. He hadn't meant to reveal that shameful fact; it had slipped out of its own accord.

'Why?'

Something in Zoe's tone encouraged him. He sensed no surprise or judgement - just a genuine interest in his reasons. Quinn let a handful of sand slip though his fingers. 'Fell overboard when I was ten, a fishing trip with Dad.' He paused, but there was no going back now. 'It frightened me witless. I almost drowned.' He cleared his throat. 'Fact is, I don't even like being here on this beach.'

Mum had known, of course, about his fears after the accident, about the nightmares. But she was gone, and nobody else in the world knew. He'd never told anyone, not even Bridget. His father had been a mad-keen fishermen, spending every spare minute out on the bay. If it became known that Quinn was scared of water, well . . . Dad's disgust would have known no bounds. This was Kiawa. People lived and breathed the sea from the day they were born. It was in their blood, their DNA. Even Bridget might find his fear hard to understand. But for some reason it hadn't bothered him to tell Zoe. It actually felt pretty good. He loved how she took it in her stride, like it was no big deal.

'At least you've got a reason,' she said. 'I'm scared of heights for absolutely no reason at all. One time I was playing this computer game, one with lots of cliffs and tall buildings. Even though it wasn't real, I was always careful not to go near the edges. So one day I got thinking — maybe I could cure my fear of heights by having my character jump off a cliff on purpose.'

'Did you do it?'

'Yep, and guess what? I fainted.'

'You're kidding.'

'True story,' she said, laughing.

'But what about that first day?' he said. 'You climbed up the lookout tower with me?'

'I got on Cobber too, when I was scared of horses. Guess you make me feel safe.'

'Scared of horses? You should have said.'

She shrugged. 'Come on, we're being beaten in a race up the beach by a turtle. Keep your distance, though. She'll spook easily until she starts laying.'

The massive reptile faced a long, tortuous climb. Hauling with fore-flippers and pushing with hind ones, she heaved herself up the beach. It was a magnificent, almost prehistoric sight. According to Bridget, sea turtles had been around since the death of the dinosaurs, sixty-five million years ago.

'She's gutsy, I'll give her that,' whispered Quinn.

The loggerhead's vast weight scored deep furrows in the sand as she followed a gentle zigzag towards a stand of casuarinas above the high tide line. Finally she paused and looked around. Maybe this was the spot? Great showers of sand flew out behind her as she started to dig. Her body had sunk quite a way into the beach when she changed her mind and methodically dug herself out of the hole she'd started.

'Why did she stop?'

'Maybe she hit a rock, or a root,' said Zoe. 'Maybe the sand was too dry, or too wet, or too hot, or too cold. The nest site has to be perfect. Loggerhead mothers are very particular.'

'Amazing,' said Quinn. 'That a turtle can figure all that stuff out.' Zoe's smiling eyes reflected the moon's glow. She looked so lovely that he almost reached out to touch the curve of her cheek.

Zoe laid a hand on his arm, her skin warm and distracting. 'Mama's trying again. No, come stand behind so you won't disturb her.' This time there was no equivocation. The turtle set to work, breathing hard as she dug a rough depression. 'Look out,' said Zoe. Sand, pebbles and bits of broken coral came flying through the air. When the turtle finished the main pit, she excavated a smaller egg chamber at the base. This was a slow and delicate task. Using the curled edge of her flippers like webbed hands, she worked with marvellous precision for such a clumsy land creature. Barely a grain of sand was spilled as she scooped it up and out of the nest. At last she'd sculpted a perfect, pear-shaped bowl.

'We can move in closer now,' said Zoe. 'They go into a kind of trance when they're laying. It'll take a while.'

'Look,' Quinn said. 'She's crying.' It was true. Tears streamed down the turtle's eyes, making little damp spots in the sand.

'Only one in a thousand of her offspring will survive until adulthood,' said Zoe. 'The old story goes that a mother turtle cries one tear for each egg she lays, in a kind of premature mourning for the babies that are doomed to die. Of course scientists say it's a way to secrete excess salt, or to keep her eyes moist, but I've always fancied the old story best.'

'Even though you're a scientist yourself?'

'Yes, even so.' Zoe turned to him, her expression both serious and sad. *'There are more things in heaven and earth, Horatio, than are dreamt of in your philosophy.'*

What a strange girl she was. Quinn took a good look at the weeping mother turtle. So helpless up here on the land, so vulnerable. Risking her life to provide the best possible start for her babies.

Instinct? Or something more? Quinn's thoughts turned to Captain's father, who died defending his litter of newborn puppies from a snake.

'Why is it,' he asked, 'that when human parents sacrifice themselves for their family, they're labelled heroes, but when an animal does exactly the same thing, people dismiss it as *instinct?*'

'Maybe we don't like admitting that animals have feelings too,' said Zoe. 'Maybe we want a monopoly on courage and self-sacrifice.'

The loggerhead settled down to lay, accompanied by deep sighs and the rhythmic rise and fall of her mottled carapace. Zoe pulled a book from her backpack, and took the opportunity to take measurements and record the number of the tag she bore on a front flipper. Then they sat down to wait.

'I meant to ask,' said Zoe, 'why Bridget couldn't come tonight. She's not sick again, is she?' He shook his head. 'Did they find out what was wrong with her?'

'It's a bit of mystery,' said Quinn. 'But she seems okay now. Bridget couldn't come because Leo needed her for something. She jumps whenever that man calls. It's bloody annoying.'

'She loves him,' said Zoe. 'She's close to her father. What's wrong with that?'

'Love is one thing.' He doodled idly in the sand. 'Slavish devotion is another.' The picture he was drawing turned into a sad face. 'What about you? I hear you're also a fan of our mayor.'

'I like Leo,' said Zoe. 'He's a lot of fun.'

'And he gave you a Lexus . . .' She laughed and punched him lightly on the arm. A sharp zing travelled through him.

'Alright, yes . . . lending me the Lexus didn't hurt. But truly, I do like him. He invites me places, trips on the yacht, dinner in Bundaberg . . . If it wasn't for Leo, I would have sat home every night researching seaweed or something. Kiawa is a beautiful place, but it can be a bit lonely.'

'So that's why you keep kidnapping my dog.' How ironic. Plenty of nights he'd watched the bright windows of the little cottage, lonely himself, wanting to knock on the door. What had stopped him?

Maybe he thought it an imposition. Maybe he was old-fashioned, and it didn't seem right for an engaged man to go knocking on a beautiful young woman's door at night. Maybe he was a little scared of her and her forthright tongue. Intrigued certainly, but still scared.

'You have to admit,' said Zoe. 'The locals are slow to warm to newbies. They haven't exactly rolled out the welcome mat.'

'What about me? Isn't this a night out?' he teased.

'It is. In fact, it's my favourite kind of night out. But since you only asked me because Bridget couldn't come, I don't think it counts.'

'And what about you?' he asked, emboldened by her closeness in the dark. 'No boyfriend waiting in the wings back in Sydney?'

Zoe laughed. 'The closest thing I've had to a boyfriend lately was a nutcase called Hugo. I met him at the gym on one of my failed attempts to get fit. He wasn't bad looking, except that his eyes were too small for his face, a bit like a dugong's.'

'What was his problem?' asked Quinn.

'For one thing, he was a foody. We spent six weeks eating our way through the *Good Food Guide* until I was the size of a house. Then one day I arrive home to find he'd let himself into my flat without permission and made a prawn and coconut curry. The place smelled like an Indian restaurant.'

'How'd he get in?'

'Sneaked the key from my bag and cut a duplicate behind my back. *I wanted to surprise you,* he said. He surprised me alright.' Quinn tensed with anger on her behalf. 'And so began my marathon effort to break up with him.' She giggled. 'Pity. The curry was excellent.'

'What, so this bloke wouldn't take no for an answer?'

Zoe laid a soft hand on Quinn's arm and shushed him with a finger pressed against her lips. 'We'd better stop talking. We'll disturb mama.'

It took more than half-an-hour for the loggerhead to lay over a hundred eggs. They gleamed like a pile of wet ping pong balls in the soft moonlight. She began to backfill the nest, making a shallow second hole in the process, using her hind flippers to press and smooth the sand.

'See how she disguises the nest?' said Zoe. 'That second hole works as a decoy to fool predators.' When the turtle was satisfied with her camouflage job, she lumbered back down the beach. They filled out the time sheet, took photos and recorded GPS coordinates. Then they dug four stakes into the sand, ran tape around them and labelled the nesting site.

Quinn checked his watch – one o'clock in the morning. When he looked up, Zoe was watching him. 'Is it time to go?'

He shrugged. 'Don't look at me. You're running this show.'

'Let's stay a while longer,' she said, 'until the tide starts going out.'

They strolled along the shore, chatting softly, eyes peeled. The pearly moon-glow lit up sea and sky alike. It was hard to tell where one ended and the other began.

'Have you given any more thought to letting Josh ride again?' she asked.

'I said before, it's not safe.'

'So he just misses out?' Darkness could not conceal the flash of disapproval in her eyes. 'You worry a heck of a lot about what's *safe* in life, don't you?'

Her words felt like a kick in the guts. They weren't said as a criticism - more as a heavy-hearted statement of fact. Was it true? Was he too caught up in keeping Josh safe? Was it only Josh she was talking about? He didn't know how to respond and they walked on in silence.

Their next find was a gruesome one. Two dead turtles, close together, partly buried in the sand. Zoe examined the smelly corpses with an impressive lack of squeamishness. 'These are green turtles, not loggerheads . . . and this one has a tag.'

'They don't look injured.'

'A lot of green turtles have been washed up lately, same as these, with no obvious wounds.'

'What killed them, do you think?' asked Quinn.

'Could be anything.' She walked around the bodies again. 'The same sort of thing happened last year up at Gladstone when they dredged through seagrass meadows to deepen the port. Dozens of turtles and dugongs starved.'

'But Gladstone's two hundred kilometres away,' said Quinn. 'And our bay's never been dredged.'

'No . . .' Zoe rested her foot on one of the magnificent mottled shells. She seemed to be thinking hard. 'If they weren't armour plated I could examine their stomachs.' She took off her backpack, and fossicked around for a pair of disposable gloves. Then she extracted a small hatchet and with one sure sweep of her arm, hacked off the fore flipper of the tagged turtle.

Quinn leaped back. 'Crikey, you could have warned me.'

Zoe fished a plastic bag from the pocket of her backpack and dropped the severed flipper in, complete with tag. She made a few notes. 'Come on. Let's keep going.'

Soon they came across another set of tracks, a metre or more wide, like a tractor had headed up the beach. 'Another loggerhead,' said Zoe. They followed the tracks and found a large turtle engrossed in laying her eggs. 'This one's tagged too.' She took some measurements and they settled down on the sand to wait.

Zoe sat close to him, so close he could hear her quiet breathing. Her hair smelled of sandalwood. They switched off their torches as the moon sailed higher. Its shining face reflected off the ocean, dimming the blinking arch of stars overhead. The polished skin of Zoe's bare shoulders shone too, tempting him to touch it. He closed his eyes, moved away a fraction, but remained intensely aware of her physical presence beside him. He opened his eyes as her hand brushed his knee. Zoe was idly combing the beach with slim fingers, sifting through the sand. Quinn swallowed hard, wanting her to touch him again. He stole a glance at her face.

'Look,' said Zoe. Just offshore, brilliant phosphorescent blazes shot through the water, accompanied by loud, percussive chuffing sounds. 'Wild dolphins, chasing schools of whitebait, then breaking the surface to breathe.' Another shower of bioluminescent flashes, like glittering underwater comets. 'I wish I was with them,' she said. 'I wish I could see what those dolphins see.'

He shivered at the thought of her swimming in that dark,

dangerous soup. 'Dolphins don't see much better than us in the dark, do they?'

'Not seeing with my eyes. I'm talking about echolocation,' said Zoe. 'Seeing the world with sound.'

'Some things out there you might not want to see,' said Quinn. 'Like tiger sharks. They kill dolphins, don't they?'

'Sometimes. Freedom has its risks like everything else, but I reckon it's worth it.'

'Then there's lionfish and sea snakes, stonefish and stingrays . . . not to mention Leo's shark nets. It's an underwater jungle out there.'

'You sound like Bridget,' said Zoe. 'She's always going on about how dangerous the reef is for dolphins. I suppose I can understand why. She told me that awful story about what happened to Hope.'

'Hope?'

'That dolphin that Bridget loved so much.'

'Right,' he said. 'I remember now. That was sad.'

'Bridget must have been devastated to lose her.'

'She did miss Hope, but we knew she was going to a good home.'

'What are you talking about?' asked Zoe. 'Hope died.'

'Oh no. Hope went to another marine park. She was a good genetic match, apparently, for one of their males.'

'I don't understand.'

'It's not complicated,' he said. 'Bridget sold Hope to Oceanworld.'

They sat in silence until the turtle finished laying and trundled off down the beach. Zoe stood up. 'You go get the stakes.'

There was a new hardness in her tone. Had he said something wrong? When he came back from the car, Zoe snatched the stakes from him and hammered them into the sand like she was trying to kill vampires.

On the trip home she stared out the window into the darkness, responding in monosyllables to his attempts to engage her. 'Two nesting turtles. Was that a good number?'

'No.'

'Did you expect more than that?'

'Yes.'

'Have you got any new thoughts on what might have killed those green turtles?'

'No.'

Quinn gave up. The charm of the unusual evening was quickly fading as they turned into Swallowdale's driveway. Captain was waiting for Zoe on the cottage doorstep. She climbed from the car without a word and the collie followed her inside. Damn that dog. Part of him wished he could swap places with Captain.

CHAPTER 17

Zoe stroked Aisha's sleek black neck while magpies carolled an early morning chorus. Josh had not ridden the mare since their disastrous ride to the river. It had been a close call that day, too close. Zoe had talked him into backing off — into giving her time to come clean with Quinn and talk him round. A sensible decision, showing how mature Josh could be. More mature than Zoe herself, perhaps. Because she'd still been getting up at the crack of dawn and spending secret mornings with the mare.

It would require a great deal of diplomacy to convince Quinn to let his brother ride again, she knew that. And to let him ride Aisha? That might be a bridge too far. She'd need the right moment and all her powers of persuasion. So far, that moment hadn't come - the brief conversation when they'd been turtle-watching notwithstanding - and it seemed a waste to let Aisha's training lapse in the meantime. So Zoe had taken it upon herself to continue Josh's good work in her own rather amateurish way. It meant no more sleep-ins, even on her days off like today, but it was worth it. There was something addictive about the beautiful black mare. The more time Zoe spent with Aisha, the more she longed to do something other than lunge her and take her for daily walks. She wanted to ride her. And she'd fought the urge long enough. Today was the day.

'Good girl.' Aisha's near ear flicked back to listen. 'Now, stand still. I'm not as nimble as some.' So far, so good. She moved the upturned milk crate closer and used it to mount. Aisha flexed her neck, nibbled Zoe's boots, then walked off sideways like a crab before her rider had found the off stirrup.

'Wait, stop.' No use. By now they were trotting towards the gate, getting faster and faster. What if Aisha decided to jump it? Zoe was loath to tug on the reins. Aisha reacted badly to heavy hands and, unlike Josh, Zoe wasn't experienced enough to fully control the mare with her seat and legs. But she'd come prepared. There was something she knew how to do just as well as Josh.

Zoe reached into her pocket for a mint and the training clicker. 'Whoa,' she said and double-clicked. Aisha propped so fast that Zoe almost fell off. 'Yes!' she yelled, startling the mare into a canter. 'Whoa,' called Zoe, and double-clicked again. This time she was ready for the sudden stop. She leaned on the mare's neck and reached forwards to give her the mint. Aisha pulled in her head and took the titbit with soft, whiffling lips. Then she relaxed, letting her ears flop comically as she sucked on the sweet.

Before long Zoe had Aisha calmly walking around the ménage in both directions, and halting on command. 'That's enough for today.' She dismounted, gave her the last mint and looked at her watch. Seven-thirty. 'Come on.' She slipped the saddle and bridle off and kissed the mare on the nose. 'We'd better hurry. I'll bring you some carrots later.' Oh dear, a distinct sweat mark showed where Aisha's saddle had been. There was no time to hose her down. What were the chances that anybody would notice? No one ever paid much attention to the mare. With any luck Aisha would roll in the grass and rub off the saddle mark herself.

.   .   .

Zoe was putting away the gear when Captain poked his nose into the tack room. 'Good morning, gorgeous,' she said.

'Good morning to you too.' Quinn came through the door.

Zoe froze, then ruffled Captain's soft ears so there was no misunderstanding about who she'd been talking to. Why was Quinn at the stables this early? Had he found her out? But then Josh pushed into the room, grinning like a Cheshire cat. What was going on?'

'I hear Cobber's foot is all healed,' said Quinn. Zoe could only stare at him. 'Are you going for a ride?' She managed to nod. 'Would you like us to keep you company?'

'I don't understand —'

'Josh and I will get the horses.'

The two of them collected halters and headed off towards the paddocks. They returned with three mounts: Duchess, Bridget's elegant grey, Yarraman, Quinn's tall chestnut and Cobber. Josh started saddling Duchess. Quinn was watching Zoe with a smile.

'Does this mean . . . ?' She smiled back at him.

Quinn lightly took her arm and led her aside. 'It means I listened to you,' he said in a low voice. 'You were right. I've seen how much happier Josh is since he's been teaching you to ride. I asked him about it. We had a good talk, first time in ages.' Quinn looked down, kicked softly at the grass. 'Josh said that just being around the horses helps him feel normal. But what he wants more than anything is to ride again. I wouldn't come at it at first. Said that I'd promised Dad to look after him. Then I thought about what you said to me on the beach, about being scared, and missing out, and playing it safe . . .'

'I could kiss you,' laughed Zoe with an excited squeal. 'Do you know what this will to mean to Josh? It could really turn things around for him.'

'Steady on.' But Quinn was laughing too, his customary seriousness banished, the tanned creases round his eyes crinkling with humour. He seemed years younger, and she could picture how he might have looked at Josh's age. 'Do you feel confident enough to ride Duchess?' he asked. 'I'd rather Josh have Cobber for his first time. It'll be safer.' They both burst out laughing again and Josh called for them to hurry up.

'I'd love to try Duchess,' said Zoe. 'You'll be able to see how well Josh has taught me.'

It took her a while to get used to the graceful grey thoroughbred – so much taller and narrower than Cobber, and not such a lump to push along. Zoe concentrated hard on all she'd learned: heels down, hands low and still, elbows close to her side. Quinn shot her an admiring glance, and she sat up a little straighter in the saddle.

After warming their mounts up in the ménage, they headed out for a ride around Swallowdale. Quinn kept a close, protective eye on them both, but the horses behaved themselves. Josh looked comical due to his long legs and Cobber's short ones, but he put up with it. It was obvious that he would gladly ride a donkey if it would satisfy his brother. Zoe focused on her own mount. It didn't take long for her to appreciate Duchess's lovely long stride, rocking-horse canter and sensitive mouth. Why Bridget always rode the mare with such a harsh bit was a mystery.

Zoe took a keen interest in the tour of the property. On their way out they passed a small metal shed that looked like a modified shipping container. 'One of our chemical stores,' said Quinn. 'We have a few of them scattered around the farm.' In a distant field, a harvester moved along rows of scorched cane, slicing up the stalks. Quinn pointed out a row of enormous wire cages on a little railway siding on the northern boundary. 'That's a collection point. See those bins?' Zoe nodded. 'Haul-out trucks fill them full of cane. Then they're collected and taken to the mill. Trains operate twenty-four hours a day, seven days a week during crushing season, and run on more than three hundred kilometres of narrow gauge track.' They rode through fields at different stages of growth. Some cane was only waist-high. Some paddocks lay fallow - expanses of rich, crumbly red soil that looked good enough to eat. In other places, black ground and charred stalks showed where fields had been burnt and harvested. Empty channels crisscrossed the farm. 'In dry times, those furrows carry water to the crop from the river and dams.' Quinn stopped and showed her a pump house. 'Though with all this rain we might not have to irrigate at all this year. The wet season's right around the corner.'

From up ahead came the sound of an engine. It grew louder, but Zoe couldn't see anything over the waving stalks of mature cane. They turned the corner. A tractor pulling a boom spray unit was pulling to a halt outside one of the little metal sheds. Duchess shied and snorted. Quinn pushed Yarraman forwards and took hold of the mare's reins. 'Easy does it. Better wait here until Rob turns off the motor.' A frail old man she didn't recognise climbed from the cabin and gave them a wave.

'Who's that?' asked Zoe.

'Rob Horton. He's worked here since my father was a boy. I promised Dad he'd always have a job if he wanted one. He got sick a few years ago, was off work for ages. Some sort of cancer. Between all the rounds of chemo and surgeries, it's a miracle he's alive. Rob's a tough old codger, though. He came back to work for me part-time last year. He runs our pest control program.'

'What's he doing?'

'Refilling the spray tanks.'

'Shouldn't he be wearing some sort of protective gear?'

'Rob knows what he's doing,' said Quinn as they turned the horses back towards the stables. 'And in any case, he's too stubborn to listen to me.' Quinn grinned. 'Don't think Rob's ever accepted that I'm in charge now. At the moment he's treating the crop for canegrubs and weeds. People think of insects and diseases like rust when they think of sugarcane pests, and the bloody beetles are bad this season – they're not usually such a problem this far south. But weeds are actually our biggest worry. They cost the industry seventy-million-dollars a year. It's a constant battle.'

Back at the stables, they were all in fine spirits. On dismounting, Quinn tousled Josh's hair and he ducked away. Quinn bounded after him and put his brother in a playful headlock. 'If you're fit to ride, Josh, I guess that means you're fit to feed the horses and hose them down.'

They collapsed on the ground, laughing and wrestling, before Josh sprang to his feet, and said, 'I'll do it for a lift to the centre and new headphones.' Quinn glanced at Zoe with raised brows, and she nodded to show she understood. There'd been no sign of Josh's halting speech pattern. Excitement had made him run his words together so he talked at normal speed. Josh tackled Quinn, who fell prone on the grass in mock defeat. 'You drive a hard bargain.' He raised himself on one elbow. 'One of the harvesters has packed up so I'm busy this arvo, but Bridget's here. She'll give you a lift. And yes, okay, new headphones it is.' Josh disappeared into the feed room, humming.

So . . . Bridget had stayed at Swallowdale last night. A rush of inexcusable jealousy made Zoe squirm. Quinn picked himself up off the grass and she had to stop herself from brushing dry leaves from his back. 'You were right about Josh and those horses,' he said. 'My brother was a different person back there.'

'He wasn't the only one,' said Zoe quietly.

Quinn's ears turned red. 'It was great having fun with him again. You know what? That's the first time I've heard Josh laugh since the accident, really laugh out loud, I mean.' He startled Zoe by taking her hand in both of his. 'Thank you.' She pulled away with an uncertain smile. 'Got anything planned for the day?' he asked.

'Mapping seagrass again,' she said. 'I know it's my day off, but it's taking forever. At the rate I'm going, the job won't be finished till Christmas. I'm finding lots of dieback and more dead turtles and dugongs. Dead coral too. Something bad's happening out there on the reef.'

'Any idea what?'

She shook her head. 'I'll know more when my samples are analysed.'

'If anybody can figure it out, it'll be you. I have a feeling you don't give up easily.' They reached the fork in the path leading to the cottage. 'How about coming to the house for a cuppa and a piece of Bridget's homemade fruitcake before you head off?'

'Okay,' she said, against her better judgement. 'I'll be up in a minute.'

Zoe wandered home, repeating the familiar two-part mantra in her head. One, she'd sworn off men and two, Quinn belonged to Bridget. Zoe let her breath out slowly, and waited for the attraction to pass. But this tried and true technique did not have its customary effect. Instead, a surge of resentment welled up inside. Who made the arbitrary *no men* rule anyway? Rules were made to be broken, and this was a self-imposed banishment.

And as for the second part of the mantra, the bit about Quinn belonging to Bridget? Well, that wasn't working today either. She didn't trust Bridget anymore. What about the contradictory stories regarding Hope? Zoe had tackled her about it. Bridget was unconcerned, swearing that Quinn was mistaken. He'd been thinking of a different dolphin, one that'd gone to Oceanworld on a breeding exchange program, one that could never be released. She assured Zoe that a young bottlenose named Hope died after being returned to the wild, and that it had been a devastating blow.

Zoe couldn't disprove Bridget's story. It happened before Karen worked at the centre, and the longer-term casuals were no help. Oceanworld's website showed that a new female dolphin had arrived there nine months ago, but her name was Rose, not Hope, and there was no information about where she'd come from. Apart from Quinn's offhand comment to the contrary, Zoe had no valid reason to doubt Bridget's version of events.

But there was more to it than that. Other things about her boss weren't ringing true. Duchess's long-shanked curb bridle, for example. If Bridget was such an expert at training animals, why did she rely on a harsh, mechanical bit to control her mare? And what about Aisha? Everybody agreed that Bridget had tried to work with the horse. Those attempts had failed, and as a result Aisha had been branded dangerous. Nobody had questioned Bridget's opinion. Yet a fifteen-year-old boy had been able to re-educate the Arabian mare. Even Zoe, an equestrian novice, had ridden her safely.

These amorphous doubts swirled about her brain as she hurriedly showered and changed. She felt guilty even entertaining such thoughts. Bridget was her boss, her friend, and Zoe wasn't a distrusting person by nature. Quite the opposite. She took people at face value, sometimes to the point of naivety. That's what her self-inflicted man drought was all about, an admission that she couldn't trust her instincts. But what if her instincts *were* sound this time? Zoe buckled her belt. All this tangled thinking was giving her a headache. There was nothing wrong with a simple morning tea.

Zoe stood before the bathroom vanity and tugged a comb through her chestnut hair. It was growing out quickly. She experimented with the part, in the middle, to the left, to the right . . . sweeping her hair back, then to the side, weighing up the effect. This new length suited her much better, but it was definitely time to drive to Bundaberg to have it styled. Having no long mirrors in the cottage didn't usually bother her; she was used to it. But Zoe had a sudden urge to examine herself from top to toe. The sunroom window should do it.

She smoothed down her top and stood in front of the floor-to-ceiling pane of glass, trying to get the angle of the light just right. There. Wow, she really *had* lost weight. Zoe turned sideways, thrilled at the smooth hollow of her hip, the lean line of her belly. She couldn't remember when she'd looked this good, and she hadn't even been trying. How many diets had she been on when she lived in Sydney? Dozens. The cabbage soup diet, the caveman diet, the Israeli army diet, and her personal favourite, the martini madness maintenance plan. She knew them all by heart, as well as the kilojoule content per hundred grams of most common foods and the equivalent amount of treadmill time to work it off. Useless information, of course, when she couldn't stay away from McDonald's or stick at the gym for more than a few weeks at a time. But here in Kiawa? Good health happened by magic. The air, when the cane fields weren't burning, was worth bottling.

CHAPTER 18

Zoe sat down at the comfy cane setting on the jasmine-laden verandah, wondering where Bridget was and hoping she wouldn't join them. Not a mug or teabag in sight. Quinn made a brew of black leaf tea in a pretty china pot and set out rose-patterned cups and saucers like her grandmother might do. Even a cuppa and cake was done with unhurried, old-style elegance at Swallowdale.

'Ah, I forgot the cake.' Quinn rose from his chair just as his phone rang.

'Don't worry.' Zoe waved him back down. 'I'll get it.'

She wandered in through the glass-panelled double doors. On her way back from the kitchen, a framed photograph of a man caught her attention. It resembled one of those paintings where the subject's eyes followed you around the room. She moved to the left and then to the right, but couldn't escape the man's magnetic, oddly familiar gaze. His dark hair was turning to grey but he still had the look of a man in his prime. He stood before a flaming field of cane, his weight on his front foot and shoulders forward, like a bear ready to attack. This must be Marshall Cooper, Quinn's father.

Zoe tore herself away and took the fruitcake outside, setting the willow pattern plate on the table and cutting two generous slices. 'Tell me about your father.'

'Dad?' Quinn put down his cake as though he'd lost his appetite. 'Everybody respected him. He was president of Kiawa Rotary, the Canegrowers' Association, the local agricultural show society . . .'

'You sound like you're writing his biography. I mean what sort of a person was he?'

Quinn stayed quiet for so long that it seemed he might not answer at all. 'Fiercely proud of his family and of Kiawa's traditions. Hard but fair, and old-school smart. Nobody ever got the best of him in a business deal. That's not to say he dudded people. Dad was scrupulously honest. He always said: *The qualities that make a man are honesty, respect and loyalty. And honesty is number one.* I feel exactly the same way.'

Zoe examined the tea leaves in her cup. Great. Quinn valued honesty above all else, and here she was lying to him about Aisha. She'd better come clean, and soon.

'That's why it was so hard for me to let Josh ride again. Dad had said no, and I promised to honour his wishes.'

'What sort of a father was he?'

'Dad was my whole world when I was a kid, larger than life. I wanted to be just like him.' A rueful smile. 'It didn't work out that way. I don't have his toughness.' Quinn shifted restlessly in his chair. 'I wish you could have met him, Zoe.'

'I'm sorry I didn't have that chance.'

'Dad was such an impressive person. Totally in charge. Absolutely fearless, even after we lost Mum. But when Josh had his accident? Well, something broke inside him and all that confidence leaked out through the cracks. It killed me to see it.'

'What would the old, fearless Marshall have said about Josh riding again?'

'The old one?' Quinn grinned shyly, like a boy. 'He would have said: *Put the kid back on a horse.*'

'Which is exactly what you've done.' She reached for his hand and squeezed it. 'Maybe you're more like your father than you think.'

A voice called from inside the house. 'Hello?' Bridget came onto the verandah. If she noticed Zoe withdraw her hand from Quinn's, she didn't show it. 'Well, this is nice. Morning tea, with my fruit cake centre stage. What's the verdict, Zoe?'

Josh followed her out and helped himself to a double-sized portion. 'I like it better without peel.' He crammed it into his mouth, dribbling crumbs.

Bridget kissed Quinn on the cheek. 'I went to the post office to collect a parcel, so I picked up your mail.' She handed him some letters and turned her attention to Josh. 'I'm heading to the centre. Fancy a lift? You can see our new turtles.'

'What new turtles?' asked Zoe.

'Karen rang to say three new rescues came in this morning,' said Bridget. 'I don't know where to put them. We're overflowing with turtles at the moment.' Bridget cut herself a thin sliver of cake. 'So, Josh, are you coming?'

'Quinn's buying me new headphones because I put the horses away.'

'You put the horses away?' She shot Quinn a questioning look.

'Zoe convinced me that Josh should be allowed to ride again. The two of them have been on at me for ages and this morning I finally caved.' Josh punched the air. 'As far as those headphones go, mate, you'll have to wait until our trip to Bundaberg on Friday for speech therapy.'

'Hey, not fair,' said Josh, but nothing could wipe the smile off his face.

'Well, that's great, Josh.' Bridget stood behind Quinn's chair with her hands on his shoulders. 'Just as long as you don't let him ride Aisha. I can tell you from personal experience that she can be danger-ous.' Josh hesitated, then opened his mouth to speak. He was going to tell for sure, and maybe it was the best thing. Maybe the time was right.

'Don't worry, Bridge,' said Quinn. 'Nobody's going to ride that horse.' He stood up and fixed his brother with a stern stare. 'Hear that, Josh? Stick to Cobber. If all goes well I'll see about getting you your own horse next year. But stay away from Aisha. If I see you anywhere near that mare, I'll sell her.'

Josh's face fell. Blinking hard, he knelt down beside Captain and furiously stroked the dog's head.

'Don't be like that, Josh,' said Bridget. 'Your brother's looking after you.' She kissed Quinn, turned on her heel and headed for the door. 'Josh,' she called. 'Let's go.' The boy gave Captain one last pat and trailed out after her.

Zoe poured herself another cup of tea and forced a smile. No, not the right time after all. Better give Quinn a day or so to get used to the idea of Josh riding again before she confessed. She'd have to warn Josh first, of course, but she was determined to do it, whether he liked it or not. Going behind Quinn's back was weighing too heavily on her.

'Josh is an amazing kid,' she said. 'He did well today.'

Quinn sank back into the chair. 'You'll get no argument from me.'

'Where did he go to school before the accident?'

'The local high school. I went there too. Dad didn't put much store in private boarding schools. Said if it was good enough for him, it was good enough for us.'

'Have you ever thought of sending Josh back there?'

'Sometimes,' said Quinn. 'Bridget thinks it's a bad idea. Says he'd be bullied and wouldn't be able to keep up.'

'At least he wouldn't be on his own all the time,' said Zoe. 'Josh is tough, and I imagine he was pretty popular. Wouldn't his old mates rally round him? What if he had an integration aid to help with school work? Josh is funny, and smart, and in some ways he's very mature. After all, you let him stay at the shack overnight by himself.'

'That's because Bridget's next door at Cliffhaven. She looks after him.'

Quinn began to clear the table. Zoe picked up her cup and saucer. 'It must have been hard for you when Bridget was away studying.'

'Josh and I missed her like crazy,' said Quinn. 'Funny thing is, she didn't really want to go, but Leo expected his three girls to get a university education. It was a point of pride.' Zoe followed him through to the kitchen. 'Her older sister studied law. She's a barrister in Sydney now. The middle one's an architect. Bridget was a bit different. Prettiest girl at school, no doubt about that, but not much of an academic, not like her sisters. Bridget's final year was really difficult: maths, physics, chemistry, all the hard subjects.' Zoe put her dishes down as far away as possible from the fearsome garbage disposal. 'She worked her guts out, terrified she'd let her father down,' said Quinn. 'Her sister would shake Bridget awake when she fell asleep on her desk at midnight, and she'd keep right on studying. Even then she didn't get into Queensland University like she wanted. Did a science degree at Armidale instead. After that she found her feet. Leo was stoked. Distinctions all the way and off overseas to study. I used to worry she wouldn't come back.'

'Plenty of international research opportunities for somebody with her qualifications,' said Zoe.

'I don't doubt it, but I think Bridget has her heart set on the Reef Centre.'

'And on you,' teased Zoe.

'Yes.' He opened the dishwasher 'I suppose so.' He turned to her with a self-effacing look on his handsome face. Zoe placed her cup and saucer into the top rack and brushed against Quinn's shoulder. A charge passed through her, a tremor deep in her gut. Did he feel it too? Well, what if he did? It made no difference. There was no future for them. Bridget stood squarely in the way. Beautiful, talented Bridget. A woman Quinn shared a history with, was engaged to for goodness sake. A woman who deserved his loyalty. She slammed the dishwasher door shut, making the stacked plates rattle and shake.

'Thanks for the cuppa, Quinn. I'd better get going. Those seagrass beds won't map themselves.'

With a cheery wave that belied her true feelings, Zoe walked out of door, straight into Bridget who was coming back in. 'I was hoping to catch you,' she said. 'I can't find my training clicker. Do you have one I could borrow?'

'Sure.' Zoe pulled a clicker from the pocket of her jeans and handed it over. She turned to go.

'Wait,' said Bridget. 'You dropped something.' Zoe glanced back and her heart stopped. Bridget was flattening out a little ball of paper. She looked at Quinn. 'This note's for you, darling. It's from Ed Owen.'

Quinn took it from her hand. His expression darkened as he read it. 'Why do you have this, Zoe?' His eyes were accusing.

'I —'

'*By the way,*' he read aloud, '*. . . saw Josh riding a black horse like the devil was after him. I couldn't catch him. Can that boy ever ride.*'

A knock came at the screen door. 'Pardon me, Mr Quinn.' It was the ancient man from the tractor. 'Someone's been riding that black horse. It's got a saddle mark, clear as day.'

'You mean Aisha?' The old man nodded. 'Thank you Rob. You can go.' Quinn's voice remained quiet but a vein began to throb at his throat. He read the note again. 'What do you know about this Zoe?'

She couldn't speak. The ugly silence yawned between them, growing fat and bloated until she could bear it no longer. 'I should have told you ...'

'Should have told me what?'

'Josh has been working with Aisha, riding her.'

Bridget gasped, her hand flying to her mouth.

'And you knew? Of course you knew. It was probably your idea.' He slammed his fist down on the table. Bridget laid a hand on his shoulder but Quinn shook it away. He waved the letter in Zoe's face. '*I met Zoe King on the river track this morning. Her horse was lame . . .*' Cobber went lame more than two weeks ago. So you and Josh have been going behind my back all this time?'

'Not exactly. Josh hasn't ridden Aisha since that note was written. We were waiting for the right time to tell you. In fact, I think Josh was getting ready to own up just before, but then you said you'd sell the mare if he went near her.'

Quinn's eyes were as cold as she'd ever seen them. He threw the note down. 'For the record, that mare is as good as gone.'

The heat of disappointment and embarrassment flushed through her like a physical pain. Tiny beads of sweat dotted her forehead. If only she'd come clean earlier.

'Where's Josh?' asked Quinn.

Bridget's hands fluttered nervously. 'Waiting for me in the car.'

'Get him.'

'Quinn, no,' said Bridget. 'Let Josh come to work with me. Talk to him tonight when you've calmed down and had time to think.'

It was good advice and Zoe hoped he'd take it. Josh was so happy. Happier than he'd been since the accident, Quinn had said so himself. It was Zoe's fervent wish that he would not cut that happiness short because of her.

Quinn nodded at Bridget. 'Go on then.' She aimed a reproachful frown at Zoe and escaped out the door.

'Don't blame Josh,' said Zoe.

'I don't,' said Quinn. 'I blame you.'

'I really am sorry,'

'The weird thing is, I believe that.' He bowed his head, dragging his hands through his hair. 'You don't stop to think though, do you, Zoe? Going through life, acting on impulse, saying whatever you feel, doing whatever you want. Not considering the effect on other people. It just doesn't occur to you.'

'That's not fair,' she said. 'You're the one who's not thinking about Josh. What about how your decisions affect him? Your brother loves that mare and he's a brilliant trainer. He has a gift, not just with horses but with dolphins too. Believe me, that kid speaks animal, and the truth is that Bridget would be lost without him. She doesn't teach those dolphins at the centre – he does. That's why she wants him there. And she uses the fact that he has a major crush on her to get her own way.'

Quinn grabbed the bentwood back of the chair in front of him. His knuckles showed pale where he gripped it. 'Get stuck into me if you want to, but leave Bridget out of it. She's the best friend Josh ever had.'

'Not much of a friend if you ask me.' Zoe's mouth was running at a million miles a minute, and she couldn't stop it, didn't want to stop it. There was a wild, cathartic pleasure in airing her doubts at last. 'Keeping Josh from going to school so she can make use of him. Telling you his horse is unsafe when it's not.'

'So now you're an expert on horses?'

'Not an expert, no, but I've seen Josh work his magic on that mare for myself. Maybe Bridget's telling the truth as she sees it. Maybe she's just not as capable as people think. Maybe she's afraid; I don't know. Look at that curb she uses on Duchess when a snaffle would do. My guess is Bridget used that awful bit on Aisha and the mare wouldn't stand for it. And I don't blame her.'

'Bridget's a professional trainer,' he said. 'And you're talking nonsense.'

'Am I? How else do you explain her complete failure to make any progress with Aisha, when Josh had the mare eating out of his hand within days? I tell you, Aisha is not dangerous, at least not since Josh started working with her. Heck, she's so quiet even I can ride her.'

'You?' Quinn snorted with disgust. 'What a liar.'

'Who do you think was riding Aisha today?' asked Zoe. 'Not Josh. He was with you all morning, wasn't he?' That gave him pause. She could almost hear him thinking. 'I won't ride your horses again, but please think about what I've said. Josh is miles more capable than you give him credit for, and you'll break his heart if you sell that horse.'

Quinn sank down on the chair and swallowed hard. 'Go home, Zoe. Please, just go.'

CHAPTER 19

Quinn stood on the verandah as Zoe's Lexus sped out the gate, wheels spinning on gravel. Clouds boiled in from the west as he walked from the house and down the line of macaranga trees along the drive. Their broad heart-shaped leaves trembled. Despite the warm breeze his skin felt cold. Bloody hell, it was going to rain again, and they were weeks behind with the harvest as it was. Wet cane wouldn't burn.

Out of habit he whistled for Captain, half-expecting the dog not to show. But he came pelting through the garden from the direction of the cottage. Captain leaped around him, all smiles and waving tail but Quinn wasn't fooled. He was the consolation prize for Captain these days. The moment Zoe arrived home the collie would desert him again.

Captain settled at Quinn's heel as he walked past the tennis courts, left towards the turnout paddocks, down the laneway and out the back. Quinn braced himself. There was Aisha, restless as ever, pacing the fence. Tail held high in that characteristic Arabian way, unsettled by the gusty wind. It was as he'd feared. The sight of her brought all the old pain crashing in and he fought the instinct to turn back. For the first time in a long time he really looked at the mare. He'd forgotten what a beauty she was, even more lovely than her mother. Aisha's championship lines showed in each stride she took.

Aisha spotted him. With a piercing whinny and arched neck she pounded forwards. Her storm-black mane lifted and tossed like the crest of a dark wave. Could this be the quiet mount that Zoe had described to him? One that a virtual beginner had ridden just this morning? Hardly. She looked more like a devil horse.

The mare galloped towards the five-railed gate at breakneck speed. If she didn't slow down soon there was no way she'd stop in time. His chest tightened. Maybe it was for the best. A fleeting memory pierced the shield he'd built around his heart: Josh's twelfth birthday, before it all went wrong. Aisha as a bold, inquisitive foal, prancing from the float behind her exquisite mother, delighting them all with her antics. He could still see the joy on his little brother's face. Josh had dedicated every spare moment of his twelfth summer to the new charges. Sleeping down at the stables with them, training Kariman tirelessly for that last fateful ride and working hard to halter-break her beautiful black filly.

A wave of nausea hit him. Quinn sprang forwards and raced for the fence. Could he turn her in time? Horse and man raced towards each other and reached the gate together. Too late. Quinn ducked aside, ready for the sickening thud of flesh and splintering timber. But instead of cannoning into the unforgiving rails, Aisha gathered her impossibly fine-boned legs beneath her and made a leap that would have made a Grand National winner proud. If not for an athletic mid-air twist, she would have fallen on top of him. Instead she landed, sure as a cat, and extended her chiselled nose to touch his face.

Quinn waited a moment for the blood to stop rushing in his ears. 'Thank you for not crushing me to death.' He rubbed the mare's pricked ears. 'Curious as ever and bold as brass, aren't you?' She nickered at the sound of his voice. He smiled with relief and something else . . . he could just as easily have been talking about Zoe. With a soothing *whoa girl* he pulled off his belt, looped it round Aisha's neck and headed for the stable.

The mare was absurdly pleased to see him, gently nudging his shoulder as they walked and nibbling his hat. She was lonely – that much was obvious – and he felt a sudden guilt. Horses were herd animals, social creatures. He hadn't banished her to a solitary existence in order to be deliberately unkind. He'd done it to protect himself from the painful memories she evoked. Out of sight, out of mind. But the flesh and blood horse before him brought home how right Zoe had been. It was cruel to keep the young animal on her own. Selling her as a brood mare would be the kindest thing, but first he would test Zoe's story.

According to Bridget the mare was dangerous and out of control, and he'd never doubted her word; why would he? It suited him to believe it, gave him a reason to exclude the mare and keep Josh away from her. But now he was about to find out for himself.

Quinn tied Aisha to the hitching rail, went to the tack room and looked around for her gear. Zoe was right. Aisha's bridle bore a savage-looking curb bit. Cobber's would do instead. He grabbed a curry comb and brushed away the tell-tale sweat mark on her back, then saddled up. The mare stood like a rock as Quinn mounted and sat still for a minute or two, trying to judge her mood. He may be an excellent rider, born in the saddle, however it didn't pay to take anything for granted. Aisha seemed calm enough, but it only took seconds for a horse to explode.

Touching his heels to her side, they set off through the cane fields towards the river. She tossed her head fretfully, fussing and chewing at the bit. He gave her a loose rein. As she stretched out her head and neck he felt the tension drain from her. Time for a change of pace. He closed his legs and Aisha launched into a contained but energetic trot. The sensation of controlled power beneath him felt good. He was enjoying himself.

The mare began to prance and throw her forelegs forwards in an exaggerated, high-stepping gait. Quinn stroked her gleaming neck. 'That's a fine imitation of a Spanish trot,' he said with a smile. 'Who said you'd never make a dressage horse?' Whenever he shortened the reins, her movement became more and more extravagant, until she was bouncing into the air and shaking Quinn about. 'Enough of that,' he said. 'If you've got all that excess energy, let's go.' He gave the mare her head, and she launched into a smooth, springy canter. They pounded out the back gate and along the river track until her neck grew damp with sweat and her sides were flecked with foam. 'Do you have some of that bounce left in you?' He aimed her at fallen log. She jumped it so gracefully and with such little effort that he barely shifted in his seat. Next came the tumbledown stone wall. The mare seemed delighted to be presented with another obstacle. She cleared it with a bold flick of her heels. Aisha was breathing harder now.

'Let's not overdo it, girl.' Aisha was breathing harder now. He reined her in with a firm, gentle hand, and turned her head for home. What a horse. What a simply marvellous horse. How could he have left her to languish in the paddock all this time? She was energetic and high-spirited, certainly. But dangerous? Not by a long shot. He had no doubt that Zoe had managed the mare in the safety of the ménage. She'd been telling the truth about that at least. Who was he kidding? She'd been telling the truth about a lot more than that. Josh, for instance, and the importance of his powerful love for the beautiful mare. And what about Bridget? It did seem strange that she'd had so much trouble with the horse. Was Zoe right about her too?

Time to be straight with himself. The years away had changed Bridget. He hadn't noticed during her brief visits back home. She'd seemed like the same lovely woman, committed to building a future together. But since her permanent return to Kiawa, the cracks were showing.

The divide between them had widened. Although their relationship appeared strong from the outside, Quinn recognised some important things were missing: communication, genuine intimacy, fun. Bridget didn't seem to notice or, if she did, she didn't say.

Bridget still played the part of the perfect partner, but something indefinable was missing. The two of them barely spent proper time together, just snatches here and there, enough to keep up appearances. And when they did go out for dinner, or drive into Bundaberg for a movie, all she could talk about were her big ideas to expand the Reef Centre. Visitor numbers had increased, yet the place still wasn't living up to her expectations. Bridget wasn't content to let it go along as it had in the past, ticking over, breaking even. She had ambitious business plans, and was aching to impress Leo with her commercial acumen.

Bloody Leo. A serial philanderer whose marriage collapsed when his wife could no longer put up with his infidelities. A ruthless legal team and deep pockets saw him retain custody of his three little girls. Their mother had died in a car crash soon after. Leo was all they had, and the children were devoted to him. Right from the start, he'd cast his daughters into some sort of sick competition to see who could make him the proudest. Although Bridget was the only one in Kiawa supporting her father's political ambitions, she always seemed to come last in his estimations.

And even for a man as old-fashioned as Quinn, it seemed strange that she was living with her father. It was a lonely life, rattling around the grand old house with only his brother for company. If you could call it company. Josh operated on a different plane. When he wasn't down at the Reef Centre, he was locked away playing online games, laughing and talking to invisible computer nerds from around the world. Quinn called them his *ghosts*, and indeed it was disconcerting, hearing those disembodied voices come through the door of Josh's room. Quinn would have loved Bridget to move in. They needed time together to mend the growing rift between them, but it seemed her devotion to Leo was greater than her need for him.

And now Leo was sniffing around Zoe, luring her with his cars and yachts. A sudden, unexpected surge of jealousy left him breathless. No, it wasn't jealousy, of course it wasn't. In spite of all her faults, Zoe was a good person and his guest. It was natural for him to look out for her. Leo was twice Zoe's age but she was a smart girl – too smart to fall for Leo's tricks.

Quinn rode on, one hand on the reins and the other relaxed at his hip. What about Zoe's assertion that Bridget was being dishonest, using his brother for her own ends, needing his help with the dolphins? It *had* been her idea to keep him at home. Josh wanted to enrol in his old school at the start of the year. His psychologist had been cautiously encouraging, providing there was proper support available. Such a big decision and Quinn had been torn, in two minds. Bridget had tipped the scales. She didn't believe Josh was ready for mainstream schooling and Quinn trusted her judgement where his brother was concerned. Bridget always had Josh's best interests at heart, didn't she? He had to believe it. One of the few things that would move him to real anger would be somebody taking advantage of his brother.

Thud— Ow. One moment he'd been pondering this disturbing question, and the next he was sitting on the ground, unharmed but red-faced. Captain had appeared from nowhere, dashing from a clump of white-flowering lilly pilly at the edge of the track, provoking Aisha into one enormous buck that Quinn had not been ready for. Right now the mare was fleeing along the river, with the dog barking at her heels. 'Oi!' bellowed Quinn. Both animals stopped and turned at the sound of his voice. Captain came racing back. Aisha stood, keen-eyed, watching. Nostrils flared, and that magnificent black banner of a tail kinked so high it fanned out over her back.

Quinn summed up the situation. Worth a try. He called the mare's name. Aisha gave a loud snort and sprang into action, for all the world like a horse from a movie. She returned to him at a cadenced, floating trot. He stroked her satin nose with its heart-shaped star. 'Well, young lady, you've certainly taught me not to take you for granted.'

Quinn remounted, walking the mare the rest of the way home without further incident. He didn't blame her for the buck. He blamed himself. A rider should always be paying attention: to the weather, the surroundings, the mood of his horse. Aisha was young and green and unpredictable, but there was no dirt in her, he knew that now.

Thanks to Zoe. He had absolutely no idea what to think about that woman, how to handle her. On one hand she'd done him a big favour, opened his eyes. He was grateful for that. But she'd also been dishonest, and all that wild talk about Bridget? Zoe had a friend and supporter in Bridget. Accusing her of some sort of hidden agenda was a poor way of repaying her. Zoe was right about his brother being too dependent on Bridget though, following her round the centre like a puppy. From now on Josh would stay home and help Quinn around the farm instead. He finally had a currency to motivate the kid – time with the horses. It would make a big difference. And he had Zoe to thank for that as well.

Quinn was waiting in the kitchen that evening when Bridget and Josh arrived home. 'We just made it here ahead of the storm.' Bridget put down her bag. 'Have you calmed down yet?' She bustled to the refrigerator without waiting for his answer. 'Did you talk to Zoe?'

Quinn shut the fridge door and took her gently by the shoulders. 'I've got dinner sorted.'

'You have?'

'The casserole's in the oven. Now . . . come talk to me.' Thunder rumbled nearby.

'I'll make some rice.'

'Already done.'

Josh might want a snack,' she said.

'Then he can get it himself.'

He took Bridget's hand, led her to the verandah and sat her down. 'Would you like a cold drink? Beer, lemonade?'

She wiped her forehead, looking puzzled. 'Lemonade.' He fetched two glasses with ice and sat down beside her. 'Is this about Zoe? I know you're upset, but don't ask me to fire her.'

'No, it's nothing like that.' He took a sip of his drink. 'I don't want Josh going to the Reef Centre each day. It's time he started working with me here at home.'

'You already tried that,' she said. 'Josh isn't capable of any real responsibility. It will end in tears like last time, I guarantee it.'

'Maybe so.' He studied Bridget's face. 'But I'll take that risk.'

'Josh is very fond of the dolphins, especially Mirrhi. He'll miss them terribly.'

'He can see them on weekends,' said Quinn. 'I'm doing this partly for you. Think how much work you'll get done when you don't have to babysit my brother.'

'I don't mind,' she said. 'I love him, you know that.'

'And he loves you too, but my mind's made up.'

For a fleeting moment there was something akin to desperation in her eyes. 'Is this about punishing Josh? I don't think that's fair. Zoe's the one —'

'It's not about punishing anybody.'

Bridget stood up, her normal composure slipping. 'Josh doesn't exactly do as he's told, especially where you're concerned. How will you get him to cooperate?'

'Simple. I'll bribe him.'

'What with?'

'With the horses . . . with Aisha.'

'What's Aisha got to do with this? I thought you couldn't stand the sight of that mare?'

'Will you please sit?' Bridget looked so flustered he feared she might walk away. 'Please?' She sat back down. 'I rode Aisha myself today,' he said. 'She's high-spirited and green, but she's not dangerous, Bridge.' He reached for her hand again but she withdrew it. 'I'll work with the horse myself, help Josh train her. Only groundwork, of course. He won't ride her.'

For a moment Bridget looked ready to argue. He almost wished she would. 'That's great,' she said at last, her voice cool and dull. 'Turning Aisha out like that must have been just what she needed.'

'Maybe.'

'So you're not angry with Zoe?'

'Yes,' he said. 'But I'm also grateful. She encouraged me to let Josh get back to what he loves, made me see my mistake.'

'As opposed to me, you mean?' She rose to leave.

'Don't be like that, Bridge.' He scrubbed a hand over his face, rubbed his eyes. 'What's happening to us? We can't even talk anymore.'

Bridget turned back to him. 'Of course we can talk.' She sat down and put a hand on his arm. 'Quinn, I had no idea you felt like this.'

'How else should I feel?' Her mouth opened, then closed again. 'You're not here, even when you are here.' The words tumbled from him. 'It's like we're living separate lives. By the time the wedding rolls around, we won't know each other at all.'

For a moment her expression was unreadable, then it softened. 'You're right,' she said. He hadn't known what to expect, denial maybe ... anger. Bridget shifted her chair a little closer to his. 'Shall I move in here, at Swallowdale?' He was too surprised to answer. 'I know I said I'd wait until the wedding, but ...'

'You want to move in?' He swallowed. 'Now?' Bridget nodded. He should be happy. Ever since her return to Kiawa, he'd been impatient for their life together to begin. Why then did he hesitate?

Bridget searched his face. A shadow of concern passed over her eyes. 'If you don't want me ...'

'No, no ...' he said. 'I'd love you to move in. How often have I asked you?

She smiled. 'Only a dozen times.'

'It's what we need, Bridge. To reconnect, make us strong again.' Quinn kissed her quickly and let her go.

'This calls for something more than lemonade,' said Bridget brightly. She went to the kitchen and returned with champagne flutes and a bottle of sparkling wine. Quinn eased out the cork, and it emerged with a soft plop. Bridget poured two glasses. 'A toast - to us!'

'To us.' They clinked glasses. Things would be better between them when Bridget moved in to Swallowdale, of course they would. Why then did he feel more lonely than ever?

CHAPTER 20

Zoe parked the car, reached over and hauled her overnight bag from the back seat. She would stay at the shack again tonight. She'd had enough of life at Swallowdale. Two weeks had passed since things had gone so horribly wrong, and she hadn't talked to Quinn since. He hadn't approached her, and she couldn't muster up the courage to go to him. She had no idea where things stood between them.

No, that wasn't right. She knew she wasn't Quinn's favourite person right now. Zoe thought about their last conversation, about how forthright she'd been, and winced. But things could be worse. Bridget hadn't fired her. In fact, she was as friendly as ever, almost as if nothing had happened. Yet Zoe did detect a subtle coolness that hadn't been there before. And this wasn't the only change. Josh no longer spent each day at the Reef Centre and she was dying to know why. Some kind of punishment, probably. Banned from his much-loved dolphins, or perhaps from her own bad influence.

As a consequence, the *Dancing Dolphins* show was rapidly going downhill. Bridget had managed for the first few days, but she didn't have the same sympathetic connection that Josh did with the dolphins. Nor did she understand the importance of timely, consistent reinforcement when they did what she wanted. Bridget missed cues, overlooked errors and randomly handed out fishy rewards whether the dolphins behaved or not.

It only took a week for the spinners to stop spinning. When Bridget blew the whistle they no longer performed their dramatic aerial twists. Instead they rushed about, jumping and splashing, receiving fish for a graceful leap here or energetic tail-slap there. It was as if Bridget didn't know how to shape specific behaviours. Little wonder she couldn't train Aisha. Hard to believe, considering her impeccable academic and research qualifications in mammalian intelligence.

Had Bridget really thought she'd forever get away with pretending the training was all her own work? To give her credit, she'd done a good job of faking it so far. People's preconceptions had helped her enormously. Nobody could imagine that Josh, the not-quite-right boy, had anything useful to contribute. Even Karen had been fooled, and Zoe enjoyed watching the truth gradually dawn on her. 'All this time I thought Lady Muck was some kind of saint, putting up with that kid. Letting him have the run of the place, even after closing. I admired her for it.' Karen snorted. 'More fool me.'

Josh's solo evening training sessions made sense now. Bridget's idea, no doubt. And it explained why she didn't want anybody staying at the shack, with its wide views over Dolphin Harbour. And why that car never turned up. Making Zoe rely on others to get to and from the centre stopped her from nosing around too much. No wonder her boss wasn't happy when Leo lent her the Lexus.

Well, the charade was over and Bridget had come well and truly unstuck. Watching her disastrous efforts to work with the dolphins, Zoe almost felt sorry for her. Baby had become so confused he withdrew from the show completely, waiting a safe distance offshore until his mother Koko finished her muddled routine. One time Kane leaped straight for Bridget, causing her to drop her bucket of fish. He scoffed the lot, and lunged more belligerently the next time. Bridget rewarded him with another fish. She really had no clue. The worst thing you could do with a dominant dolphin was to try to appease him. It only served to increase his aggression, and Zoe became even more frightened of Kane.

Karen tried to step in when she realised what was happening. Although more competent than Bridget, she still let the animals get away with sloppy performances. She didn't have Josh's feel for the task, his hunches, his split second-timing — his intuitive ability to get into the animals' heads. Most of the audience members were none the wiser. They seemed happy just to see dolphins up close, doing anything at all. But the animals were growing more and more out of control and the punters were bound to notice eventually.

Zoe tried to help, but she was no expert either. Just because she recognised Josh's uncanny ability didn't mean she could emulate it. Nobody was on the same page. The dolphins were getting mixed signals from too many people. But even when Zoe followed the strict scientific rules of operant conditioning and achieved a degree of success, something was still missing. That indefinable connection that trainers called rapport, when an animal responds intuitively to a person's body language and emotions, and vice versa. In time she hoped it would come, but the *Dancing Dolphins* didn't have time. At the rate things were going, it would only be a few more weeks before they stopped performing anything remotely recognisable as a *show*.

None of this bothered Zoe too much. Her passion was for conservation, not training. The more she came to know about dolphins, the less she approved of them turning tricks for crowds, day after day. Learning was a useful enrichment tool for the bored captives, nothing more. Sometimes she wondered how the centre was tracking financially. Visitors brought in money, and dolphin shows brought in visitors. Gate takings would drop pretty quickly once the dolphins stopped performing. But that wasn't really her problem, except for the fact that she hadn't been paid this month. Leo was loaded. He'd bail his daughter out if needed. Zoe had more important things on her mind, namely her stalled research project.

The seagrass specimens she'd given to Bridget for analysis after her first day out on the boat with Josh were taking forever to come back. Growing impatient, Zoe had sent some samples off independently to the University of Sydney. The results were startling. Dangerous levels of chemicals had shown up in water, sediment and tissue samples across all the seagrass monitoring sites. Even more disturbing was that the banned pesticide Dieldrin had also been detected. The worst contamination was in near-shore meadows around the river mouth. This pointed the finger directly at run-off from Kiawa's sugarcane farms. She hadn't discussed any of this with Bridget, and not just because of the subtle frostiness between them. Her boss had shown a distinct lack of interest in the project all along, which was strange, considering it was her idea in the first place.

Zoe headed through the centre gates and hurried towards the hospital compound. Good, the vet's jeep was parked up ahead. She'd asked George to do two autopsies. One subject was a juvenile dolphin found dying by snorklers at Turtle Reef. The other was a dugong calf washed up in mangroves not far from the river mouth. Today was reporting day.

Zoe had to wait more than two hours for the results. The compound was chock-a-block with close to twenty sea turtles, apparently three times more than this time last year. They were coming in malnourished, dehydrated and underweight. X-rays revealed a few had swallowed plastic, leading to *floater's syndrome*. Trapped gas in the gut kept the turtles stranded on the surface, so they couldn't dive to feed. George treated these impactions with fibre, Metamucil and vegetable oil. Sometimes it worked. Sometimes they needed surgery, like when fish hooks were caught in their throats or intestines. But a surprising number of otherwise healthy sea turtles were simply starving for no apparent reason.

'It's the same with your dugong, and another one I dissected last week,' said George, as he administered antibiotics to a young loggerhead while Zoe struggled to hold it still. 'Half the expected weight and no food in its stomach. It's quite a mystery.'

Zoe bit her tongue. No mystery to her. Confirmation of the disappearing seagrass meadows was mounting by the minute, but she didn't want to go off half-cocked. All the pieces of the puzzle needed to fit.

When George finally finished his rounds, Zoe made him a coffee and they sat down with the autopsy results. He handed her a few stapled pages. 'As I mentioned, your dugong died of starvation.' Zoe began to read through the report. 'But your dolphin's a different case altogether.' George handed over the second set of results. 'She was a very sick animal when she died. Anaemic. Terrible lesions all over her body and respiratory system. White blood cell count through the roof. Bacterial, fungal and viral infections – she had the lot.'

Zoe looked up sharply. 'Viral?'

He looked grave. 'I'm afraid so. Morbillivirus. The first confirmed case I've seen.' He looked grave. 'It's a very potent pathogen. More animals are likely to be affected on the reef in the coming months.'

Zoe shook her head in shock. A potent pathogen. That was an understatement. Morbillivirus had been ravaging overseas dolphin populations for years, and there was no cure. The first record in Australia involved a stranded bottlenose at Marion Bay in Tasmania in 1997. She'd studied the case in first-year marine biology. Morbillivirus was still rare in Australia, but had been linked to mass mortality of inshore bottlenose dolphins in Perth's Swan River.

Zoe leafed through the detailed report, not really taking it in. George drained his coffee. 'It's all there.' He rose to leave.

'Wait.' She put the pages down on the table. 'What else did you find?'

George sat back down. 'There was a banned toxin in the dolphin's tissue samples.'

'Dieldrin?' He raised an eyebrow and nodded. It was all adding up. Healthy, older animals could often fight off the morbillivirus, but juveniles had little resistance. If the Turtle Reef dolphins faced added stress factors, like pollution in the environment? Well, the younger generation could be wiped out. 'I found Dieldrin too,' said Zoe. 'In seagrass sediment samples. Along with high amounts of Diuron – fifty times the safe levels.'

George whistled low through his teeth. 'That wouldn't surprise me. Kiawa's a funny place. The locals have some old-fashioned ideas when it comes to farming.'

'I've noticed that,' said Zoe with a frown 'They're a pretty traditional bunch.'

George snorted. 'Traditional? More like stuck in a time warp. Farmers here don't take any notice of current rules and regulations about how to handle their chemicals. *If it was good enough for my father and for my grandfather, then it's good enough for me.* I hear that all the time. Somebody needs to drag them into the twenty-first century.' He stood to go. 'I'll be reporting my findings to the department. I suggest you do the same.'

Zoe followed him to the door, his words repeating in her head. *Somebody needs to drag them into the twenty-first century.* 'Thank you, George.' He nodded goodbye, grim-faced. She trailed after him, weaving through people heading in the direction of Dolphin Harbour where the day's performance was about to begin. The music started. Zoe checked her watch. She'd be pushing it to feed the seaquarium fish tanks before the Octo Show. Bridget kept saying she'd hire someone else to help in the mornings, but it hadn't happened. Zoe ran fingers through her untidy hair and apologised to a small boy in front of her who she'd just walked into. When would she learn? Even after everything that had happened, she was still trusting Bridget's promises.

Zoe set about preparing daily feeds for the smaller aquarium residents. Chopped squid for the blue-spotted rays. Vitamin-soaked shrimp for the baby cat sharks. Blood worms for the striped angelfish. She made up fresh reef blocks from plaster mixed with peas, pellets and chopped spinach. Specialised coral feeders like pufferfish, parrot fish and triggerfish used their beak-like teeth to bite off chunks. Then they ground up the plaster and filtered it for the nutrients, like they would with living coral in the wild.

When she finished, Zoe selected a few choice pilchards from the fridge. Time to head for *Tentacle Town*, the catchy name she'd chosen for the darkened storeroom with the red light bulb, where she kept the cephalopods. Technically octopuses had arms, not tentacles, but nobody had pulled her up on it. Archie seemed to enjoy bringing them to her, and Zoe had quite a collection now, along with cuttlefish and some big-fin reef squid. The beautiful and mysterious nautilus, with its pearly spiral shell, was next on her cephalopod wish list.

'Good morning, gang.' At the sound of her voice, Einstein flowed out from under her rock and glowed green in greeting. She'd become quite friendly, and enjoyed having her arms stroked after being fed. But not in front of an audience. That little intimacy was reserved for when they were alone. 'Hope you're hungry,' Zoe said. 'I've saved the fattest pilchard for you.' Einstein's arms snaked towards the top of the tank. 'Not yet,' she said. 'We've got a show to do first, and you're growing a little bit lazy.'

Zoe moved down the rows of tanks, checking on the wellbeing of her charges. She stopped to watch the reef squid ripple through the water. Surprisingly beautiful, with scintillating bands ranging in colour from black to almost transparent, and pairs of iridescent spots on their billowing mantles. All well and healthy. Next was her new mangrove display. Since many estuarine creatures were active at night, it made sense to set up a tank in the nocturnal room to show-case this vital ecosystem. She'd stocked it with mangrove seedlings, snails, sea cucumbers and an assortment of mud, hermit and fiddler crabs. Archie was on a quest to find her some mudskippers. The lightning-fast little fish were equally at home on land as in water, making them particularly difficult to catch. Slogging around on foot in smelly mud with a hand-held net wasn't the sort of thing the veteran deep-sea fisherman was known for, but he'd vowed not to return empty-handed. Bless his heart. Zoe was growing quite fond of the rough old man. She inspected the mangrove tank. What? Half a dozen empty shells lay piled in the corner. Something had been eating her crabs.

'Einstein,' said a voice. Zoe jumped a foot in the air. Josh was standing behind her, right up close in that unsettling way he had. But she didn't mind. She was far too glad to see him. 'Einstein climbs out at night and goes into the other aquariums.' Josh took her hand and led her to the tank. He pointed to where the lid was askew, just the tiniest bit, but an octopus could squeeze through something the circumference of its beak.

'Are you certain?' Zoe got the stepladder for a closer look. Sure enough, there were traces of dried octo-slime outside the glass at the top. So that's why fish had been disappearing. At night the place had become an all-you-can-eat octopus buffet.

'Einstein needs more food now that she's having babies.'

Zoe looked at him in horror. Babies? She peered into the space beneath the rock. It was impossible to see properly in this strange red glow. Zoe fetched a bright white torch and directed it into the tank. Oh no, Josh was right. The startled octopus dived for cover, but not before Zoe spotted dozens of pale, teardrop-shaped eggs hanging from the underside of the rock by delicate stalks. She turned off the torch. Einstein shimmied forwards and placed one glowing, suckered arm against the glass. Zoe pressed her hand against it, her eyes swimming with tears.

Josh added his own hand into the mix. 'Don't cry, Zoe.' His tone was puzzled.

She checked her watch and wiped her eyes. Time for the show. Outside the room a dozen people had gathered.

'Welcome everybody,' said Zoe, her voice catching. She cleared her throat. 'Today will be a bit different from usual. I'm debuting a new octopus, Houdini – his first public performance.'

'We want Einstein,' said a redheaded woman. 'I saw the show last week and it was fantastic. I've brought my husband along this time.'

'You'll still be able to see Einstein,' said Zoe. 'but she won't be performing any more. As of today she's on permanent maternity leave.'

'Permanent? I don't understand.'

'Come with me and I'll explain.'

A curious group of people, including Josh, stood watching Einstein eat a plump pilchard. Zoe pointed to the tank. 'Underneath that rock are a clutch of newly laid eggs,' she said. 'It's a sad reality that bringing new life into the world is a death sentence for octopus mothers. They're the definition of maternal self-sacrifice. Einstein will devote all her time and energy to those eggs from now on. Protecting them twenty-four hours a day. Aerating them with gentle jets of water, grooming them to keep them clean and stop algae growing. In a little while she'll stop eating altogether for fear of fouling her den with food waste or faeces. Einstein will slowly starve herself to death.' She could hear the break in her own voice and the redheaded woman gasped. A murmur ran through the crowd. 'It sounds like a Greek tragedy, doesn't it?' she continued. 'But it happens to every female octopus in the world who lays eggs. So whenever you see an octopus, spare a thought for the mother who gave her life to bring it into the world.'

Josh turned on his heel and left. Houdini proved himself a capable understudy, but he didn't have Einstein's panache or gift for improvisation. After the show, Zoe went looking for Josh. She found him playing with Mirrhi, spraying her with the saltwater hose. The boy swam to the lagoon edge when he saw her, and she sat down with her legs in the water. Dark clouds rolled in off the bay above her.

'I don't want Einstein to die,' Josh said.

'Neither do I,' said Zoe. 'But I'm afraid it's nature's way. She'll love and care for her eggs until the little octopuses are born. Then she'll die happy, knowing that she gave her babies the best start in life that she possibly could.'

'Like my mother did.'

The hairs lifted on the back of Zoe's neck. Of course, she'd forgotten. Josh's mother had died in childbirth. 'We'll release Einstein's babies on Turtle Reef so that part of her will always live there.'

Josh nodded, then patted Mirrhi as she nosed her way into his arms. 'Dolphins don't die when they have babies, do they?'

Zoe smiled. 'You know they don't.'

'Good,' said Josh. 'Because I'd die too if anything happened to Mirrhi.'

'That's quite enough talk about dying. Mirrhi won't have a baby anytime soon. Now hop out of there before the rain starts.'

'Mirrhi is so going to have a baby. Bridget said.'

Zoe examined his face for any sign of pretence and found none.

Oh dear, poor Mirrhi. This was certainly a day for unpleasant surprises. In the wild, living with a family pod of mature females: mothers, grandmothers, aunties . . . well, a dolphin as young as Mirrhi would never fall pregnant. But here at the centre, bored, confined all day with only an eager male like Echo for company? Things were bound to happen. Once more Zoe questioned Bridget's decision not to release the young dolphins. They might be safe and well fed in this gilded cage, but at what cost?

Karen arrived with eye drops, and cheered when she saw Josh. 'Have we ever missed you, mate.'

'Did you know Mirrhi was pregnant?' Zoe asked her.

Karen nodded. 'George confirmed it last week with an ultrasound. If you ask me, Mirrhi's too young. Chances are she'll never successfully raise a calf.'

'What about Koko?' asked Zoe. 'She managed. Maybe Mirrhi can learn from her?'

'Koko's a totally different case,' Karen said. 'She was already an experienced mother when Baby was born.' Mirrhi rolled onto her left side for an eye drop. 'And Koko's a spinner, not a bottlenose. Mirrhi needs females of her own species, don't you, darling?' As if in answer, the young dolphin uttered a series of plaintive high-pitched whistles and rolled the other way for the second drop. 'There, all done.'

Karen rubbed Mirrhi's back and gave her the last fish. Josh jumped back in the water. Boy and dolphin began a noisy splashing game. 'Hop out, Josh,' said Karen. 'Bridget could use a hand with Kane. You too, Zoe. I'll go on ahead.'

Josh kissed Mirrhi's rostrum and climbed from the water. 'Since you've been missing in action,' said Zoe as they followed Karen, 'this place has been falling apart.' Josh looked around, as if he expected to see buildings literally tumbling down. 'I mean that, without you, the dolphins aren't doing their tricks the way they should.'

Josh gave her a shy grin, as if secretly pleased to hear how indispensable he was. 'Quinn's letting me drive the cane haul-out.'

'That sounds like fun. And you're riding the horses?'

'Every day,' said Josh. 'I'm not allowed to ride Aisha though.'

'Give it time. Now let's finish up here before the storm hits.'

'I miss Mirrhi,' said Josh.

'I'm sure she was thrilled to see you today.'

'I miss you too, Zoe.' The words were so sweet, so unexpected, that they stopped her in her tracks. 'Why don't you come to the house anymore?'

'I've been very busy.'

'I wish you would come. Quinn and Bridget don't fight when there are visitors.'

Zoe couldn't help herself. 'Fight? What about?'

'Me,' said Josh. 'And sometimes you.'

Zoe was dying to know more, but there wasn't time. Bridget and Karen were waiting up ahead, standing by the disused pens at the far end of the lagoon, where a low sea wall and steel mesh gateways cut the park off from open water. It was a fragile separation. Winds ahead of the approaching storm were whipping up waves, sending them crashing over the barrier. In combination with the high tide, it seemed like the ocean was trying to reunite its divided parts into one awe-inspiring whole.

Bridget's eyes lit up when she saw Josh. 'Kane's got himself in here somehow and now he won't come out.' The big dolphin prowled around the enclosures, veering away whenever Bridget tried to tempt him through the rusty gate with fish.

'What are these old ponds for?' asked Zoe.

'Years ago they used to lock dolphins up here at night and sometimes even in between shows,' said Karen.

'How awful,' said Zoe. 'And what about those metal grates?'

'Before the pumps were installed, they relied on those grates to let fresh seawater into the lagoons.'

Kane swam close and slapped his tail as he went past, splashing them. 'Now, can we get on with it?' said Bridget. 'I need him out of there. The show starts in fifteen minutes.'

Or what's left of it, thought Zoe. 'Right, Josh, what do we do?'

Bridget glanced at Zoe sharply, obviously unhappy to hear her talk to Josh as if he was in charge. Too bad. She wouldn't play Bridget's game anymore.

Kane cruised up and down the sea wall like a caged tiger. 'Kane's mad,' said Josh. 'I can't do anything when he's mad. Nobody can.' He started up a nervous humming.

'Don't be ridiculous.' Bridget waved a useless herring in the dolphin's direction. 'And will you stop that bloody humming.' Josh went quiet. 'Maybe I can chase him out.' She slipped into the water. 'Hand me your target pole.' Karen obliged, and Bridget swam after Kane, waving the stick to urge him forward.

Kane made a pass at the gate. A crack of thunder made Zoe jump, and the heavens opened. 'Leave it,' called Karen.

'I've almost got him.' Bridget lunged at the dolphin and he rapped her arm hard with his head as he rushed past.

Josh pulled at Zoe's arm. 'Tell Bridget to come out.' His face had turned grey with worry.

'Get out,' yelled Zoe.

Bridget ignored her. She probably couldn't even hear through the pounding rain. Kane tried to double back, but Bridget headed him off. He was trapped between Bridget and the open gate. Surely he'd take the exit into the lagoon now?

Bridget looked up at them with a smile of triumph, rain streaming down her face. For once she didn't look at all glamorous. Kane floated, watching her with one baleful eye, rhythmically slapping the water with his fin in a menacing way. 'Go on.' Bridget poked Kane with the pole.

Zoe could hear Josh's sharp intake of breath as he jumped into the pool. Too late. Kane rocketed straight for Bridget, jaws open. She lunged sideways, missing the full force of the powerful ramming motion. He swung his head towards her, teeth snapping. Bridget's scream was almost drowned out by a deafening crack of thunder. Almost. Blood stained the water. Josh helped her to the side and they hauled her out. She seemed in shock, staring at the bloody lacerations that ran across her left shoulder.

Karen examined her. 'The wounds don't look too deep,' she said.

'Zoe, can you take her to the hospital in Bundaberg? I'll ring Quinn and get him to meet you there.'

'Sure.' Zoe rubbed Josh's back. He was choking back sobs. A dark blur beneath the water caught her eye. Kane, dashing towards them where they huddled at the water's edge. 'Move!' They scrambled back, struggling to keep their footing in the rivers of rain. Kane sprang for them, snapping his jaws twice, almost beaching himself with the force of his attack. Then he turned and raced for the sea wall. A vicious squall sent waves crashing over it as he made his leap for freedom. For a moment they couldn't see a thing. All was sea spray and surging breakers. When the wind and waves abated, Kane was gone.

They were all hypnotised, staring out at the stormy seascape, oblivious to the driving torrents of rain. Scanning the waves for a dark shape beneath the surface, or a tell-tale dorsal fin. But there was no trace of Kane.

Practical Karen was the first to break the spell. She took Bridget by her uninjured arm. 'Come on. Can't have you bleeding to death.' Josh looked horrified. 'I'm joking, Josh. She's going to be fine.'

She didn't look fine. Bridget's colour had drained away, leaving an odd pallor beneath her tan. She shivered uncontrollably. Karen and Josh supported her as they made their way to cover, and Zoe ran to get the car. By the time she returned for Bridget, Karen had expertly cleaned and bandaged her shoulder.

'Easy does it,' said Zoe. Josh helped Bridget into the passenger seat, then opened the back door.

'No, you stay here to help Karen.' Bridget's voice quavered.

'Don't worry.' said Karen 'We'll look after things, won't we, Josh?'

Josh reluctantly let go of the door. He stood out in the pouring rain, waving until they were out of sight. Zoe put the heater on. The gale tugged at the car, trying to wrest away control on the rain-slicked bitumen. It took all Zoe's concentration to stay on the road. It some ways it was a relief, this excuse not to speak. What to say?

Bridget broke the silence. 'You must be wondering why I'm having so much trouble with the dolphins lately.'

Zoe didn't know how to respond. She wasn't wondering at all. She knew exactly why.

'I'm ashamed to admit it, but I've never been able to translate my academic knowledge of learning theories into practice.' Bridget wore an expression of transparent honesty that was very engaging. The colour was returning to her face. 'I've been trying to hide my total incompetence, with Josh's help. Trying to impress you and Dad, I guess, not wanting you to know what a failure I really am.' She heaved a big sigh. 'Please accept this as my official apology.'

Zoe glanced across at Bridget, who was dabbing at the blood seeping through her bandage with a tissue. Her naked sincerity was disarming. It cut through Zoe's defences. 'I don't understand,' she said. 'Why would you want to impress me?'

'You're a talented researcher, Zoe, with a great future and your good opinion matters. I happen to admire you very much.'

The conversation had taken a surprising turn, and a wave of compassion washed over her. Zoe understood all too well about feeling inadequate. But she'd never imagined that it could also be a problem for the illustrious Bridget Macalister. 'And I admire you,' said Zoe. 'You've worked with some of my greatest heroes, the leading professors in their field. You're director of your own marine park, pursuing absolutely vital marine mammal research —' She stopped herself before saying, *and you have Quinn*. 'I couldn't care less about who trains the dolphins. I don't care if nobody trains them at all, as long as they're happy.' She swerved to avoid a fallen branch, bumping along the rutted edge of the road. Bridget groaned and Zoe winced in sympathy. 'Sorry.' She slowed down. 'And as for Leo, he thinks the world of you.'

Bridget made a quiet sound, a soft sob of pain. 'Zoe, if you only knew. I've spent my entire life trying to impress that man and I don't think I've succeeded once.' Bridget suddenly sat forwards and gripped Zoe's arm. 'You won't tell him, will you?' Her voice rose. 'Leo, I mean. You won't tell him about the dolphins?'

'Of course not,' said Zoe. 'It's none of my business.' Bridget collapsed back into her seat. 'I don't know what you're worried about.

Your dad's already super proud of you. Why wouldn't he be? There's the Reef Centre, your outstanding academic achievements, your research work — it doesn't matter to him whether you train the dolphins yourself. Nobody expects you to be good at everything.'

'Dad does,' said Bridget. They drove on in silence for a few minutes, while the storm ripped viciously at the windscreen. 'You seem to know a lot about what my dad thinks.'

'Leo's been kind enough to show me round, take me out a few times. We're friends, that's all. He's been really lovely to me.'

'And generous,' said Bridget.

'Yes, and generous . . . But remember, a car was always in my contract.'

'Of course,' said Bridget. 'Dad's entitled to do what he likes, and so are you. I don't mind a bit.'

Zoe exhaled. 'I have an apology to make too,' she said. 'I shouldn't have gone behind Quinn's back like that when it came to Aisha and Josh. It was wrong.'

'You've caused me a lot of problems,' said Bridget. 'Quinn's decided that his brother needs more supervision. He's keeping Josh home, when I could really use him at the centre.'

It felt good to get everything out in the open. Perhaps they could rebuild their relationship? She pushed thoughts of Quinn from her mind: sitting together under the jasmine on the verandah, sharing stories on moonlit Kulibari beach, riding with him and Josh before it all went wrong.

'Let's start afresh,' said Bridget. 'As friends. No more secrets.'

'Deal.' Zoe pulled into the hospital emergency lane, where Quinn was waiting for them. Her heart beat faster and she willed it to stop. 'No more secrets.'

CHAPTER 21

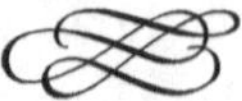

It had been weeks now, since she'd patched things up with Bridget. Zoe was spending most nights at the shack. With Josh kept busy at Swallowdale, the quaint little house perched on the cliff was empty and available. Zoe loved drifting off to the lullaby of waves. She loved waking each morning to a sun-spangled sea or the dramatic swell of breakers before a storm. The magnificent, old-fashioned shower rose that didn't know the meaning of *water-saving*. The dolphins private play in the lagoon before the gates of the centre opened to other eyes.

There were things she missed about Swallowdale, of course: Josh's off-beat company; the weight of Captain's comforting body pressed against her in the early hours; the earthy smell of Aisha's warm neck. And Quinn. Her feelings hadn't changed; she still desired him, still dreamed about him. But he was living with Bridget now. How was that going? Were they still arguing, like Josh had said? Whatever the case, she would do nothing to spoil things for them.

It was a relief to step away, to get some distance from all those conflicted feelings. Zoe threw herself into her work, mapping and sampling the remaining seagrass meadows in record time. Thank goodness she'd had the presence of mind to get her own sampling done, because Queensland University was still dragging its feet. She was tired of waiting for confirmation of what she already knew. Time for a bit of sleuthing, a bit of private investigation work, and she would start right in her own backyard, so to speak – in the Swallowdale chemical shed.

Zoe parked her car at the cottage and headed off on foot down the central laneway, the same path she'd ridden a few weeks earlier with Quinn and Josh. She kept a close lookout for curious eyes, but appeared to be all alone in this part of the farm today. When she reached the little converted shipping container where she'd seen Rob refill the boom spray, Zoe donned a pair of disposable gloves and pulled a booklet from her pocket: *Code of Practice for the Storage and Use of Chemicals in Rural Workplaces*. She flipped to the checklist page and put a red cross next to the first point. The door was not locked with a childproof latch as it should have been. In fact, the door wasn't locked at all: it stood wide open. She glanced about nervously before going inside. The light didn't work when she flicked the switch – another cross. Ventilation seemed good, thanks to the line of spinning whirlybirds installed along the roofline. She ticked that box. *Are chemicals protected from moisture?* Tick. *Is storage area fire-resistant?* Tick. *Are herbicides separated from insecticides and fungicides?* This was a more difficult question. A few containers didn't have labels at all, earning another cross on the page.

Zoe didn't know brand names, but she recognised ingredients, and they added up to a toxic chemical cocktail: Aldicarb and Atrazine, herbicides banned in the European Union; 2 4-D, a known groundwater contaminant; Diuron, a carcinogen found at fifty times safe levels in her seagrass sediment samples. Fungicides were stored higgledy-piggledy among drums of pesticides such as Carbofuran. There were containers of liquid Chlorpyrifos – an insecticide known to kill off coral larvae – instead of the much safer slow-release granules. Another unreadable label.

Zoe moved further into the darkened shed, her vision taking time to adjust. How Rob managed to see a thing in here with his old eyes was a mystery. On a steel shelf lay piles of grimy two-ring binders. She picked one up, and the resulting cloud of dust made her sneeze. It was filled with forms. She scanned one of them, and the information it required. Chemical usage records, dates and times, field numbers, chemical and quantity used, application rates, wind and speed directions, weather conditions. The list of questions went on. If filled out properly, the completed form would have added up to a thorough and detailed record of chemical use on the farm. Problem was, the form was blank – they all were. She flipped through another folder, shaking her head at the multiple-choice final question. *Tick the box beside Protective Equipment Used.* Options included apron, gloves, face mask, goggles, respirator, filtered air tractor cab – as far as she could remember, Rob hadn't even worn a hat!

She wandered around, ticking and crossing her checklist, mainly crossing it. Two rusty steel drums smeared with gobs of dried mud stood near the door, their labels too faded to read. The screw cap of one was rusted on. She tried the cap on the second drum and managed to twist it open. Zoe took out one of the unused forms and dipped its corner into the liquid inside, shuddering involuntarily as she did so. Then she clipped it back into the front of the folder. Nearly done. A quick look outside and round the back, in case she'd missed something. Nothing much to see, just an old corrugated-iron dunny. Trust Rob. Blank chemical use forms were impaled upon a bent nail on the wall – bush toilet paper.

Zoe set off back home, folder under her arm. Maybe she should stay at the cottage tonight and tackle Quinn on the state of his shed. She wasn't looking forward to it. Seeing that man, caring for him like she did, knowing she could never have him . . . and then starting another fight. Captain came bounding along the path towards her. Zoe kneeled down to hug the big collie. 'I've missed you.' She ruffled his silken coat. 'It's been too long.'

'It certainly has.'

Zoe looked up to find Quinn smiling down at her. Her mouth went dry.

'Long time no see,' he said. 'Where've you been hiding?'

Zoe shrugged. 'Staying at the shack.' When she stood up, Captain sat on her foot, leaning against her leg like he was trying to keep hold of her. 'I wanted to give you and Bridget some space.' A shadow of sadness fell across his face. Why on earth had she said that? It sounded so presumptuous. Their relationship had nothing to do with her.

'Will you come up to the house for a cuppa?'

She squirmed inside. Quinn's close presence caused her a physical ache. Every instinct screamed *No, spare yourself the pain!* But this was the perfect opportunity to tell him what she'd found. It had to be done. Surely Swallowdale wasn't the only farm in Kiawa not following the code of practice for chemical use? And as president of the local Canegrowers' Association, Quinn had a lot of influence. If she could convince him to change, then others might follow his lead. What was more important – her bruised heart or the safety of Turtle Reef National Park?

Zoe braced her shoulders. 'Okay.' She felt like howling. How would she cope sitting opposite this man, feeling the way she did, and keep the conversation to herbicide use and record-keeping?

Zoe watched Quinn pull the cellophane packet open and empty chocolate ripple biscuits onto the plate. 'No homemade Anzacs today.' He gave a little laugh of apology. 'Bridget finally moves in and she's too busy to cook.'

Zoe was dying to ask how things were going between them, but managed to hold her tongue.

Quinn poured the tea. He seemed to move in slow motion, expertly raising and lowering the sky-blue pot as the arc of amber liquid poured into her dainty cup. 'Milk?'

She smiled. 'Do you ever just throw a teabag into a chipped mug and drink it with the little tag hanging over the side?'

'Not when I have special visitors.'

Special? For a moment Zoe's heart leaped with happiness. She wished his words really meant something, instead of being just a figure of speech. 'How's Josh going? I hardly see him anymore.'

'He's going great guns. Those horses are really turning things around for him. He's happier, friendlier, talkative . . . more normal, I guess. I rang our local school principal to ask whether they could swing an integration aide if Josh enrolled next year. She reckons there's a good chance.'

'Great . . . that's just great.' Zoe sipped her tea but couldn't seem to force it down her throat. His physical presence was overwhelming, the undercurrent of attraction so strong, her pulse so swift that surely he must hear the blood throbbing in her veins. Quinn had never affected her this powerfully before. How was she supposed to tackle him about on-farm procedures when what she really wanted to do was kiss him? She pushed the thought away. Time to take the bull by the horns.

'I've taken a look at your chemical store. Well, one of them anyway.' Quinn looked taken aback, and why not? It must have seemed an unlikely thing to come out of her mouth. 'You know about my research project?'

'Where's this going?'

'Some pretty high levels of contamination are turning up: 2 4-D, Atrazine, Diuron – cane chemicals. They're killing off the seagrass, Quinn. Dugongs and turtles out in the bay are starving to death.'

He scratched his jaw. 'So, what, you're blaming me?'

'Not you in particular, of course not.' He looked a little happier. 'But I am blaming cane farm run-off in general. I'm wondering . . .' She took another sip of tea, giving herself time to choose her words carefully. 'How much attention do local people pay to chemical use guidelines? You know, codes of practice, that sort of thing?'

Quinn took a chocolate ripple and offered her one. She shook her head. He bit his biscuit in half. 'Folks round Kiawa - we have own way of doing things.' He popped the rest of the biscuit in his mouth. 'And we don't put much store in government rules and regulations. Never have and never will.'

His cavalier attitude helped to break the spell of wanting to kiss him, wanting to be held by him, wanting more than that. A different sort of heat rose in Zoe's body. 'What about the reef? What about the turtles – the ones we saw that night?' Her breath caught, and she felt herself beginning to tremble. 'What about the dugongs, minding their own business, trying to raise and protect their calves the best they can? How are they different from you, trying to raise and protect Josh? How would you like it if he was starving and you went to somebody for help, and they said, *We don't put much store in feeding kids, never have and never will?*'

He shifted in his seat. 'Aren't you being a bit melodramatic?'

'How so?'

'Dugongs aren't people.'

'Makes no difference. They've as much right as anyone to be here, more actually. They were here first.'

Quinn fixed her with those penetrating grey eyes of his and Zoe felt her presence of mind slip. It was like he could see right into her soul. 'How are the dolphins in the bay doing?' he asked her. 'Are they in trouble too?'

'As a matter of fact they are.'

'Dolphins don't eat seagrass.'

'But loads of fish do, and they use it for shelter and a nursery for their young. Everything's connected. Chemicals build up in fish, and dolphins are top of the food chain – apart from us.' At least he was listening: that was something. 'I don't blame cane chemicals directly for the dolphin's predicament. A virus is killing them off, but something's lowered their immunity and let this disease take hold.'

'Like what?'

'Banned toxins have shown up in the tissue of dead dolphins, including Dieldrin.'

Quinn whistled through his teeth, inadvertently summoning Captain to his side. 'Dieldrin. Dad used that before it was banned. Nasty stuff. ' He offered her more tea. She nodded, calmer now. Quinn was paying attention. Maybe she was getting through to him.

'Let's take Swallowdale as an example. There are problems with the way you store your chemicals.' She showed him her checklist. 'And records don't seem to have been filled out. Unless Rob's handing them on to you?'

Quinn fondled Captain's ears. 'I'm lucky if Rob passes the time of day on to me. I'm afraid he's never seen me as a fitting heir to Dad's throne.'

'Why not?'

'Maybe my management style isn't tough enough.'

'Rob should be more worried about his own management style,' said Zoe. 'Without records, there's no way of telling what particular chemicals are being used on the farm, or when or how heavily they've been applied.'

Quinn's brow furrowed as he examined the sheets of paper. 'There's a legal obligation on farmers to comply with this stuff?'

'Yes, you've got some work to do.'

'I'll look into it, Zoe, but please don't go poking around here without asking. You shouldn't have done that.'

'Okay,' she said. 'But in return, will you talk to your canegrowers, remind them of their obligations? Let them know how harmful their chemicals are to the reef. There's more to it than safe-storage and record-keeping,' She flipped through the check-list, reading out topics as she went. 'Subsurface fertilising, slow release pelleted pesticides, waterway exclusion zones, bans on wet-weather spraying – it's all in here.' She handed him the booklet.

Quinn frowned and put it down. 'Stick to what you know, Zoe. My blokes won't appreciate being dictated to, especially by a blow-in from Sydney.'

'Is that how you see me?' The heat was back again; her eyes flashed flame. 'As a blow-in?' Captain whined and came to sit beside her. She was too angry to pat him. She'd misread Quinn. He hadn't been listening at all. 'Maybe Josh was right. ' she said.

'Why? What did he say?'

'That you're stubborn and don't listen. Just like your father.'

Quinn's nostrils flared. 'You know nothing about my family.'

'And you know nothing about the reef. But you have no right to harm it just because you and your mates aren't willing to drag your-selves into the twenty-first century.'

Quinn laced his fingers and flexed his knuckles. 'This conversation is over.'

'Only for now.' Zoe threw the checklist at him as she shoved back her chair. 'I'm not finished, not by a long shot.'

A lump lodged in Quinn's throat as Zoe stormed off, taking the timber steps two at a time and marching down the path to the cottage. Captain stared longingly after her. 'Don't you dare,' said Quinn. The collie gave him a reproachful look, barked twice and then ran after Zoe.

Quinn dug his fingers into his fist. He didn't blame the dog. He wanted to go after her himself. This wasn't meant to happen, not at all. He'd missed Zoe, missed her a lot. Hadn't been able to stop thinking about her. Several times a day he checked the cottage carport. Felt his blood surging in his body whenever he heard a motor, hoping to see the Lexus turn into Swallowdale's gates. He'd started to worry that she might not come back at all. And then today, there she was, flashing that beautiful smile, wanting to have tea with him. A tide of relief and happiness had washed through him, startling in its power, making him feel like singing. And now he'd gone and ruined it.

He never knew quite how to react to Zoe. She was so full of surprises and yes . . . bloody aggravating at times. Today was a prime example. Unbelievable, that she'd gone rummaging through the spray shed uninvited. A city girl like her. What would she know about farm chemicals? And then she had the hide to criticise him for what she'd found, as if somehow he was in the wrong instead of her. And she'd talked about his father, a man she'd never met? Just as well too. He could only imagine the sort of row those two would get into.

A breeze blew the booklet with its attached checklist off the table and he picked it up: *Code of Practice for the Storage and Use of Chemicals in Rural Workplaces*. He'd never seen it before. Dad had his tried and tested ways of doing things around the farm, and since his death nothing had changed.

There was no reason to, was there? Quinn opened the booklet. *Chemical storage areas must be locked and secure.* That was actually a good idea. If he'd locked the shed, Zoe wouldn't have been able to snoop. Quinn read on. He didn't know about half this stuff. Regulations covering bunding, record keeping, chemical mixing, spraying. Accreditation. *Ensure all operators have up-to-date training and relevant accreditation.* A list of recommended courses followed. That was a good one. Quinn imagined sending Rob off to enrol in a chemical management course. Heaven help anyone who tried telling that old bastard what to do.

He flipped over a few pages. *Reef Wise Farming. Obligations and Penalties For Non-Compliance.* This was something he did know a bit about. Canegrowers in the northern catchments had been saddled with onerous new regulations governing chemical and fertiliser use, all designed to protect the Great Barrier Reef. The protocol did not extend as far south as Kiawa, which was the cause for much celebration in the ranks of the Canegrowers' Association. Still, the controversial changes had many local farmers up in arms. They saw it as the thin end of the wedge, government gone mad.

They were particularly enraged about growers having to undergo random farm audits by reef protection officers. With the price of sugar in the doldrums, the financial burden of implementing the resulting reforms had been the last straw for some of their northern neighbours, sending them to the wall. To stay in business and ignore the new rules risked large fines. A farmer in the Burdekin had shot and killed a compliance officer who'd tried to inspect his property late last year. Some Kiawa growers, especially the older ones, had quietly applauded.

Not Quinn, of course. The murder had stunned him with its savagery. But as far as the new *Reef Wise* regulations, he'd been as angry about them as his peers.

He imagined how wild Dad would be about the changes, then checked himself. Dead for two years, and he was still viewing things through the prism of his father. Quinn hadn't seen this as a problem before. Reacting as his father would have reacted was one way of honouring him, of keeping his memory alive. But something Zoe said had struck a nerve. A taunt purportedly based on Josh's words. *'You are stubborn and you don't listen. Just like your father.'*

Quinn put the booklet down and rubbed his forehead. The seed of a headache was germinating behind his eyes. Why had he snapped at Zoe like that? He knew what she was like, and shouldn't have been surprised by what she'd done. He'd wanted so much to talk with her, share a laugh, something that never seemed to happen with Bridget.

Bridget. The thought of her intensified the pain in his temple. The things Zoe said about her had been going round and round in his head. He couldn't silence them, not when he was hauling cane out to the siding, not when he was arguing with the manager at the mill . . . not when they were in bed together at night.

He had no first-hand knowledge about what had been going on at the Reef Centre. But the tenor of Zoe's words, the implication that Bridget had been dishonest somehow, holding things back – that rang true. And if Josh really was the one training the dolphins? It meant Bridget had been using the boy, something Quinn could not forgive.

Funny, he'd always imagined that the day Bridget moved in would be the happiest day of his life. He'd dreamed of it during her years away studying, longed for it while she stubbornly insisted on staying with Leo at Cliffhaven. Spent night after sleepless night craving the press of her flawless, perfumed body against his. And yet, now she was here, a vague and terrible disquiet had taken root. Something was wrong with Bridget.

She seemed oddly detached, as if living in her own little world. Oh, she was going through the motions alright. She came home each night, ate dinner, watched television – was a willing partner in the bedroom. She rose early each morning to shower and change, kissed him goodbye and left for work.

But they didn't talk about anything, not really, not about what mattered. They didn't laugh and joke, or tell silly stories, or discuss their hopes and dreams. Whenever Quinn tried to engage her, she put on that perfect smile and allowed the conversation to grind to a halt. Or she changed the subject, steering the discussion safely back to shallow waters.

'How about we turn off the television tonight, go sit out under the stars and talk,' he'd say.

'What about?'

'I don't know. What our lives might be like in five years' time? Do you want to see Paris one day? If somebody handed you a magic lamp and gave you three wishes, what would they be? Anything.'

'Quinn, you're being silly.' Her smile was ambiguous. 'Let's watch a movie instead.'

The truth was, he was profoundly lonely. The physical passion they shared was a hollow delight. It was like making love to a stranger. Afterwards he couldn't sleep. He'd wait until Bridget had drifted off, then get dressed and go walking, restless and dissatisfied. And more and more during these solitary nocturnal interludes, his thoughts would turn to Zoe: beautiful, fascinating, infuriating Zoe.

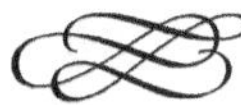

CHAPTER 22

'Think about it,' said Zoe. 'Without turtles and dugongs and dolphins, without healthy fish and coral — what sort of an eco-resort will the Bennett's have on their hands? If something isn't done about run-off from the cane farms, your deal's dead in the water.'

Leo stabbed the meat on the barbecue grill with a fork and turned it over, the aroma of seared steak competing with the salty scent of the sea. He swung around to face her. 'And you're sure about it – this contamination problem?'

Zoe brandished a sheaf of stapled papers at him. 'It's all here in these reports. Analysis of samples, pollution levels, effects on wildlife. I'm expecting independent results from Queensland Uni any day now. I'm certain they'll confirm these findings.' Leo poured a glass of wine and handed it to her, his expression unreadable. He might not be much of a greenie, but he was an astute businessman. An appeal to commercial reality was her best bet. 'I don't need these to prove my point.' She tossed her notes aside. 'In the last thirty years we've already lost fifty per cent of the Great Barrier Reef. Now the Bundaberg *Guardian* is reporting fish kills, algal blooms . . . dead dolphins and dugongs washing up on our doorstep. You're the mayor, Leo – freshly re-elected what's more. It's your job to do something, and fast.'

'Dugongs are dying too, you say? Let me show you something.' Leo disappeared through the French doors of the patio for a few moments, returning with a folder. 'Carla Bennett sent this through. Mock-ups of their proposed resort logo.' Zoe opened the cover to reveal an elegant emblem of coral white and sapphire green, *Mermaid Cove* emblazoned across it in a fancy typeface. *Where Dolphins and Dugongs Dance* in smaller letters. A stylised silver dolphin and dugong waltzed together to complete the graphic. 'Your story about sailors mistaking dugongs for mermaids intrigued her. She wants to feature the theme right through the resort. It won't bloody work if there aren't any dugongs, will it?' Leo frowned. 'And you say you've gone to Quinn about it?'

'Yes, but it didn't go well. We both got a bit hot under the collar. I think me going through his chemical shed shocked him so much that he didn't really listen after that.'

Leo snorted in derision. 'Don't get me wrong, Quinn's a lovely bloke. I wouldn't have let my daughter marry him if he wasn't. But he's not a decision maker. Marshall always had to do the thinking for him.'

Zoe wanted to leap to Quinn's defence. As far as she could tell, Marshall Cooper never gave his son a chance to decide anything at all. But this wasn't the time, not when she was winning Leo over.

Leo checked underneath the steaks. He grimaced and forked them onto plates while Zoe fetched the bread, salad bowl and cutlery. They sat down and Leo investigated his scotch fillet further. 'Bloody hell, it's overdone. Where's my daughter when I need her? She normally does this sort of thing.'

'Don't look at me,' said Zoe. 'I'm no chef, not like Bridget.'

'Bridget is a great little cook, I won't argue with you there.' Leo sawed at the corner of his scotch fillet. 'It's the one thing she's really good at.'

Zoe put down her forkful of food. 'Why do you run her down like that?'

'Paternal privilege.' Leo laughed. 'She knows I'm joking. But don't you worry. Anyone else says something against her? They'd better watch out.'

Now Zoe wanted to stand up for her boss. Point out the sad irony that Bridget could cope perfectly well with criticism from anyone – anyone *except* her father. She gulped her wine, refusing to get distracted.

Encouragingly, it was Leo who steered the conversation back on track. 'I'll support you to the hilt when it comes to tackling this pollution problem, Zoe. I've been in cane myself most of my life, still lease out some farms, so I know what I'm talking about. Kiawans are a fiercely independent bunch. They don't take government regulation seriously.'

'You have some responsibility here yourself, Leo. Archie rescued a dolphin mother and calf from your shark nets last week. They drown turtles too. You'll have to get rid of them.'

'Of course, I'll be guided by you on such things.' Leo waved his hand expansively. 'This town has a great future, an exciting future. But the biggest growth will be in tourism, not cane. Tourists mean jobs, trade, money for the local economy.' He drained his beer, lit a cigarette and winked. 'Don't tell Bridge about the fag, okay?'

'Okay,' said Zoe. 'Now keep talking.'

'The price of sugar's at a five year low and cheap overseas suppliers are flooding the world market. It's time to be smart – play to Kiawa's strengths. And with a world-class reef on our doorstep? Well, you'd be mad not to protect a potential money-making asset like that.' Zoe nodded, smiling on the outside, troubled on the inside to hear Turtle Reef described in such calculating, economic terms. Leo was charming, flattering even, and a great deal of fun to be with. But there was another aspect to Leo: a greedy, selfish side. 'So,' he said. 'What do you want to do?'

'Let's wait until the second set of samples are analysed. Once my initial results are confirmed, I'll tackle Quinn again, try to talk him round.'

'Tell him to stop those bloody cane fires while he's at it. Simon won't want smoke blowing over his resort.'

'Absolutely,' agreed Zoe. 'But we need to bring the whole farming community along with us. As president of the Canegrowers' Association, Quinn has a lot of clout.'

'No idea why – the man's not a patch on his father. Hasn't got his backbone.' Zoe's smile was tight-lipped. 'But I reckon the growers will go along with what he says. And don't forget that I'm mayor of this town. I have clout too.'

'I know you do.'

'Good girl.' Leo rose from his seat and moved to stand behind Zoe's chair, massaging her shoulders with firm fingers. It took her only a moment to stand and slip sideways.

Since Zoe had been staying at the shack, she'd taken to spending the occasional evening with Leo. She was lonely; so was he. She'd even toyed with the idea of taking things further, of turning her flirtation into a fling.

But it couldn't go any further; Zoe knew that now. Although grateful for his support and friendship, today she'd come face to face with all the things she didn't like about Leo. What would it have been like for Bridget, growing up with such a man for a father? Without the support of a mother. Depending on Leo's brand of casual, qualified love to shore up her fledgling confidence. How many times would Bridget have heard Leo belittle her, ridicule her, compare her unfavourably to her sisters?

Zoe couldn't imagine her own father behaving in such a way, not for a second. And to think that a few short months ago she'd been jealous of Bridget. Zoe wouldn't want to swap places with her now for anything – except in one regard. Bridget had Quinn. For once Zoe dared an honest examination of her heart. The truth was blindingly clear. It wasn't just attraction she felt for him. She was in love with the quiet cane king.

Leo heaved a deep, theatrical sigh, as if he somehow guessed at the tumult within her. 'Am I wasting my time here, Zoe? Do I have any hope with you, any hope at all?'

She shook her head. 'I'm sorry.' He clasped a hand to his heart in mock despair. 'You've been a good friend to me, Leo. Lending me the car, keeping me company, making me smile.' He shrugged. 'Letting me stay at the shack . . .'

'I have an ulterior motive there.' Leo stroked his moustache rakishly. 'One of these nights I'll be round to change your mind.' As Zoe laughed good-humouredly, Leo's brashness slipped away for a moment and he looked genuinely deflated. 'You must think me a silly old fool,' he said, 'chasing after you like this.'

'No, I'm flattered. But we both know you're not serious. It's nothing more than a flirty game.'

'Not to me.' He held up a hand for silence. 'I've fallen for you, Zoe, and not only because you're the most gorgeous woman in town. It's your courage, your sass, your honesty. The way you speak your mind and hang the consequences. The way you wear your passion on the outside. I was talking to Quinn the other day about what a breath of fresh air you are. Stuffy old Kiawa is far too set in its ways. *This town needs a good shake-up*, I said, *and Zoe King is just the one to do it.*' Leo crossed his arms. 'Quinn agreed with me.'

'He did?'

'Oh yes. He seems quite taken with you. I don't think you'll have too much trouble bringing him round to your way of thinking. If Quinn wasn't already spoken for, I reckon he'd be after you himself.' Zoe's mouth went dry. She tried to clear her throat, but needed a glass of water to regain her composure.

Leo looked at her shrewdly. 'Is there something I'm missing here?'

Zoe wandered away to the patio railing to avoid his searching eyes. To the east, Cliffhaven's infinity pool met the sea in a seamless expanse of blue. Something moved out on the reef: vast shadows, a spume of spray, a tipping tail. 'Leo,' she called. 'Whales.' An awe-inspiring and timeless scene. She longed to be out there with them, to dive into the warm azure blur, to be lost in the majesty of migrating ocean giants.

Leo's voice came from close behind her. 'What are we waiting for?' He'd read her mind. She followed him down to the boat, her body buzzing in anticipation; already one with the humpbacks in the magical waters of her imagination.

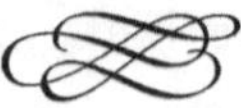

CHAPTER 23

Loud barking heralded a visitor. The noise reverberated around the massive engine block of the haul-out, making Quinn's ears ring. Not Zoe. Captain would never bark at Zoe like that. Who then?

'Morning.'

Great— Leo. Quinn swore softly. He hauled himself from under the chassis, face dripping with sweat. The air was unseasonably humid, so humid he could have wrung it out like a towel. Quinn mopped his neck with a rag and nodded a greeting.

'How about this weather, eh?' Leo glanced up, where a bank of threatening clouds hung low in the west. 'Damn wet starts earlier and earlier each year.'

Quinn frowned at the sky as thunder rumbled near. Leo was right. How on earth were they meant to bring in the cane when it never stopped raining? Fields too soggy to burn, too muddy for the heavy harvesters? This season had been a difficult one, starting with the wettest June in thirty years. The mill had been forced to shut down until the paddocks dried out, and they'd had precious few windows in the weather since. A crush that should have been almost finished was only half done. He'd been forced to bring in special wet weather machinery, tracked harvesters and high flotation haul-outs. But the smaller growers, the close-knit community of farmers he'd known all his life? They couldn't afford it. It tore him up to see despair, even fear, in his friends' eyes.

'What's up, Leo?'

'We need to talk.'

'Shoot.'

'Not here.' Leo gestured towards the house. 'You got some time?' Captain erupted in another flurry of barking, and Quinn called him to his side. The dog didn't like Leo any more than he did. Thunder cracked, and here came the rain.

Quinn looked around, hoping some urgent task would reveal itself. The afternoon might be a washout but there were plenty of things he'd rather be doing than chatting with Leo. Quinn kicked at the haul-out tyres. The reality was that Leo was going to be his father-in-law, and he'd better learn to put up with him. 'You head up to the house before the rain gets any heavier,' said Quinn. 'I'll be along in a minute.'

Leo eyed the growling Captain before turning to go. Quinn wiped his hands on an oily rag, feeling more aggravated than usual by Leo's visit. He put away his tools and tried to ignore the little nagging voice in his head. The reason he felt so hostile . . . was he jealous of the man? Perhaps. It sure riled him to think of Zoe spending so much time around Leo.

The ancient tractor chugged past with Rob aboard, oblivious in his oilskin to the downpour, heading for the fresh plantings by the railway line. That bloke was tough as old boots. Quinn gave him a wave, wondering what on earth he was planning to do. He couldn't top-dress, not in this rain. It would just end up in the creek, a waste of good fertiliser. Quinn walked bang into the back of the quad bike, rubbed his throbbing shin, and his mind wandered again — to that booklet of Zoe's. Leafing through, he'd seen a section on fertiliser run-off and the reef. He wished she was here so he could ask her about it.

Quinn rubbed his stiff neck. What was the use? He'd accused her of interfering, justifiably as it happened, and now she was gone.

Where was she spending her nights? The red Lexus was rarely parked at the cottage anymore. She was staying at the shack, or maybe at Cliffhaven itself – with Leo. The idea evoked a flash of anger. Quinn tilted his head one way and then the other to relieve the tension in his shoulders. Zoe deserved better than that old wolf. 'Come on, Captain.' He whistled the dog. 'Let's see what the bastard has to say.'

Quinn plonked a mug of instant coffee down in front of Leo, who wrinkled his nose and took a sip. 'This stuff's rough as guts.' He made a face and pushed the mug away. 'I'll have some brewed, if you've got it.'

'All out, mate. There's tea?' Quinn knew very well that his prospective father-in-law didn't drink tea.

Leo swatted at a fly with his hat and shot Quinn a dark look. 'How's my daughter treating you?' He didn't wait for an answer. 'I sure do miss Bridget's cooking. I'd kill for one of those risottos of hers.'

'Bridget's fine,' said Quinn. 'Thanks for asking.' Apparently the irony was lost on Leo. 'What's this about, mate? Do you need a hand with something?'

Leo clasped his hands together on the table. 'I won't beat around the bush,' he said. 'I've been having a yarn with Zoe King.' What? That was the last thing Quinn expected to hear. 'She has some concerns about the way you're running your operation.'

'Does she just?' Quinn was a private person. He took a deep, disappointed breath. So Zoe had gone running off to Leo, telling him Swallowdale's business. Irritation rose in his throat.

'I'll let you in on a secret, since you're soon to be my son-in-law. Keep it under your hat, though, eh?' Leo glanced around as if someone might be eavesdropping. The rain redoubled its efforts, drumming on the verandah roof, almost drowning out the conversation. 'There's a deal in the works, something big. Something that could well and truly put Kiawa on the map.'

'I don't want it on the map,' said Quinn. 'I like things fine just the way they are.'

'You'll change your mind when you hear this.' A dramatic pause. 'Plans are in the works for an international resort development on the foreshore north of town. What do you think of that, eh? A coup or what?' A yawning silence. 'I can't have agricultural run-off affecting the bay. You understand that, don't you?' said Leo. 'Tourists will be coming to see a healthy reef, not a bunch of cane farms and dead turtles.'

Quinn stiffened, hoping he hadn't heard right. Not in Kiawa. Not in their little jewel of a town, the best-kept secret on the Queensland coast. What was Leo thinking? Quinn crossed his arms. The locals wouldn't stand for it. There'd even been rumblings of discontent when Bridget decided to revamp the Reef Centre, complaints about the odd busload of sightseers. How much more up in arms would people be at the prospect of a large resort?

'Have you told Bridget about this?'

'Not a word,' said Leo. 'Nobody knows, apart from Zoe and a couple of councillors who are sworn to secrecy. Oh, and now you, of course.' He looked immensely pleased with himself. 'Well, what do you think?'

Quinn got to his feet. He wanted to punch the triumph off Leo's face. 'You can take your bloody international resort, mate, and shove it where the sun doesn't shine.'

Leo thrust back his chair and stood up. 'Wait Quinn, hear me out—'

'This time you've gone too far, Leo, you and your council mates. Getting some juicy kickbacks are you, some sweeteners in return for ramming through the planning permits?'

'Now hold on. Everything's legit and above board, which is more than I can say for your chemical procedures.' Quinn gave a snort of laughter. 'I thought better of you, Quinn, I really did. Thought you had some vision, some feel for the future. But you're as bad as the rest of them in this backwater of a town. Stuck in the past, clinging onto the idea that Kiawa is some sort of Shangri-La, to be preserved under glass like a museum piece.'

'I don't like change,' said Quinn. 'So shoot me.'

'Have you heard the saying, *nothing is permanent but change?*'

Quinn sighed and shifted on his feet. He shouldn't have responded to Leo's rant. It had only served to encourage him.

'Things aren't perfect in this town,' said Leo, 'and you damn well know it. Kids can't get jobs. Growers going bust. And now your sloppy, out-of-date farming practices are threatening to wreck the one thing this place does have going for it – the reef.' Leo put on his hat. 'I'm warning you, Quinn. You'd bloody well better get your act together pronto, and tell your country bumpkin mates in the Cane-growers' Association to do the same. I could make life extremely diffi-cult for you lot.'

Captain was growling and crouched low. 'You'd better go,' said Quinn.

Leo's face reddened. 'You haven't heard the end of this.' He headed off into the driving rain.

Captain whined and pressed against Quinn's leg, while keeping an eagle eye on Leo's retreat to his car. Quinn fondled the collie's ears. So nobody in Kiawa knew about the plans for the development, including Bridget. Leo hadn't told his own daughter. But he'd told Zoe, made her his confidante. How long had she known? He groaned and buried his face in his hands. What did it matter? It was perfectly clear whose side she was on. He'd been a bloody fool to get so sweet on her. The dog put a muddy paw on his knee. 'You and me both, eh, Captain?' Quinn stroked his head. 'Whoever said animals were good judges of character?'

CHAPTER 24

It was one of those sparkling mornings of early summer, diamond-bright, just past daybreak. Zoe couldn't get out of the habit of rising early, even though there were no horses waiting for her anymore, shifting like shadows in the dawn light. She pushed down the longing in her heart. How she missed them.

She carried her tea and toast out onto the little balcony, filled with melancholy, still dressed in her cotton nightie. A deep breath. These days she took every opportunity to confront her aversion to heights. Staying at the shack made that easy, and this self-imposed desensitisation program seemed to be working. The fear she used to feel sitting out on the deck had turned into a half-giddy kind of delight.

And she needed all the happiness she could muster this morning, because the rest of the day wasn't looking too promising. Time to start mapping the northern quadrant of Kiawa Bay. She gulped her lukewarm tea and took in the view. Low tide, with whorls and channels etched into the sand. Seaweed lay exposed in the intertidal zone, lacing the beach with green. To the north, a patch of dying seagrass lay like a bruise on the water. Depressing to think that this afternoon she'd be seeing the devastated meadow up close. She looked instead out to sea, where a pod of a dozen wild dolphins frolicked at the edge of the reef. Was Kane with them? She hoped so.

Voices floated up from below. Down at the lagoon, Bridget was feeding the dolphins and attempting to put them through their paces. Two men in khaki shirts and shorts stood beside her. They must be somebody special. The place didn't open until ten. Well, if Bridget was trying to impress them, she wasn't succeeding. The show had descended into chaos. Dolphins, not humans, set the agenda now and they'd become rather creative. Zoe liked the way each animal carried out a variety of its own favourite tricks, generally ones based on natural behaviours like tail-slapping, leaping and breaching. Bridget randomly rewarded their stunts, no doubt grateful that the dolphins were performing at all.

The slender spinners rose from the water and twirled as one in a spectacular aerial display for the two men. Nice. Bridget was so happy she threw half the bucket of pilchards in their direction. Unfortunately the larger, lazier bottlenoses snapped up the treats, leaving the acrobats unrewarded. No matter. The spinners leaped again in synchronised grace. Zoe smiled. Their behaviour was voluntary, born of spontaneous *joie de vivre*, and she much preferred it that way.

Bridget picked up her bucket of fish and led her visitors to the adjacent pool containing Mirrhi and Echo. Echo kept to the far side, swimming robotically up and down, up and down, keeping as far away from the strangers as possible. Now that Josh was no longer working with him, the young male had retreated into himself. He showed little inclination to interact with the staff, and Zoe was becoming concerned about him. Depressed captive dolphins had been known to suicide by simply deciding not to breathe.

But it was Mirrhi that the visitors seemed interested in, pointing at her and raising their voices in animated conversation whenever she drew near. Bridget coaxed her to the poolside. The men gathered round, stroking the young dolphin and taking photographs. Who were they? She made a mental note to find out.

Zoe finished breakfast and went inside to get dressed. A quick check of her emails first. Still no report from Queensland University on the seagrass samples. Unbelievable. It was time to give them a call. Bridget had contacted the lab twice to hurry them up, so far with no result. Apparently they were short-staffed. Even so, the delay had dragged out for more than a month. Maybe she'd have more luck than Bridget had.

Zoe checked her account. Last month's pay still wasn't in the bank. She may be living with free accommodation and petrol, but she did have some expenses and they were beginning to eat into her meagre savings. She'd better have another talk to Bridget. Everything seemed to happen in slow motion in Kiawa.

A knock came at the door. 'Are you decent?'

'Come in, Leo.' He must be on his way to work, already looking hot in his tailored suit. 'What's up?'

'Any chance of a coffee?'

'Sorry.' Zoe felt his eyes on her legs and pulled her skimpy nightie down over her knees as she sat at the kitchen table. 'No coffee. I'm hooked on tea.'

'Not to worry.' He sat down opposite her. 'Thought you might like to know that I saw Quinn. Tackled him about chemical run-off on the reef.'

'How'd that go?'

'I didn't get much joy. He has his head stuck in the sand, same as most other folks around here.'

'Ignoring the problem won't make it disappear.'

'Quinn's trapped in the past and as stubborn as a mule to boot. Takes after his father. Don't get me wrong – Marshall Cooper and I were friends, and good ones at that, but I won't gloss over his faults. He belonged to a bygone era.'

'What about Bridget?' said Zoe. 'Why not enlist her help? Surely if anybody can get through to Quinn, it's her.'

'I'd rather not drop her in the middle of a fight between her father and her fiancé if I can help it. She tends to take my side and that could cause them problems.'

Problems? There were already problems aplenty in that relationship. Still, the thought and compassion behind his comment surprised her. Leo may be overbearing and insensitive, but it was clear he loved Bridget in his own way.

'But I have told her about the chemical misuse at Swallowdale,' he said. 'She didn't know you'd had water and seagrass samples independently analysed. I think she feels a bit sidelined. After all, it is ultimately my daughter's research project.'

Yes, that was true. And it was a research project that Bridget seemed strangely uninterested in.

'Any reason why you didn't fill her in?'

Zoe fiddled with the sugar bowl. How could she explain it to Bridget's father, of all people, when she didn't understand it herself? Zoe might have superficially patched things up with her boss, but the trust had gone. She wasn't about to share any independent research with Bridget until she had a few answers. Her stint in this quiet coastal town had taught Zoe to believe her gut instincts, the way animals did, and her instincts told her that Bridget was still dodgy.

There'd been too many contradictions. Dozens of little inconsistencies that made her question her boss's motives. Bridget had accomplished something nobody else had ever been able to: she'd cured Zoe of her naivety, taught her that common sense and discernment were important qualities, and that trust needed to be earned. But this was hardly a breakthrough she wanted to share with Leo.

'The original tests were delayed, so I organised a second set to ensure the research project stayed on track. Bridget had a lot on her plate,' said Zoe. 'I didn't want to bother her.'

Leo studied her, and she made herself hold his gaze. 'Fair enough.' He stood to go. 'You might have some explaining to do, though.'

Zoe groaned inwardly. That was going to be fun. 'Bridget's leaving this morning for Brisbane, but we're going diving together on Friday. I'll talk to her then, and I'll talk to Quinn too. Have another go at getting through to him.'

Leo seemed satisfied. 'Pop in when you're done. Let me know how you go.' He turned to leave, then swung back around for a parting shot. 'And you can give Quinn this warning: if he doesn't move to clean up his act, I'll report him and his mates to the Department of

Environment myself - future son-in-law or not. Those blokes will swoop in so fast it'll make his head spin.'

Zoe climbed from the seaquarium and headed for the change rooms, stopping to admire her reflection in a window. Amazing, how much her figure had changed since taking this job. She'd gone down two wetsuit sizes, and looked so lithe and fit – like somebody else. Shame there was no lover waiting in the wings to be impressed.

Karen came in as she was changing. 'Good crowd today. How'd it all go?'

'Fine,' said Zoe. 'The moray eel seemed a little off-colour. We'll have to keep an eye on him. Maybe he's intimidated by all the new turtles.'

Zoe had to hand it to Bridget; she was doing a great job with the stream of rescues pouring in. Two more turtles had arrived yesterday and they were running out of places to put them. Every tank and holding pen was crammed full. As Zoe slipped into shorts and shirt and hung up her wetsuit, an unsettling thought hit her. It must be costing a fortune to care for so many new animals. Feed bills would be going through the roof. The dolphins alone each ate fifteen kilos of fish a day. Was her missing pay really due to an accounting mix-up as Bridget had said, or was the centre in trouble financially?

'Who were those blokes here this morning?' she asked Karen.

'What blokes?'

'Bridget was showing two men the dolphins. Early, like six-thirty.'

Karen shrugged. 'I didn't see her before she left for Brisbane.'

'Did George come to look at those new turtles?'

'Yep. Reckons there's not much wrong with them that a good feed won't fix. By the way, he left something for you.' Karen tossed an envelope onto the table and gave Zoe a curious look.

She shoved it in her pocket. 'See you later. I'm out on the reef again this afternoon.' She hurried away before Karen could quiz her about the letter. George had analysed the substance from the rusted drum in Quinn's shed for her. This could be the results.

Zoe slipped out the side gate and scaled the stone steps to the shack. Opening the letter, she skimmed through to the bottom line. Oh, no . . . Dieldrin. She needed a drink. She poured herself a glass of wine from a half-finished bottle in the fridge, then sat down to read the report again. Zoe couldn't believe it. Swallowdale had a chemical sitting in its shed that was so toxic it had been banned in Australia since the 1980s. Zoe helped herself to another glass of wine, and sat for a while, thinking it through.

The seagrass could wait. She rang Quinn: something she'd rarely done before. 'It's Zoe. Where are you?'

'Why, what's wrong?' The background roar of machinery almost drowned out his voice.

'I have to see you. Can you meet me at the house in ten minutes?'

A deafening clash, a shudder and then silence. Had he hung up? 'Make it fifteen,' he said at last.

Zoe gulped down the last of her wine and dashed out the door.

Quinn stood in the driveway with Captain at his heels, staring at her in disbelief. 'Impossible,' he said. 'I admit we used Dieldrin in the past, when we didn't know any better. Everybody did. For grubs, wireworms, funnel ants, soldier flies – pretty much any pest you can think of. We even put ratoons of cane through Dieldrin baths before we planted them. But that was back when I was a kid. After they banned the stuff, Dad got rid of our leftover stock.' Zoe handed over the report. He ran his hand through his hair as he read it. 'Where did this come from?'

'When I went through your shed I took a sample from one of the drums. It was all rusted, so you couldn't read the label. I wanted to find out what was in it, so I had George analyse the sample. There's no mistake.'

'Rusted drums?' He sounded bewildered. 'In my shed? Show me.'

Zoe followed Quinn to his jeep and they headed for the shed. This time she had to wait for him to unlock it. That was an improvement, at least. But when she looked inside, the two mystery drums were nowhere to be seen. 'You've moved them,' said Zoe. 'Where are they? Those things are terribly toxic. They have to be disposed of properly.'

'I haven't moved anything.'

Zoe inspected the steel floor. Faint circular rust marks showed where the drums once stood. 'There, see?'

Quinn gave the floor a cursory, disbelieving glance. 'I haven't got time for this,' he said, his voice tight. 'You come over here like you're on some kind of mission and throw wild accusations around. Then when I show you there's nothing here, you still don't believe me.'

'What about the lab report?' said Zoe. 'That's proof.'

'It's proof the lab analysed something. How do I know it came from my shed?'

'Because I told you it did.' Tears welled up unexpectedly and she blinked them back. 'Believe me, Quinn, those drums were here.'

'So what, you think I've gone and hidden them?

'I don't know what to think.' Zoe buried her face in her hands, rubbing her eyes until she saw spots. 'Maybe somebody else moved them.'

Quinn's expression softened. 'I don't know what you think you saw,' he said. 'But I can guarantee you, nobody's been using Dieldrin at Swallowdale.'

'There are other sheds, right? Will you show me?'

For a moment he looked like he was going to argue, but then his body relaxed. 'Come on,' he said. 'If it's the only way I can convince you.'

An hour later and she followed Quinn from the last shed. 'That's it.' He locked the door behind him.

Zoe examined his face. Clear, honest grey eyes without a hint of deceit. Yet somebody had moved the drums. 'Talk to Rob. Please. It must have been him.'

Quinn couldn't quite disguise his frustration. 'Okay, okay, I'll talk to Rob.' His tone was soothing, as if he was pacifying a fractious colt. 'Now will you come and have a cuppa? I'm parched.'

. . .

Josh was as pleased to see her as Captain was. The boy bounced around the kitchen while Quinn made the tea, telling Zoe all about Aisha, and how he'd been helping with the harvest.

'He's doing a great job too,' said Quinn.

'Wow,' she said. 'I'm impressed.' She looked from brother to brother. Pride was reflected in both their faces.

'Can I go back with Zoe?' asked Josh. 'I want to see Mirrhi.'

'I don't see why not —' started Quinn.

Zoe put her hand on the boy's arm. 'I have to talk to your brother.'

'Go on then,' said Josh.

She shook her head. 'In private.'

Quinn picked up the tray and headed outside. 'Hop it. I'll run you down to the centre myself later on.' Josh shot him a mutinous glance.

'Please,' said Zoe. Josh frowned and stomped from the kitchen, slamming the door behind him.

She joined Quinn outside on the verandah underneath the jasmine, trailing her fingers through its soft leaves. The sweet scent of freshly cut cane wafted on the breeze. Quinn poured the tea, eyes neutral, his face a mask. They were unsure of each other, on different sides of something important. She felt her knuckles tighten. It was painful, being here like this. Her feelings towards him hadn't changed: one look at him was enough to tell her that. If only things were different. If only she was here to go riding, or to walk by the river, or for a long, lazy afternoon to chat about nothing and everything. She craved the warm, easy bond they once shared, and desperately wanted it back. Instead she was getting ready to rip apart their uneasy truce.

'I hear Leo came to see you,' she said. The mere mention of Leo's name provoked a flare of anger in Quinn's eyes, before his expression grew guarded again. 'He said you're against the Mermaid Cove resort.'

'Damned straight. I don't want hordes of ignorant tourists overrunning the town. Kiawa would never be the same.'

Would that be such a bad thing? she wanted to say, but managed to hold her tongue. 'It will be a real boost for Bridget and the Reef Centre.'

'Bridget's stressed out and run off her feet as it is.' He swatted at a fly on the table, and swore when he burned his hand on the teapot. His control was slipping. 'I don't get it, Zoe. You're the last person I thought would want a development on the reef. Leo's really gotten to you, hasn't he? It's amazing how his wealth can turn heads.'

'Nice to know you think so little of me,' she said. 'I don't think you understand. The resort will target eco-tourists and pump part of the profits into education programs and reef conservation. I'm all for it.' The bitterness in his glare cut deep, and for a moment her resolve almost slipped. No, however much this hurt personally, it had to be said. 'Let's put the Dieldrin issue aside for a moment.'

'There *is* no Dieldrin issue,' he said, his voice rising. 'Why can't you leave things alone?'

Zoe struggled to stay calm. 'Quinn, you're in a position of leadership and influence in this town. It's your responsibility to do the right thing.' A pulse was throbbing in his cheek. 'If you and your mates don't tackle this chemical run-off problem before the wet season kicks in properly, it'll be out of my hands. Leo won't risk his investment – he'll bring in the authorities. There are substantial fines and even criminal sanctions for what's happening around here.'

Quinn stared at her with wild eyes. 'Why did you have to go shooting your mouth off?' He jumped to his feet and paced the verandah. Long fields of cane stretched out beyond him, like an emerald ocean. 'I'm doing nothing wrong at Swallowdale, but bring those government fellers in and they're bound to find fault. Do you know how many growers in Kiawa are *this* close to selling up? They can't afford to pay any fines. I've seen what the cost of compliance did up north. Put some small farms right out of business.' He paused, ran his fingers over his eyes. 'Just about every local farmer I know kept a disabled worker on after the government funding ran out for *Project We'll Show You*. They're paying those wages out of their own pockets. Ramp up their costs and guess who'll be the first to go. Is that what you want? To put kids like Josh out of work?'

'Of course not,' said Zoe. 'But Turtle Reef must be protected, no matter what.' Her throat was tight and dry, barely allowing the words out. She took a mouthful of tea. 'I've heard there are grants for farmers to help them transition to best practice. Maybe you could look into —'

'I don't need any more advice,' said Quinn. 'I think you've helped enough.'

His sarcasm made her want to cry. She should plead with him, plead for herself as well as for the reef. For a split-second the desire almost won.

Zoe forced her mouth to remain shut. No, emotion would not rule her, would not weaken her. She stood up. 'Think about what I've said, Quinn. One way or another, Kiawa will move with the times. You can bring the local growers along with you. Help them adjust, learn new ways of doing things. Protect the reef at the same time. Or you can all flounder in the past and get washed away by the tide of progress. Your choice.' At least he was listening now. 'And those drums of Dieldrin *were* in your shed. Somebody moved them. You'd better find out who.'

CHAPTER 25

Zoe slipped into the seaquarium and headed for *Tentacle Town*. She wanted to check on Einstein before work, and was delighted when the octopus emerged to take her favourite meal. 'There's my girl.' Zoe briefly fondled Einstein's arm as she accepted the fat prawn. 'You need to keep up your strength.' She was rewarded with a gentle squeeze of her hand.

A month had passed since Einstein laid her eggs. She'd lost a lot of weight and was responding less and less to Zoe's visits. She still ate sometimes and her eyes remained bright. But they looked far larger and wider than before, a sure sign that her skin was shrinking away. The only colour change she made anymore was to a defensive shade of red.

Einstein finished her meal and hurried back to her den. She pulled two clam shells across the entrance. It was hard to find definitive information on the length of time it took hammer octopus eggs to hatch. Zoe's own report on the subject was being eagerly awaited by the cephalopod curator at Sydney Aquarium. However a comparison with similar species suggested that Einstein had perhaps another month left to live. Zoe would miss her. She took one last look at the devoted little octopus before heading for the kitchen. With Bridget away in Brisbane they were short-staffed. Zoe would be preparing the morning feeds single-handed.

When Zoe opened the kitchen door, an awful sight confronted her. She'd forgotten to put the defrosting bags of fish into the fridge. They'd been sitting out on the bench since yesterday and were already smelly. She dared not feed them out. Zoe looked ruefully around. She'd been the last one to leave last night, and Karen was out collecting yet another sick sea turtle. There was no reason why anybody should find out what an idiot she was.

Zoe pulled out two fresh bags of fish from the freezer. Now, how to get rid of the evidence. Didn't Karen dispose of dead specimens by bagging them in plastic and throwing them into the big skip in the utility yard? It was Friday tomorrow, pick-up day. That would work.

She hauled one of the spoiled bags onto the feeding trolley and wheeled it out the back. Bummer, the bin was padlocked. Maybe the key was in the maintenance shed? Yes, there it was, on a nail behind the door.

Zoe shoved the heavy metal lid up and anchored it open, holding her nose. Nobody would notice another foul smell in all that stink. With great difficulty Zoe hauled the slippery, twenty-kilo bag up and over. So far, so good. But when it came to closing the lid, she couldn't. It was jammed somehow. She climbed up the side and holding on with one arm, jiggled the mechanism with the other. What was wrong with the thing, it was so stiff. Sitting precariously on the edge of the skip, she tried to shift the hinge mechanism with both hands. Almost . . . but just when Zoe thought she had it, she lost her balance and slipped. Argh . . . how disgusting. In the bin, half-buried by rotting fish and garbage.

As she struggled to her feet, something caught her eye. A small, labelled plastic bag with something green inside. Zoe struggled across to it, shuddering as her leg sank into the stinking mess. She picked up the little bag. No, it couldn't be. One of the seagrass samples she'd painstakingly collected from the bay and prepared for analysis. She wiped away some crud so she could read the date. First of December, just last week. She'd personally handed this bag to Bridget. How on earth had it wound up in the rubbish?

Zoe searched around. There, beneath a carton of slimy lettuce, another one of her samples. Forgoing all squeamishness, she dug deeper. More bags . . . four, five, six of them. She collected each one into a cracked, plastic tub. Deeper again. Incredible, right near the bottom was a whole box of them, dated two weeks ago. She flipped through the sample bags and did the calculations. As far as she knew, the skip was collected once a fortnight. Her brief bin audit accounted for nearly every sample she'd handed over to Bridget during that time. They were all here. Thrown away. Discarded. Not sitting in a queue at Queensland University at all. She shook her head in disbelief.

The chug-chug of an approaching motor; the maintenance man on his little golf cart. Zoe ducked and held her breath, stifling a coughing fit. He turned off the engine. Would he notice the skip was open? Would it matter if he did? After all, she wasn't really doing anything wrong. But as that thought was born, a more knowing one pushed it aside. How naive could she be? Whatever the explanation, her boss was up to some serious no-good. That much was plain. Did she really want someone telling Bridget about this? Zoe needed to stay on the front foot, maintain her advantage. The element of surprise could be crucial to figuring this thing out. A few clangs and bangs sounded from the maintenance shed, then the noise of the retreating golf cart.

Zoe was gagging on the stink. She had to get out of there. One last look around to make sure nothing had been missed. She heaved herself onto the side of the skip, reached for the plastic tub, and jumped awkwardly to the ground. Good, nobody in sight. Zoe hurried to the kitchen, stowed the tub under a bench, and then disposed of the second bag of spoiled fish. This time she managed to close the bin lid. She snapped on the padlock and put the key back in the shed with a sigh of relief.

Despite the warm morning Zoe couldn't stop shivering. The seaquarium residents could wait for their breakfast. What she needed was to go home, wash off the filth under the shack's magnificent shower, and store away the rescued sample bags. They were the proof she needed to turn her vague misgivings into genuine suspicion. Something was dodgy at the Reef Centre, very dodgy indeed. Bridget had been lying all along about getting the samples tested, and Zoe was determined to find out why.

It was two o'clock before she finished the morning chores. The animals were finally all fed and clean, the shows all done and Karen was back on board.

'Are you coming down with something, Zoe? You look terrible,' said Karen as they slid the new turtle into the quarantine pool 'Very green around the gills. I'm surprised you haven't scared off our visitors. Go home. I can manage here.'

'Are you sure?' Zoe kicked herself before the words were out. The afternoon off was precisely what she needed.

Karen grinned. 'Clear out before I change my mind.'

Zoe sat hunched over the computer, googling dugong research projects. She found plenty of them, but no reference to any based at Turtle Reef National Park. Next she tried the Queensland University *Centre for Marine Science* website. It was packed with interesting information, and she kept getting distracted by the great openings on offer. Heron Island and Moreton Bay Research Station scholarships. Grants and postgraduate opportunities. Genuine opportunities. In some ways she wished that she'd never set eyes on Bridget Macalister. But then she would never have rediscovered her love of horses. She would never have got to know Mirrhi or Baby or any of the other extraordinary resident dolphins. She wouldn't have met Josh . . . or Quinn. Quinn. She had to tell him about Bridget. She pushed aside the ugly thought that this might be a self-serving act. Quinn was getting ready to marry Bridget, wasn't he? He had a right to know what she was up to – whatever that was.

Zoe stood up, stretched, and went to fetch a jumper. She felt stiff all over, and cold too, in spite of the warm afternoon. Probably just nerves, but her head was heavy and starting to ache. Maybe Karen was right? Maybe she was coming down with something. That would be problematic. She had no time to be sick.

Zoe poured herself a drink and sat back down to search for promising email contacts or phone numbers. She scrolled down the website's home page. *One of the largest and most diverse group of marine scientists and engineers in Australia, with over fifty independent research group leaders, fifty postdoctoral researchers and two hundred PhD students.* Where to start?

Zoe emailed any likely contacts and then began making phone calls. 'Yes, that's right, I need a list of all your current research projects . . . Great, I'll try his number.'

It was harder than she thought to pry information from people, but two hours and three glasses of wine later, she struck gold with the secretary of the Director. 'I'd rather not send that information to a private email address,' he said. 'However if you have one associated with the Reef Centre, I can send through a complete list of our current projects. You said it's urgent?'

'That's right.'

'I'll see what I can do, but I'm afraid it might not be until tomorrow.'

'My work email is *z.king@reefcentre.com.au.* I look forward to hearing from you.'

Zoe put down the phone. Tomorrow — how would she wait? She craved to confront Bridget this very instant, show her the discarded sample bags, demand an explanation. But that was hardly strategic. She'd seen too many movies where the hapless hero confronts the villain on the moor. *When we get back to town I'll expose you for the monster that you are!* It never ended well. No, better to keep her powder dry until she had undeniable proof that Bridget was up to no good. Good grief, they were diving together on the reef first thing in the morning. Could she really last the whole day pretending nothing was wrong?

CHAPTER 26

Zoe packed the last of their gear into *Seafarer*'s starboard storage. She was twitchy and on edge after a restless night. Exhausted too — as if a university would send information through after hours. But she'd still obsessively checked her emails until late, and it was past midnight before she got to bed. Too much wine, a mind that wouldn't turn off and a headache led to a sleepless night. But none of that could erase the shiver of excitement she always felt before a dive on the outer reef. Or did she shiver because she had a temperature? Her throat was scratchy and sore, and it hurt to swallow. What a day to be under the weather.

'Ready?' Bridget was already seated at the wheel with the motor running.

'Ready.' Zoe cast off the lines. The sky was bright and cloudless, with a freshening breeze, a perversely beautiful day. They were heading for Bora, a small outer reef. She sat in the stern, as far away from Bridget as possible. Staring out to sea, letting the salt air revive her and blow away the cobwebs. Zoe checked her phone for emails. Still nothing, and soon they'd be out of the range of her ancient mobile. She scoffed some Panadol and tried to put on a brave face.

This wouldn't be so hard. Keep the conversation light, avoid anything contentious, get through the day whatever way she could — then get home for some answers.

Bridget called her name. Zoe groaned. She'd been hoping to make the trip out without having to talk. She forced a smile and moved forwards. As usual, her boss looked stylish and elegant. Not a hair escaped from her shining ponytail. Zoe still wondered how she did it, but was no longer envious, even though her own hair was swirling round her face in an unruly, tickling tangle – too short to tie back and too long to stay put. So what. Who'd want to be a lying snake like Bridget?

'Good to get this job out of the way,' said Bridget. 'A storm's forecast for early next week.' Zoe pretended to see something off the port bow. She did not intend to be lured into small talk. 'How did things go while I was away?'

'Fine,' said Zoe.

Bridget abruptly increased the speed and the outboard purred louder. They skipped over a larger-than-usual wave and Zoe's stomach dropped alarmingly. The small boat, the growing swell, feeling sick to begin with – not a good combination. She lurched to the side and vomited.

'Are you alright?'

Zoe raised her hand and gave a wave without turning round. Her head still hung overboard in case there was more to come.

'You poor thing,' said Bridget. 'You should have taken seasickness pills before we left. What an awkward problem for a marine scientist to have.'

There was a sarcastic, almost hostile edge to Bridget's words. Or was she imagining it? Things had been okay between the two of them ever since the day Kane escaped and they'd had that heart to heart. *Let's start afresh,* Bridget had said. *No more secrets.* And Zoe had believed her. What a monumental sucker. Well, not anymore. Her eyes were wide open.

Zoe stood up a bit shakily, wiped her mouth with an old tissue she found in her pocket and sat back down. 'I'm fine. Bit of an upset stomach is all.'

Bridget gave her a sympathetic smile that didn't fool Zoe for a second. 'Better out than in, that's what Dad always says.' She cast her a sideways glance. 'How is my father? I hear you two are seeing a lot more of each other since I moved in with Quinn.'

So that was it. Bridget was snooping. Should she put her mind at rest? No, let her squirm. 'Your father's very well. He sends his love.' Zoe went back to staring at the sea and thinking about the day ahead. Bridget would be collecting specimens. Zoe's job was to photograph bommies: the great, mounding outcrops of coral forming the boundary of Bora Lagoon. Normally she would have been asking lots of excited questions about the purpose and possibilities of their trip to the outer reef, where bleached areas of coral had visibly grown, even in the few months that she'd been there. Damage that normally healed on its own did not mend when colonies were near pollution sources on land, and a scientific sampling program and photographic record could help establish that. But Zoe didn't believe their dive trip had anything to do with science. For all she knew Bridget merely wanted some new coral for her tropical display tanks.

They didn't talk for the rest of the trip. When they reached Bora Reef, Bridget killed the motor. Zoe gazed around at the sparkling water and far horizon. Frigate birds, those supreme acrobats of the skies, soared overhead and a pod of dolphins frolicked in the distance. A place as remote as it was beautiful. At that moment it was easy to believe that she and Bridget were the last people left on Earth.

'Shouldn't we be moored near a marker buoy?' asked Zoe.

'This is the spot I want,' said Bridget. 'Don't worry, we have a GPS.' They dropped anchor and changed into dive gear. Zoe couldn't resist a small, shallow surge of satisfaction when she realised they were wearing the same size wetsuit.

'Shall we synchronise our watches?' Bridget turned her wrist to check her Meridian dive computer. The little beauty did everything but hold your hand underwater. An LCD display showed depth, water temperature, remaining air time – it even suggested decompression stages on ascent. A far cry from Zoe's discount store specimen. Still, her watch was waterproof to fifty metres and reliable enough. 'I make it nine-thirty,' said Bridget. 'Meet me back here in an hour.'

'Righto. You go first.'

Bridget fell backwards into the blue. She orientated herself on the surface for a few seconds, then vanished beneath the strengthening swell. Zoe began to cough. She popped a butter menthol in her mouth. A glorious reef dive lay ahead of her and she wasn't going to let any cold steal away the joy of it. Now, where was her camera?

Zoe slid beneath the waves and exhaled. Freedom, beauty, danger, bliss – sinking into the sea was always a spiritual experience. Like being in heaven, but on borrowed time. A backbone of large bommies flanked the lagoon, offering deep diving on one side and shallow on the other. Zoe headed for the outer shelf, where giant groupers faced into the current. Marine life was more abundant here than inshore. Turtles, wrasse and rays abounded. On the sand below sat five fat brain corals, a colonial species, prime indicators of an expanding reef. A promising find. Passing shadows caught her eye. In deeper water cruised a pair of tiger sharks. Fond as she was of sharks, the sight of these sleek predators frightened her. She had to pull herself together, concentrate on the job at hand. Zoe found a patch of bleached coral and started taking photographs.

Here was trouble. Two crown-of-thorns starfish, bristling with spines and much larger than she'd imagined. The first she'd seen. They weren't normally found this far south. A native species, crown-of-thorns fed on vigorous corals like plates and staghorns, allowing slower growing brain and boulder corals to take hold. But sometimes their numbers burgeoned out of control, devastating whole reefs. Outbreaks had been linked to polluted waters. Zoe snapped some more photos.

Diving was an inherently forgetful experience. A weightless world, dreamlike, views blinkered by the margins of the mask. Things drifted mysteriously on the edge of vision, and a brand-new window on the underwater world appeared with each turn of the head or change of direction. Angelfish and bright blue sea stars browsed among forests of staghorn coral. Purple sea fans seemed to wave in an underwater wind and massive giant clams lurked in deeper water, large enough to close on a foolish diver's arm if examined too closely.

A deadly banded sea snake swam by, breaking the spell. She checked her air tanks. Getting low. Must be time to go. Oh no, according to her watch only five minutes had passed. The bloody thing wasn't working. She thought longingly of Bridget's wrist computer. Some day.

Keeping the bommie wall on her left, she retraced her footsteps, so to speak, ticking off remembered landmarks in her mind: the overhang that looked like a horse head, the underwater arch. Finally Zoe arrived at the distinctive pillar-like outcrop where she'd started. She took one last photo of a particularly grand fire coral resembling a miniature castle, then headed topside. Her throat was parched and her head throbbed. She could use some more Panadol.

No matter how much she loved diving, it was always a relief to break the choppy surface, to bury her head into that vast dome of life-giving air. The sun shone bright and hot, warming her chilled bones. Zoe removed her mask, shook out her hair and gulped down a great lungful. Much better. An hour underwater always left her disorientated and she badly needed a drink of water.

She looked around for the shadow of the *Seafarer*, squinting in the strong light. Wait a minute, where was it? She spun slowly around. Not left, not right, not behind her. Not anywhere. She was all alone on the wide, wide sea.

Zoe struggled to control a surge of panic. It was every diver's nightmare to be left behind. Where was the boat? Maybe the anchor had failed and it had drifted during their dive. That meant Bridget would be stranded too. Zoe looked wildly around for her. Hard to pick a bobbing head in this swell. If only the wind would die down, then she might be able to see something. Out of habit she looked at her watch. Useless thing. What time was it? She tried to judge by the position of the sun in the sky. At a guess, she'd say ten-thirty. That would tally with the amount of air left in her tanks. But knowing the time didn't help her. She needed to find Bridget and the boat.

A wave washed over her. Zoe spat the saltwater from her mouth, trying to ignore her thirst. Dread was creeping into her bones. Had she lost her bearings, completely misjudged the underwater landmarks, surfaced miles away? It seemed unlikely, but not as unlikely as the boat just disappearing. She fumbled for the whistle built into her buoyancy vest. The shrill note sounded loud in her ear, a scream for help lost on the vast ocean. She blew it again and again, hopelessly, knowing as she did that she was wasting precious breath.

Time passed. A dreadful reality was settling on Zoe like sea-spray. There was nobody to hear her. Bridget wasn't nearby, lost and alone somewhere in the water. She wasn't desperately searching for her dive companion. Bridget was safely on the boat, heading for home. Zoe dropped the camera and it sank from sight.

Another wave doused her, pushing her under. There wasn't even a buoy to cling to. She struggled to breathe, fear sapping her strength. Being left behind wasn't an immediate death sentence. Like most divers she wore an emergency lifejacket and had enough air in her tank to inflate it. People had survived overnight in such circumstances, and surely somebody, somewhere, would come looking for her. But any search would rely on Bridget reporting Zoe missing and faithfully relaying her last known position. A slim hope.

She couldn't stop thinking about what had happened to two American divers a few years ago. They disappeared on the Great Barrier Reef after their boat's crew bungled a roll call. The alarm wasn't raised for two days, when the captain discovered their belongings in a dive locker. Despite a massive search they were never found. Ten days later some of their gear washed up down the coast, and a dive tablet bearing a chilling message: *Please help us or we will die. January 26, 8:00 a.m.* They'd survived the night, only to drown the next day— or worse. Zoe tried to put the large sharks cruising the reef out of her mind.

This kind of thinking wasn't getting her anywhere. Was there something practical she could do? She scanned the horizon again for a boat. Bridget may be gone, but other people must dive Bora Reef. She might get lucky . . . no, she *would* get lucky. Positive thinking could well mean the difference between life and death. The most important thing was to conserve heat and energy. She could feel the current moving her. Instinct said to swim back to her original position, but was that really the best strategy? And what was her original position anyway? Struggling against the sea sounded like a good way to exhaust herself. She paddled sideways instead, angling back in an arc during lulls in the swell, working with the waves to stay vaguely in place.

What tools did she have at her disposal? Not much. The whistle, a signal mirror and a light. What about her weights? She should have dumped them ages ago. Zoe began to jettison them one at a time, planning to hold onto the weight belt. She could use it to tie herself to . . . to what? With a sinking heart she unfastened the whole thing and let it slip into the depths. She hesitated to ditch the cylinder. They were expensive. The absurd irony of this thought actually made her smile. Bridget had left her to die, and yet here she was wanting to save the bitch a couple of bucks. Still, it might be best to keep the tank. It was almost empty and not weighing her down. If the life jacket leaked, she could at least use the last of her air to pump it back up again.

Zoe wracked her brains for anything else she could do to gain an advantage. Nope, that was it. She pulled her knees to her chest to conserve body heat. Nothing for it but to endure. Now that she'd run out of things to focus on, her mind ranged in terrifying directions. She was constantly pulling it back from the brink of despair. Don't think about Bridget, don't think about sharks, don't think about what will happen if nobody comes.

Time wore on. Her head throbbed as the blazing sun travelled across the sky. It became harder and harder to judge how long she'd been waiting. Minutes? Hours? She dared not swallow for the pain in her parched throat and her thirst raged. Exhaustion was claiming her and she found it harder and harder to concentrate, to resist the buffeting swell. Her mind drifted along with her body. Why hadn't she rung her mother lately, or talked to Dad? So caught up in the excitement of her new job, she hadn't bothered to make the time. Next week, always next week. Well, maybe there wouldn't be a next week. If she ever got out of this alive, that was a lesson she wouldn't forget.

Never had the ocean seemed so vast, so trackless, so filled with grand indifference. That was somehow a comforting thought. There were worse endings. If the sea took her, no malice would lie behind her death.

This last, morbid thought roused her, brought her to her senses. Of course there would be malice behind her death. Malice that belonged not to the great, thoughtless ocean but to Bridget Macalister. And what about Quinn? She must go to him and confess her true feelings. She could not die without him ever knowing that she loved him. That would be a shame. That would be a terrible, terrible shame. And he would marry a murderer and ruin his life, along with Josh's. She couldn't let that happen. She must hold on.

But how? She allowed herself a mouthful of seawater, swirled it round, gargled and spat it out. It briefly eased her burning throat and she felt a little brighter, bright enough to take a look around. Maybe a boat had come? But what she saw stopped her heart.

A five-metre tiger shark lurked so close she could touch it. She prayed it would sail past, pay no attention, but her luck was out. It made a U-turn, curious about this strange, clumsy creature bobbing in the ocean. Tiger sharks were adventurous about their diet. Rubber boots, bags of charcoal, boat cushions, hubcaps and pets, among other things, had all turned up in their stomachs. They were known to investigate what came their way in the ocean by taking an investigative bite. Sea snakes, turtles, even dolphins and dugongs were on the menu – and tigers came second only to great whites when it came to attacks on humans. But they also didn't like their prey to fight back, and adrenaline was giving her strength.

The shark approached again, bumping her leg with an inquisitive nose. Zoe willed herself not to flail about, fighting an urge to scream. A combination of watching the movie *Jaws* and having studied sharks at uni gave her an idea. She slowly undid her air tank and held it in front of her, struggling to grip with icy fingers. Don't drop it now.

Sharks had tiny receptors speckling the skin of their noses. These pores were filled with conductive jelly that detected the electrical currents around fish. Hitting sharks' faces disrupted that unique sense and could sometimes deter them. It was worth a shot. The tiger nudged closer, and closer still until they were face to face. Now! She pounded the cylinder down on its sensitive nose and it veered away. Oh no, the tank had slipped from her grasp. The tiger approached again, more cautiously this time. Zoe made a fist and rained down blows with all her strength, using fingernails to rake its skin and jamming a knuckle into its eye. The shark thrashed its massive head, throwing her sideways. Then it yawed left and swam away. For now.

Zoe gasped for breath, every muscle burning, her energy gone. She felt like a soggy rag doll. Her head throbbed so loudly she couldn't think anymore. Wait, it wasn't just her head throbbing. A white helicopter was flying in from the west. She fumbled for her whistle, waved wildly, screamed to the sky for help. Why was it flying so high? How would the crew spot her from way up there? Time seemed to stand still. She willed the copter to dip and turn, willed it so hard that it felt as if her brain was bursting.

The helicopter did not deviate from its course. They hadn't seen her. Tears welled in her eyes as it vanished from view — a crushing disappointment. No, don't cry, don't waste precious water. But perhaps it didn't matter. A tell-tale dorsal fin had appeared in the distance, slicing through the water. More than one this time. She couldn't go on, she had no more strength. Zoe closed her eyes.

It was then she sensed it, an odd prickling energy, like she was being zapped on the inside. Then a series of whistles and clicks, louder underwater than above. She opened her eyes and looked at the fast-approaching fins, at their shape, their curved trailing edge. Fear had made her brainless. Not sharks - dolphins.

Zoe laughed like a maniac and rinsed her mouth out with water again. Dolphins were symbols of good luck at sea. Maybe the copter had seen her after all? Maybe help was on its way? The pod arrowed straight for her, lifting her flagging spirits. Silly as it was, she didn't feel alone anymore. There must have been nine or ten of them. *Please let them stay around.* The nearest dolphin bore a distinctive drooping dorsal fin. It came closer, and closer again. Zoe's smile broadened. She felt her lip split, it was so dry, but she didn't mind the pain. Kane. The dolphin with the drooping dorsal fin was Kane.

CHAPTER 27

It seemed inconceivable that not too long ago she would have viewed Kane's approach with apprehension, would have quailed at the memory of the bloody rake marks across Bridget's shoulder. To see him now, porpoising around her, was like coming face to face with a dear old friend.

Countless legends and, in more modern times, news reports told of dolphins helping humans in peril. Zoe had studied this phenomenon during her course. Victims of shark attacks described dolphins rushing to the scene, fending off the predators with high-speed rams. Drowning swimmers spoke of dolphins raising them to the surface to breathe, as they might do with one of their newborn infants. Was this what was happening? Was Kane here to save her?

How different these circumstances were to when they'd last met. Then Kane had been captive in a human world, performing tricks in a zoo. But they were in his realm now and she was the helpless one. She could feel the buzz of Kane's sonar beneath her skin, something she'd never experienced back at the centre. Could he read her terror, her vulnerability? Were Zoe's blood, lungs and beating heart as clear to Kane as if they lay on the outside of her body? He drew close and she rubbed his warm back, thankful for the companionship and the heat beneath her frozen fingers.

Her mind was drifting: her parents' faces before her, then gone; an image of Quinn and Josh. Then a moment from her studies came to her, something she'd read: that the rescue behaviour of dolphins was not automatic or instinctive. Dolphins made conscious decisions about whether to intervene or not. They were selective about who and in which circumstances they would help. Zoe prayed Kane might deem her worthy.

He bobbed beneath her. Would he allow it? Zoe scrambled to rest her weary body on his and absorb his warmth. She clung to him, clutching his dorsal fin, overwhelmed by the gravity of the moment. Kane's fin was firmer than it had been back at the centre, recovering from its droop. A life of freedom in the open ocean suited him. Kane's heartbeat seemed to echo through the hollow shell of her body, bestowing strength and courage where there had been none.

How long she waited like that, sheltered and protected by the big dolphin, she couldn't tell. From the vantage point of Kane's back she twice saw tiger sharks in the distance. But there was safety in numbers, and the sharks steered well clear of the pod. Neither humans nor dolphins would be on the menu today. Clouds were building in the east, scudding across the sun, bringing some shady relief. Of course she couldn't go on like this forever. Eventually she'd have to find land, but this failed to distress her. She was caught in an extraordinary moment, aboard a wild dolphin that was also a patient friend, floating free in the wide blue ocean. And whether she lived or died seemed somehow unimportant.

Later, exhaustion claimed her. Zoe's hands locked onto Kane in an involuntary death-grip. She drifted into semi-sleep, a blessed respite, and roused some minutes later to find they were on the move. The pod was travelling towards a shadow on the ocean. Zoe's vision was blurry and she blinked to clear it. Yes, a boat, and they were heading straight for it. Zoe looked again. Not just any boat. The *Seafarer,* A shudder of fear passed through her, and she fought against it. She had to believe that Bridget would help.

Zoe fell forwards to hug the big dolphin's neck, losing balance, slipping from safety. The heedless pod continued, but Kane turned back and circled close. She reached for him, lunging again and again until her slight strength was spent. Each time he dodged away. 'So I guess this is the end of the road for us.' A mere murmur through chapped lips. The boat was drawing near. Zoe scrabbled for the whistle, fumbled for the signal mirror. Since losing Kane's body warmth, her legs and arms were cramping up. She tried to whistle, but her mouth was dry. Stiff fingers lost hold of the mirror. It didn't matter. Bridget had seen her, was waving and shouting. Kane sidled past one last time, allowing her to stroke his side. Then he vanished into the waves.

Minutes later Bridget hauled her onto *Seafarer*'s rear dive platform.

Zoe's legs were like jelly. She couldn't stand. Crawling onto the shaded deck, she was only dimly aware of the horrified expression on Bridget's face. Zoe tried asking for a drink, but her voice didn't work. She pointed to a water bottle sitting on the seat.

Bridget passed it to her.

Water had never tasted so good. 'More.'

Bridget filled up the bottle, wrapped a blanket around Zoe's shoulders and handed her a tube of Vaseline.

Zoe smoothed the soothing ointment on her lips, ran her tongue over them. 'How long was I out there?' she managed, though it hurt to talk.

'Five hours maybe . . .'

Five hours? It had felt like five days. 'Why?' she whispered.

'The anchor failed,' Bridget said. 'And the boat drifted without me noticing. When I tried to start it, the engine kept stalling and . . .' Zoe stared into the middle distance, barely listening to her cockamamie explanation. 'I called search and rescue,' said Bridget. 'Didn't you see the helicopter?'

Zoe shook her aching head. 'No . . . I mean why did you come back?'

Bridget fell silent. The look in her eyes was unmistakable. They understood each other. Her further protestations were merely for show. Were those tears tracking down her high cheekbones? Was she sorry? Zoe pulled her knees into her chest and drew the blanket tight around her. You couldn't tell with Bridget. In some ways Zoe had felt safer with Kane, all lost at sea.

When they arrived at the dock, nobody was waiting. Zoe didn't know what she'd expected, her mind was so fuzzy. An ambulance maybe?

Bridget helped her from the boat onto the pier. Zoe's legs were still wobbly but at least she could walk now. 'Sit down,' said Bridget, guiding her to a timber bench. 'Do you feel well enough to go home or do you want to see a doctor?'

How to answer? She did want to see somebody, desperately, but it wasn't a doctor. She wanted to see Quinn: to warn him, to tell him his girlfriend was a mad woman, a homicidal maniac.

'Wait here,' said Bridget. 'I'll go get the car.' She hurried away.

Zoe rose unsteadily to her feet. What a relief to see the back of Bridget. Now, to get home, ring Quinn. She tried to run, but her legs failed her, so she started for the shack at a shambling walk. Was that a car? Zoe concentrated on walking faster, putting one foot after the other, her fear building There was no way she was going to accept a lift from that woman.

A jeep pulled up beside her. Not Bridget - Quinn. He rushed to her, his face a mask of concern. 'Zoe, are you okay? Bridget rang to tell me what happened.' Kneeling before her, he tenderly brushed back the hair from her sunburnt face. She'd daydreamed about that same gesture many, many times. In her imagination he'd always followed it with a kiss and, in her dazed state, she was surprised when the kiss didn't come. 'Get in,' he said. 'I'm taking you to the hospital.'

. . .

It was early evening before they pulled up at the rear of the shack. Quinn had wanted to take her to the cottage at Swallowdale, but Zoe had resisted. She didn't want to stay anywhere near Bridget. Physically she was much improved, apart from an overarching exhaustion. The need to sleep was almost irresistible, but first she had something to say.

Quinn opened the door and carried her, actually carried her, inside. Despite her fatigue, she felt a shock of pleasure to be in his arms. He deposited her on the living room couch and fetched a blanket and pillow. Then he pulled up a chair and sat very close. 'Are you hungry.' She'd had nothing to eat except a biscuit at the hospital, and her depleted body craved nourishment, but her mind was somewhere else. Zoe propped herself up and leaned on Quinn's arm. This was it. She was ready, more than ready to tell him the truth about Bridget, however ludicrous it sounded, however much it hurt him. But when she went to speak, something in his expression gave her pause.

Quinn's tongue traced his lips, as his eyes grew bright and urgent. 'There's something important I want to say.' The intensity of his expression confused her, chased away her resolve. 'I've kept my feelings to myself for too long.' What was this? 'You're always on my mind Zoe. Always. You're there in the cane fields and the clouds, the river and the rain. And then today, when I almost lost you ... well, it's time to be honest, time to stop playing it safe.' She dared to hope. 'I'm ending things with Bridget, tonight.' Quinn took hold of her hands, his eyes tender now. 'I love you, don't want to be without you. I need to know if you feel the same way.'

It took her a moment to catch her breath. 'Can't you tell?'

He exhaled and squeezed her hands. 'I wasn't sure. You're a hell of a change for me, Zoe King. Each time I thought we were getting close, you'd start a bloody big fight. First Aisha, then Josh, and the chemicals and Bridget ...'

'And the lungfish ...' she said.

'Of course.' He smiled. 'How could I forget the lungfish?'

A knock came at the door, startling them both. Quinn released

Zoe's hands as Bridget entered uninvited. 'How are you, Zoe?' she asked. 'What did the hospital say?' Zoe huddled down and pulled the blanket higher.

Quinn stood up. 'She has to rest up for a day or two, but there's no lasting damage.'

'Excellent.' Bridget spoke with a brittle gaiety. Her searching gaze travelled over their faces. 'I'll make us something to eat, shall I? What would you like Zoe? Something light? An omelette perhaps, or a toasted sandwich?'

The thought of eating food prepared by Bridget made her gag. It would probably be poisoned. Bridget went into the kitchen. This might be her best chance. Zoe clutched Quinn's arm. 'It wasn't an accident.' Her voice was scratchy and weak.

'Want some water?'

She grabbed his arm tighter. ' Listen to me. It wasn't an accident. Bridget left me out on the reef deliberately.'

Quinn's expression grew troubled. 'You're in shock— '

Zoe shook her head. 'Something's wrong with Bridget. You have to believe me. I nearly died today.'

'Zoe . . .'

'She's been throwing away the samples I collected for the dugong project. I found them in the bin.' Zoe picked up her phone from the table, then took hold of his hand, bracing against his arm to help pull herself to her feet. 'Come and look.'

Zoe shuffled to the bedroom still wrapped in the blanket. She pulled open the wardrobe door and pointed to the cardboard box on the floor. 'There.' Quinn flipped through the labelled sample bags inside. 'I gave those to Bridget,' said Zoe. 'She said she'd sent them for analysis, but instead she threw them away. I don't believe there *is* any research project. I don't believe a word Bridget says.'

With clumsy fingers she checked the emails on her phone again. Still nothing from Queensland Uni. Where was the list of projects she'd been promised? She could really do with some concrete proof right about now.

'I don't know what to think,' admitted Quinn. 'But to say she left you out at the reef on purpose - do you realise what you're saying? Bridget was the one who called in the search and rescue copter. You said yourself that you saw it. She was the one who found you. Bridget saved your life.'

Zoe shut the bedroom door. She'd had plenty of time to think this through, had thought about nothing else. 'I don't think that helicopter was looking for me at all. It was way too high for one thing, and the wrong colour to be from Queensland Search and Rescue. I can picture the pattern beneath.' She scrolled through Google images until she found a photo of a blue and white Channel Nine News helicopter. She showed it to Quinn. 'I think this was it. No, I'm sure of it.'

Bridget knocked on the door, causing Zoe to jump. 'What's going on in there? Your sandwich is ready.'

'We'll be out in a minute,' called Zoe.

Quinn scratched his beard. 'Television station copters often help out with searches.'

'Yes, but if that was the case, why wasn't it on the news? The television at the hospital was tuned to Channel Nine the whole time we were there. Not a word about a missing diver.'

'If Bridget meant to leave you out there,' said Quinn, 'why did she then turn round and rescue you?

'I think it was a coincidence that the helicopter flew overhead,' said Zoe, keeping her voice low. 'When Bridget saw it she panicked, thinking that it might have spotted me. She couldn't afford *not* to go back.'

The door swung open and Bridget walked in. Her face was white, giving the lie to her smile. 'Anything I should know about?' The cardboard box of samples lay on the floor in full view. Zoe moved in front it, stumbling as she did. Quinn offered her a supportive arm. Bridget's eyes gleamed keen as a hawk. She did not miss the look that passed between them, and the smile died on her lips. 'What has Zoe been saying.' She saw the cardboard box. 'What's that?' Her voice grew shrill. 'What are you trying to hide?'

Bridget pulled the box out from behind Zoe and picked up one of the bags.

'Do you recognise that?' Zoe was too tired to pretend anymore. One way or another she wanted some answers.

Bridget stared, open-mouthed. Zoe could see her mind working frantically to come up with a plausible explanation. Quinn was no fool; maybe it was best to say nothing at all, let Bridget dig herself in deeper. 'Karen was meant to post those off. I have no idea how they wound up in the bin. Maybe she mixed them up somehow. I hope the university didn't get bags of dead fish instead of Zoe's specimens.'

'How did you know they were in the bin?' asked Quinn quietly.

'What do you mean?'

'Just what I said. How did you know Zoe found the sample bags in the bin.'

'Didn't she say? Well, it's obvious, isn't it?' Bridget inspected some of the bags. 'They have crud all over them.'

Blood surged to Zoe's head in an angry rush. She couldn't listen anymore, couldn't stand one more lie. 'You left me out on the reef deliberately. I know that, you know that ... I'm going to the police.'

'Now, hang on,' said Quinn,. 'There must be some explanation.'

'There is.' Bridget fastened cold eyes on Zoe. 'She's a born trouble-maker, who loves throwing wild accusations around. We both know she's done the same thing to you, Quinn, threatening to report you to the authorities, accusing you of using Dieldrin.' She spoke as if Zoe wasn't in the room. 'Don't listen to her, Quinn. She can pack her bags and go back to Sydney. I don't want that woman to ever set foot in Kiawa again. '

Zoe sank down on the bed. This last barb came as a jolt. She hadn't properly thought through what exposing Bridget might mean. To never again work with the dolphins, or see the tilt of their head while they watched her. To not see Echo released. And what about the turtles? And what about Einstein? Tears brimmed in her eyes and her waning headache returned with a vengeance. She couldn't bear it. It would shatter her heart into pieces so tiny she wouldn't be able to see them.

'Can we all please calm down?' Quinn put the box of samples back in the wardrobe. Then he took hold of Bridget's hand. The gesture provoked in Zoe a furious resentment, but she remained silent. Her exhausted brain had enough insight left to temper her tongue. She mustn't act on impulse. There was nothing left to say without proof. Tomorrow, one way or another, she would get find the hard evidence to show that Bridget was lying.

Quinn said, 'I'd like to take Bridget home.' His grey eyes were so serious, so solemn. 'Is that okay with you, Zoe? Will you be alright?'

'Will you?' asked Zoe. 'No, I'm serious. Be careful of her, Quinn.'

He guided Bridget out of the door. A minute later Zoe heard the jeep start up. She fell back on the bed. Quinn loved her. He was taking Bridget home to tell her, but it still rankled to have them leave together. A thought nagged at her tired mind. One thing in particular was bothering her. She thought she'd been so clever. Not telling Bridget about finding the discarded samples, not confronting her boss with her suspicions. Bridget had no reason to suspect that Zoe was on to her, and they'd been diving together plenty of times. So why had she chosen today to abandon her? Bridget didn't like her seeing Leo, and she probably guessed Zoe had feelings for Quinn. But was that motive enough for murder?

The answer wouldn't come. Zoe's eyelids grew heavy; sleep was claiming her. But first . . . she found her phone and scrolled through for the number. 'Mum? How are you?'

Daylight filtered through the bamboo window shade. Zoe lay half-awake, going through the events of the previous day, marvelling at what they meant. It was no dream, Quinn had declared his feelings. He loved her. That sweet thought scrubbed the pain from her aching limbs.

The clock radio turned itself on, offering the local forecast. '*A low off the coast will progress to a tropical storm by tomorrow.*' The wind moaned on cue and the little shack creaked alarmingly. Thank goodness the bad weather hadn't hit yesterday when she was on the reef. Scraps of the previous day's ordeal tumbled into her consciousness, fragments of a nightmare. Zoe was drifting back to sleep when the phone rang. She found it in the folds of the blanket. 'Hello?' It was Quinn. Glancing across at the dressing table mirror, she rubbed her eyes and smoothed her hair, as if he could see her.

'How are you this morning?'

'Still pretty wrecked,' she said. 'And starving, but my headache's gone.'

'I'm coming to make you breakfast, and for once in your life, don't argue with me. See you in ten.'

Argue? She wanted to weep with joy.

Zoe climbed stiffly from the bed and took a shower, letting the steaming water iron smooth her creased body. Hurry, there wasn't much time; he'd be here soon. Stepping from the shower, towel drying her hair, she felt almost human again. Get dressed – shorts and a shirt tied at the waist that she now had. Into the kitchen – boil the kettle, eggs from the fridge. No bacon? Oh well, mushrooms would do. Bread? Yes. Stale, but that didn't matter for toast. Was there time to wash the few dirty dishes? She'd just finished filling the sink with hot sudsy water when the knock came. She checked herself in the mirror and ran to answer it. Today she would see him without the guilty idea of Bridget hovering over her head.

Quinn stood, hat in hand, on her doorstep. She stood back to let him in, but he dropped his hat and pulled her into his arms. With a shock of pleasure she let herself go loose, melding into his body as if tailor-made to fit. He swept back her hair, a half-smile on his face, and this time he kissed her the way she'd imagined so many times. The way she needed to be kissed.

When Quinn finally let her go, he said, 'I ended it with Bridget. She's moved out, gone back to Leo.'

'How did she take it?'

He picked up his hat. 'Badly. Bridget insisted that what happened yesterday on the reef was an accident. She was desperate for me believe her.'

'And did you?'

He looked down and twisted his hat. 'Blind Freddy wouldn't believe her, Zoe. I've been in touch with the search and rescue boys and you were right. No emergency call was logged about a missing diver yesterday.'

Relief flooded her body, making her tremble. Quinn circled her waist with an arm, guided her to the couch and sat down beside her. 'Bridget abandoning you like that? Pretending to care for Josh, when she was just using him? I can barely bring myself to think about it.'

'I don't know how responsible she is for what she's done,' said Zoe.

'She tries to kill you and you're making excuses for her?

'I'm just saying that Bridget must have some major psychiatric problems.'

Quinn frowned and stood up. 'You're far too forgiving for your own good. Stay there while I make that breakfast. Can't have you wasting away on me. You're getting too skinny.'

'Too skinny?' She couldn't help laughing. 'That's the first time a man's said that to me.'

'What about Leo?' he said. 'What does he say to you?'

'Leo?' she said. 'Leo's just a friend.'

'Truly?'

She went into the kitchen and twined her arms round his neck. 'Truly. Now kiss me again.'

An hour later Zoe's stomach was full, and so was her heart. She sat on the couch, leaning against Quinn, legs tucked beneath her and nursing a cup of tea. Fairly bursting with happiness. In spite of the fact that she was still physically drained. In spite of the fact that she no longer had a job. In spite of the fact that she had no hard evidence against Bridget. It didn't matter. For the moment, nothing mattered but the weight of Quinn's arm around her shoulder.

'I can't bear to think of you alone out there on the reef — facing tiger sharks, no less.' She felt a shiver run through him, and moved her hand to hold his.

'I wasn't exactly alone.' She thought of Kane, wondered where he was now.

'Woman rescued by dolphins. What a headline. I sure do owe Kane and his mates.'

'Well, then do something about it,' said Zoe. 'Help make Turtle Reef safe for them again.'

'When I leave here – not that I want to go . . .' He kissed her until it felt as if they were floating together in a soft, warm ocean. Her body felt weightless, weightless but aching for him. 'When I leave here I'm going to talk to old Rob.'

Zoe tried to pull herself back to the shack, to the conversation, when all she wanted was to lead him to her bedroom.

Quinn's body shifted away a fraction, and her breathing slowly returned to normal. 'I've done some asking round,' he said. 'When Dieldrin was banned all those years ago, a lot of it was illegally dumped in the bush. Word is some blokes are salvaging the drums and flogging them. It's cheap and effective, and growers round here are doing it tough. I reckon there's probably been a black market in the stuff for years.'

'And you think Rob's involved?'

'Could be. He's pretty old school.'

'That's appalling,' said Zoe. 'But at least it's an explanation for what I saw.'

He smoothed her hair. 'Whenever we argue, it turns out that you're right. I'll try to remember that.' The phone rang and he frowned. 'Don't answer that.'

But Zoe was already up and reaching for it. 'Yes, this is Zoe King.'

'My name is Professor Perry Armstrong. I'm . . .'

'I know who you are.' She was unable to contain her eagerness, even if it seemed rude. 'You're the Director of the Marine Science Centre at Queensland University. I've been waiting for an email from your secretary.'

'You haven't received it? Just as well I rang then. Junk mail folder, perhaps? I sent the list of our auspiced research projects through to you the very same day you requested it. If I may be so bold . . . were you curious about a dugong study proposed by Bridget Macalister? Is that why you wanted the information?'

'It is.'

'This is rather tricky to get into, but you won't find that project on the list. It was never approved.'

A wave of relief washed through her. 'Thank you *so* much, Professor. I've been suspicious for a while.' This remark was met with a long silence. 'Can you tell me why the study wasn't approved?' she asked at last. 'Not sure if you realise, but I work for Bridget.'

'I am aware of that.' More silence. The professor seemed reluctant to continue, which was odd considering that he'd rung her. Zoe was beginning to think they'd been cut off when he finally spoke. 'My department conducted investigations into Bridget Macalister in January of this year. I'm afraid she isn't who she purports to be.'

'I don't understand,' said Zoe. 'I know her father.'

'Oh, I don't mean that her name isn't Bridget Macalister. I mean her application for a study grant was fraudulent and was rejected on that basis. She also applied for standard government funding, and a grant from the department of environment to employ you, Ms King. They referred the claims to us. We recommended they be rejected as well.'

'Why?'

'Ms Macalister holds none of the qualifications that she claims to.'

Zoe steadied herself by holding onto a chair. 'What, none at all?'

'No.'

She sat down. She could feel Quinn behind her, curious. 'No PhD or postdoctoral fellowship at the Californian Marine Mammal Institute?'

'No.'

'No grant from Curtin University to study dugongs in Shark Bay?'

'Bridget Macalister never even finished her undergraduate degree. She failed first-year science at the University of New England and, as far as we can tell, never returned to study. When my secretary said a request for information had come from Ms Macalister's marine park, it raised alarm bells. You must pardon me for taking the liberty of verifying your own credentials, Ms King. I was delighted to discover that you, at least, are a genuinely talented and promising young researcher. But I feel it's only fair to warn you about Ms Macalister. Be extremely careful of any dealings you might have with this woman.'

'Incredible,' said Zoe. 'Inventing a life like that, a whole history.'

'It's an extremely troubling case,' said the Professor. 'But not as uncommon as you might think. Last year a man worked for three months at a country hospital as a doctor before being found out. Other staff became concerned about his treatment of patients and raised the alarm. He claimed to be a graduate of Queensland University and had, in fact, attended this institution, but failed to complete his course. A faked degree was sufficient, however, for him to receive conditional registration to work as an intern.'

'That's amazing,' said Zoe. 'How do people get away with it?'

'With surprising ease,' he said. 'In spite of our modern cynicism, on the whole we still trust people to be who they say they are. It leads to a kind of imposter blindness, making us slow to suspect. And as for Bridget Macalister, I believe her father owns the privately run Reef Centre, so her qualifications are probably unimportant. It's not a case of conventional fraud. But sever your association with the place, Zoe. It will taint your CV.'

Zoe said goodbye, put down the phone and met Quinn's gaze. She heaved a big sigh. 'You're not going to believe this.'

Half an hour later she farewelled Quinn with a lingering kiss. 'I'll be back after my talk with Rob,' he said. 'And we'll go to see Leo. He needs to know about Bridget. Then together we'll work out what to do.' Zoe nodded, her mind awhirl. How hard must this be for Quinn? Coming to grips with Bridget's lie of a life, a lie he'd lived along with her for years. She clasped her hands behind her neck and stretched until her spine ached.

A wave of exhaustion washed over her. Maybe she should go back to bed? Though that made her think about Quinn and the promise of his body beside her . . . She shook the image away and fetched her laptop, climbed under the covers and opened her emails. It still puzzled her why Bridget had chosen yesterday to leave her on the reef. She browsed her inbox again, and her junk mail, searching for the missing email from Queensland University. She went through her conversation with Professor Perry and with his secretary. Then it struck her. *'I'd rather not send that information to a private email address,'* the secretary had said. *'However if you have one associated with the Reef Centre . . .'* Of course. Bridget had access to the Reef Centre network, to everybody's emails. She would have seen the request for a list of approved research projects and realised that Zoe was onto her. She could have accessed Zoe's inbox and deleted the Professor's reply. Abandoning her at sea had been Bridget's final, desperate attempt to prevent her world from tumbling down.

The familiar music of *Swan Lake* drifted in through the billowing curtains. With a pang Zoe pulled a chair up to the open window to watch. Down below, the dolphins were performing their show, or what was left of it. How beautiful they were, how splendid. Bridget looked beautiful too, standing tall in her trademark gold bikini, silhouetted against the dark water. Something seemed different about her. Only a dozen people sat in the audience under the grey sky, but Bridget performed as if there were a thousand – strutting the lagoon's edge and gesturing with theatrical flourishes worthy of the greatest stage star. Even the dolphins seemed impressed, flipping and spinning with a semblance of their old grace. Zoe almost admired Bridget, toughing it out until the bitter end, knowing that any minute her charade would crumble around her ears.

Who was that interrupting the show? Was that Josh? Yes, pulling at Bridget's arm and arguing with her, although Zoe couldn't hear what they was saying. How extraordinary. She'd never seen Josh as much as disagree with Bridget, let alone quarrel with her in public.

Curiosity got the better of her. Zoe slipped out the side door and down the stone stairs, grimacing at each step, leg muscles still sore from yesterday. A tugging gust of wind caused her a flurry of fear. Zoe's dislike of heights wasn't entirely a thing of the past, and she held tight to the handrail. By the time she reached the gate at the bottom, Bridget had shaken Josh off, and was persevering with the show. Josh stood beside the portable grandstand, watching.

'Josh?' He turned to face her, fists clenched by his side, eyes red and swollen from crying. She took his hand. 'Come with me, and you can tell me what's wrong.' He followed her out the gate and up the steps. When they reached the little balcony Zoe looked down to find Bridget staring up at her.

She hurried Josh inside. 'What's happened?'

'I heard Bridget on the phone this morning. She's selling Mirrhi.'

'What?'

'I heard her.'

Zoe wrapped her arms around his stiff shoulders and hugged him tight. 'We won't let her,' she said. 'I don't think Bridget will be in charge of the Reef Centre for very much longer. Quinn and I are going to talk to Leo about that today.'

'No.' He pulled away, not looking at her, and paced restlessly about the room. 'Bridget always gets her own way. Always. You won't be able to stop her.'

'Yes,' said Zoe firmly. 'I will. I promise.' He stopped abruptly and shoved his hands in his pockets. 'What exactly did you hear?' she asked him. 'Maybe you misunderstood.'

Josh shook his head violently. 'No, Bridget said the people could come get Mirrhi.'

Zoe thought back to when Bridget had shown Mirrhi to the mysterious visitors. Were they from another oceanarium? Australian marine parks hadn't been allowed to capture wild dolphins since 1994. They had to rely on captive-bred animals or rescues like Mirrhi, deemed unsuitable for release by an independent body such as Parks and Wildlife. Mirrhi was a healthy, pregnant, trained young female with wild-caught genes. A dolphin like her would be highly sought after.

'Josh, I'm taking you back to Swallowdale.'

'No.'

'Yes.' She grabbed her car keys. 'I won't let anything happen to Mirrhi. You have to believe me.' Josh gave her a mutinous glare. 'No arguments. Come on, and if you see Quinn when you get home, tell him I've gone to see George Fairthorn the vet. Okay?'

'Okay,' said Josh in a surly voice. He didn't trust her; that much was obvious. Well, it couldn't be helped. He'd see soon enough. Nothing bad was going to happen to Mirrhi or the other dolphins. Not on her watch.

CHAPTER 29

George came into the waiting room and took off his gloves and mask.

'I thought you didn't do surgery on a Saturday,' said Zoe.

'Tell that to the little French Bulldog that just had a caesarean.' A plump middle-aged woman followed him out, glowing with pride and cradling two tiny, wriggling black puppies.

'I can see how busy you are, George, but could you spare me a few minutes? It's important.'

'I'm all yours. Come into the office.' He closed the door behind them. 'What's up?'

'I have some questions about the dolphins at the centre.'

George washed his hands in a corner sink. 'Fire away.'

'Who deemed them unfit for release? Was that you?'

'Me? No. I've told Bridget more than once that half those animals could be released tomorrow. She doesn't listen. They're crowd-pullers. I think she relies on them to pay the bills.'

'Did Parks and Wildlife examine them?'

'I doubt it.'

'You mean nobody has looked into the possibility of their release?'

'Not as far as I know.'

'Do you remember Kane?' George nodded. 'Bridget told me a stingray barb permanently damaged his jaw, so he couldn't catch his own fish. That can't be right, because I saw him at Bora Reef yesterday, looking terrific. His dorsal fin was starting to stand up again.'

George shrugged. 'I don't know what more to tell you, Zoe. Kane was fighting fit, and I told Bridget exactly that. His fin was fine when he came in, by the way. It drooped after a few months in captivity. That happens a lot.'

'Was he ever declared a public nuisance?' George raised his eyebrows. 'And does Mirrhi have seizures? No, of course not.' How stupid was she? 'What about a dolphin named Hope. Do you know what happened to her?'

'Hope went to Oceanworld,' he said. 'In return, they funded Bridget's sea turtle rescue program for twelve months.'

Zoe left the surgery with a new spring in her step. Some of the dolphins had a chance for freedom after all. Echo certainly, and Mirrhi. A chance for Mirrhi's baby to be spared the life sentence that birth in captivity would bring. She imagined the dolphins fishing out on the reef, basking in the sun, echo-sounding the depths with their mysterious sixth sense. Zoe gave a little skip as she neared her car. Here was the chance to be involved in a genuine rehabilitation and soft release study. First the dolphins would need a dose of the new morbillivirus vaccine. Young dolphins like Echo and Mirrhi were most at risk from the virus ravaging the bay. But all these things were doable. There was just one minor problem. She didn't work at the Reef Centre anymore. She had absolutely no say in what happened there.

Zoe sat out on the deck, watching the waves build at sea, waiting for Quinn. The storm was lurking offshore, playing cat-and-mouse with the coast. In the foreground, Archie's old fishing boat, *Rambler*, tacked expertly across the dark water, taking wind and waves at an angle.

First broad on the bow, then broad on the quarter. Zoe's scalp prickled. Thank goodness she wasn't out there. It would be some time before she'd feel like braving the bay again.

It was mid-afternoon before Quinn's knock came at the door. He pushed it open. A quiver of anticipation ran down her spine and through her legs. They sank down on the couch, wrapped up in each other; kissing long and hard and with satisfying attention to detail. She hadn't felt this way with a man before – this odd combination of excitement and safety.

'What happened with Rob,' she asked at last.

'You're not going to like it.' Quinn touched her face. 'He and his cronies have been salvaging drums from an illegal dump site.'

'No! Where's the dump site?'

He put an inch of space between them on the couch, and rearranged his long legs. 'In that patch of rainforest along the river.'

'What – on Swallowdale land?'

'I'm afraid so.' Quinn swallowed hard. 'Seems my father didn't want to pay for proper disposal. Said it was a waste of money. He bulldozed a track into the bush and used it as a tip. I've had a look. Neighbours from miles around must have used the place. There's still a heap of drums left.'

'What will you do?'

'I've sacked Rob, for starters. Wasn't planning to. Promised him a job for life and, after all, it was my Dad who did the wrong thing in the first place, not him. But the old bloke argued the point with me. Said I was making a mountain out of a molehill, and that my father would turn in his grave.' Quinn stood up and paced the room. 'I told him how farms were moving to new ways, better ways to protect the reef. Rob wouldn't hear of it. He'll never change.'

She jumped up and laced her hands around his neck. 'You did the right thing, firing him — for his own good as much as anything else. He never uses protection. For all we know, it was those chemicals that made Rob sick in the first place.'

'I hadn't thought of that.' Quinn kissed Zoe again, sitting her down on the couch, drawing strength from her body. 'There was a time I was as set in my ways as old Rob,' he said. 'But I've changed, Zoe, I've opened my eyes.'

His words stirred in her a deeper passion than she'd ever known. A fire-in-the-belly hunger to explore the future with this man. Both of them innocents in some ways, innocents who'd opened their eyes.

Leo cleared his throat and looked lost. 'Can this be true?'

Zoe handed him the letter from Professor Perry. It detailed the full extent of Bridget's fraudulent academic record. Leo reread the letter, his face ashen. 'No mistake, then?'

'I'm afraid not,' said Zoe.

'There's more.' Quinn squeezed her hand. 'When Bridget realised Zoe was onto her, she took her diving at Bora Reef and abandoned her. Zoe could easily have died. Bridget only came back when she thought she'd been found out.'

Leo buried his head in the heels of his hands.

'We didn't want to go to the police until you knew,' said Quinn.

Zoe glanced at him sharply. He hadn't mentioned the police before. 'There are two sides to this,' she said. 'Bridget's done a lot of good at the centre. Saving dozens of turtles, educating people about the reef, staying up half the night to feed orphaned pelican chicks. Paying expenses out of her own pocket. That cormorant she released last week didn't care whether she had a qualification or not. Bridget isn't a truly bad person, she just painted herself into a corner with all the lies. Desperate people do desperate things.'

Leo rubbed his face. 'I still don't understand why.'

'You'll have to ask her that,' said Zoe.

Leo took his phone from his pocket and made a call. 'She's not answering.'

'I saw Bridget from the window this morning,' said Zoe. 'Down at the lagoon. She was arguing with Josh. I spoke to him about it later. Apparently Bridget's planning to sell Mirrhi to help pay the bills.'

'Mirrhi?' Quinn's brow creased with concern. 'Josh is head over heels in love with that dolphin. Mirrhi and Aisha – they're all he talks about. It would kill him to lose either one of them.'

Zoe smiled, thrilled and proud to hear those words. The look of love was in her eyes and Leo didn't miss a thing. He gazed at Quinn with undisguised envy. 'So that's how it is? Would have been nice to know.'

'We didn't really know ourselves until yesterday.' Quinn's expression was so earnest, so sincere, it melted Zoe's heart. She finally had herself a genuine keeper. 'But you have my word, Leo. I was never unfaithful to your daughter.'

Leo made an expansive gesture with both arms. 'Oh, don't worry, Quinn, I believe it. You always were so darn honourable. Used to drive me mad sometimes.' He winked at Zoe. 'I suppose the best man wins, eh?' For once Zoe kept her mouth tactfully shut. 'What I don't understand, though, is why Bridget didn't come to me for money? She knows I'm not short of a quid.'

Zoe shrugged and glanced at Quinn. He picked up his hat, gave her a nod and gravely shook Leo's hand. 'Talk to your daughter. Let me know how it goes.'

They made the brief walk back to the shack in silence. 'I'd better go home,' said Quinn. 'Get a few things sorted before the storm hits tomorrow.'

'Let me know how Josh is,' said Zoe. 'He was pretty upset this morning. Tell him we won't let anything happen to Mirrhi.'

'Will do.' Quinn kissed her long and very thoroughly. When he released her, she took a faltering backwards step. He smiled. 'Don't know how long it's been since I had that kind of effect on a woman.' He turned to go, then changed his mind and returned to kiss her again. His phone beeped with a text message. 'I'm rostered on *Turtle Watch* tonight,' he said. 'Care to come?'

. . .

Zoe watched Quinn walk down the path to the carpark, climb in his red jeep and drive away. She sagged against the doorframe, overcome with an odd combination of elation and weariness. Going to her room, she climbed back into bed, dizzy with possibilities, until precious, dreamless sleep finally claimed her.

CHAPTER 30

Zoe stood at the tideline, staring out to sea. Winds whipped up the waves. The storm still hovered offshore. Quinn admired her silhouette against the fading glow of a cloudy, twilight sky. She swung around to face him, her tangled chestnut hair framing her smiling face. How lovely she was, how unique. No Barbie doll. No fake shell of a person. Flawed, but adorable. Real.

He set the basket down on the sand. Here they were, back on Kulibari Beach, close to the turtle nest they'd roped off almost two months ago. It could almost have been a rerun of that first night, when together they'd watched the giant, prehistoric-looking logger-head lay her eggs by moonlight. When he'd been so intrigued by the beautiful Zoe King. When he'd unexpectedly opened up to her about his life, confessing his disgraceful fear of the ocean. But tonight was different in some very significant ways. Tonight they had a chicken and champagne picnic, and an understanding.

Quinn shook out the blanket and sat down, beckoning Zoe to him. She sat close, hugging her knees. The lacy strap of her purple singlet slipped a little. He kissed her bare shoulder, hardly daring to believe this evening was real. Her skin tasted of salt and sand and sin. He breathed in and flexed his thighs to still the stirrings in his loins.

Zoe opened the champagne and poured two flutes. 'Here's to us.'

'To us.' As they clinked glasses Quinn caught a small movement from the corner of his eye. 'And to our little friend.'

She looked puzzled for a moment, before following his gaze. A miniature, sand-encrusted turtle sat on the beach within the roped-off area. Impossibly tiny. It couldn't have been more than four centimetres long. 'Oh wow,' whispered Zoe, jumping to her feet. 'They're hatching.' She produced two red-light head-torches from her bag and handed him one.

Seconds later, the beach began to boil, erupting in an explosion of loggerhead hatchlings. They swarmed from the nest and toddled towards the ocean. One flipped on its back, exposing a soft pale-ochre underbelly. Quinn gently picked it up, examined its nut-brown body, marvelled at its miniature flippers, delicately edged in white. He put the baby back down and it scurried away with startling energy. Another group of hatchlings piled up behind a driftwood barrier. A couple of them set off sideways. Quinn quickly moved the obstacle and set the babies back on course.

Astounding that he'd lived here all his life and had never witnessed such a miracle. There was something profoundly moving about the tiny creatures' intrepid march down the beach. Flippers working furiously. Weak and vulnerable, yet so eager to cast themselves into that vast, perilous ocean. They put him to shame.

Zoe was busy smoothing their path to the water. Quinn fetched the champagne and handed her a glass. 'Here.' She straightened up, eyes shining in the torch-glow, face flushed with pleasure and excitement. They made another toast, this time to new beginnings.

'Is it true they come back to the same beach to lay their own eggs?' Quinn asked. 'I wonder how they know?'

'It's magical,' said Zoe. 'Those little turtles, just minutes old, somehow detect the magnetic field and orientation of the earth at the exact place where they enter the ocean. They never forget it.'

'And only one in a thousand make it?'

'That's right.'

'Then I suppose we'd better clean up their bay.' He pulled her to him. 'Shorten the odds for the little tackers.' Zoe's face lit up. Her kiss was eager and full of promise. A knockout. He wanted to pull her down to the sand then and there. But instead he went to rescue a hatchling stranded behind some kelp. 'I know what my father would make of all this,' he said, as he set the baby back on course.

'It doesn't matter what he'd think.'

'You don't understand.' A confessional fervour was taking hold, a desperation to tell. 'My family did terrible things, Zoe. Clear-felling thousands of acres of rainforest. Shooting koalas for the fur trade. Selling turtles and dugongs for oil and meat to a factory at Hervey Bay. Harvesting turtle eggs. When Dad was a boy they were still considered delicacies. And there are huge polished shells stashed under the house somewhere. My grandfather exported them for tortoise-shell at five guineas a pound. We Coopers saw the wild as simply something else to exploit for a profit.'

She gave his leg a little kick, hard enough it hurt, as the moon vanished behind a cloud. 'Stop it. Quinn, this is your life. You can do things your way - make up for the wrongs of your family.'

Zoe's words hit home more than she could have known. 'Remember that old stone wall, down by the river?' he said. 'The one you admired so much? It was built by Kanakas – South Sea Island labourers brought over here to work the cane fields. Slaves they were, treated like dirt, sold like cattle on the docks.' He swallowed to clear the lump in his throat. 'Swallowdale was built on the backs of those blokes. I talked to Dad about it once. He couldn't see anything wrong with it, wondered what all the fuss was about. *Where's the harm in giving a few black bastards an honest day's work?* That's what he said.' Zoe stroked his arm. 'Some of them died here. Never got proper funerals. They weren't allowed in Kiawa cemetery apparently, so they were buried out here at Swallowdale. Dad showed me the graves once, when I was a kid. Their mates had made beautiful engraved head-stones from the local basalt. It gave me the creeps. I thought that place was haunted. Never went back.'

Zoe's face lay in moonshadow. 'Where are they buried?' she asked softly.

His mouth turned to sandpaper. 'In that patch of rainforest by the river.'

'What, where the— ?' Zoe's question slid to a halt.

'That's right. Where Dad cleared land for a chemical dump. I've had a look. He bulldozed right through the graves, headstones and all.' He gave a hollow laugh. 'And I've wasted my whole life trying to live up to a man like that.'

She squeezed his hand. 'You're a good person, Quinn Cooper. A kind and honest one. You'll make a difference with your life. You already have – look at those kids you found jobs for. Look at what a wonderful brother you've been to Josh. And now you have a chance to bring Turtle Reef back to health, and lead others to do the same. Every one of those little baby turtles owes you a debt of gratitude.'

Her touch, her smile, her words – everything about her served to comfort him. 'Let's have another toast.' He fetched their glasses and refilled them. 'To the future.'

The moon burst through the clouds. They held hands until all the hatchlings disappeared beneath the waves. Quinn toasted the babies with the last of his champagne. 'Long may they swim with the dolphins.'

'Hear, hear.'

Then he kissed her, sweet and slow, running fingers through her hair. The tilt of her head, the taste of her lips, her half-lowered lashes in the rosy torch light – all combined to make his craving unbearable. He led her up the beach and lowered her to the soft sand. The slim pandanus palm above them bent low in the wind, as if it wanted to kiss her too.

The moment swelled. She undid the top button of her shirt and loosened the tie at her waist. Quinn was shy as a school boy with his first date. Zoe was from Sydney. She was clever and confident and desirable. How many lovers had she known? He, on the other hand? He and Bridget were childhood sweethearts, and he'd never had another woman.

Zoe twined her arms around his neck. 'I love you,' she said. 'I've loved you for ages. I knew it wasn't right, because you were with Bridget. I knew I shouldn't fantasise . . .'

'You fantasised about me?'

'Oh, all the time.' She kissed the tip of his nose. 'I think you loved me too, but you're so bloody principled, you wouldn't admit it.'

His nerves evaporated. 'You're right. You always are.'

'No, I'm not.' She nipped his ear. 'Sometimes I talk too much.'

He quivered, on the threshold of something wonderful, something life-changing. She switched off their torches and they undressed each other, exploring unfamiliar flesh with fingers and lips. Finding their night eyes, they made urgent love to the sound of the incoming tide.

Long after midnight, they lay together on the moon-bright beach. Quinn traced the hollow of her hip with his finger. 'I hate to go,' he said at last. 'But Josh will be worrying himself sick over Mirrhi. He shouldn't be alone.'

'The contract of sale might already be signed.'

'Leo will find a loophole,' said Quinn. 'He's as slippery as they come. And, if not, we'll break the contract and pay the price. Mirrhi isn't going anywhere.'

Zoe reached for her clothes. Quinn admired her naked form, outlined against a faintly glowing sky. This lovely young woman who'd turned his life upside down. Zoe King had blazed across Kiawa's landscape like a fearless shooting star, shining the light of change into the town's dark corners. Transforming lives. To have won this extraordinary woman. To have her love him. He was the luckiest man in the world.

CHAPTER 31

Zoe woke to the ringing phone, rattling windows and the steady drum of rain on the roof. For a moment she was back in Sydney, fighting from a fog of sleep, dreading the routine of the engineering library that awaited her. Then she stretched like a contented cat, remembering, and answered the call.

It was Quinn. 'Good morning, gorgeous.' She smiled and checked the time. Six o'clock on a Sunday morning. He was keen. 'Is Josh there?'

'Josh?' It wasn't what she'd expected him to say. 'I don't think so. Let me check.' She got out of bed and did a quick sweep of the shack. 'No. He's not home then?'

'No.'

'Has he gone riding?'

'The horses are all in their paddocks.' There was an edge of real concern in Quinn's voice. 'And my jeep's missing.'

A knock came at the door. 'Wait,' she said. 'That could be him now.'

Not Josh, but Leo on the doorstep, almost blown away by the wind. 'I don't suppose Bridget's here?'

Zoe shook her head. 'It's not him,' she told Quinn. 'It's Leo. Should I come over?'

'No, I'll come there. Josh is probably somewhere at the centre.'

Zoe put down the phone. Leo was sitting in the kitchen with his arms folded. For once he well and truly looked his age. 'Put on the kettle,' she said. 'I'll have a shower and then we'll talk.'

Zoe poured the coffees and sat down at the end of the table. She'd expected Quinn to ask for tea instead, but for once he didn't seem to care. He and Leo sat opposite each other, faces rigid with worry. 'Have you heard from Bridget?' Leo asked. 'She won't answer her phone.'

'It's not Bridget I'm concerned about.' Quinn couldn't disguise the anger in his voice. 'She'll be lying low somewhere. Josh, on the other hand ...'

'We'll search the centre,' said Zoe. 'Maybe he's hiding there somewhere.'

'I shouldn't have gone out last night.' Quinn swigged the hot brew and made a face. 'I shouldn't have gone out.' His phone rang and everybody held their breath. 'I'll be right there.' Quinn skulled his coffee. 'That was Karen. She's found my jeep parked around the back. Apparently Mirrhi's gone missing too.'

A squally gust of wind drove rain into the pool at an angle. Echo patrolled the boundaries, occasionally slapping the water with an angry tail and biting the bars of his gate. It broke Zoe's heart to see it. 'I think he's cracked a tooth,' said Karen. 'But he won't let me near him to check.' Karen pulled the hood of her raincoat over her head. 'Mirrhi was having an ultrasound first thing, so I put her in the veterinary compound overnight. When I got here this morning, the gates out to the bay were wide open and she was gone.'

It was pretty clear what had happened. Josh must have released Mirrhi, unaware he was putting her in danger. Unlike the much older and tougher Kane, Mirrhi was vulnerable to the virus ravaging the bay's dolphins. She'd been in captivity for years and would have no immunity to new pathogens. Exposure to wild dolphins could mean a death sentence.

Leo and Quinn arrived on the scene, having searched the centre with no luck. Zoe filled them in, trying hard to stay positive. 'If Mirrhi hangs round the fringe of the centre's lagoon, she'll be alright,' said Zoe. 'We'll have a good chance of getting her back. I'll take the boat and have a look for her now.'

'Not in this weather you won't,' said Quinn.

'I'm afraid the boat's gone too,' said Karen. '*Seafarer* — it's missing from its moorings. Must have come loose in this wind.'

The blood drained from Quinn's face as Karen's phone rang. She quickly turned as pale as Quinn. 'That was Archie,' she said when the call ended. 'He's just seen our boat in the bay. It's heading out to sea with Josh at the helm.'

CHAPTER 32

Driving rain and thick blankets of cloud obscured the noon-day sun. Quinn shivered as the wind jostled the sleek cabin cruiser against its wharf. The gusts grew stronger, with lulls in between, as if some monstrous living thing was giving birth to the storm. What a coward he was. His little brother, all alone on the bay. Perhaps lost and in trouble ... or worse. And yet the idea of heading out on this search filled him with dread. Quinn pulled himself together as best he could and stowed away the last of their gear in *Flipper*'s hull.

Zoe ran down from the house. 'I've rung the lot – police, search and rescue, coastguard . . . They're sending out boats, but helicopters can't go up in this weather.'

Quinn saw something more than compassion in her eyes — he saw understanding. He looked away. He didn't deserve understanding, especially not from someone like Zoe. Someone who'd confronted vertigo on that very first day and climbed the lookout tower anyway. Who'd overcame her fear of riding. Who'd challenged herself daily by living in a house perched high on a cliff. Someone who'd nearly lost her own life just two days before, and yet was prepared to brave the ocean again for Josh.

'Will you be alright?' she asked.

'I'll have to be.'

Zoe slipped a couple of tablets into his hand. 'For seasickness,' she whispered. 'They might help.' Quinn was not too proud to pop them in his mouth. He could use all the help he could get.

Leo got off the radio. 'Archie's heading out too. It would help if we bloody well knew where to look. What on earth was Josh thinking, heading out in a storm like this?'

'I know where he'll be.'

The three of them turned to see Bridget standing there, dressed in wet weather gear. Leo marched forwards and hugged her, didn't let her go.

A burning anger flared in Quinn's chest. 'You're not welcome, Bridget.' He moved onto the dock and positioned himself between her and Zoe.

Bridget broke away from her father's embrace. 'Please, Quinn.' Her voice rose higher. 'Let me come. I can help.'

'Help? You're lucky you're not in jail.'

'Now hold on —' said Leo.

'Hear her out,' said Zoe. 'What if she really does know where he is?'

'I do,' said Bridget. 'Josh is heading for Bora Reef, I'm sure of it.'

'Why there?' asked Quinn.

'Mirrhi's missing too, right? She's originally from the Bora Reef pod. Josh knows that. He used to talk about taking her back to her mother . . .'

'Josh thought it was his last chance to reunite Mirrhi with her family before she was sold.' Zoe turned to Quinn. 'It makes sense.'

He thought it through. Knowing Josh, there was a certain logic to the theory. 'Would Mirrhi follow Josh's boat?'

'Trust me —' said Bridget.

'Bad choice of words.'

She ignored him. 'Mirrhi would follow that boy anywhere.'

'Bridget's right,' said Zoe. 'And there is a pod out at Bora. Kane's joined them.' She took Quinn's arm, disregarding the pain in Bridget's eyes when she touched him. 'Give her a chance to put things right.'

Quinn opened his mouth, then closed it again. How could he allow it? It would be like forgiving Bridget: for his brother, for Zoe, for making a lie of his life. But how could he deny her if there was a chance she'd lead them to Josh?

'Well?' asked Leo. 'Is Bridget coming or not? I'd just as soon my daughter stayed on dry land in this weather, but since she wants to help, well . . . I reckon it's up to you, Quinn.'

They all stared at him expectantly. 'Get on board then, the lot of you,' said Quinn. 'We should be able to catch Josh up in this old tub.'

Quinn sat with Zoe on the rear bench seat, scanning the dark ocean with binoculars, grateful the cabin cruiser rode so high in the water. That small degree of separation was a comfort. Bridget sat up the front, talking on the radio. Occasionally Quinn glanced at Leo, reassured by his calm competence at the helm, determined not to let his rising panic show. High above them, sea swallows recklessly rode the wild winds.

'Barometer's dropping,' called Leo. 'Weather's closing in.' Great. Leo sounded almost cheerful, like he was enjoying the battle with the sea. 'Let's hope we spot Josh before he reaches the Pass. Visibility's shocking and getting worse.' Quinn didn't need Leo to tell him that. He could barely make out the shore, or even the lighthouse on the cape.

Zoe put a hand on his knee, which was shaking. 'Are you okay?'

He managed a smile. 'I'm sweating like a pig, sick in the guts and scared stiff of drowning. But mainly I'm terrified we won't find him.' Quinn clasped her briefly to him. 'How could I live with that?'

'We'll find him.' She squeezed his hand. 'I'm sure of it.'

The sky grew blacker as the sea grew rougher. *Flipper* lurched between waves, crashing down between them with stomach-churning, bone-jarring jolts. Quinn imagined the damage those waves would be doing to the little *Seafarer*: at the very least flooding her deck; at the worst, flipping her right over. But then Josh was a capable, level-headed skipper, who understood the ocean and her moods – loved them even. He had an even chance.

'There!' yelled Bridget. 'Up ahead, near the neck of the channel.'

Quinn ran to the bow of the boat, full of a wild and hopeful joy. 'Well, if the little beggar isn't still powering out to sea.'

Leo grinned and gave him the thumbs up. 'A cocky one, your lad. Though if he makes it to open ocean he'll have his hands full.' For a moment they watched the runabout framed by the grey sea and grey sky. 'Let's head him off at the Pass,' yelled Leo, and then more quietly: 'I've always wanted to say that.'

Ten minutes later they caught up with him. Josh made a valiant attempt to escape up the channel, but the runabout was no match for a twin-engine, fifteen-metre cabin cruiser. Leo blocked him at every turn. What *Flipper* lacked in manoeuvrability she made up for in sheer horsepower and stability. Quinn held his breath. If Josh strayed too far onto the shallow inshore reef, the razor-sharp coral could puncture *Seafarer*'s thin hull. 'Watch it,' called Quinn, as Leo brought the bow dangerously close to Josh's boat. A wave broke over it. 'You'll capsize him.'

One more drenching and Josh gave up the game. Leo executed a final, skilful movement with a hard starboard rudder. Now *Seafarer* lay on the lee side of *Flipper*'s hull, sheltered from the worst of the weather, almost within reach of the mid-ship boarding ladder. 'Tie her on,' screamed Quinn, but the wind whipped his words away. 'Where's the loudhailer?' Zoe ran to a locker and returned with a megaphone. Quinn turned it on. 'Josh!' His words boomed loud and clear across the dark choppy waters 'Tie on your boat.' But although Josh was tantalisingly close, he made no effort to secure the offered line or grab hold of the dangling lifebuoy.

'Look,' yelled Zoe. 'There's Mirrhi.' The dolphin emerged briefly from behind *Seafarer* and then ducked round the other side.

'Give it to me,' said Zoe, snatching the loudhailer. 'Josh, listen, you have to bring Mirrhi home. She'll get sick out here . . . '

Josh's expression remained defiant. 'It's no use,' said Quinn. 'I know that look. I'll have to go after him.'

'There are no safety harnesses onboard,' she said. 'I've already asked.'

'Have you now?' he said. 'Planning to do me out of my hero status, were you?'

She favoured him with a faint smile. 'But you're —'

'Terrified to be even standing on this deck? That's right.' He tested a lifebuoy rope. 'So things can't get any worse, can they?' He pulled her in for a kiss. 'Give Leo the heads-up. Tell him, steady as she goes.'

Zoe ran to the cockpit to deliver the message as Quinn tied a rope around his waist.

Taking a bottomless breath he tried to calm himself, calm the racing nerves, and the hammer of his heart against his ribs. Then he climbed over the side, holding fast to the ladder as *Flipper* pitched and rolled.

Quinn looked up. Much safer that way. Bridget was leaning over the rail, holding the loudhailer. Rain streamed down her face. Her eyes were red and puffy from crying. He hadn't seen her like this since they were children, stripped of composure, raw emotions on show for all to see.

'Josh,' called Bridget. 'Mirrhi's not going anywhere. The sale's off.'

Quinn dared to turn and face the water. Josh stared back at him, almost on a level now, but still out of reach. 'She's lying.'

'No, she's not, mate,' His own voice sounded echoey and far away, like it belonged to somebody else. 'We have to get that dolphin back home quick smart. There's a disease out here.' The knot in his gut tightened. 'Chemicals from the farm have been leaking out to sea, making the animals sick.' He could see Josh's resolve weakening. 'Mirrhi's not safe out here. Will you help us bring her home?'

'And Bridget won't sell her?'

'No, mate.' Mirrhi surfaced and uttered a loud series of clicks and whistles. 'See? She says she's homesick.'

A smile sneaked out around Josh's eyes. 'You don't speak dolphin.'

Quinn pointed to his watch. 'My secret dolphin translation device.' A huge wave crashed in, blinding him and stealing his breath. But surprise, not terror, was his overwhelming emotion. He'd been so intent on coaxing Josh on board that he'd forgotten his fears. When Quinn could see again, Josh was tying the line to *Seafarer*'s bow. Faint cheering floated down from *Flipper*'s deck.

Quinn grabbed the lifebuoy. 'Ready?' Josh nodded and Quinn flung it across. 'Quick, before your stern swings wide.' Josh wriggled into it, tested it once with his weight, then swung like a monkey across to the ladder. 'Come on,' said Quinn, grabbing him tight. 'Let's go home.'

Zoe and Quinn sat at the round teak table, basking in the comfort and warmth of Leo's living room. Helping themselves to pots of steaming coffee and plates of chocolate biscuits. Through wide bay windows, the storm still raged across Turtle Reef.

Sirens and explosions sounded from the next room. 'Turn that racket down, Josh,' called Quinn.

Bridget sat in the corner, sobbing softly. She'd barely stopped crying since they'd found Josh. It seemed a lifetime of dammed-up grief was overflowing.

Leo and Quinn were deep in conversation. They'd been talking for what seemed like hours now, a wide-ranging exchange that began with Bridget, moved onto the reef, and now extended to the future of their little town.

'So that's the proposal,' said Quinn. 'An alliance between the Kiawa business council, the new eco-resort and my canegrowers. Promoting best-practice on farms and showcasing Turtle Reef National Park at the same time.'

'Does this mean no more filthy fires?' asked Leo.

Quinn made an open-handed gesture of resignation. 'Seasons are changing, getting wetter and warmer. Three shockers in a row and the long-range forecast is for another one next year. We'll have to move to green trash-blanketing around here anyway.'

Leo slapped him on the back with his free arm. 'I love it. The press will love it. The Bennetts will love it. Why don't you get in on the action yourself, Quinn? Open up Swallowdale for cane farm tours, horse rides to the Hump, rainforest picnics . . .'

Bridget moved to sit beside Zoe. Leo and Quinn's conversation ground to a halt. 'I want to explain.' Bridget's breath came in shuddering sobs. 'You were so clever, so brilliant with the animals. And then my father fell for you, and so did Quinn . . . I tried hard to keep it together, to keep up the show. But you knew what a fraud I was from the start, the only one to see straight through me. You, who had what I wanted – an authentic life.'

Zoe was stunned. 'And to think I wanted to be more like the beautiful Bridget Macalister.'

Leo gave Quinn a perplexed look. 'Women,' he said, 'who can figure them?'

Bridget smiled grimly. 'I was jealous of you before Zoe, terribly jealous, but now I'm grateful. I've been scared for years, scared I'd be found out, scared Dad would hate me.'

'That could never happen, sweetheart.' Leo wrapped an arm around her. 'Don't worry, love, we'll get you the help you need. Now, how about a lie-down, eh?' He helped her gently to her feet and led her out. She turned as she reached the doorway. 'I was coming back for you, Zoe. I always was.'

Josh came in from the next room. 'The movie's over. I'm going to check on Mirrhi.'

'Why not wait until the rain stops?' called Quinn as Josh disappeared out the door.

Zoe laughed. 'Your brother just took a boat all the way to the outer reef, by himself, in the middle of a storm. I think he can handle a little rain.'

'You're right,' said Quinn. 'Of course you are. I've been wrapping that kid in cottonwool. Projecting my own fears on to him.' He pulled her to him and they joined together in a dizzying kiss. 'Know what?' he said, when they came up for air. 'I'm going to let Josh ride Aisha again. After all, he just took a boat all the way to the outer reef, by himself, in the middle of a storm. I think he can handle a little trot down the road.'

CHAPTER 34

Josh hummed happily as the vet gave Aisha the all clear.

'Now, remember what I told you?' said Quinn. 'Start out slowly. Let the hyped-up horses get out of your way. Don't worry when people pass you. Your goal is to finish, that's all.' Aisha stood like a statue while Josh mounted. 'And yield the trail to over-taking riders. Don't try to be first.'

'I won't.' Josh trotted a circle around Quinn on a loose rein, warming up his mount.

'And don't ride too close to other horses. I don't want Aisha kicked.'

Josh rolled his eyes.

'He'll be fine,' said Zoe.

Quinn slapped Aisha affectionately on the rump. 'Off you go then.'

It was a heart-warming scene. Josh, his brother and the summer-sleek, shining black mare, working as a team. What a difference these last months had made to all their lives.

Zoe sat on the stockyard rail, hand on hip, brimming with pleasure and pride. Josh had worked hard to prepare for today's ride. He'd built up Aisha's fitness with lots of slow, long-distance work, accompanied by Quinn on Yarraman. The pair were always off somewhere. Down at the beach, riding the picturesque network of cane-train trails, or just going bush. Plenty of time for talking during those long hours together in the saddle. A perfect way for the brothers to reconnect. A perfect way to begin the new year.

Next week Josh faced another momentous step forward. Starting school at Bundaberg High, three days a week, with a modified curriculum and the assistance of an aide. Studying basic maths, English and one unit of a certificate in sugar production. He'd be boarding with the family of an old school friend for half of each week. Already the two boys were getting on well, going to the movies one day and laser-tag on another. Josh had complained that he barely had time anymore for his online computer games. That remark had made Quinn *very* happy.

And then, of course, there was his cool weekend job. In her capacity as director of the Reef Centre, Zoe had hired Josh to help with their newly-funded research project, *Freedom Fins*, a program to return dolphins to the wild. Mirrhi and Echo had received their morbillivirus vaccinations in readiness, and Zoe was having the other dolphins assessed as potential candidates.

Dr Wendy Hossack, a marine mammal specialist, was consulting on the project. She'd overseen the successful rehabilitation and release of two long-term captive dolphins late last year. So far they'd exceeded all expectations. Satellite transmitters had tracked the pair hundreds of kilometres in their first weeks of freedom. They'd begun hunting fish as a team and interacting with wild dolphins. Exciting stuff.

The *Dancing Dolphins* shows continued, but with a new emphasis on education and natural behaviours. Visitor numbers were rising, and hundreds of people had signed on to sponsor Mirrhi and Echo's release program. The money proved very handy, as the dolphins were learning to catch live fish again and Archie was flat out keeping up supplies.

A loud enthusiastic whoop brought her meandering thoughts back to the present. Quinn was waving his hat in the air. 'They're off.' Aisha and Josh were leading a bunch of riders out of the start gates. 'Cheeky little beggar. I told him to start off slow.'

~

'There's one,' said Josh.

Zoe aimed the turkey baster at the oyster shell in the tank, trying to hold her hand steady. She squeezed the red bulb between thumb and forefinger, slowly does it, then suddenly let it go. 'Gotcha.' The tiny octopus was sucked into the glass tube. 'How many inklets is that?'

'Sixty-two.' Josh updated his octo-count notes.

'Inklets?' asked Quinn.

'That's what newborn octopus are called. Cute, eh?'

Quinn took the turkey baster from her and peered in. 'Beats me how you can even see them.' The brown-spotted baby was less than a quarter the size of his thumbnail. It settled on the glass, eight miniature arms and big dark eyes, blue blood on show through translucent skin.

Zoe was knuckling back tears. Einstein had died last night. Thirty-five days without eating, of total devotion to her brood. There was a theory that as mother octopuses approached death, they gave off chemical signals to their eggs. *Hurry now, babies. I'm growing weak. I can't look after you much longer.* However it happened, Einstein's death coincided with the hatching. Shortly after blowing the last inklet clear of the nest, she curled up and passed on.

It had been a long, sad time coming. An ordeal for Zoe, as well as for Einstein as she wasted away. She grew thin and uncoordinated, with bulging eyes and painful-looking skin lesions that wouldn't heal. Her death had come as a blessed relief for them both.

'Are we going to catch all of them?' asked Josh.

'We're going to try.' Zoe emptied the baster into a glass jar of seawater. She'd spotted another inklet.

'Couldn't I keep one as a pet?'

'Octopuses are very hard to grow from eggs in an aquarium,' she said. 'And I owe it to Einstein to give her babies the best possible start. That's why we're taking them out to the reef.' Josh looked glum and Zoe took pity on him 'The truth is,' she said, 'that I'm bound to miss one or two. They're so tiny and well-camouflaged. We'll keep any that are left behind and try to raise them. How's that?'

Josh looked much happier and immediately stopped helping her spot more babies.

An hour later Zoe called it a day. 'How many is that?'

'Ninety-five,' said Josh.

'That'll do us.' Zoe refreshed the jars with oxygenated water. 'I'll stock the tank with brine shrimp before we go, so there's food for any leftover inklets.'

Quinn picked up the tray of jars and the three of them headed down to the jetty. He carefully stowed it beneath *Seafarer*'s rear seat, while Zoe fussed about like a mother hen. 'I can't believe I'm on an octopus rescue mission,' said Quinn, taking the helm. 'Turtle Reef, full speed ahead.'

Zoe had chosen the release site with great care – a shallow sunlit coral garden, full of cracks and crevices where inklets could hide. Quinn stripped down and began sorting through fins. He selected a mask, then a snorkel, and tried them on. 'Do you think these fit?'

Zoe's eyes widened. 'You mean you're coming in?'

'Of course,' he said. 'I'm kind of like their godfather, after all. I need to say goodbye to the little tackers, don't I?'

'Yes.' Zoe wrapped her arms around his neck for a quick kiss. 'You certainly do.'

The three of them entered the water, carrying their precious cargo in string bags. Clouds of colourful fish parted before their eyes. Zoe led them through the warm translucent water to a broad shelf of table coral, just a metre below the surface. She held up her hand. 'This is the place.'

Quinn helped open the jars. The babies needed encouragement to let go of the glass before scooting into open water. One blink and they were gone, back where they belonged, part of the timeless circle of life on Turtle Reef. The future looked bright for Einstein's little inklets. Zoe and Quinn joined hands. The future looked bright for them all.

ABOUT THE AUTHOR

Bestselling Aussie author Jennifer Scoullar writes page-turning fiction about the land, people and wildlife that she loves.

Scoullar is a lapsed lawyer who harbours a deep appreciation and respect for the natural world. She lives on a farm in Australia's southern Victorian ranges, and has ridden and bred horses all her life. Her passion for animals and the bush is the catalyst for her bestselling books.

Visit Jennifer's website to enter the monthly prize draw! If you enjoyed this book and have a moment or two, please leave an online rating or review. Reviews are of great help to authors.

ACKNOWLEDGEMENTS

Writing a book is never a solo exercise. Thanks go firstly to the team at Pilyara Press — especially Kathryn Ledson, Sydney Smith and Kate Belle.

Thanks also to my agent, Clare Forster of Curtis Brown, and to my family for their support and help.

Writing can be a lonely business, but not with fabulous writer friends like the *Darklings* and the *Little Lonsdale Group*. It means such a lot to have you guys in my corner.

I pay special tribute to the Australian Marine Conservation Society and the Australian Conservation Foundation. These organisations work tirelessly to protect the Great Barrier Reef and its marvellous marine life. The reef is one of the natural wonders of the world, the only living thing visible from space. Let's not ruin it!